Razzle Dazzle Unicorn

Another Phoebe and Her Unicorn Adventure

Dana Simpson

Andrews McMeel Publishing®

a division of Andrews McMeel Universal

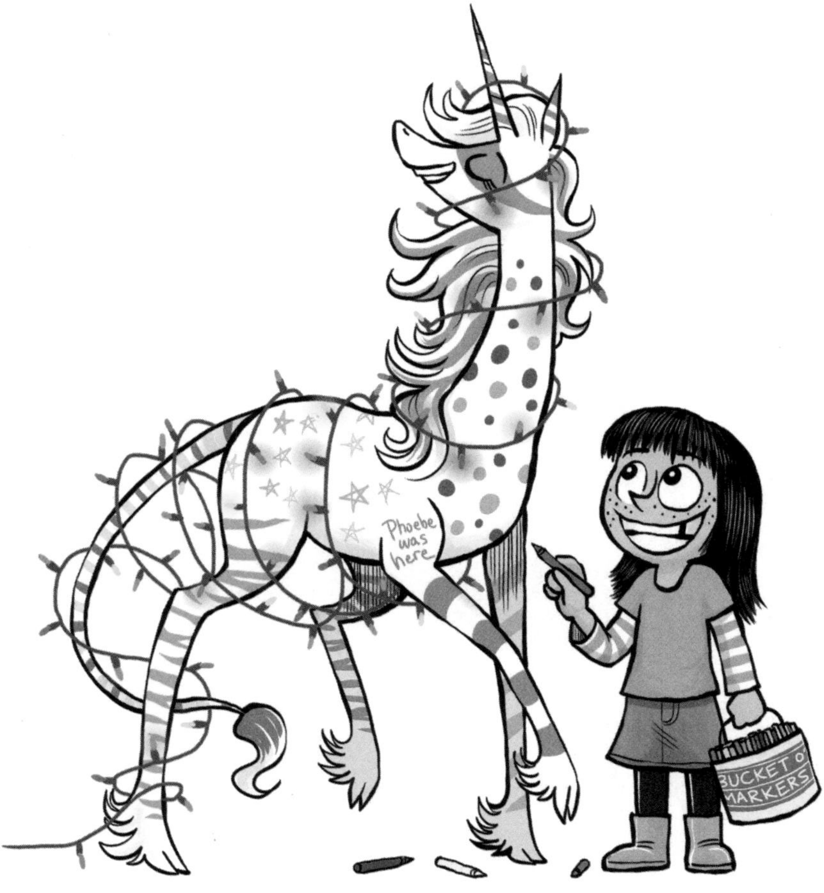
Phoebe was here
BUCKET O' MARKERS

INTRODUCTION

Sometimes a unicorn shows up in your life and makes everything better.

I wasn't really expecting one. A few years ago, I had nearly realized an ambition I've had since age twelve: I had scored a contract to develop a comic strip for newspaper syndication. I won that contract in the Comic Strip Superstar contest, which was sort of an *American Idol* for aspiring comic strip artists (without the surrounding glamour). I won with a comic strip called *Girl*, which starred a little girl who would eventually acquire the name Phoebe Howell. She ran around in the woods behind her house and hung out with talking animals.

I thought I'd just draw a bunch of *Girl* strips, and that would be that, and I'd be syndicated and happy forever. What happened instead was, I sent my required thirty strips in every month, and I got back a lot of notes explaining to me why the work I was doing wasn't good enough to launch in syndication.

My editor at the time, John Glynn, was blunt. "The work you're doing is better than some currently syndicated strips," he told me, "but in a market this tight, your work needs to be transcendent."

I was, as far as I could tell, doing my best. If it wasn't transcendent already, I didn't have the faintest idea how to make it transcendent. I wasn't even sure what I was being asked to do.

A year of my two-year development contract had passed. Despair began to set in. And that's when the unicorn made her appearance.

One day I wrote a strip with a unicorn in it. It was a one-off joke, riffing on a theme that was looming large in my life at the time: knowing what counts as a reasonable expectation. Phoebe was conversing with a voice off camera about whether her ideas about her life were realistic. Final panel: pan out, and look, she's talking about this to a unicorn.

And then the unicorn wouldn't leave. Once she was there, she was there. She more or less announced herself as the second main character in the strip.

Being a unicorn, she wanted attention. She needed to shine in front of an admiring audience. This dovetailed nicely with my own goals. I named her Marigold Heavenly Nostrils, a name I got by typing my own name into an online unicorn-name generator.

The strip must, at last, have transcended, because it launched in over a hundred newspapers. The books have done pretty well, too, as evidenced by the fact that this one is the fourth.

Every year I've spent in the company of Marigold Heavenly Nostrils has had more magic in it than the last.

Unicorns are around. The one I found was the best thing that ever happened to me.

— Dana Simpson
September 2016

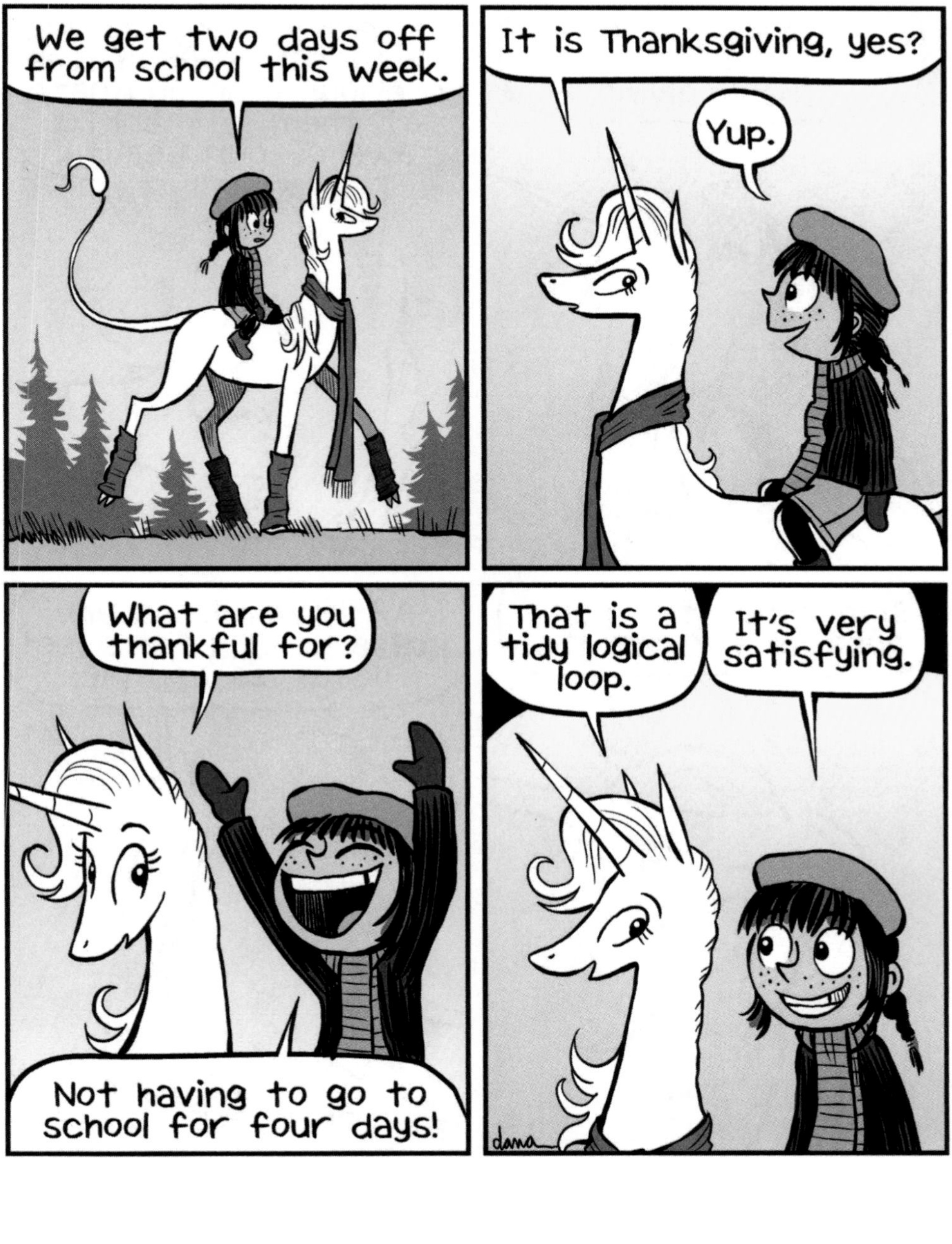
We get two days off from school this week.
It is Thanksgiving, yes?
Yup.
What are you thankful for?
Not having to go to school for four days!
That is a tidy logical loop.
It's very satisfying.
dana

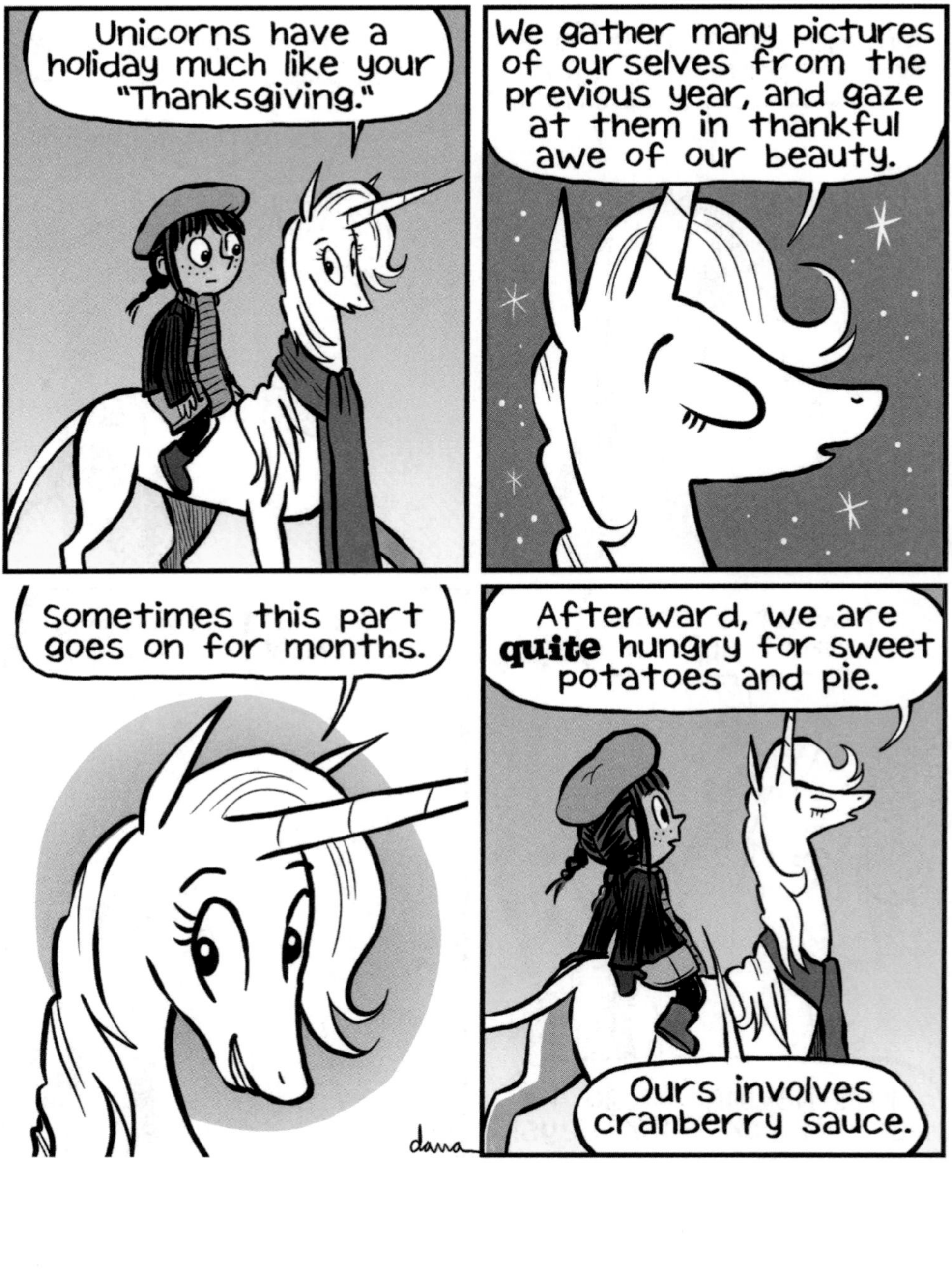
Unicorns have a holiday much like your "Thanksgiving."
We gather many pictures of ourselves from the previous year, and gaze at them in thankful awe of our beauty.
Sometimes this part goes on for months.
Afterward, we are **quite** hungry for sweet potatoes and pie.
Ours involves cranberry sauce.
dana

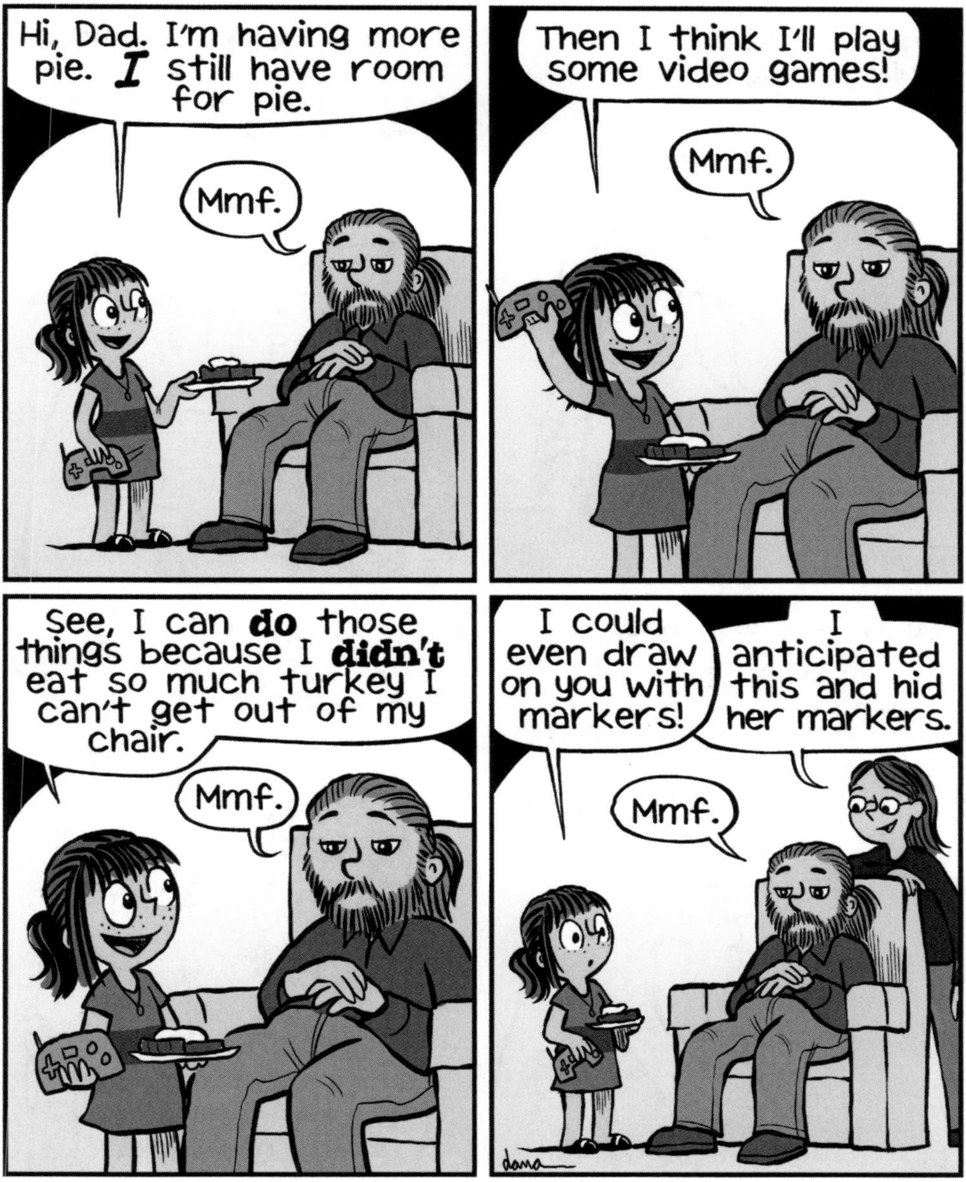
Hi, Dad. I'm having more pie. **I** still have room for pie.
Mmf.
Then I think I'll play some video games!
Mmf.
See, I can **do** those things because I **didn't** eat so much turkey I can't get out of my chair.
Mmf.
I could even draw on you with markers!
I anticipated this and hid her markers.
Mmf.
dana

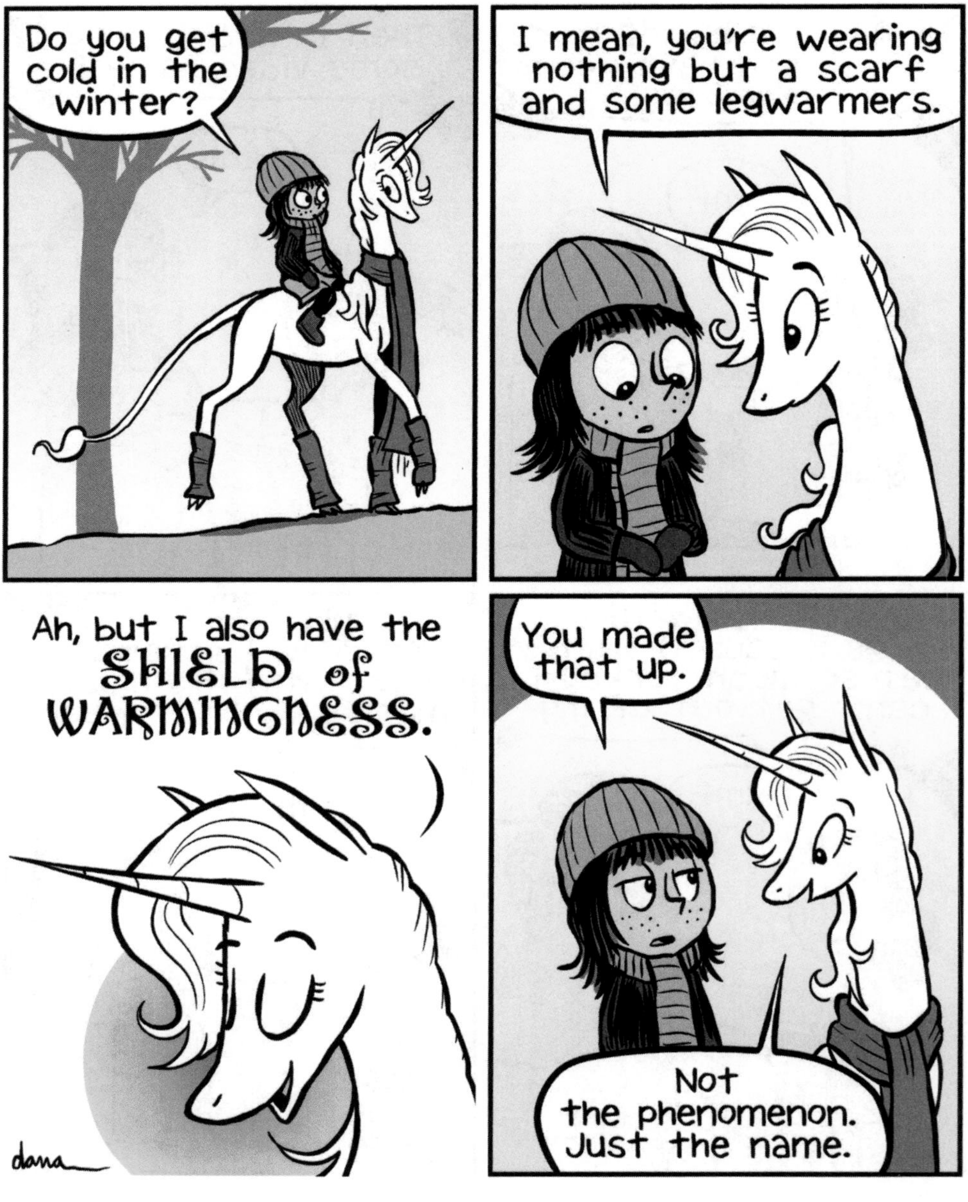
Do you get cold in the winter?
I mean, you're wearing nothing but a scarf and some legwarmers.
Ah, but I also have the SHIELD of WARMINGNESS.
You made that up.
Not the phenomenon. Just the name.
dana

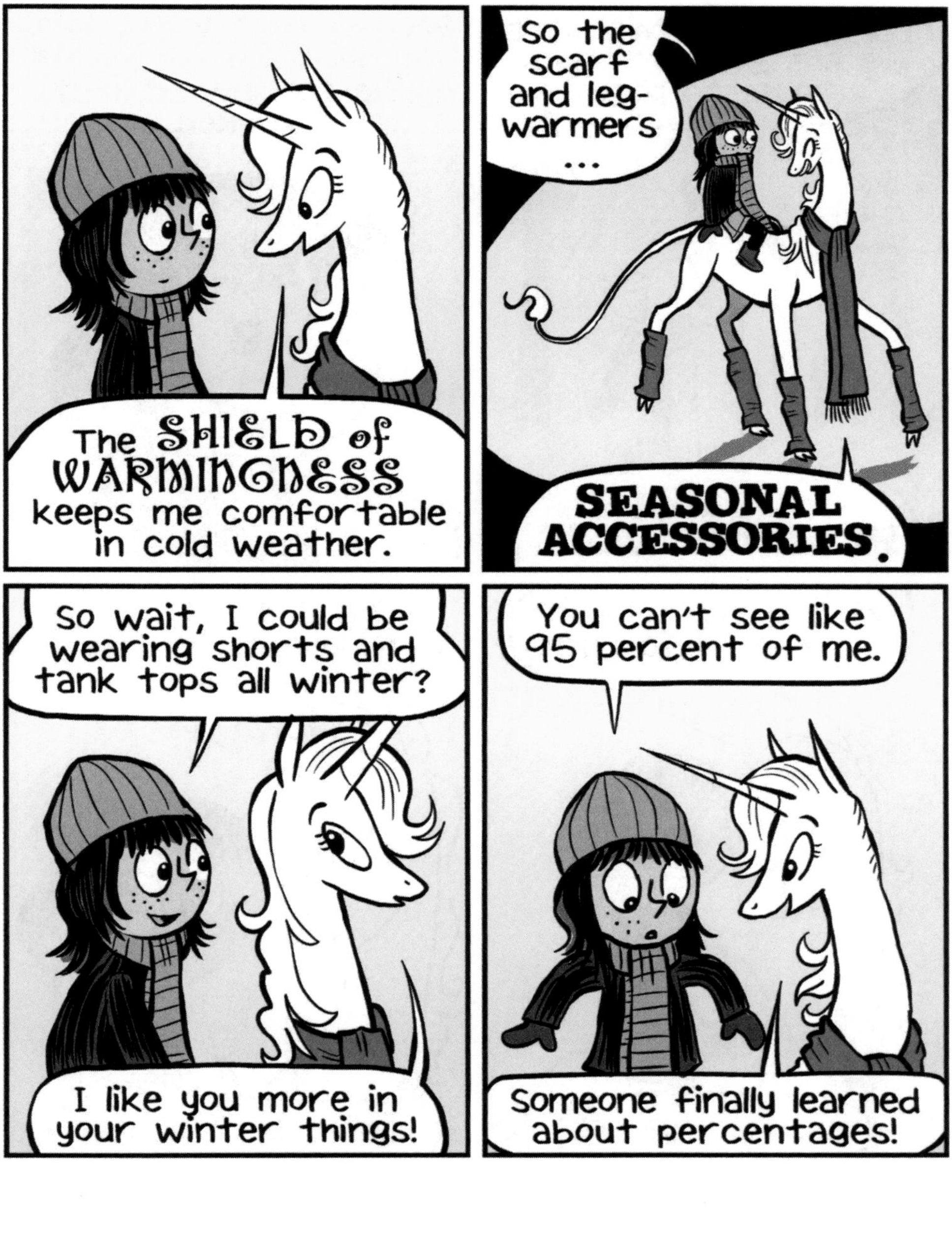
The SHIELD of WARMINGNESS keeps me comfortable in cold weather.
So the scarf and leg-warmers ...
SEASONAL ACCESSORIES.
So wait, I could be wearing shorts and tank tops all winter?
I like you more in your winter things!
You can't see like 95 percent of me.
Someone finally learned about percentages!

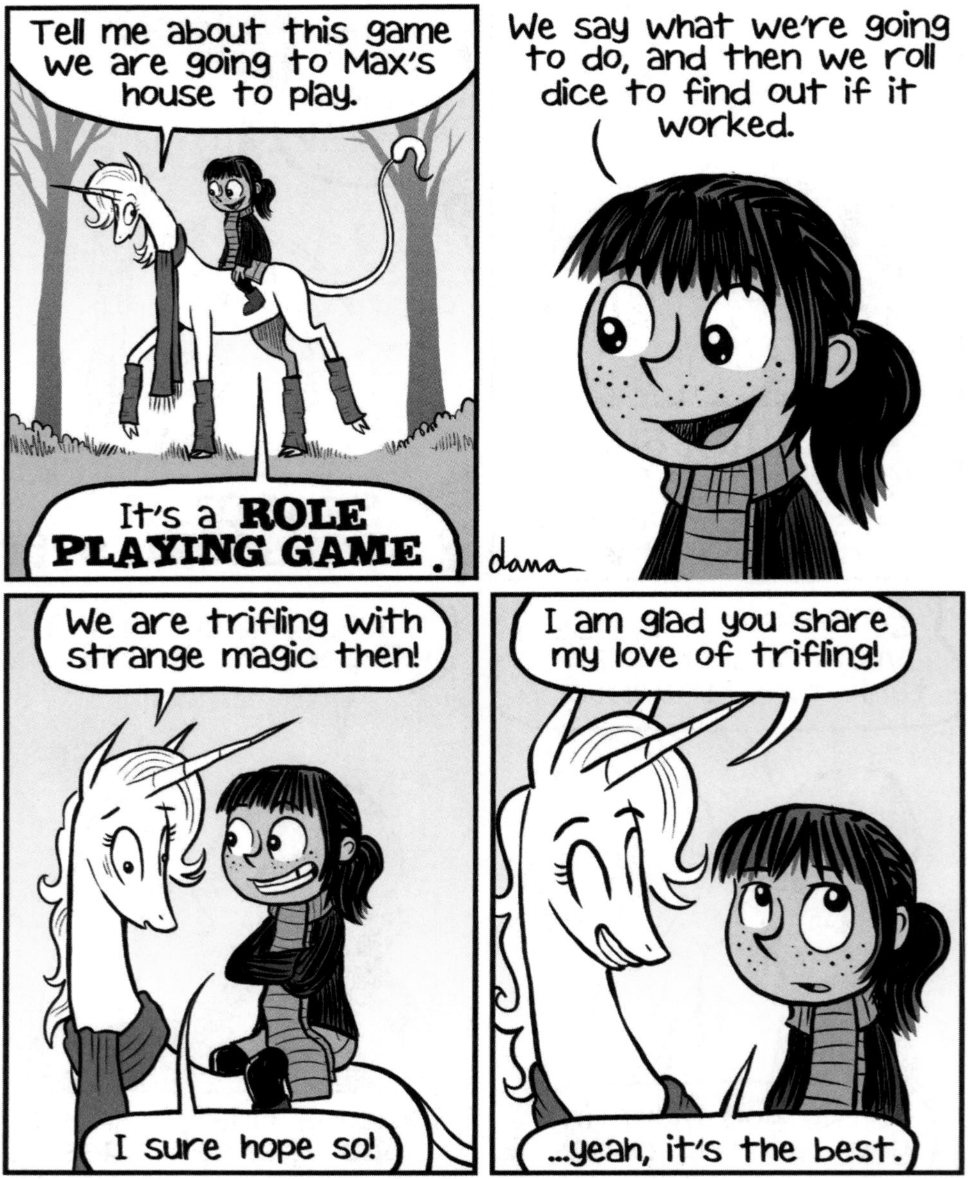

Tell me about this game we are going to Max's house to play.
It's a **ROLE PLAYING GAME**.
We say what we're going to do, and then we roll dice to find out if it worked.
dana
We are trifling with strange magic then!
I sure hope so!
I am glad you share my love of trifling!
...yeah, it's the best.

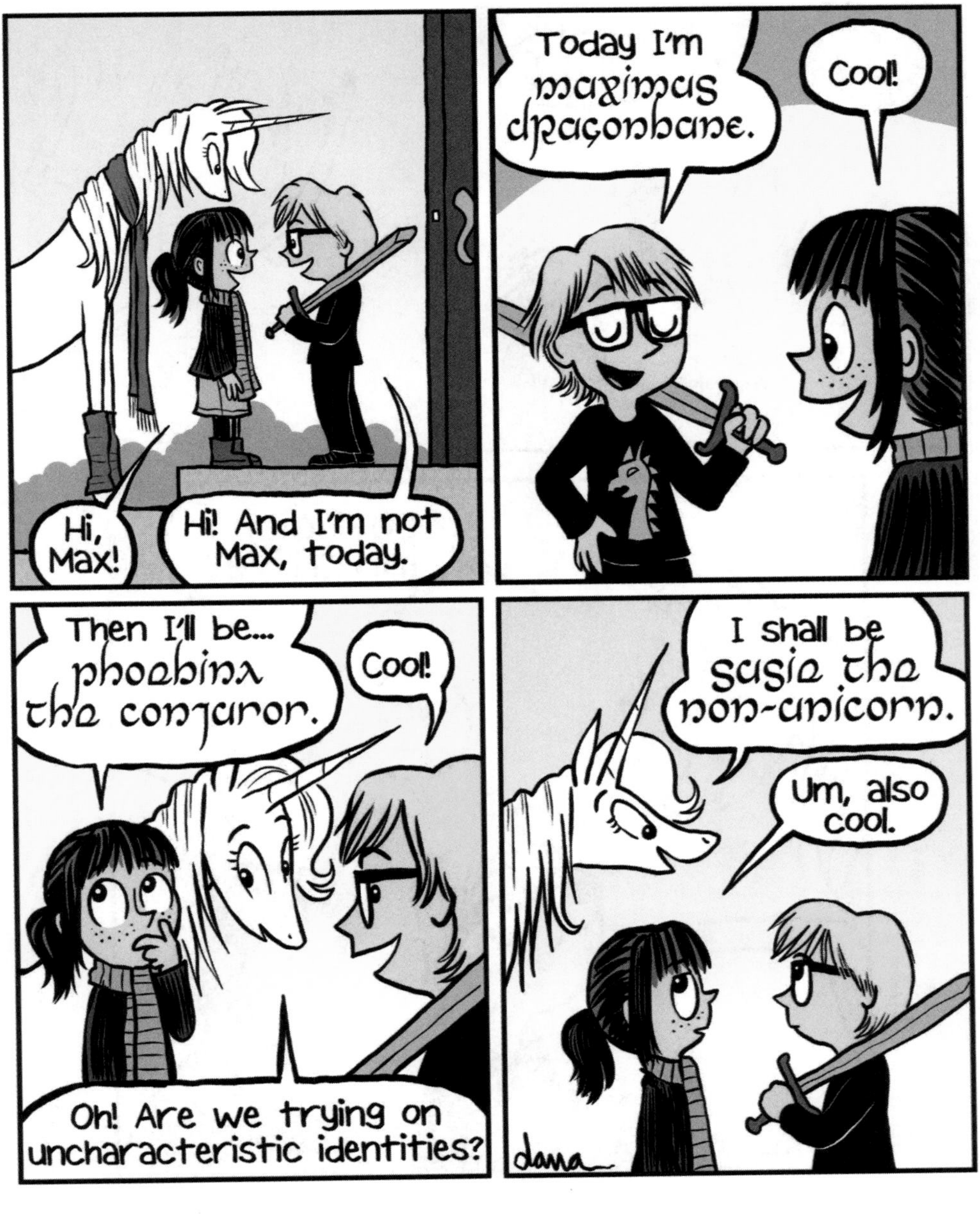
Hi, Max!
Hi! And I'm not Max, today.
Today I'm maximus dragonbane.
Cool!
Then I'll be... phoebina the conjuror.
Cool!
Oh! Are we trying on uncharacteristic identities?
I shall be susie the non-unicorn.
Um, also cool.
dana

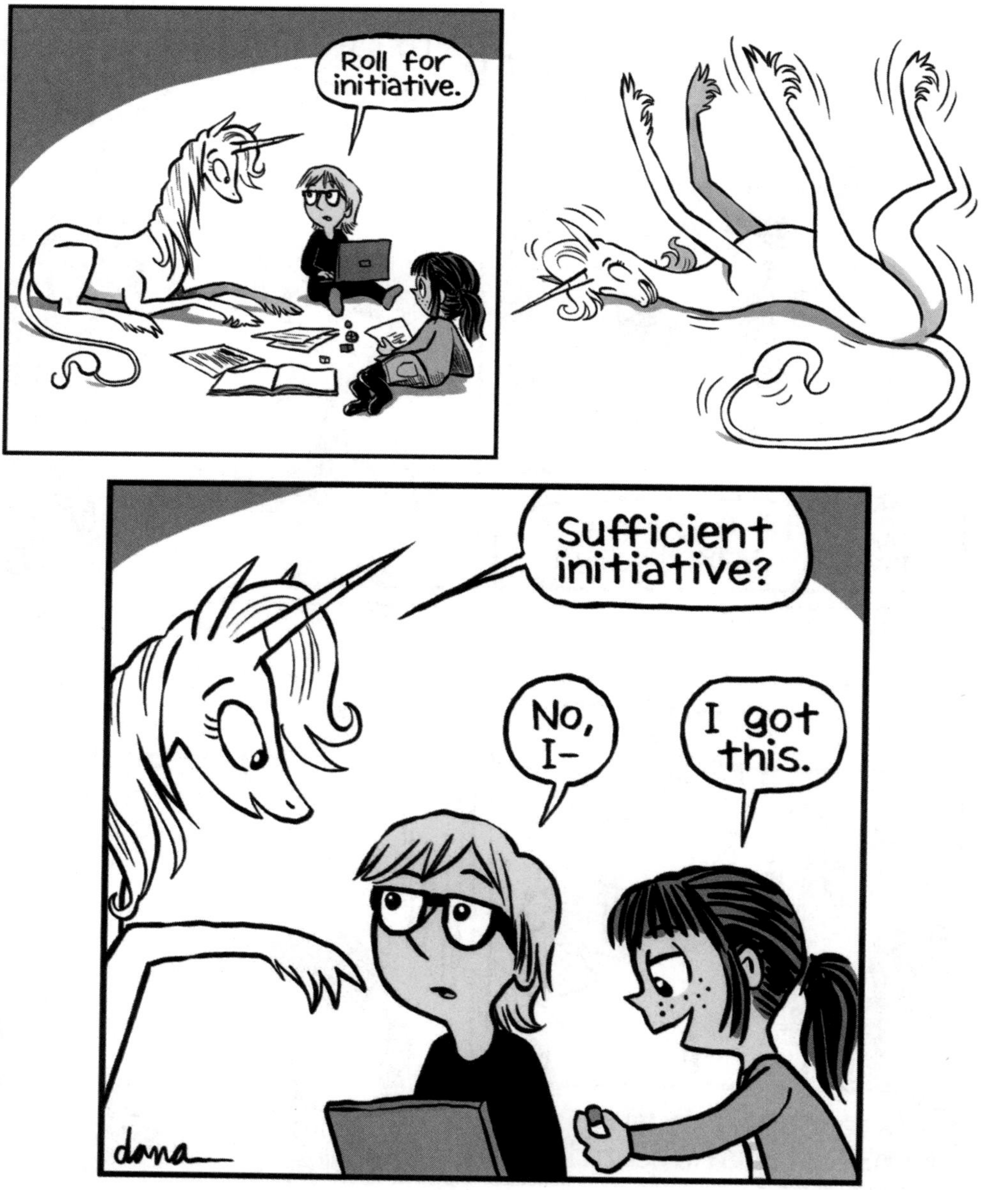

Roll for initiative.
Sufficient initiative?
No, I-
I got this.
dana

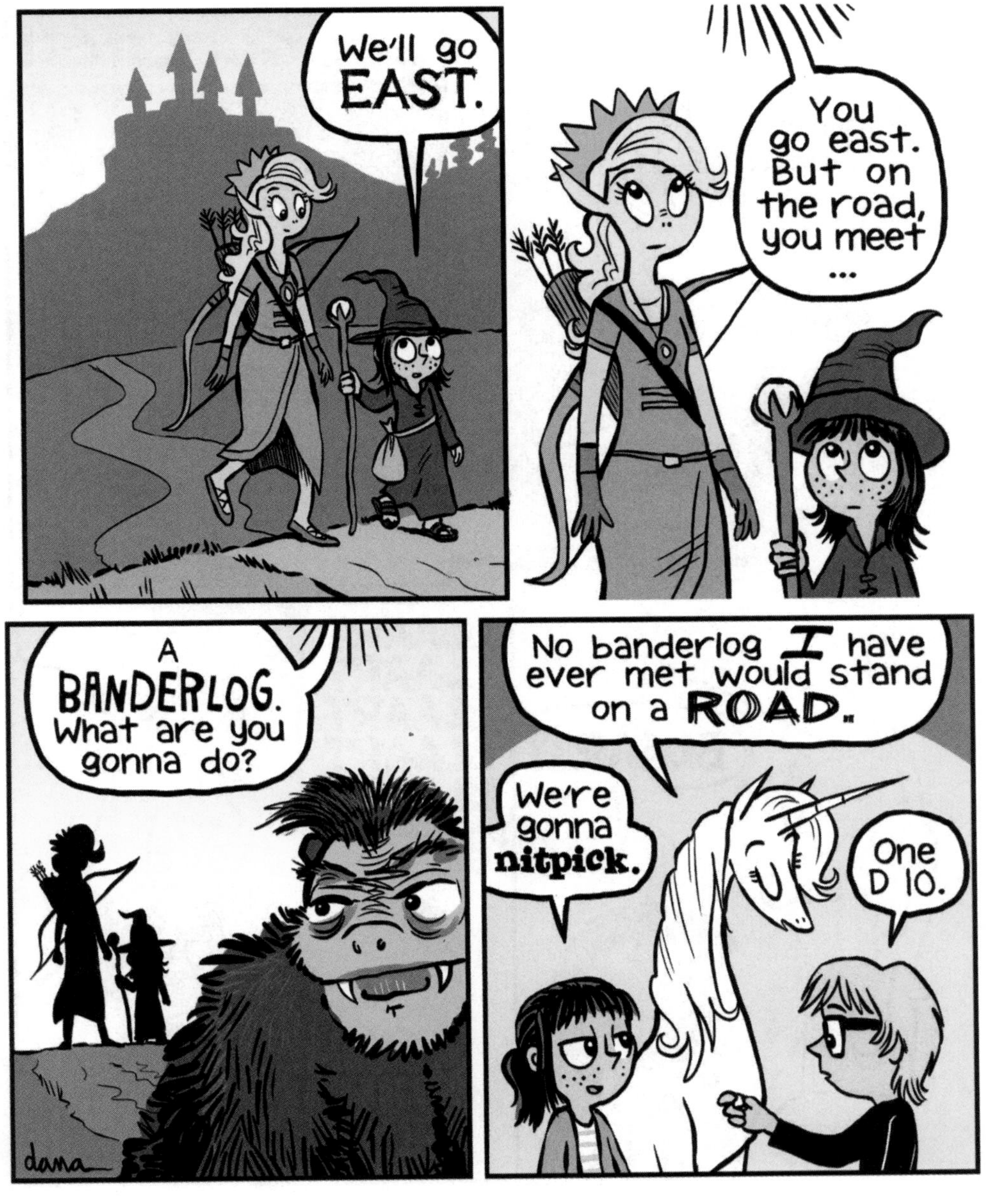
We'll go EAST.
You go east. But on the road, you meet ...
A BANDERLOG. What are you gonna do?
No banderlog I have ever met would stand on a ROAD.
We're gonna nitpick.
One D 10.
dana

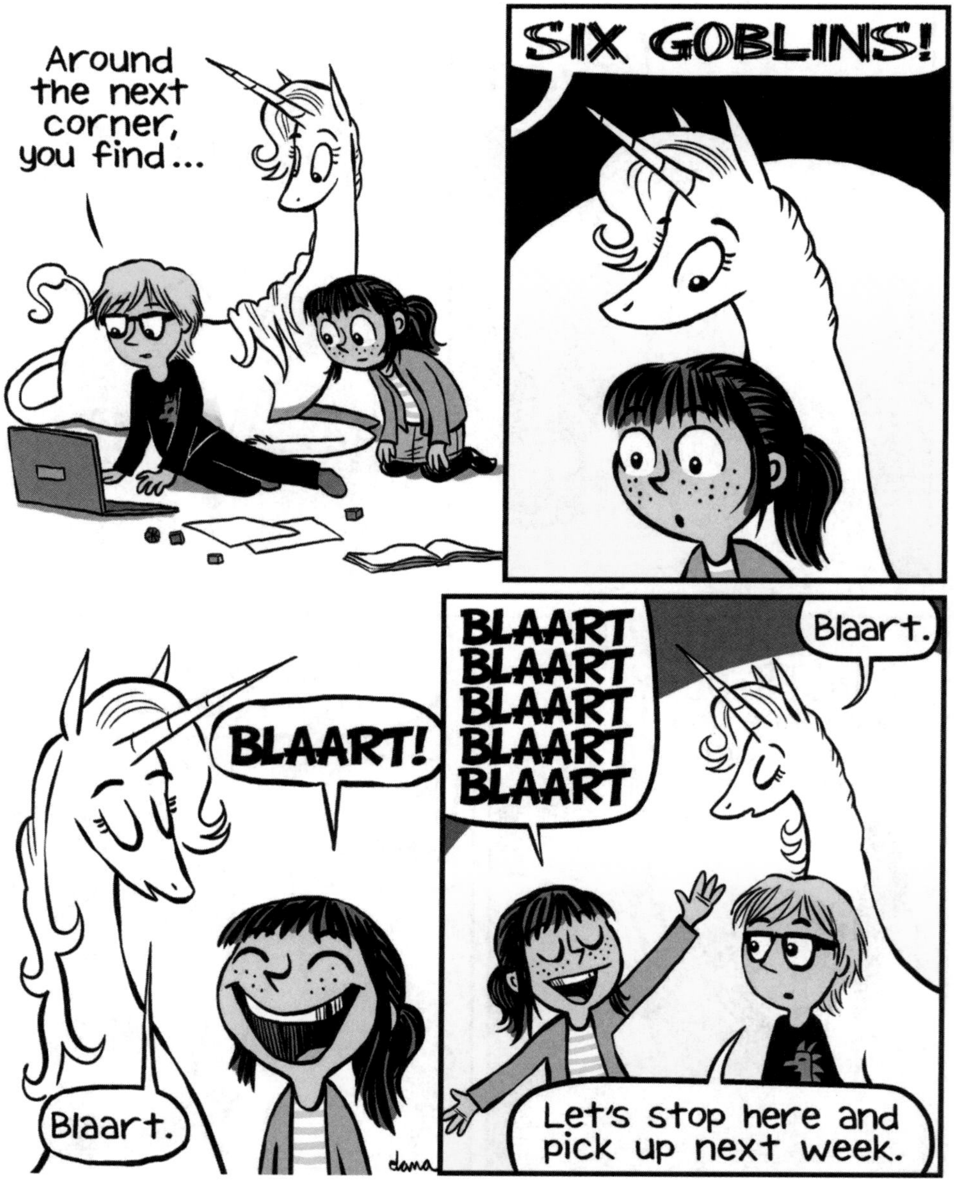
Around the next corner, you find...
SIX GOBLINS!
BLAART!
Blaart.
BLAART BLAART BLAART BLAART BLAART
Blaart.
Let's stop here and pick up next week.
dana

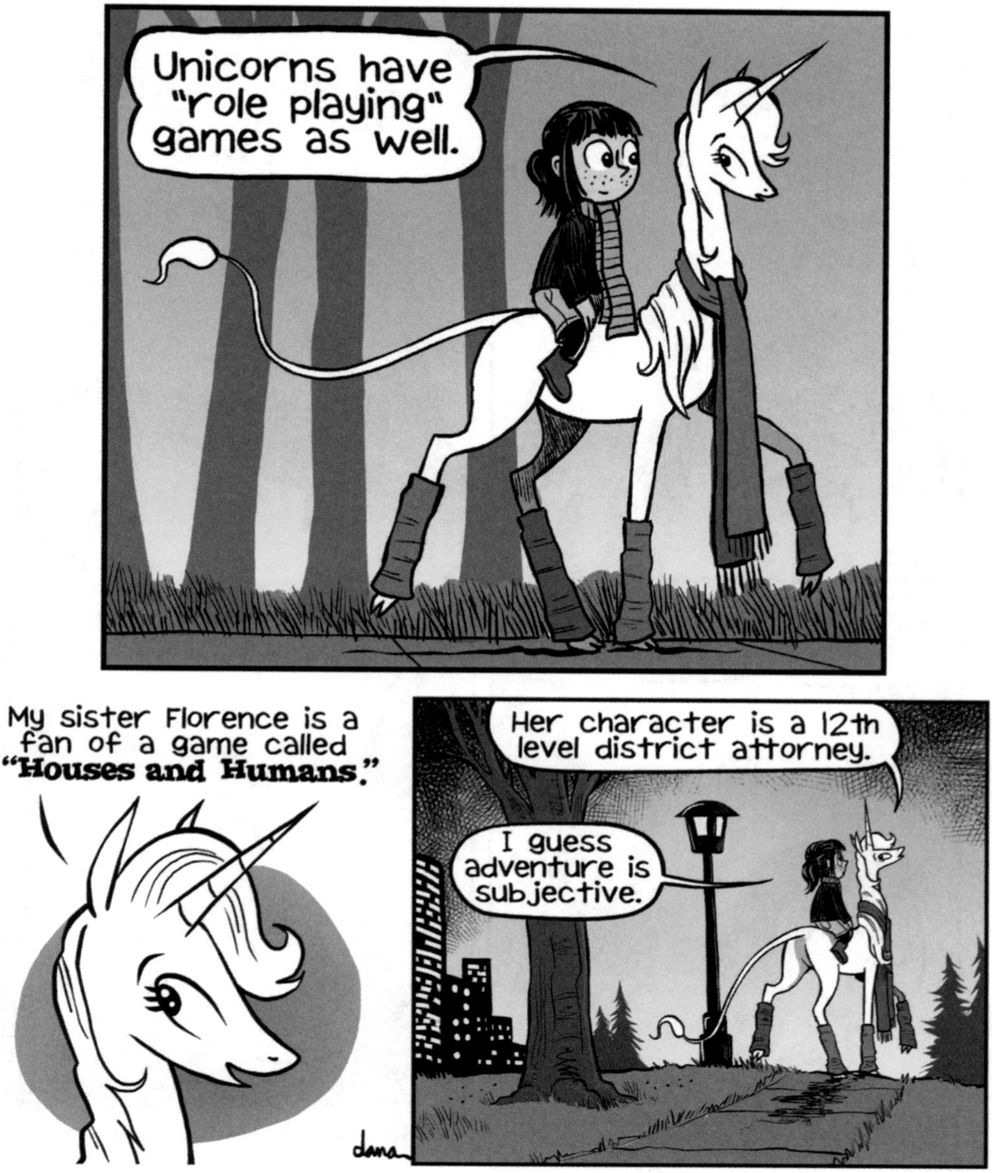
Unicorns have "role playing" games as well.
My sister Florence is a fan of a game called "**Houses and Humans**."
Her character is a 12th level district attorney.
I guess adventure is subjective.
dana

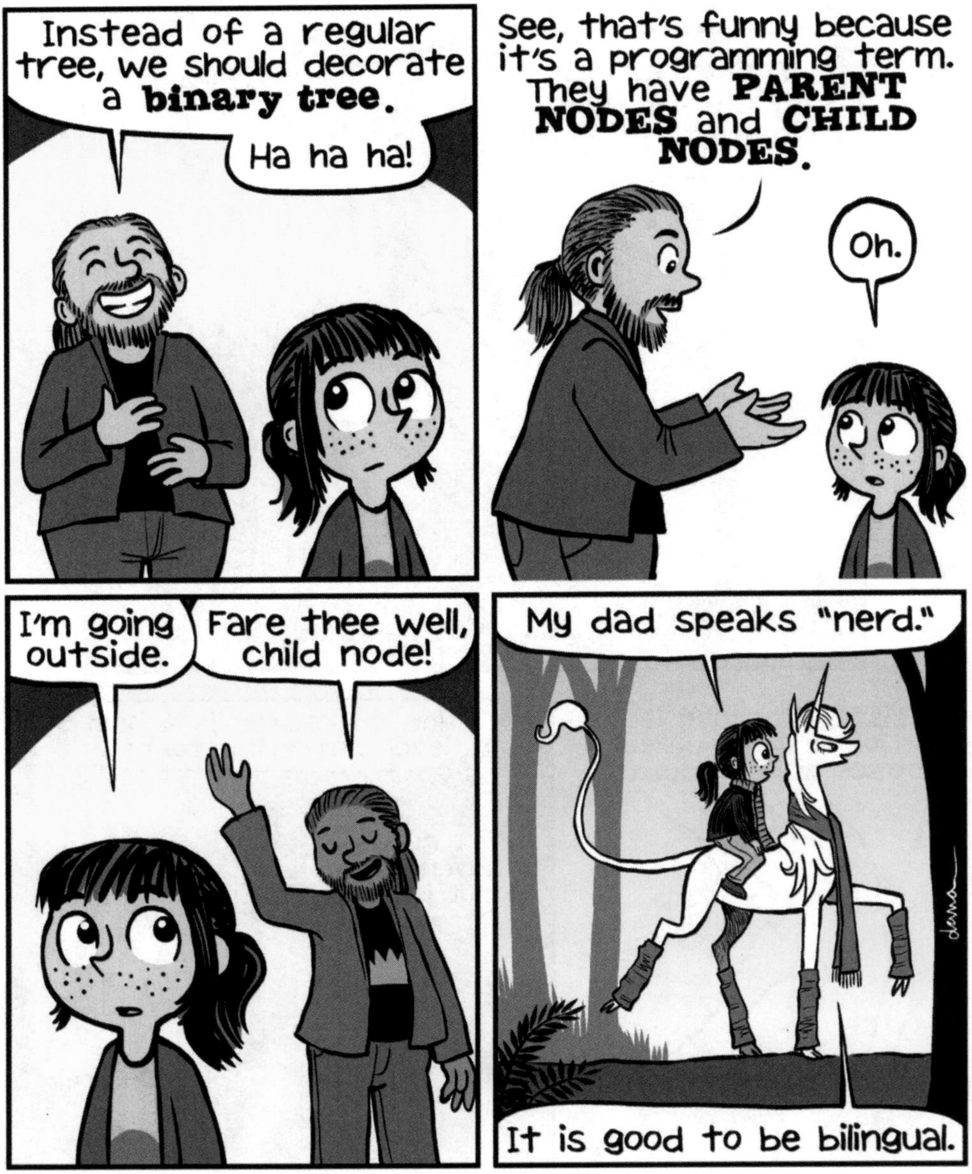
Instead of a regular tree, we should decorate a **binary tree**.
Ha ha ha!
See, that's funny because it's a programming term. They have **PARENT NODES** and **CHILD NODES**.
Oh.
I'm going outside.
Fare thee well, child node!
My dad speaks "nerd."
It is good to be bilingual.

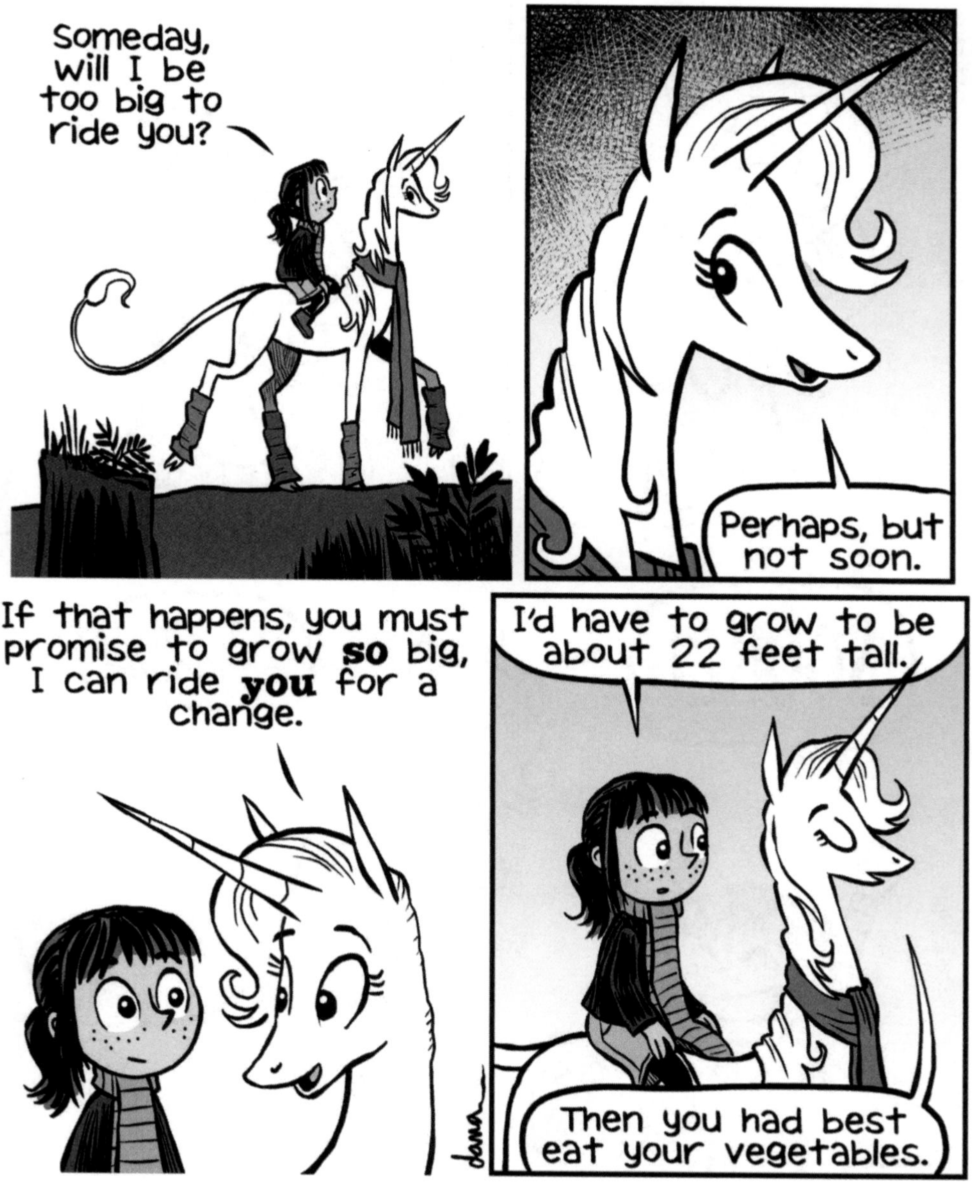
Someday, will I be too big to ride you?
Perhaps, but not soon.
If that happens, you must promise to grow **so** big, I can ride **you** for a change.
I'd have to grow to be about 22 feet tall.
Then you had best eat your vegetables.
dana

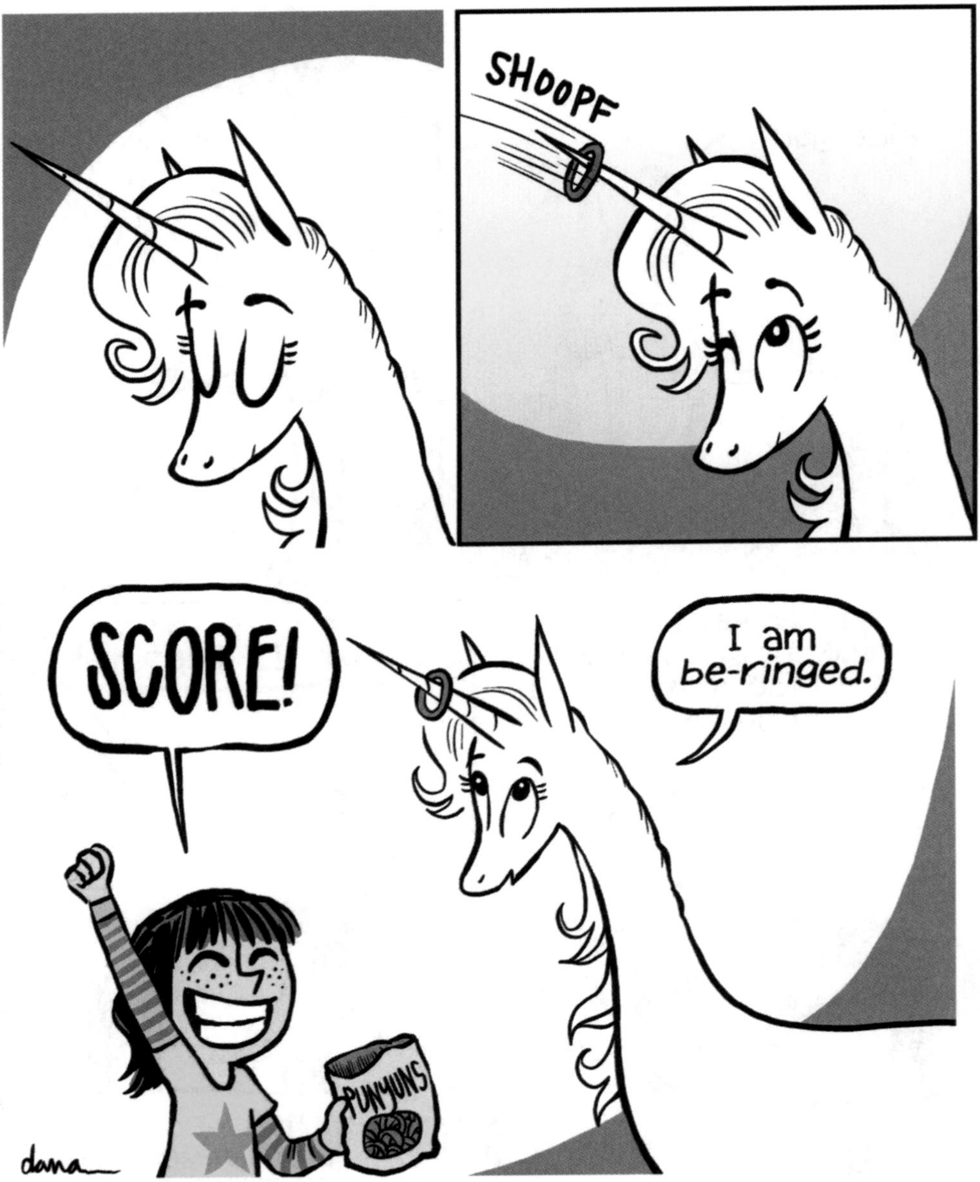
SHOOPF
SCORE!
I am be-ringed.
PUNYUNS
dana

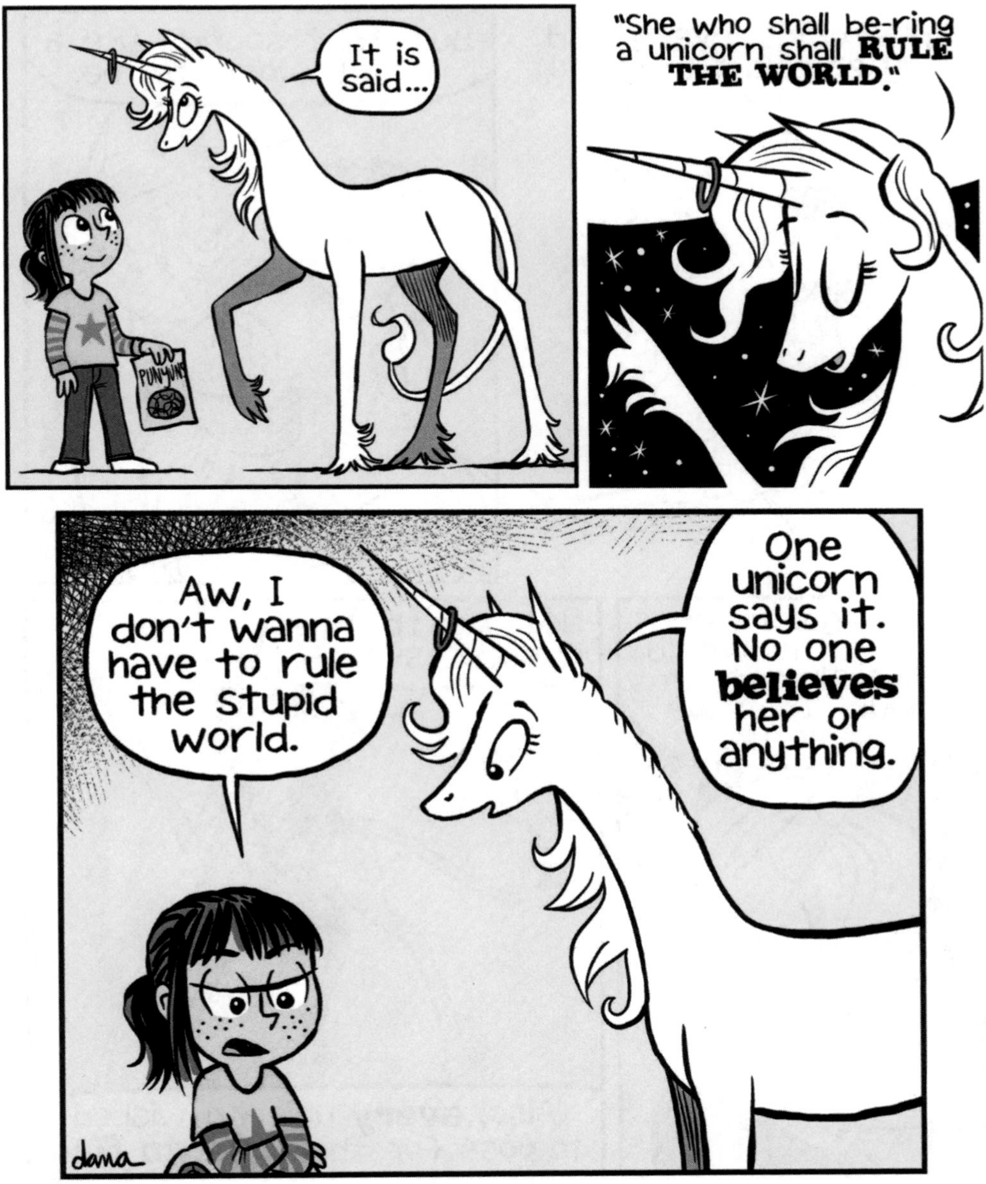
It is said...
"She who shall be-ring a unicorn shall **RULE THE WORLD.**"
PUNYUNS
Aw, I don't wanna have to rule the stupid world.
One unicorn says it. No one **believes** her or anything.
dana

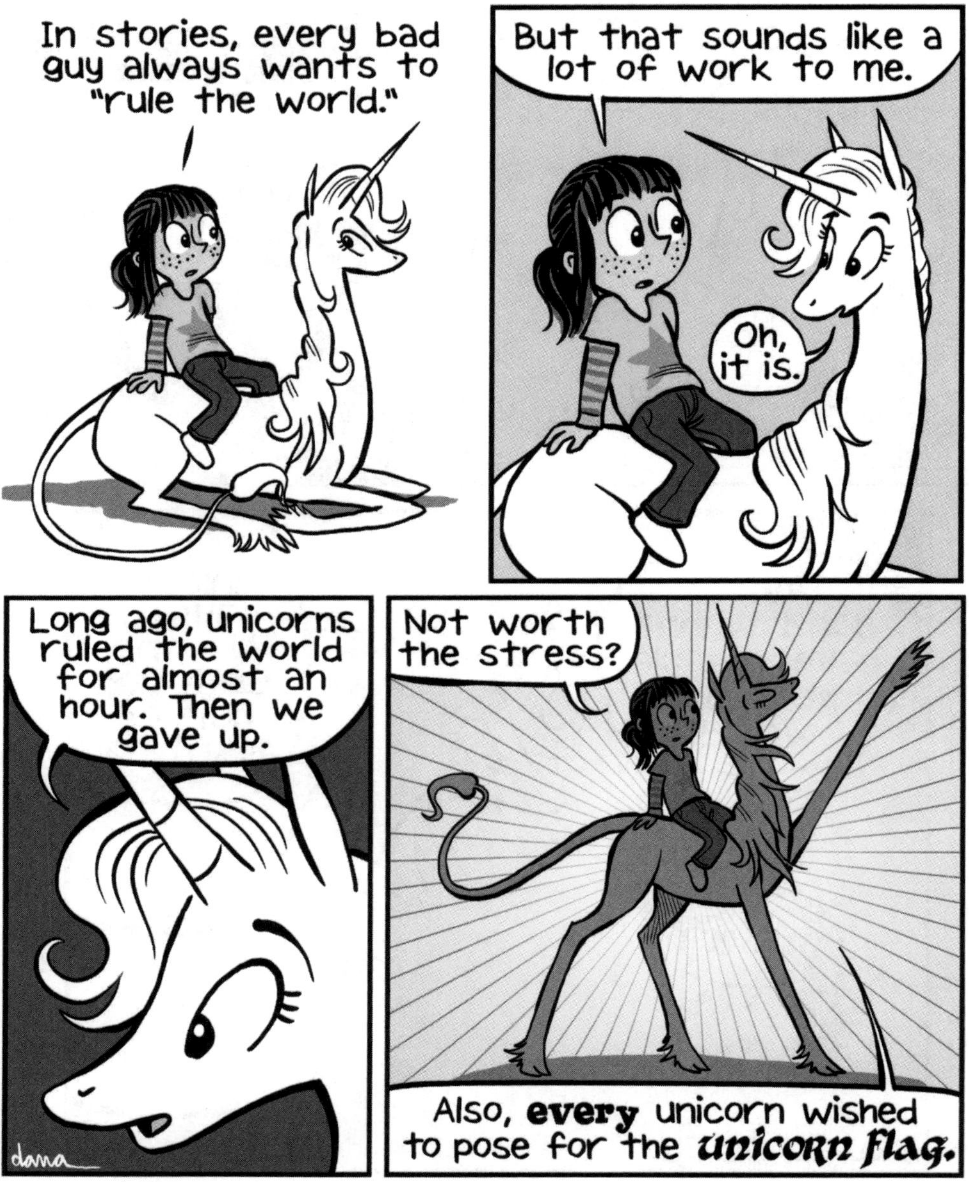
In stories, every bad guy always wants to "rule the world."
But that sounds like a lot of work to me.
Oh, it is.
Long ago, unicorns ruled the world for almost an hour. Then we gave up.
dana
Not worth the stress?
Also, **every** unicorn wished to pose for the ***unicorn flag.***

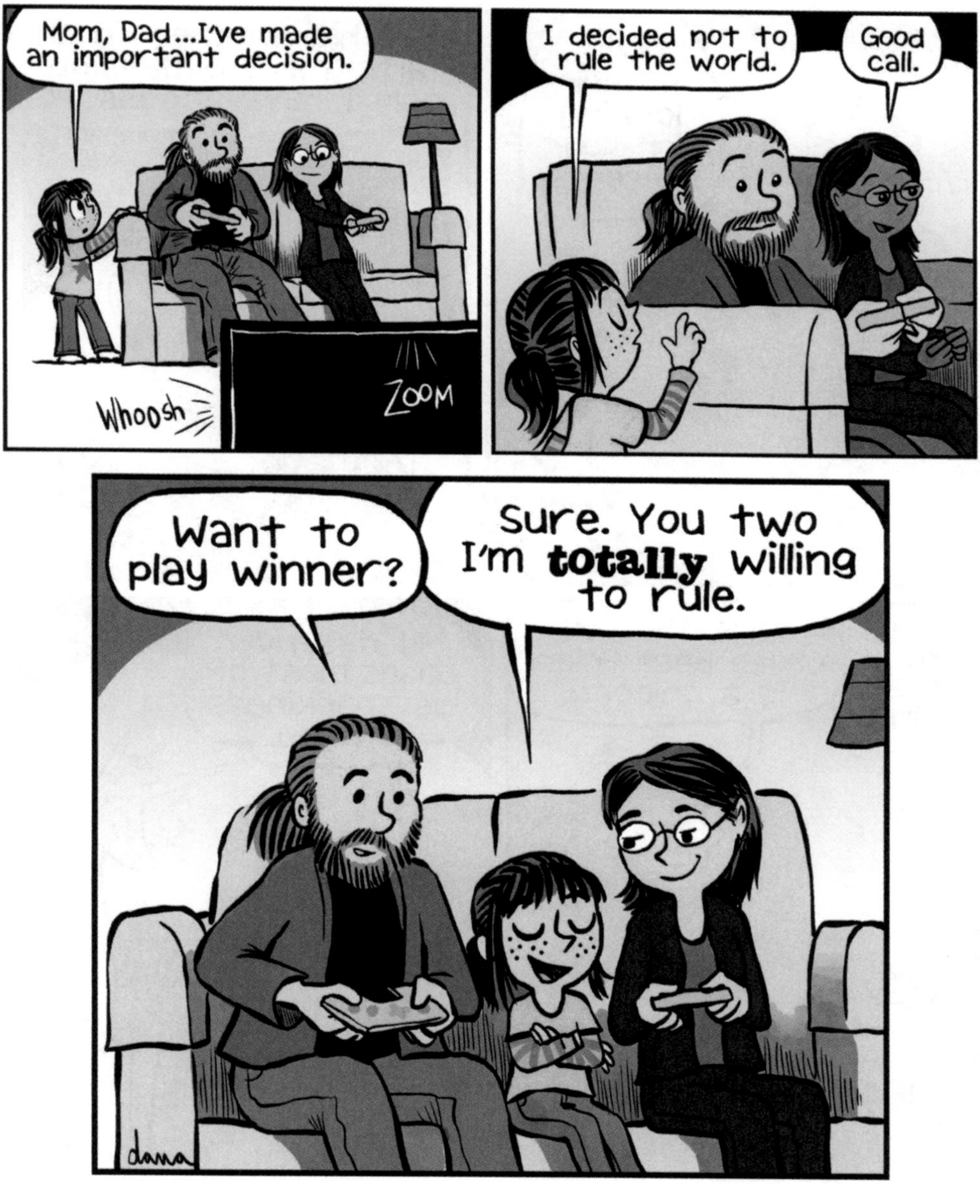
Mom, Dad...I've made an important decision.
Whoosh
ZOOM
I decided not to rule the world.
Good call.
Want to play winner?
Sure. You two I'm **totally** willing to rule.
dana

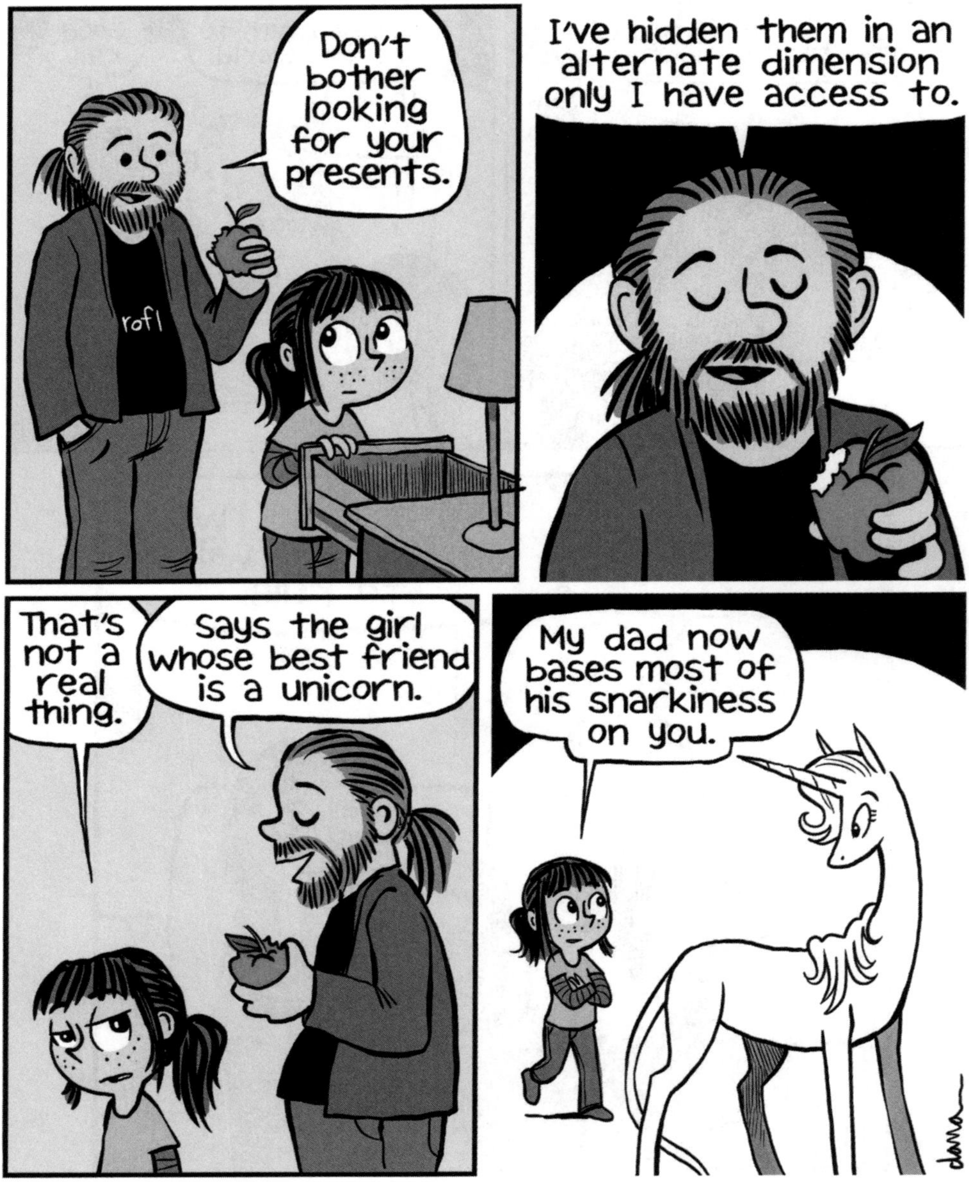

Don't bother looking for your presents.
rofl
I've hidden them in an alternate dimension only I have access to.
That's not a real thing.
Says the girl whose best friend is a unicorn.
My dad now bases most of his snarkiness on you.
dana

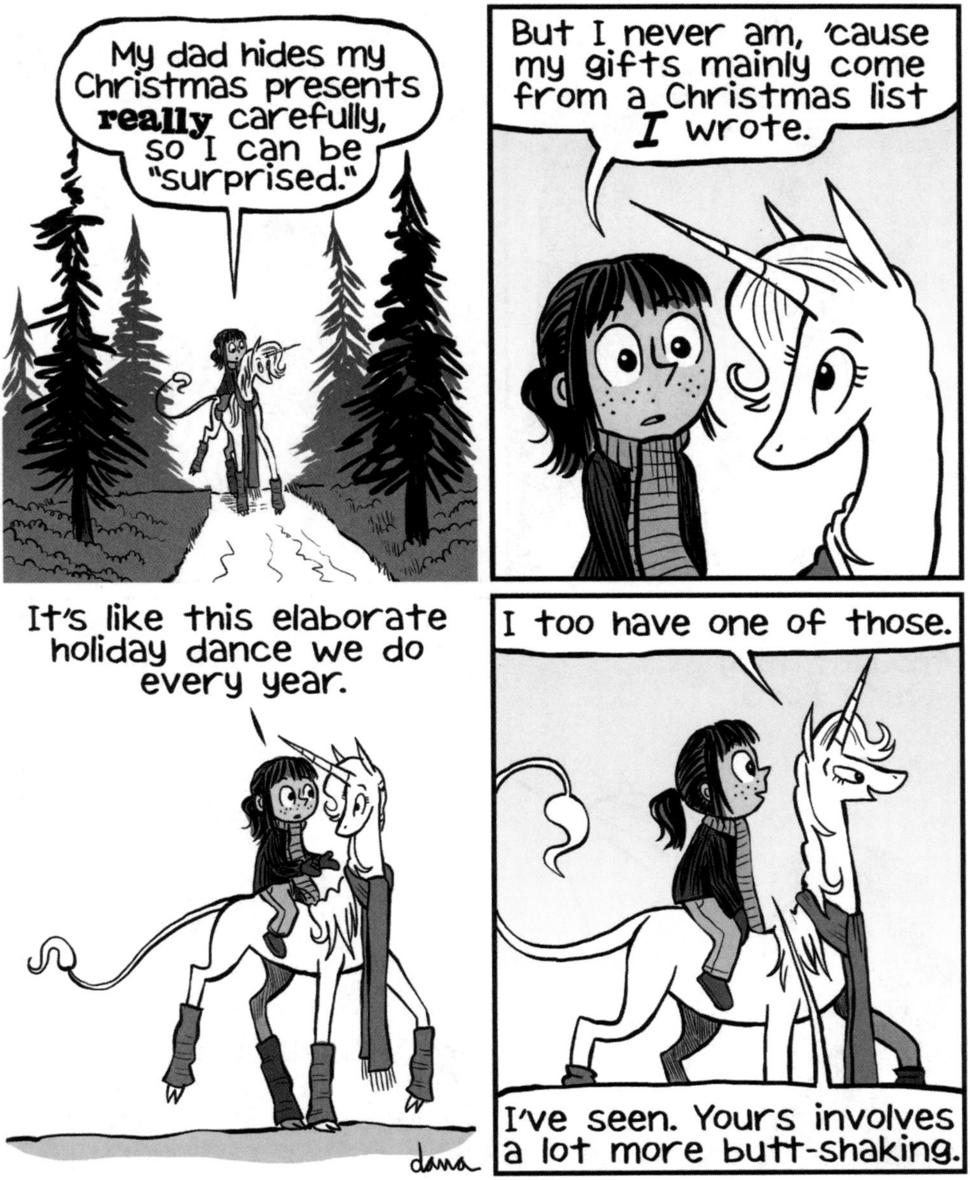
My dad hides my Christmas presents **really** carefully, so I can be "surprised."
But I never am, 'cause my gifts mainly come from a Christmas list *I* wrote.
It's like this elaborate holiday dance we do every year.
I too have one of those.
I've seen. Yours involves a lot more butt-shaking.
dana

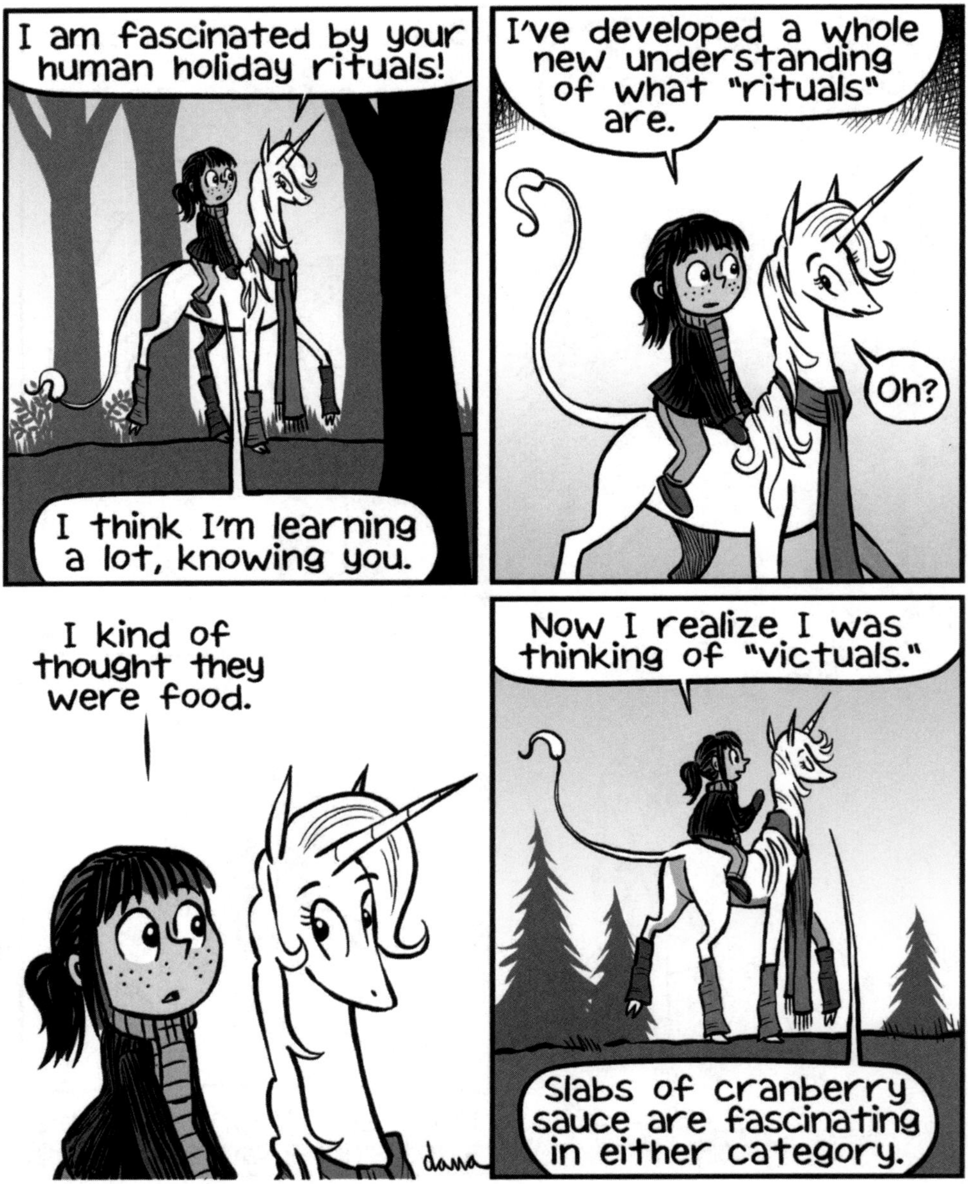
I am fascinated by your human holiday rituals!
I think I'm learning a lot, knowing you.
I've developed a whole new understanding of what "rituals" are.
Oh?
I kind of thought they were food.
Now I realize I was thinking of "victuals."
Slabs of cranberry sauce are fascinating in either category.
dana

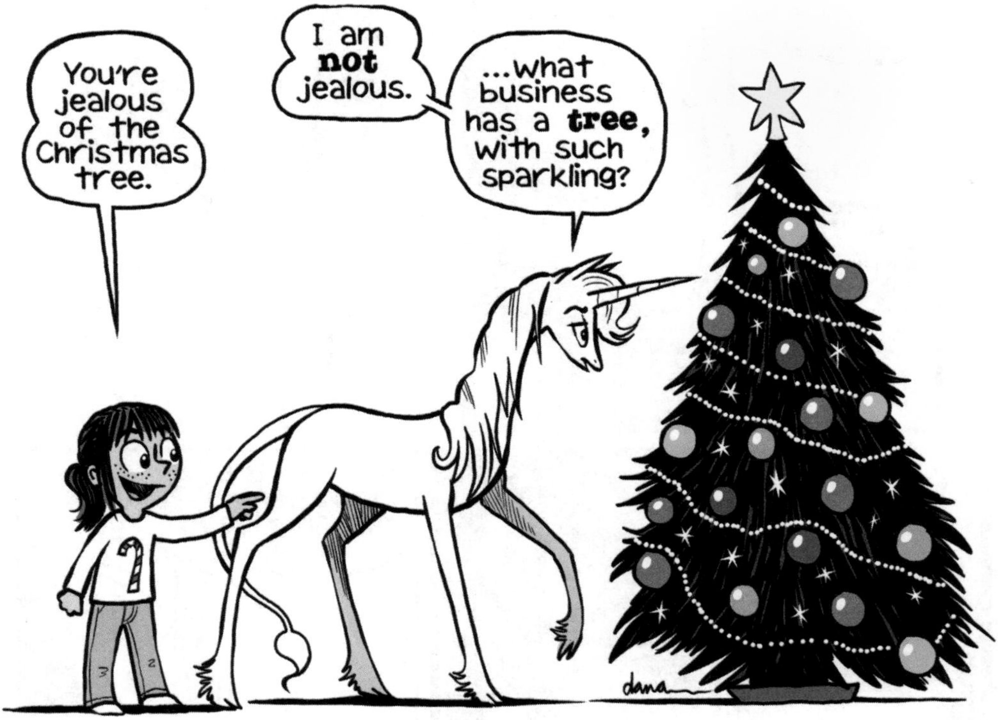
You're jealous of the Christmas tree.
I am **not** jealous.
...what business has a **tree**, with such sparkling?
dana

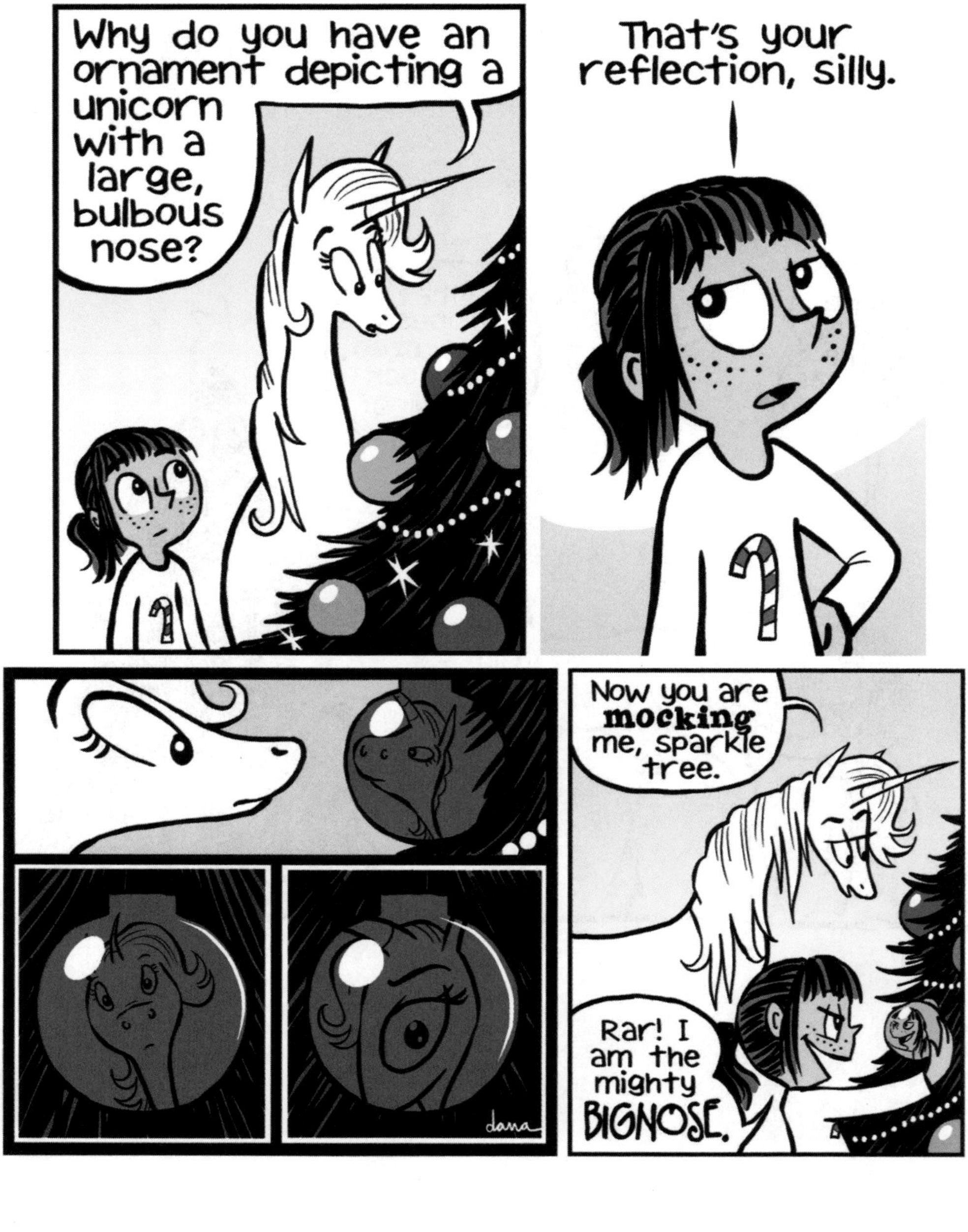
Why do you have an ornament depicting a unicorn with a large, bulbous nose?
That's your reflection, silly.
Now you are **mocking** me, sparkle tree.
Rar! I am the mighty BIGNOSE.
dana

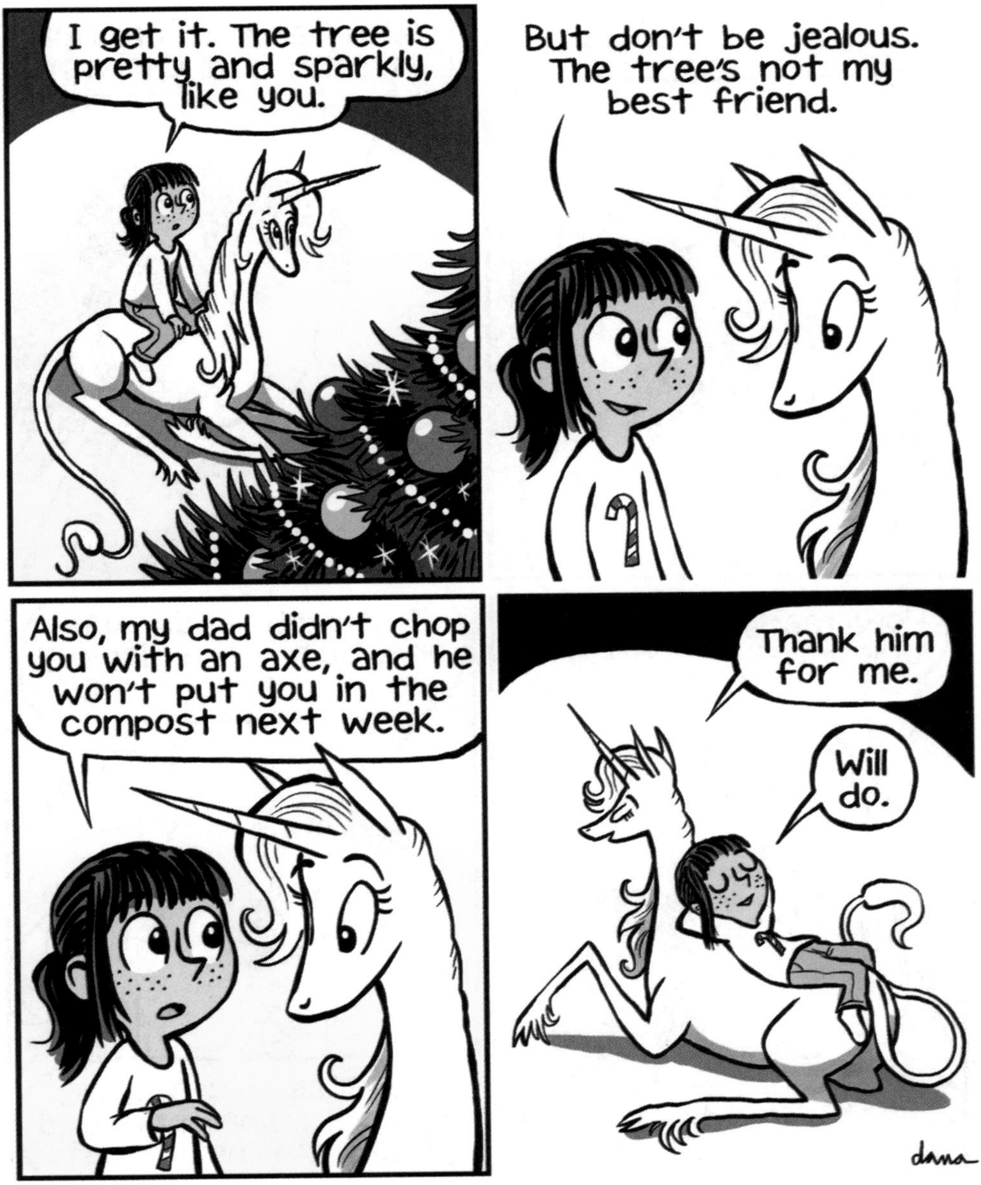
I get it. The tree is pretty and sparkly, like you.
But don't be jealous. The tree's not my best friend.
Also, my dad didn't chop you with an axe, and he won't put you in the compost next week.
Thank him for me.
Will do.
dana

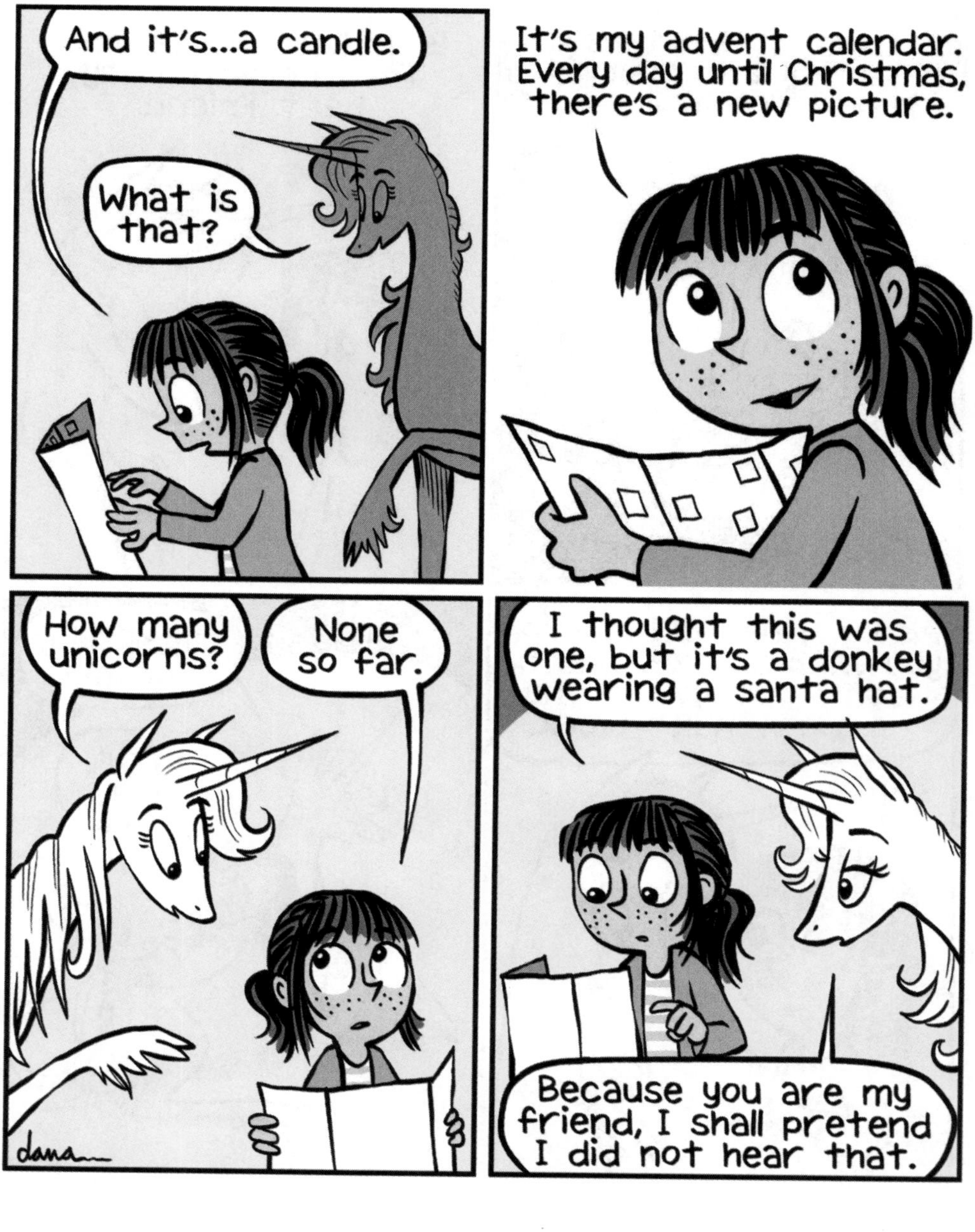
And it's...a candle.
What is that?
It's my advent calendar. Every day until Christmas, there's a new picture.
How many unicorns?
None so far.
I thought this was one, but it's a donkey wearing a santa hat.
Because you are my friend, I shall pretend I did not hear that.
dana

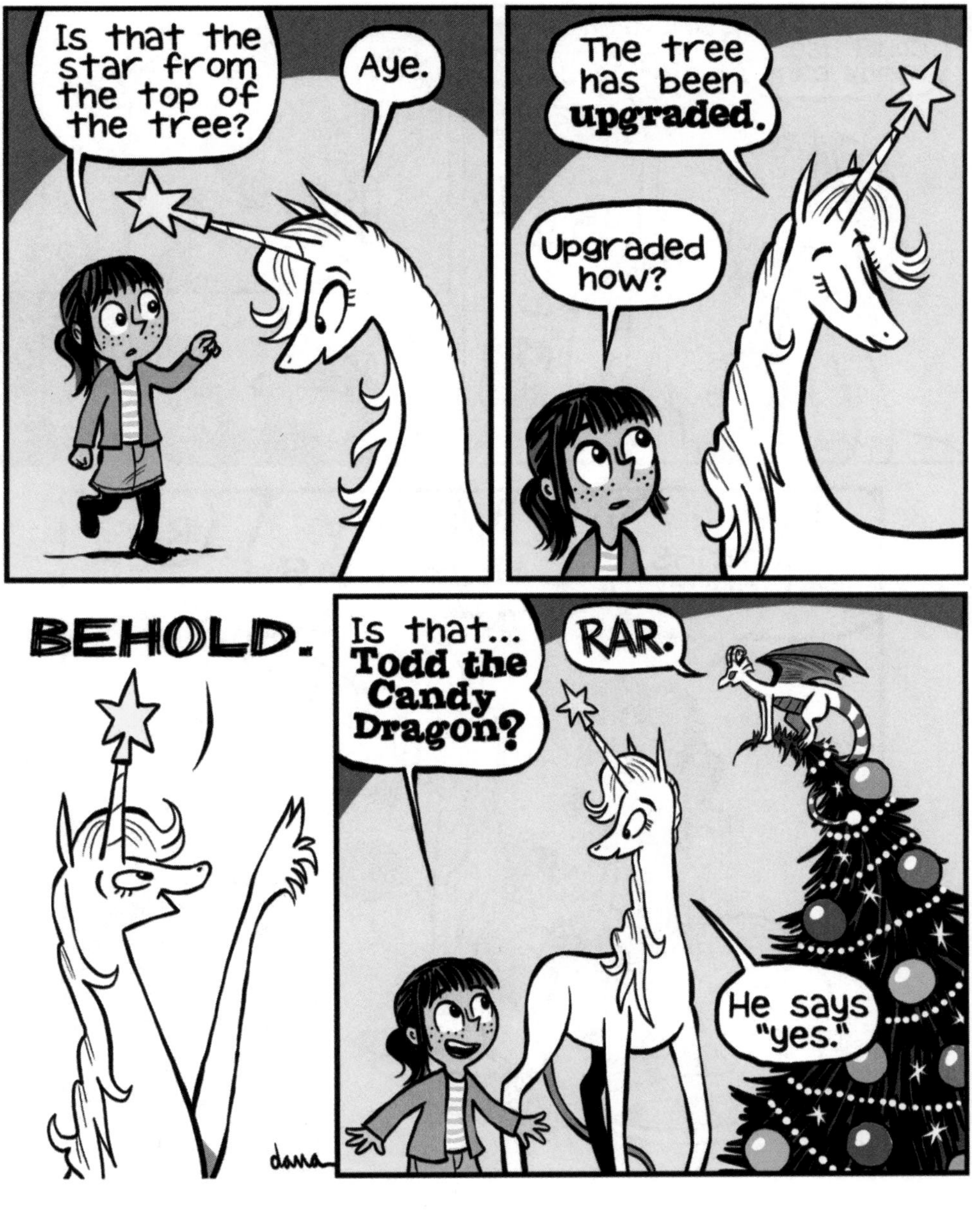
Is that the star from the top of the tree?
Aye.
The tree has been **upgraded.**
Upgraded how?
BEHOLD.
Is that... **Todd the Candy Dragon?**
RAR.
He says "yes."
dana

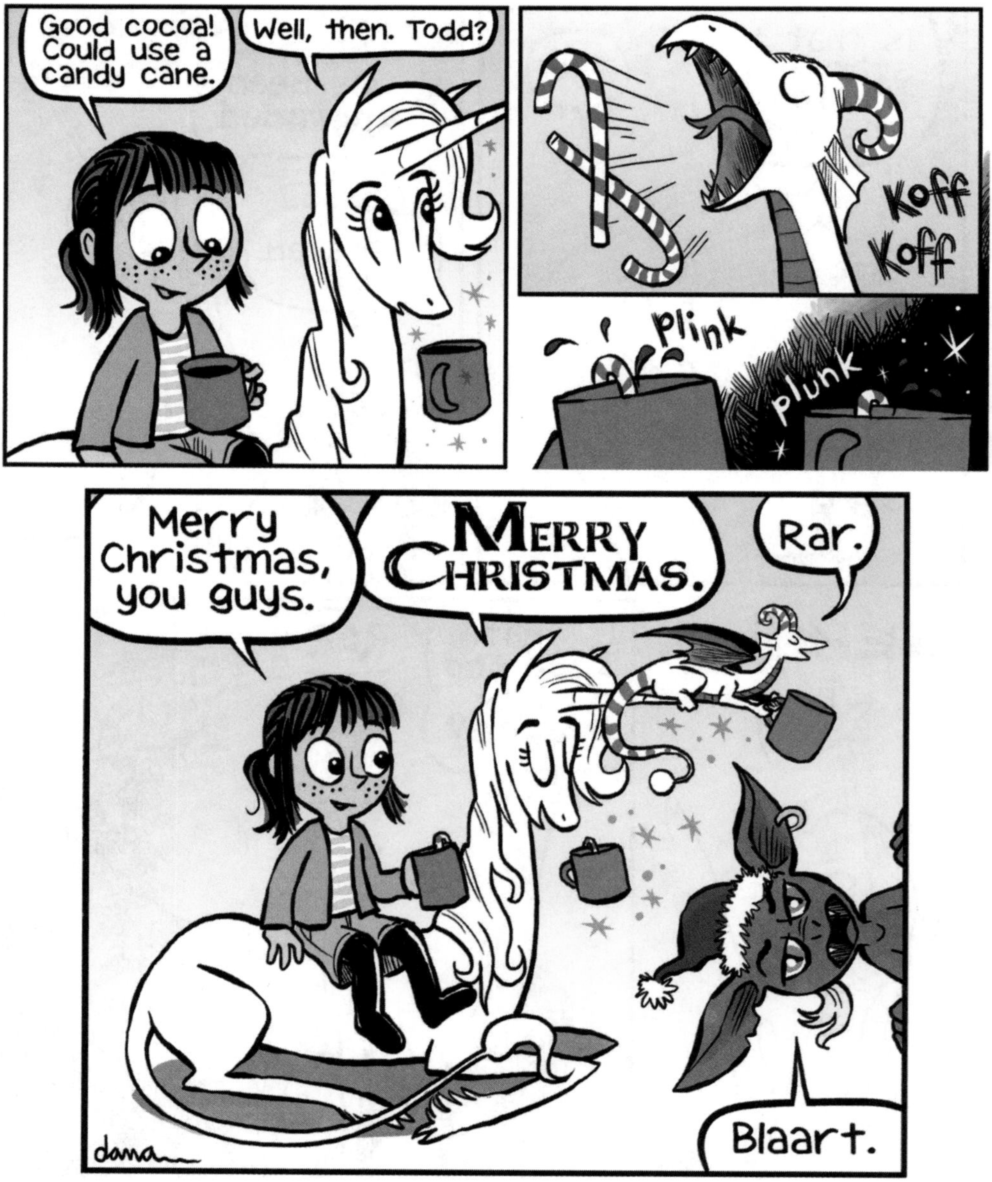
Good cocoa! Could use a candy cane.
Well, then. Todd?
Koff Koff
plink
plunk
Merry Christmas, you guys.
MERRY CHRISTMAS.
Rar.
Blaart.
dana

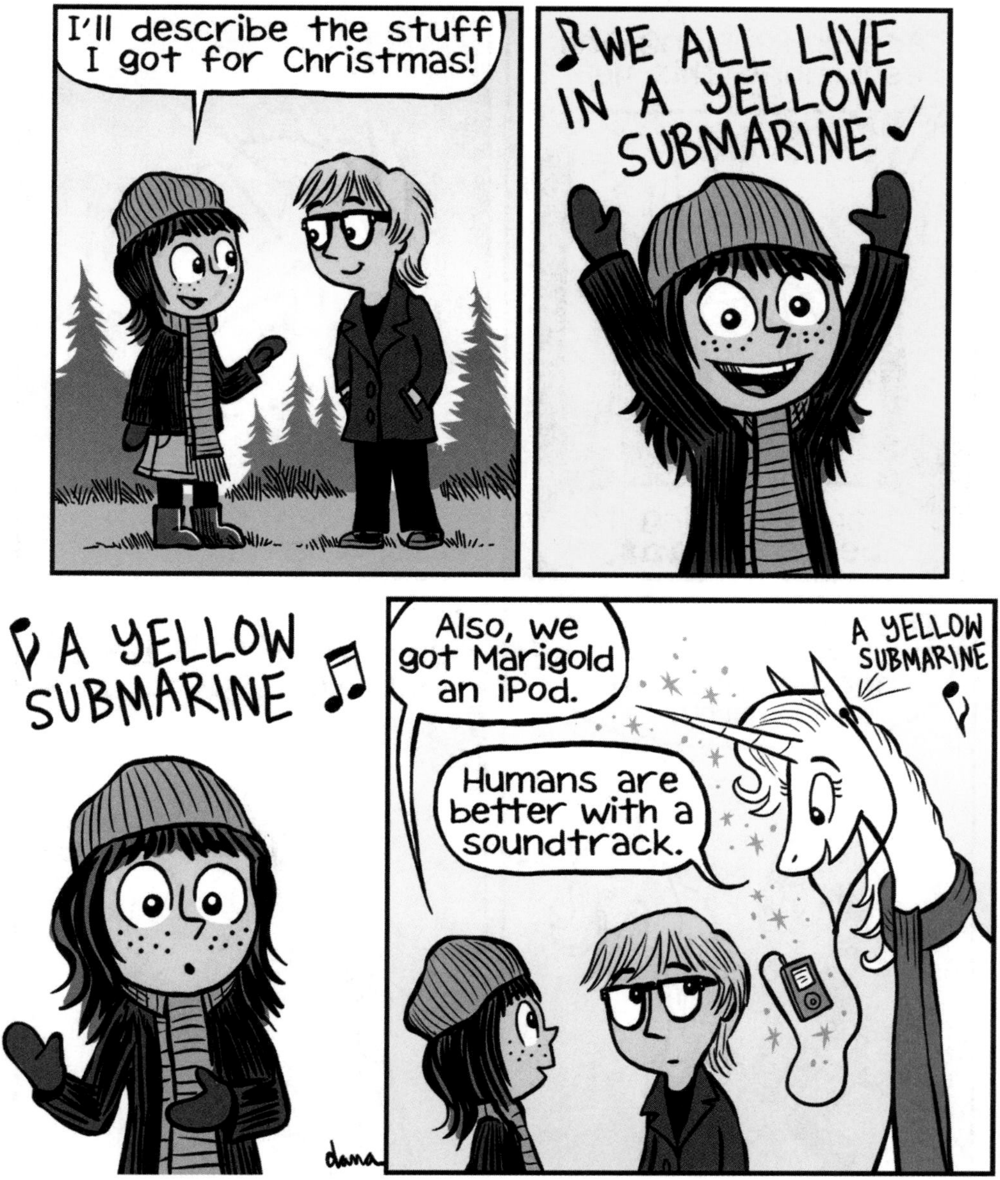

I'll describe the stuff I got for Christmas!
WE ALL LIVE IN A YELLOW SUBMARINE
A YELLOW SUBMARINE
Also, we got Marigold an iPod.
A YELLOW SUBMARINE
Humans are better with a soundtrack.
dana

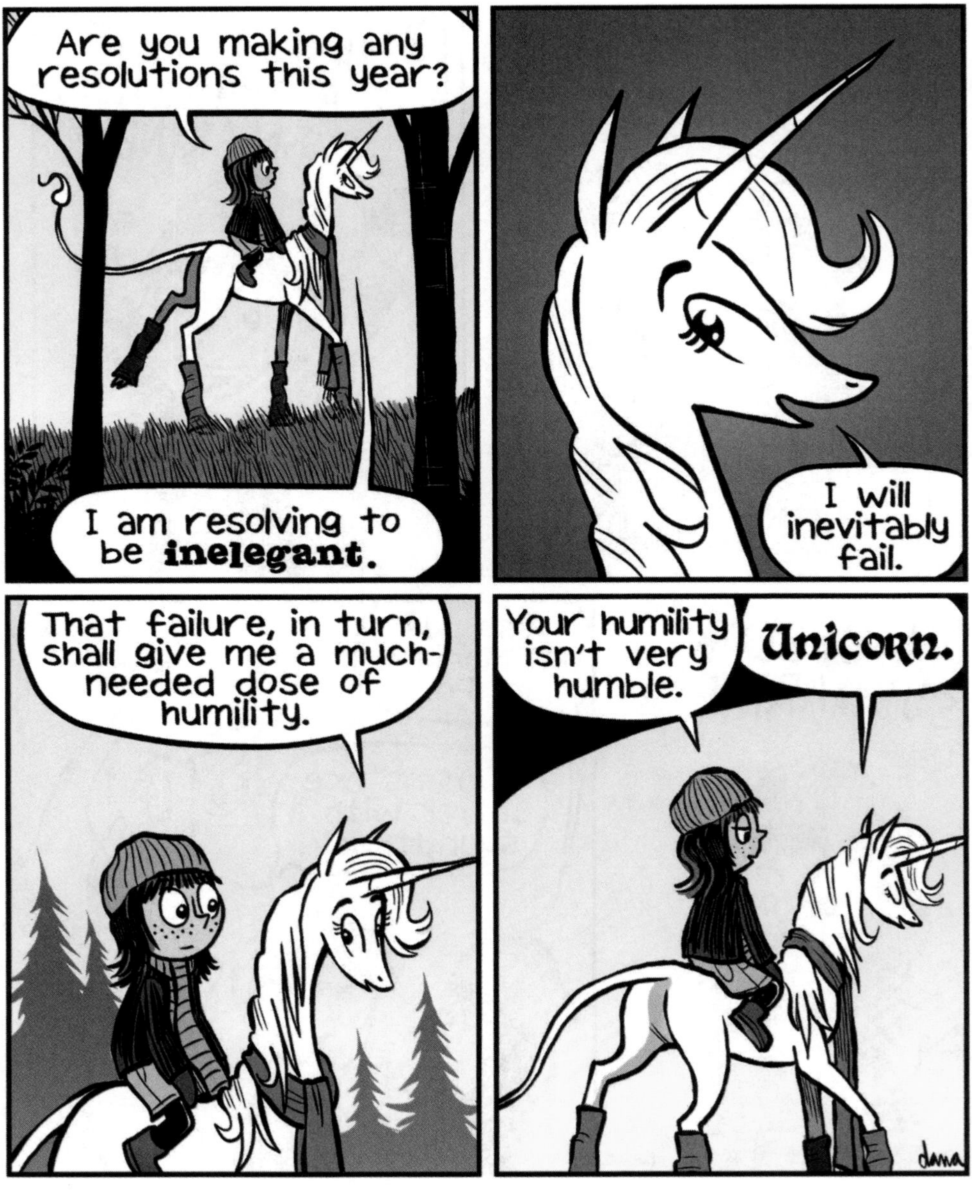
Are you making any resolutions this year?
I am resolving to be **inelegant**.
I will inevitably fail.
That failure, in turn, shall give me a much-needed dose of humility.
Your humility isn't very humble.
Unicorn.
dana

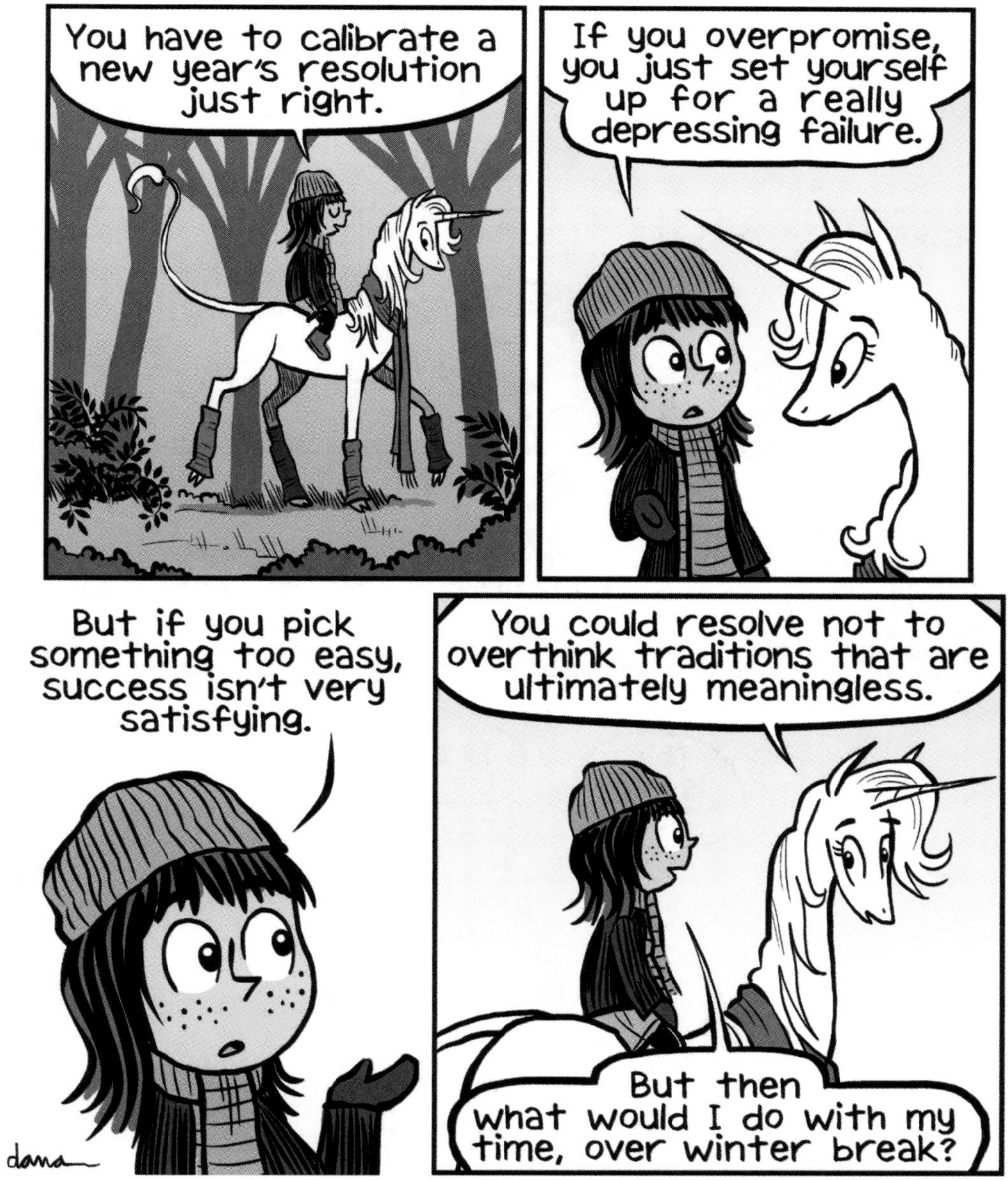
You have to calibrate a new year's resolution just right.
If you overpromise, you just set yourself up for a really depressing failure.
But if you pick something too easy, success isn't very satisfying.
You could resolve not to overthink traditions that are ultimately meaningless.
But then what would I do with my time, over winter break?
dana

crumple crumple

Meatball!

crumple crumple

Asteroid!

crumple crumple

Um...crumply thing!

That is not origami.

It's a kind I invented.

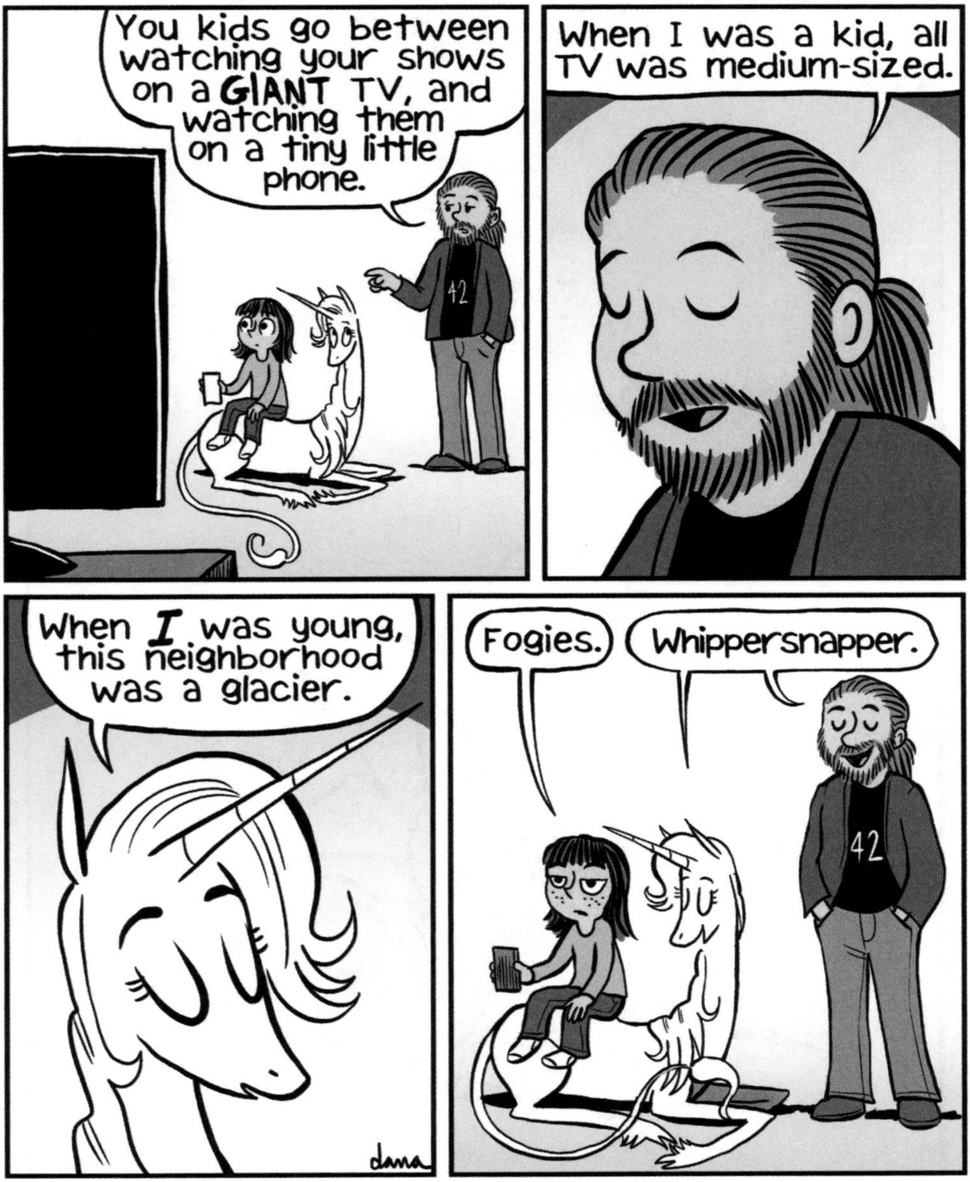
You kids go between watching your shows on a GIANT TV, and watching them on a tiny little phone.
42
When I was a kid, all TV was medium-sized.
When I was young, this neighborhood was a glacier.
dana
Fogies.
Whippersnapper.
42

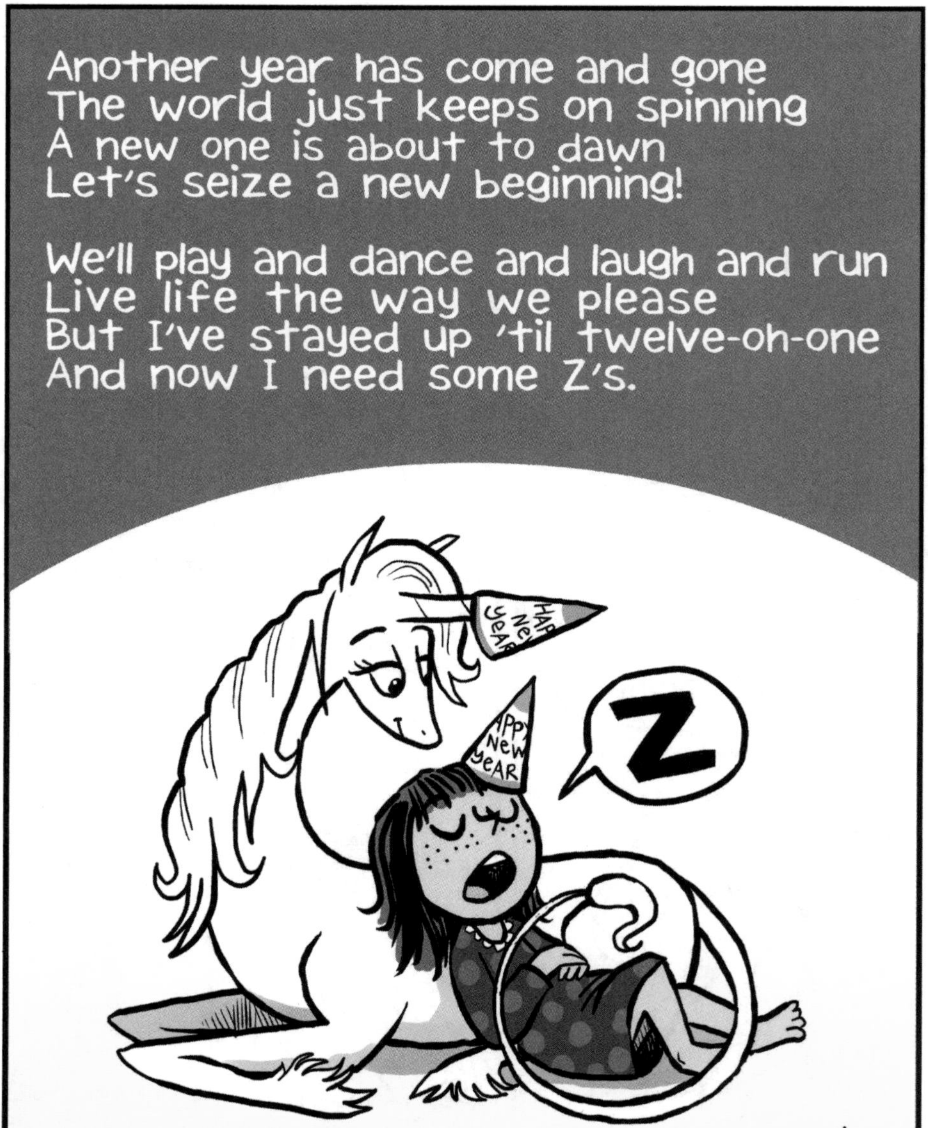
Another year has come and gone
The world just keeps on spinning
A new one is about to dawn
Let's seize a new beginning!

We'll play and dance and laugh and run
Live life the way we please
But I've stayed up 'til twelve-oh-one
And now I need some Z's.
Z

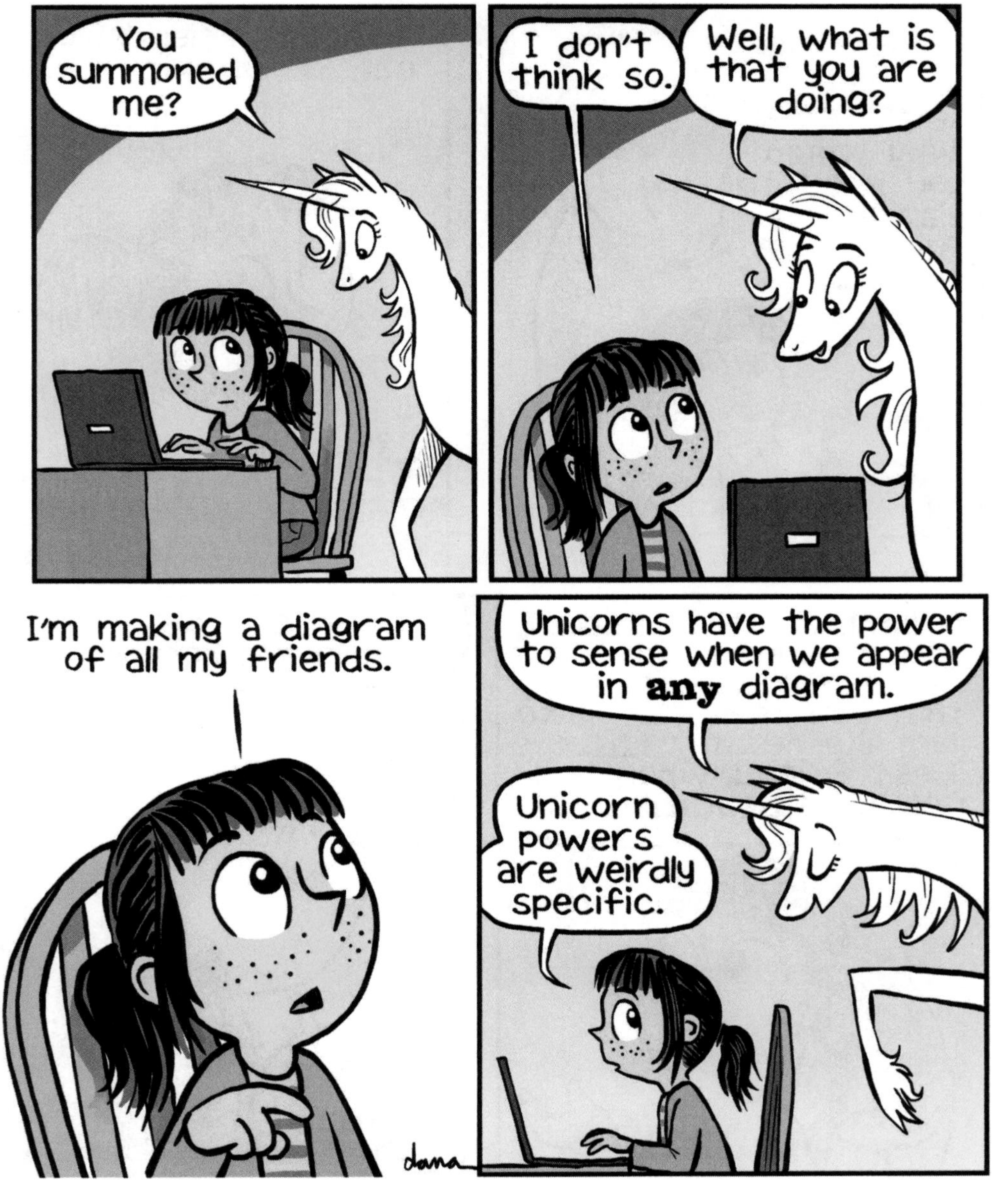
You summoned me?
I don't think so.
Well, what is that you are doing?
I'm making a diagram of all my friends.
Unicorns have the power to sense when we appear in **any** diagram.
Unicorn powers are weirdly specific.
dana

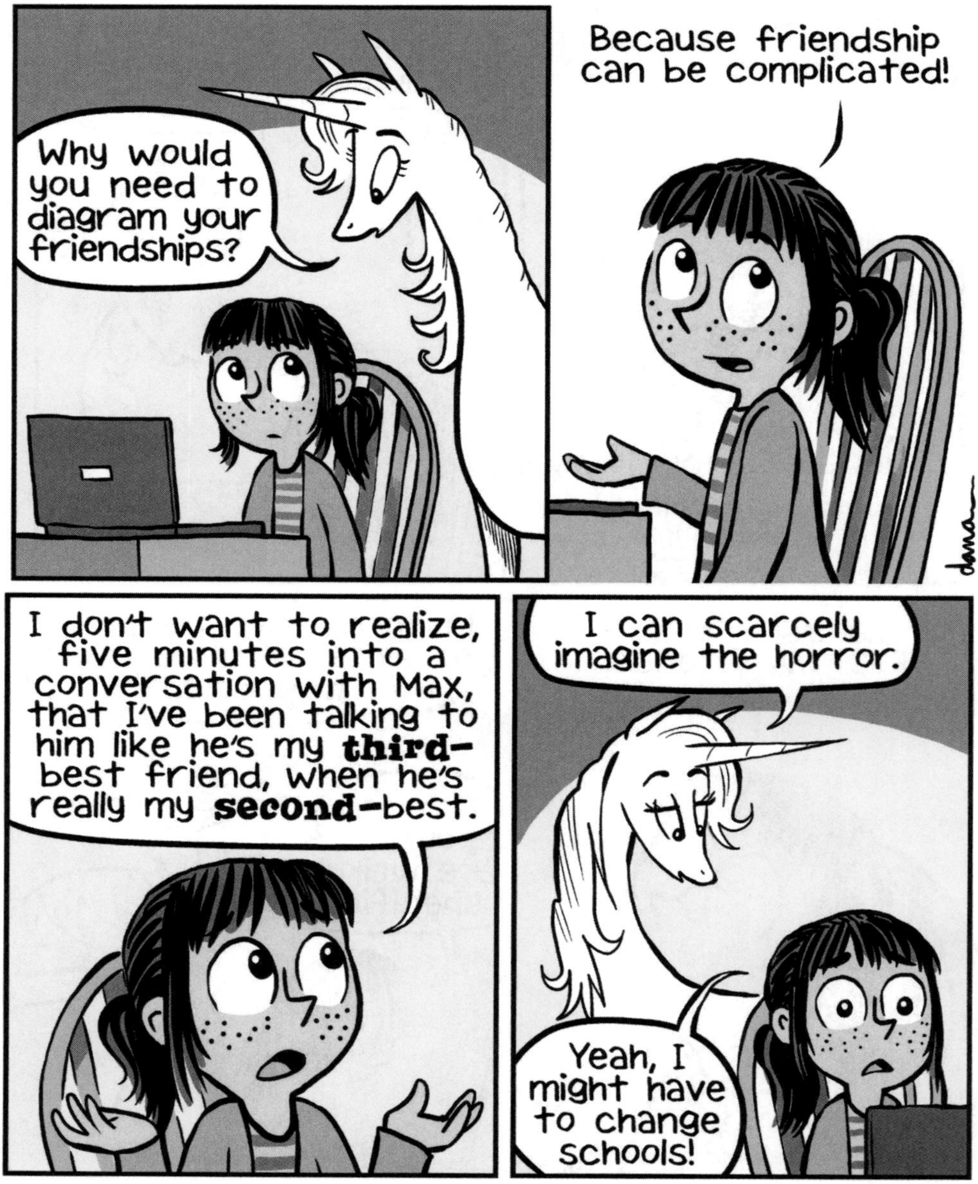
Why would you need to diagram your friendships?
Because friendship can be complicated!
dana
I don't want to realize, five minutes into a conversation with Max, that I've been talking to him like he's my **third**-best friend, when he's really my **second**-best.
I can scarcely imagine the horror.
Yeah, I might have to change schools!

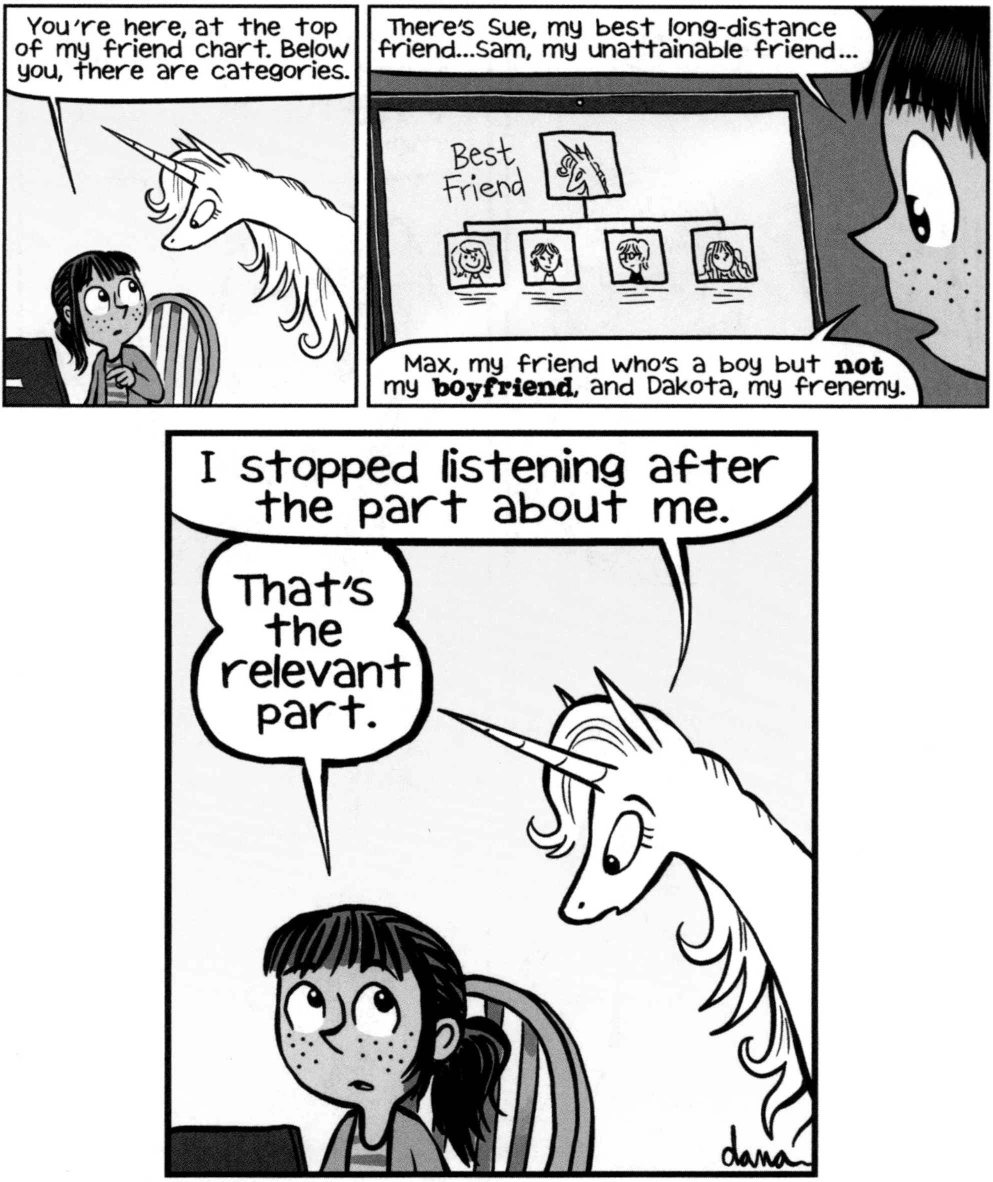
You're here, at the top of my friend chart. Below you, there are categories.
There's Sue, my best long-distance friend...Sam, my unattainable friend...
Best Friend
Max, my friend who's a boy but **not** my **boyfriend**, and Dakota, my frenemy.
I stopped listening after the part about me.
That's the relevant part.
dana

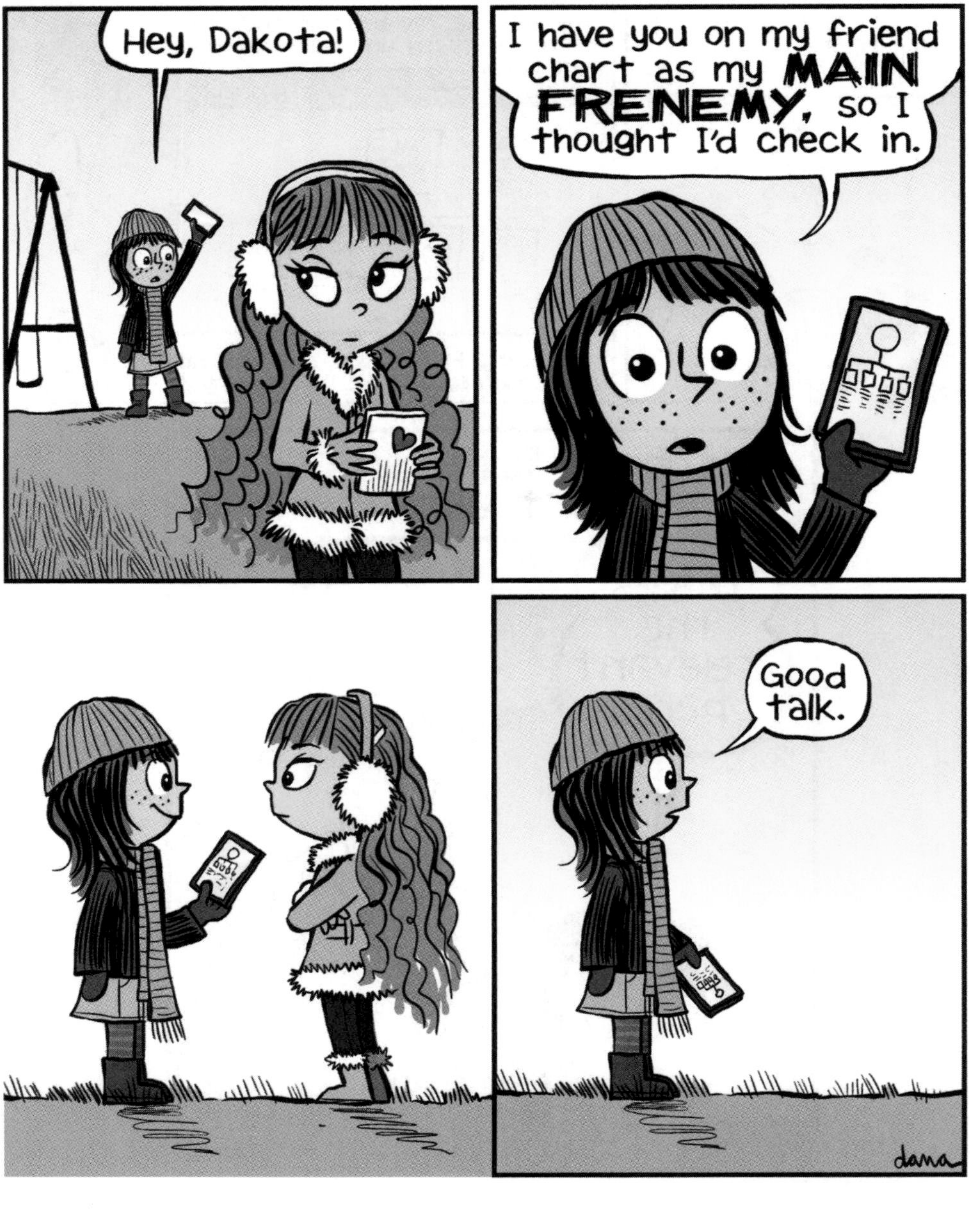
Hey, Dakota!
I have you on my friend chart as my MAIN FRENEMY, so I thought I'd check in.
Good talk.
dana

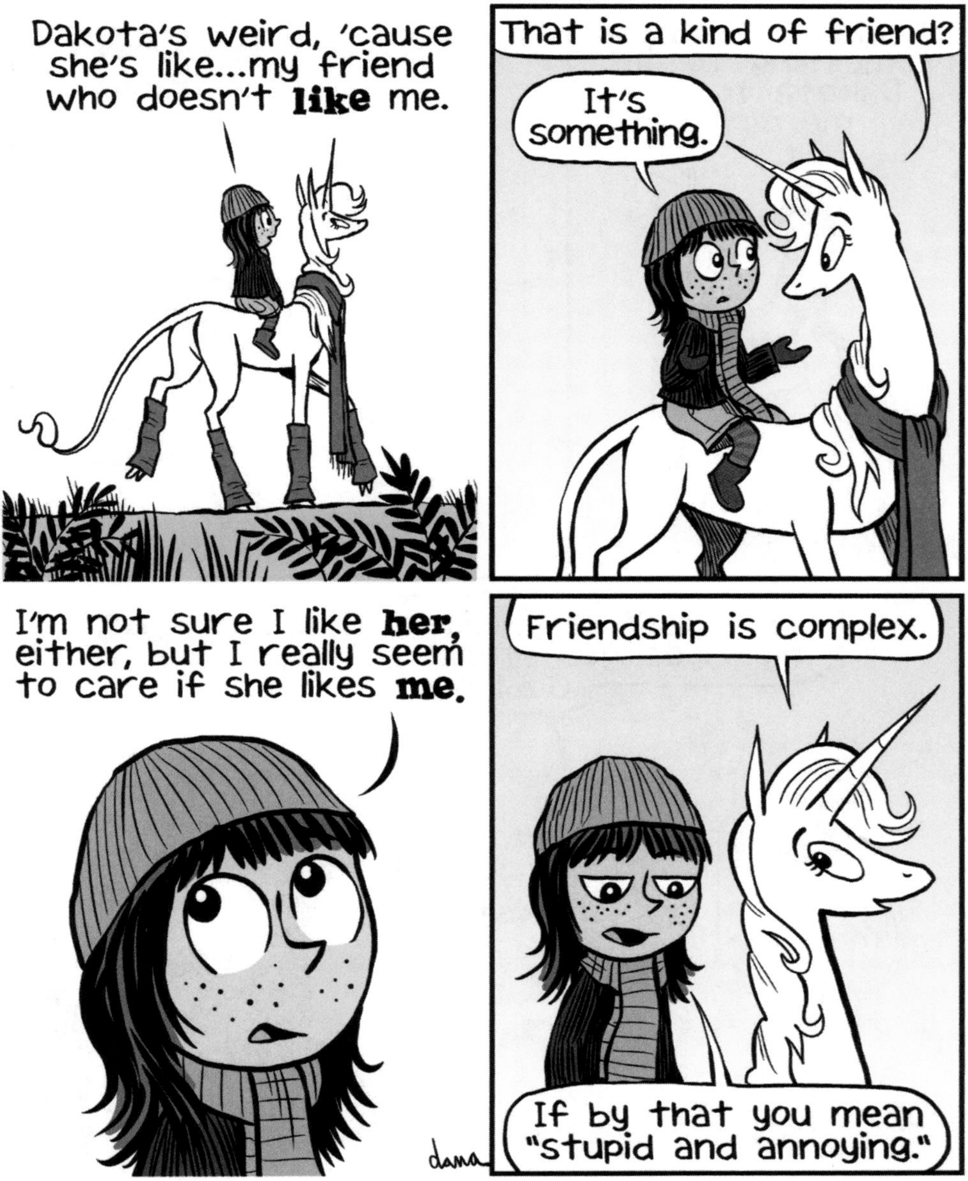
Dakota's weird, 'cause she's like...my friend who doesn't **like** me.
That is a kind of friend?
It's something.
I'm not sure I like **her**, either, but I really seem to care if she likes **me**.
Friendship is complex.
If by that you mean "stupid and annoying."
dana

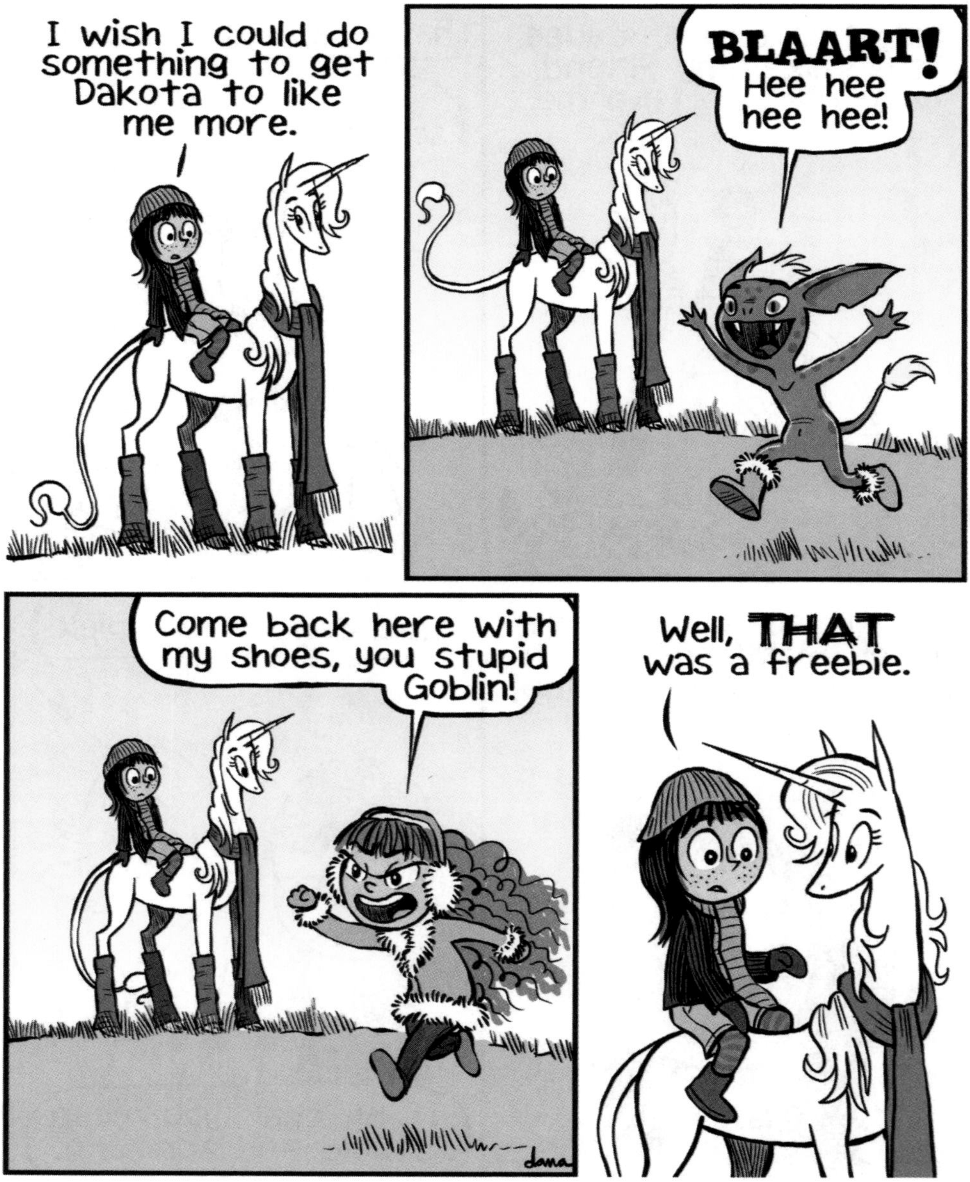
I wish I could do something to get Dakota to like me more.
BLAART! Hee hee hee hee!
Come back here with my shoes, you stupid Goblin!
dana
Well, THAT was a freebie.

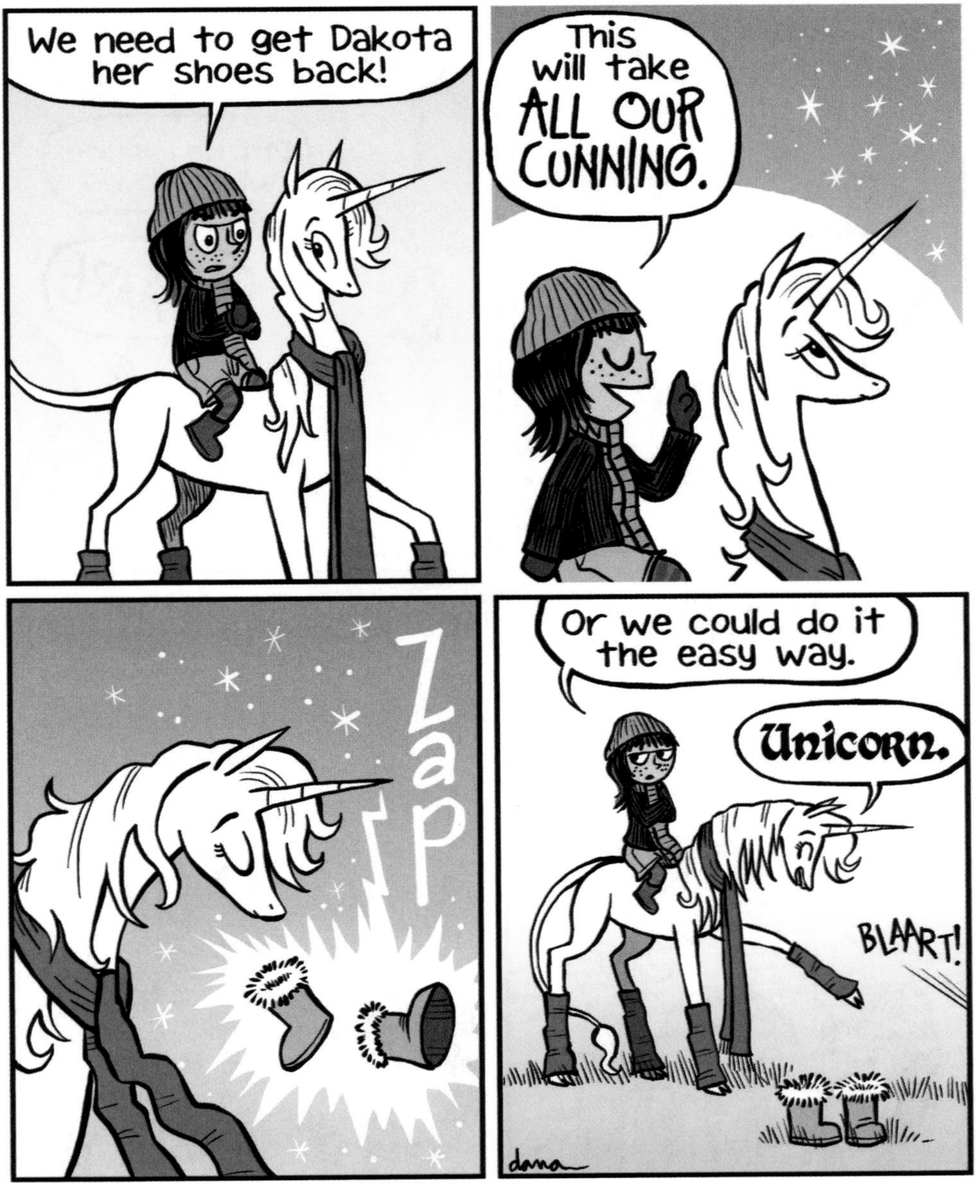
We need to get Dakota her shoes back!
This will take ALL OUR CUNNING.
Zap
Or we could do it the easy way.
Unicorn.
BLAART!
dana

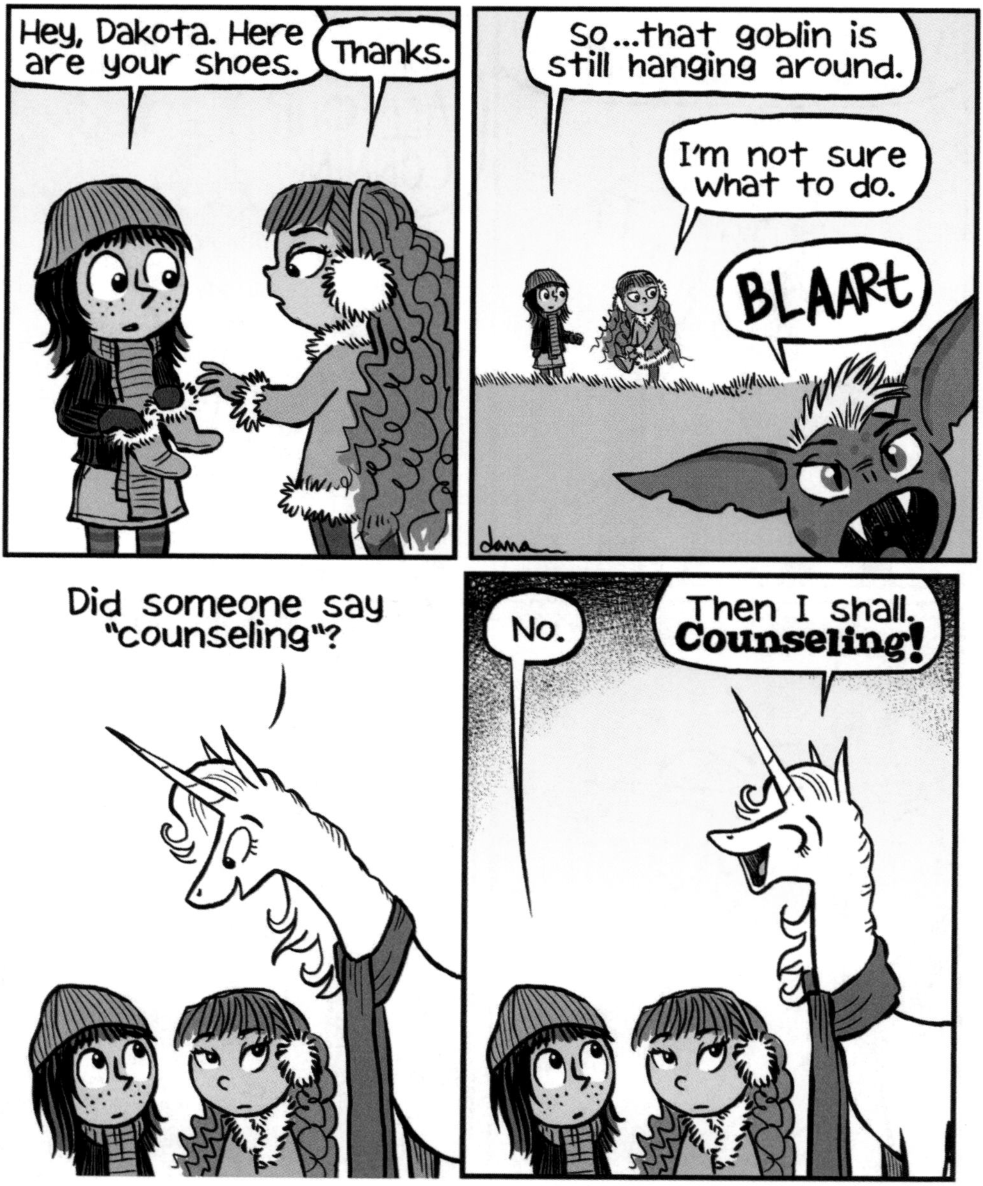
Hey, Dakota. Here are your shoes.
Thanks.
So...that goblin is still hanging around.
I'm not sure what to do.
BLAARt
dana
Did someone say "counseling"?
No.
Then I shall. **Counseling!**

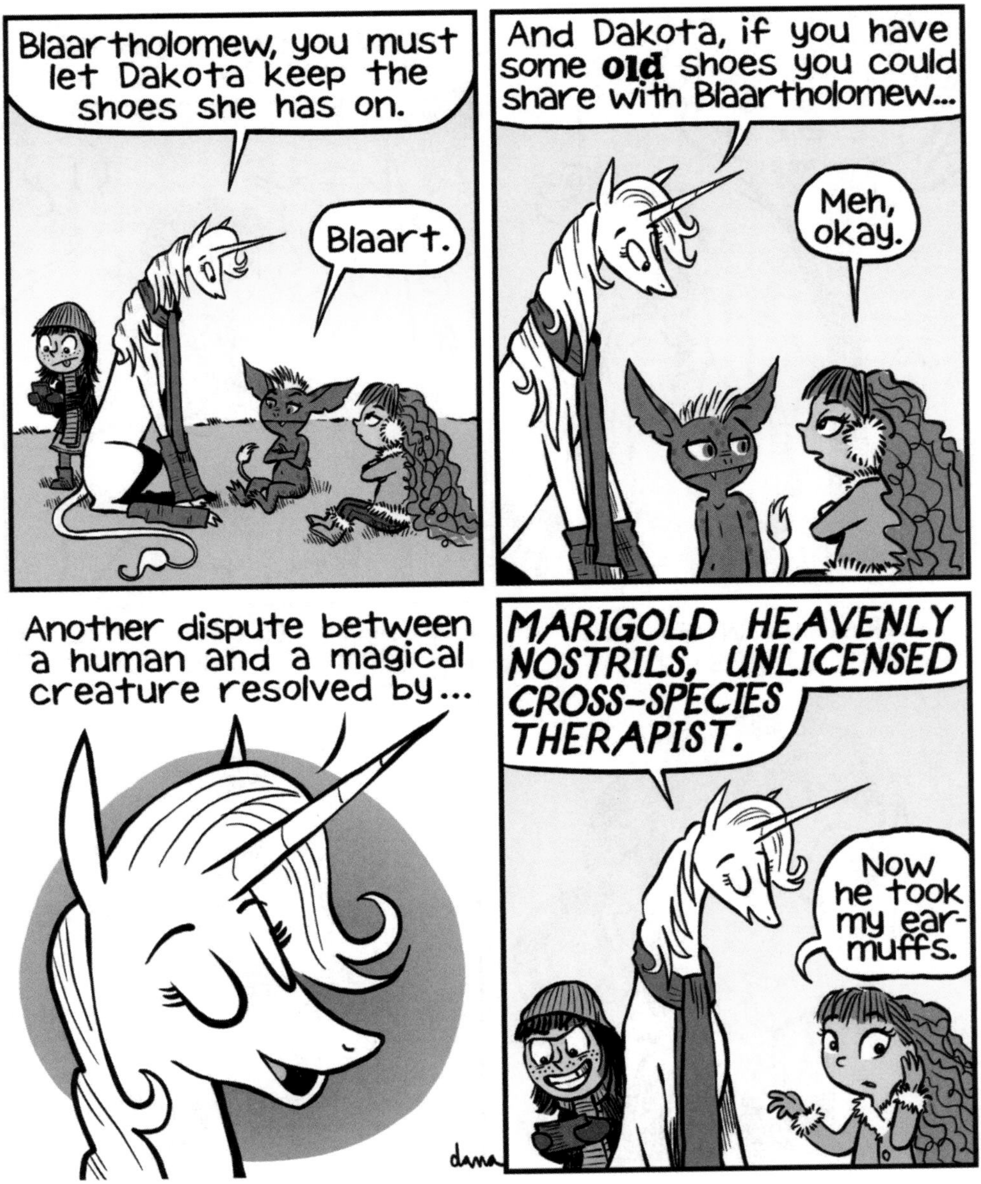
Blaartholomew, you must let Dakota keep the shoes she has on.
Blaart.
And Dakota, if you have some **old** shoes you could share with Blaartholomew...
Meh, okay.
Another dispute between a human and a magical creature resolved by...
MARIGOLD HEAVENLY NOSTRILS, UNLICENSED CROSS-SPECIES THERAPIST.
Now he took my ear-muffs.
dana

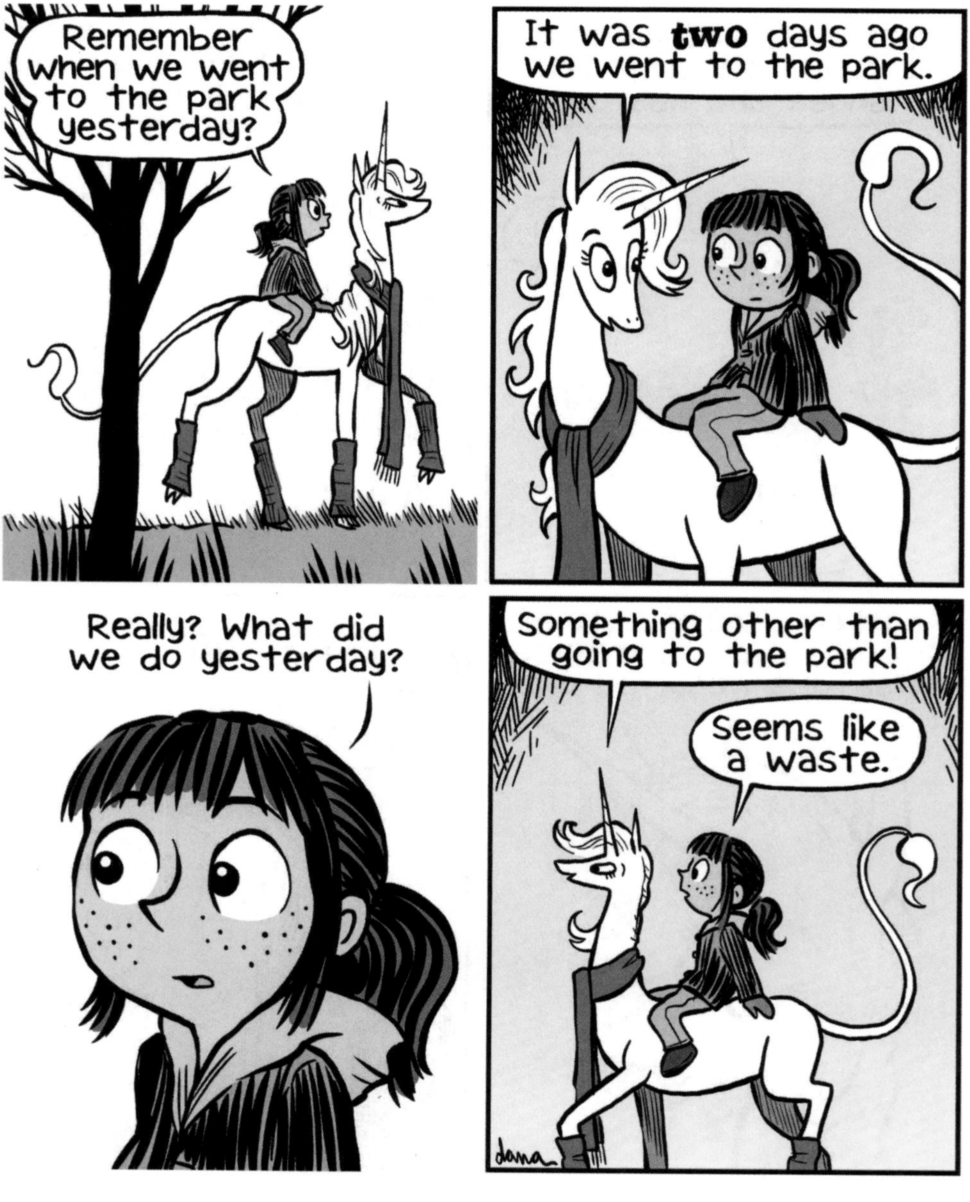
Remember when we went to the park yesterday?
It was **two** days ago we went to the park.
Really? What did we do yesterday?
Something other than going to the park!
Seems like a waste.
dana

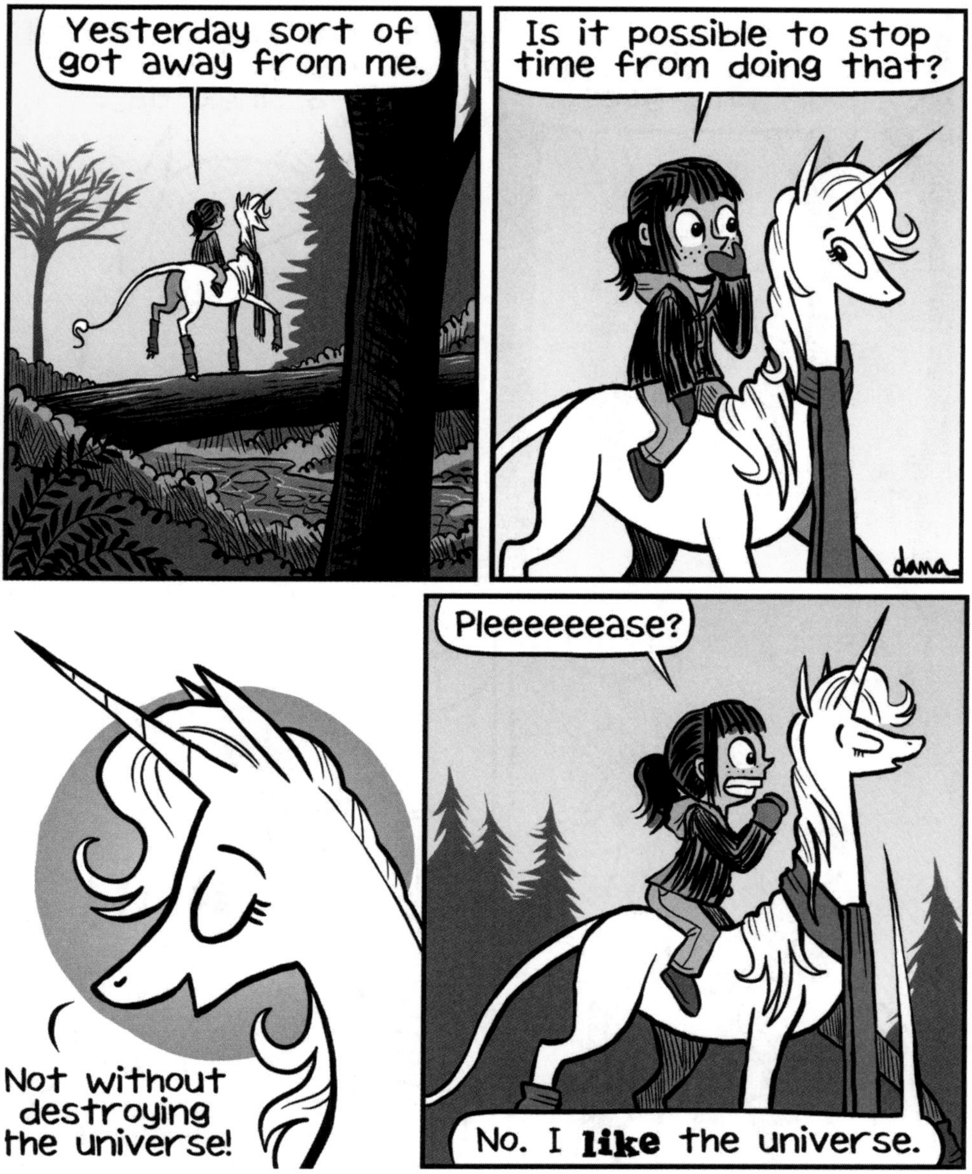

Yesterday sort of got away from me.
Is it possible to stop time from doing that?
dana
Not without destroying the universe!
Pleeeeeeease?
No. I like the universe.

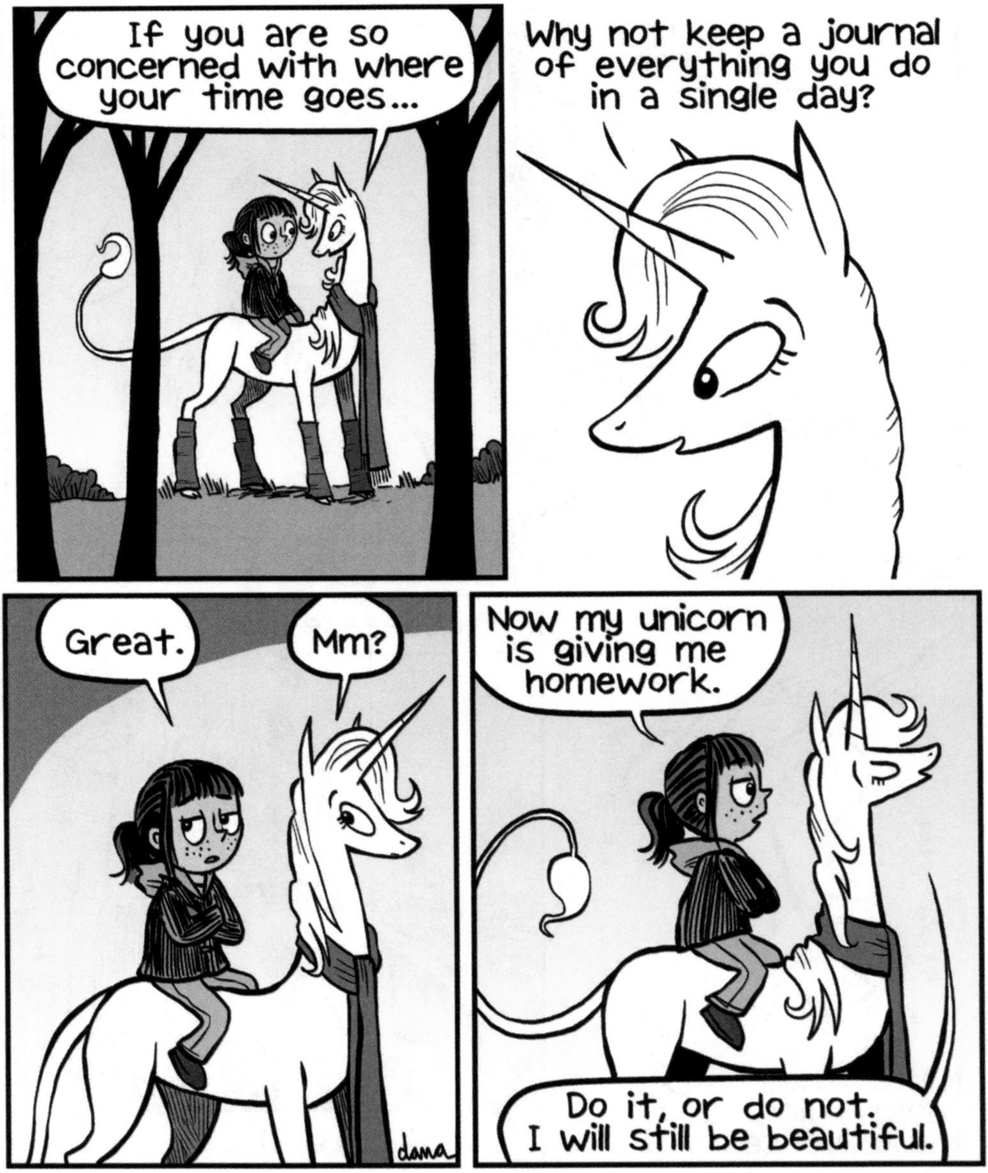
If you are so concerned with where your time goes...
Why not keep a journal of everything you do in a single day?
Great.
Mm?
Now my unicorn is giving me homework.
Do it, or do not. I will still be beautiful.
dana

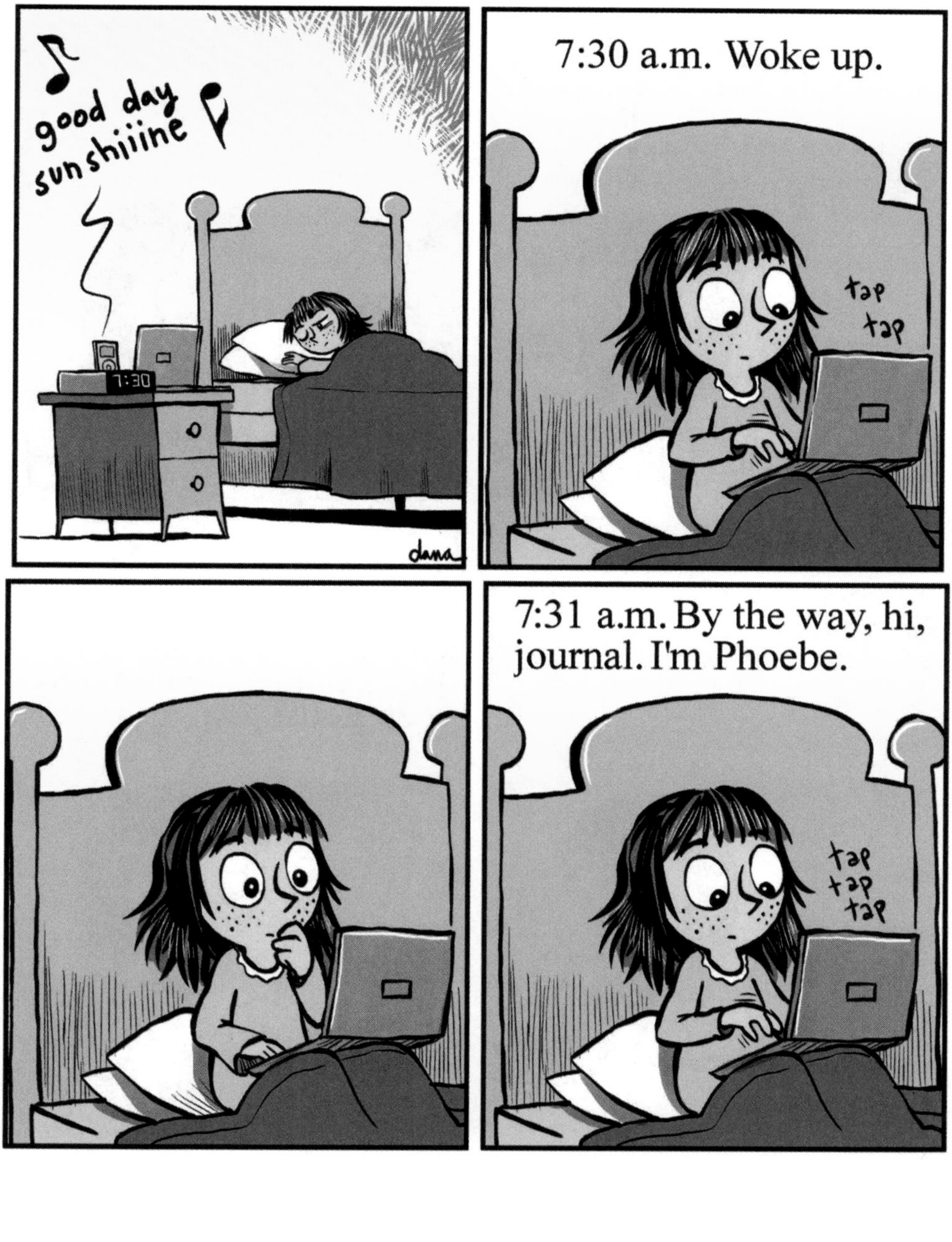
good day sunshiiine
7:30
dana
7:30 a.m. Woke up.
tap tap
7:31 a.m. By the way, hi, journal. I'm Phoebe.
tap tap tap

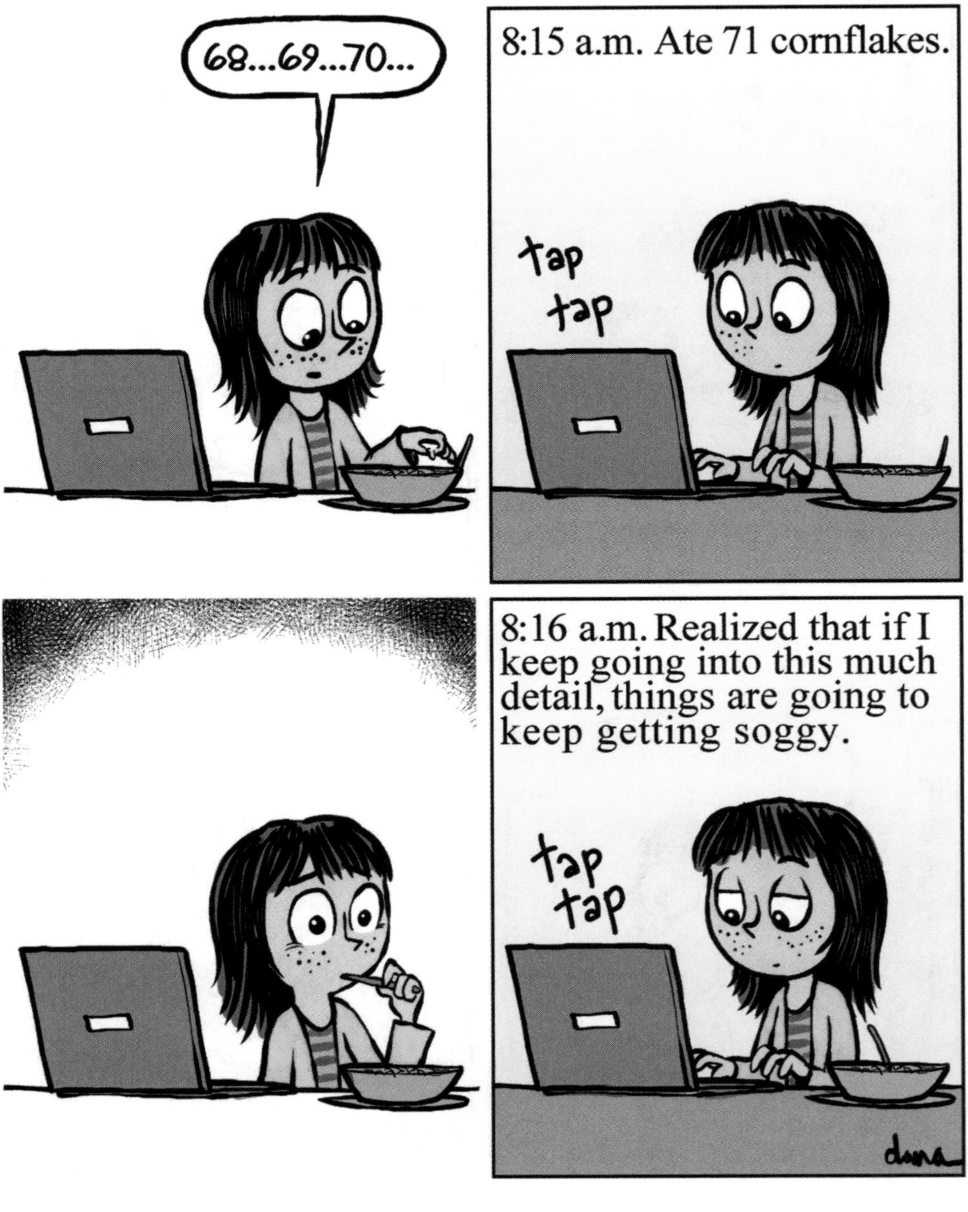
68...69...70...
8:15 a.m. Ate 71 cornflakes.
tap tap
8:16 a.m. Realized that if I keep going into this much detail, things are going to keep getting soggy.
tap tap
dana

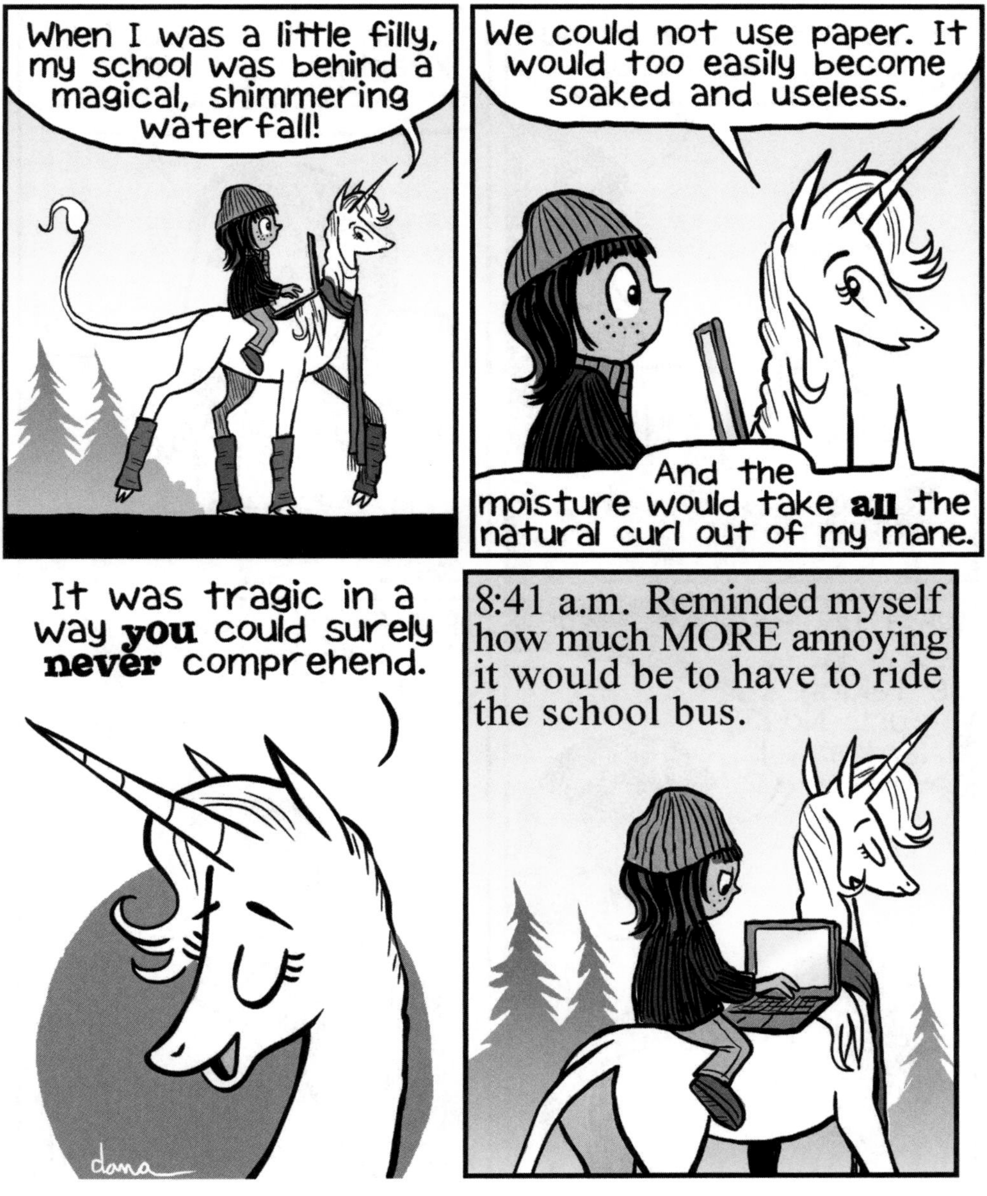
When I was a little filly, my school was behind a magical, shimmering waterfall!
We could not use paper. It would too easily become soaked and useless.
And the moisture would take **all** the natural curl out of my mane.
It was tragic in a way **you** could surely **never** comprehend.
dana
8:41 a.m. Reminded myself how much MORE annoying it would be to have to ride the school bus.

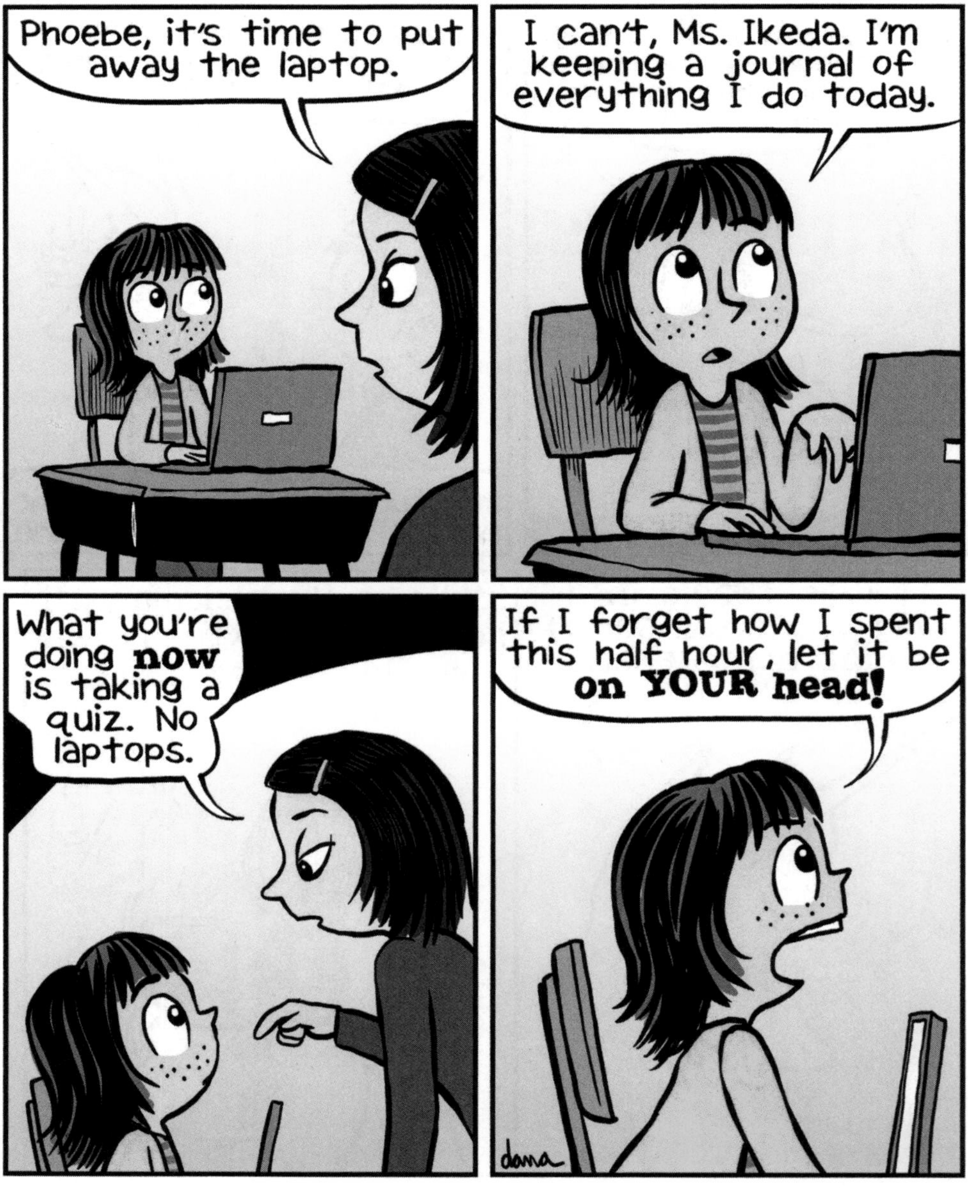
Phoebe, it's time to put away the laptop.
I can't, Ms. Ikeda. I'm keeping a journal of everything I do today.
What you're doing **now** is taking a quiz. No laptops.
If I forget how I spent this half hour, let it be **on YOUR head!**
dana

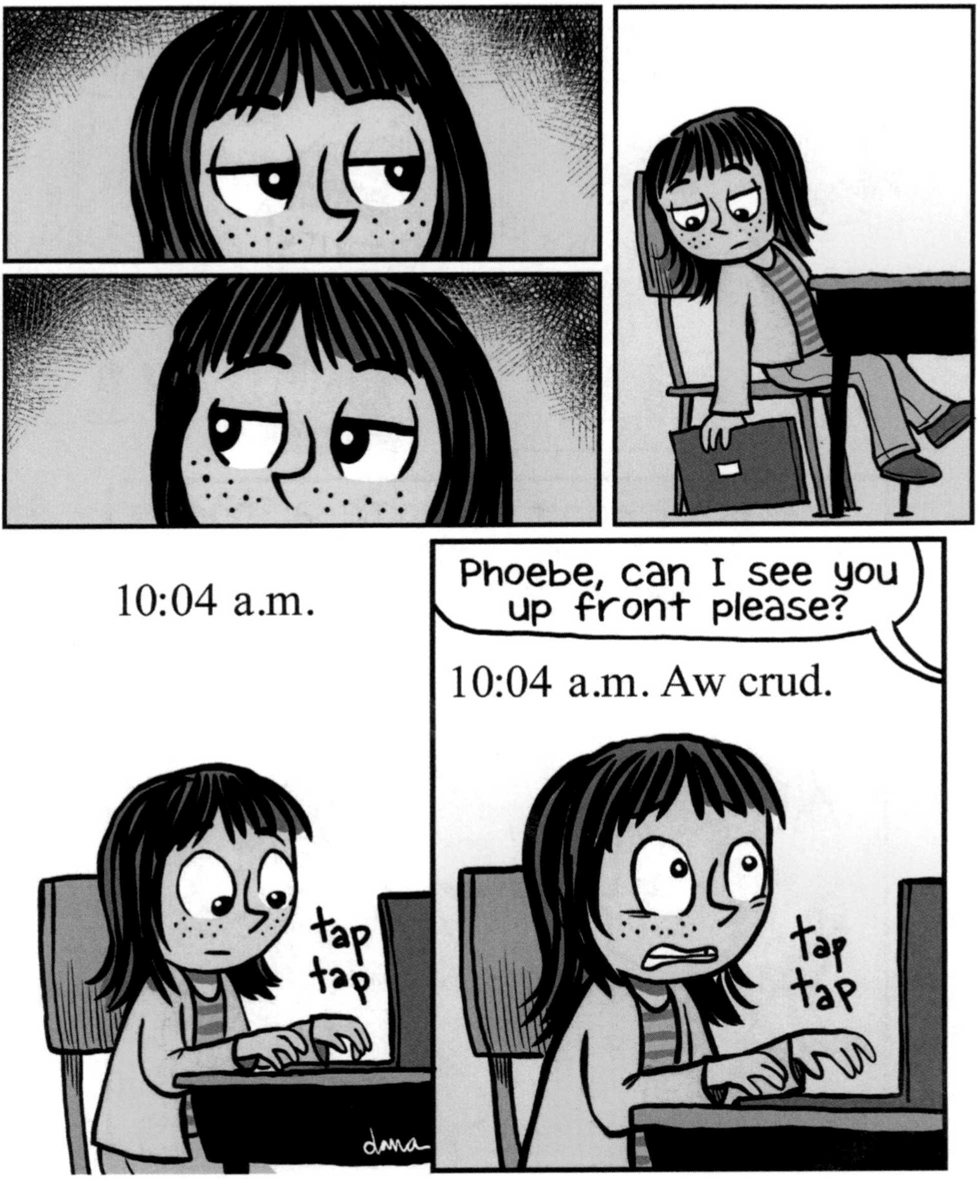
10:04 a.m.
tap
tap
dana
Phoebe, can I see you up front please?
10:04 a.m. Aw crud.
tap
tap

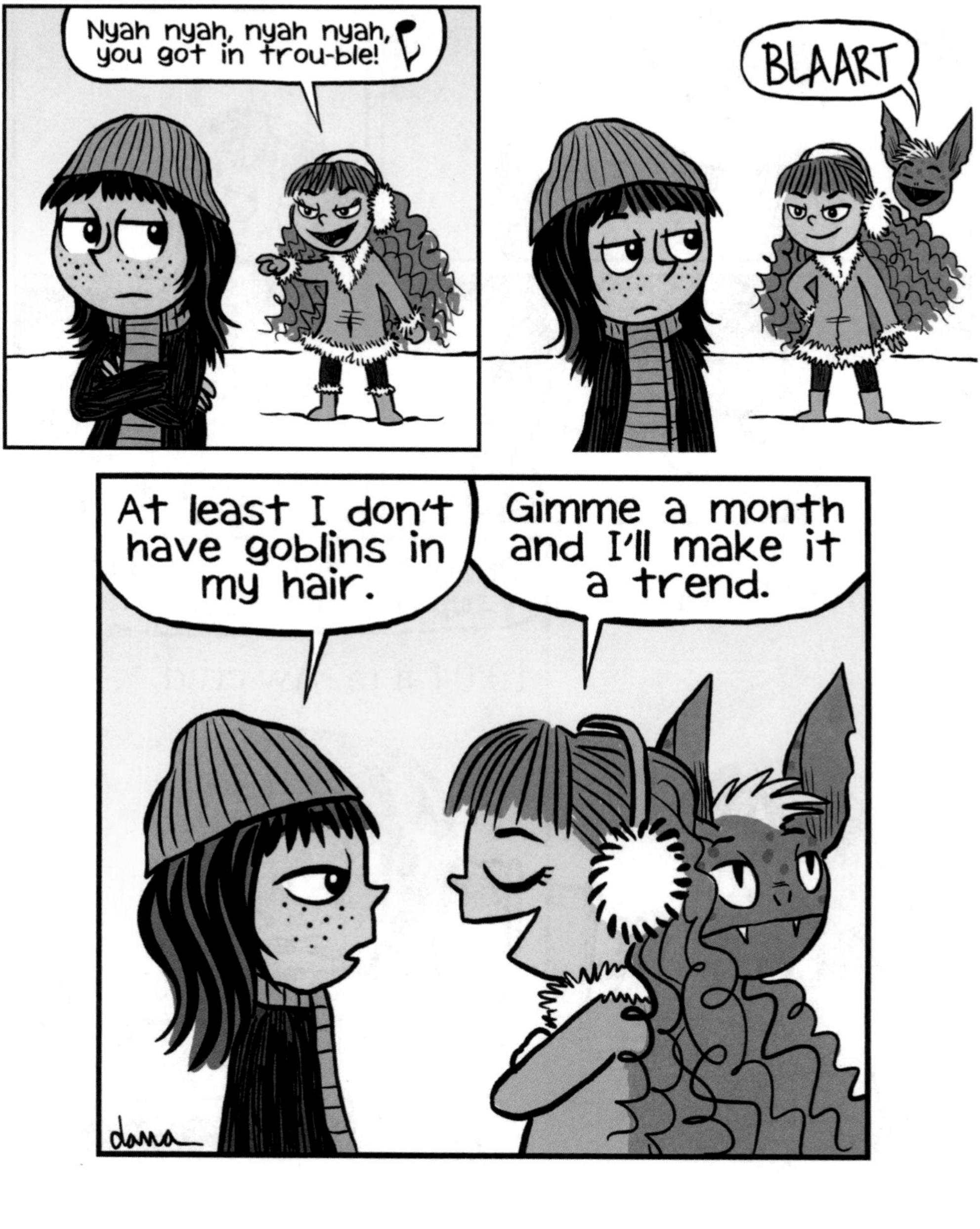
Nyah nyah, nyah nyah, you got in trou-ble!
BLAART
At least I don't have goblins in my hair.
Gimme a month and I'll make it a trend.
dana

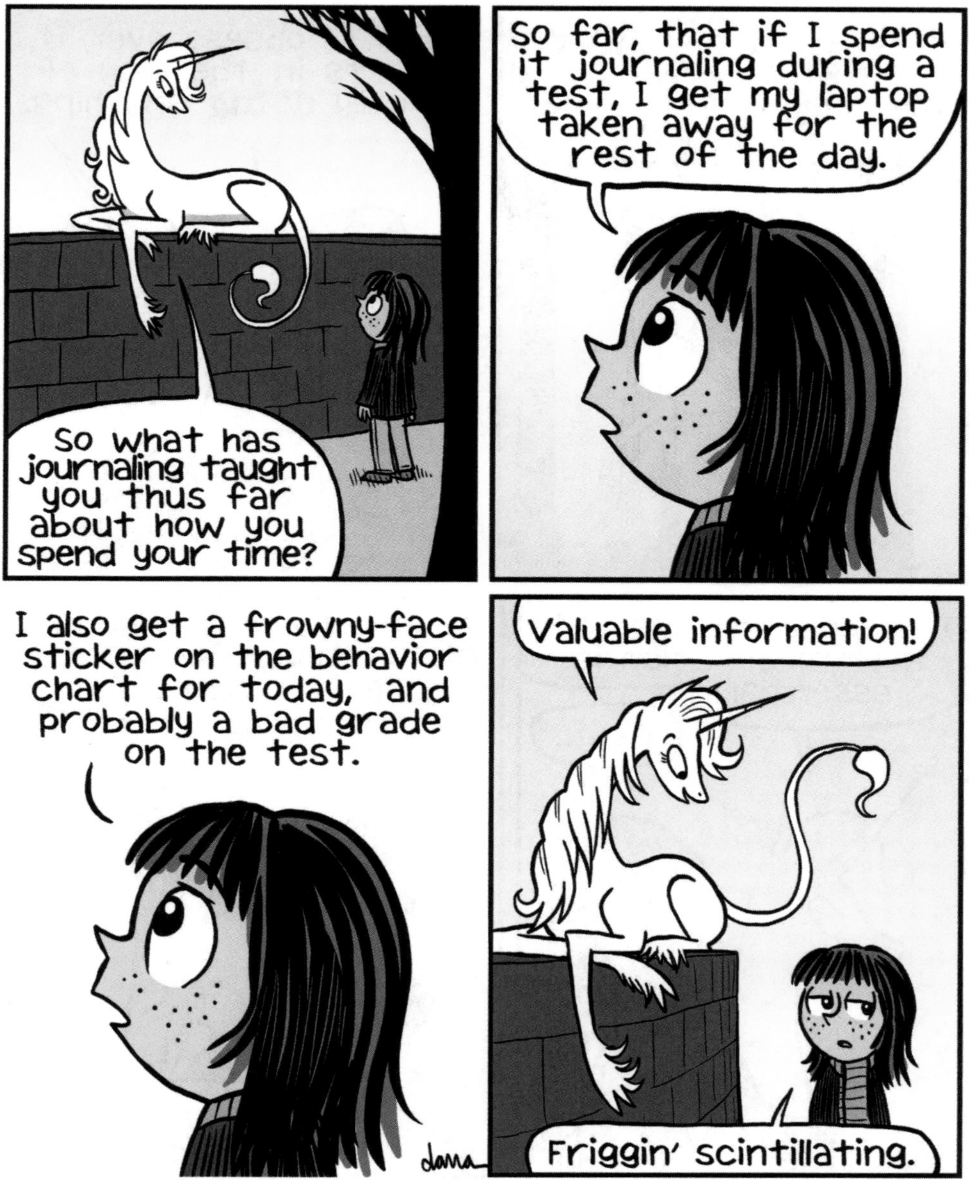
So what has journaling taught you thus far about how you spend your time?
So far, that if I spend it journaling during a test, I get my laptop taken away for the rest of the day.
I also get a frowny-face sticker on the behavior chart for today, and probably a bad grade on the test.
Valuable information!
Friggin' scintillating.
dana

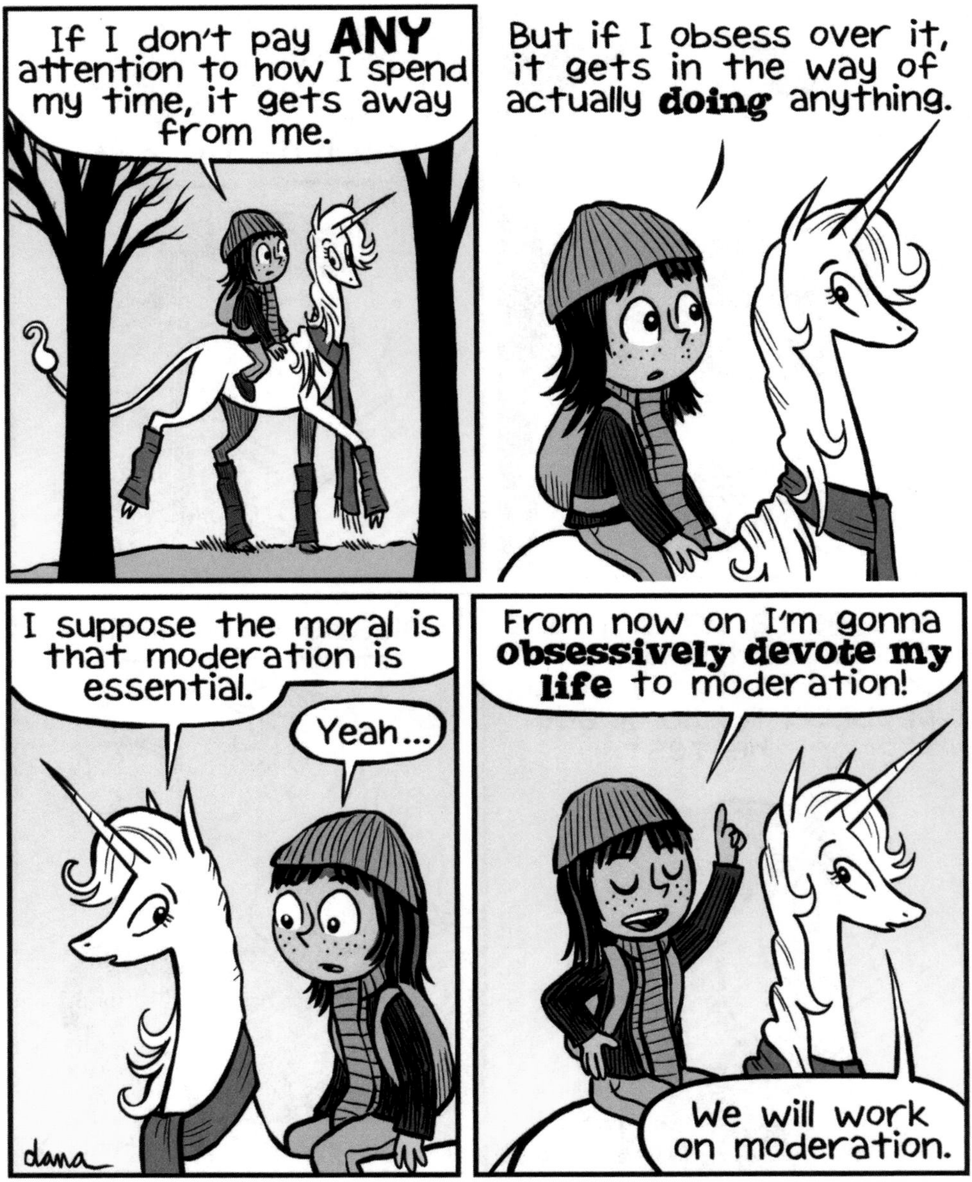
If I don't pay **ANY** attention to how I spend my time, it gets away from me.
But if I obsess over it, it gets in the way of actually **doing** anything.
I suppose the moral is that moderation is essential.
Yeah...
dana
From now on I'm gonna **obsessively devote my life** to moderation!
We will work on moderation.

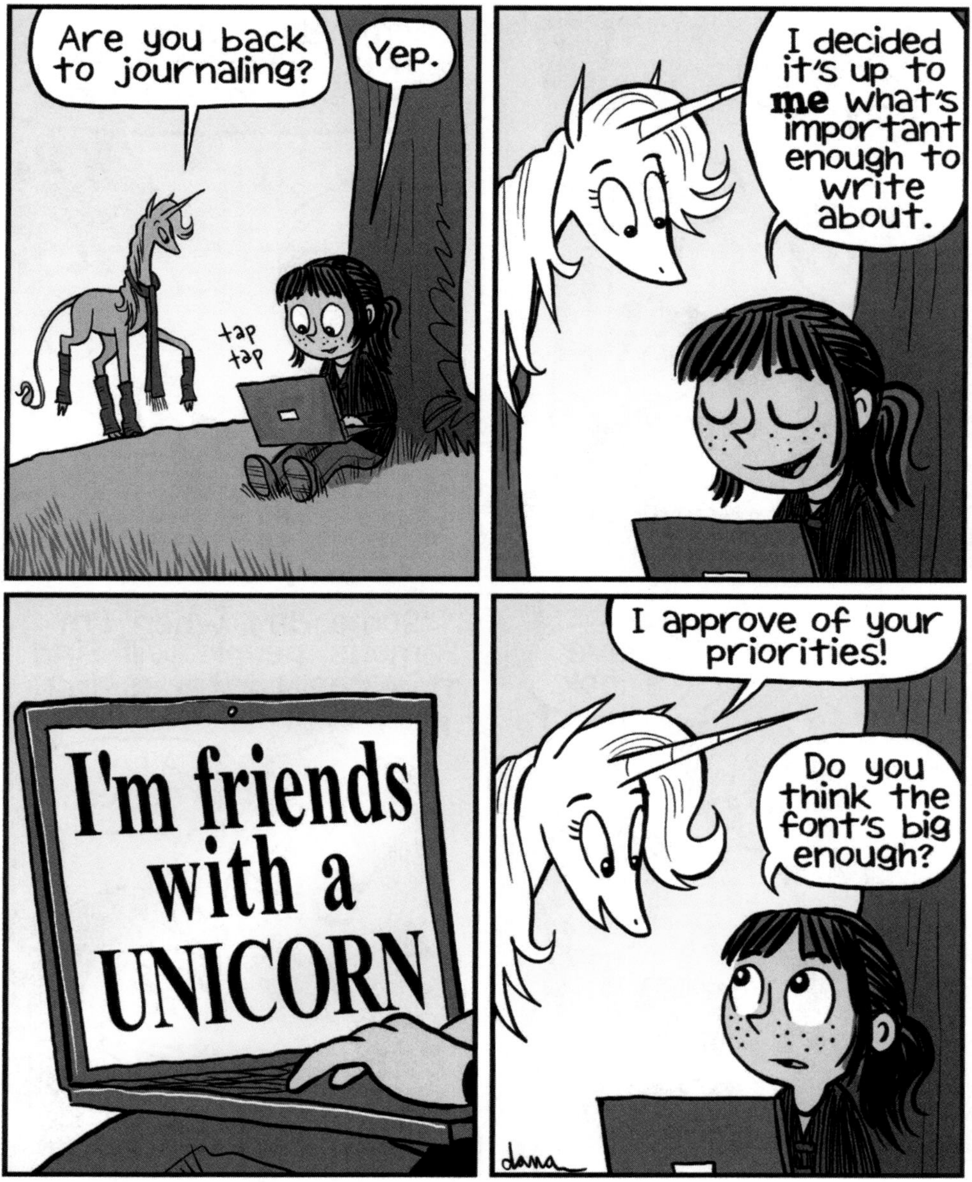
Are you back to journaling?
Yep.
tap tap
I decided it's up to **me** what's important enough to write about.
I'm friends with a UNICORN
I approve of your priorities!
Do you think the font's big enough?
dana

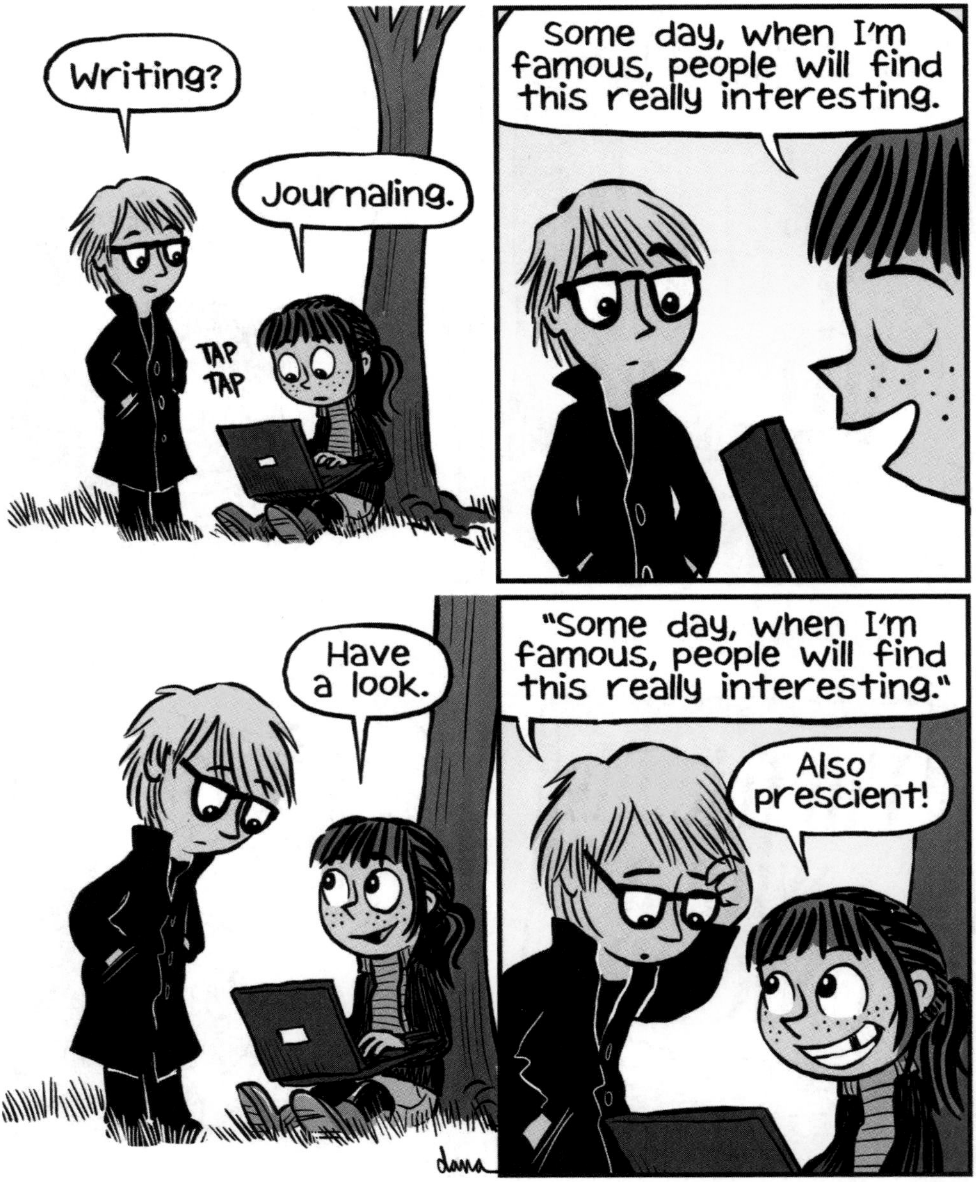
Writing?
Journaling.
TAP TAP
Some day, when I'm famous, people will find this really interesting.
Have a look.
"Some day, when I'm famous, people will find this really interesting."
Also prescient!
dana

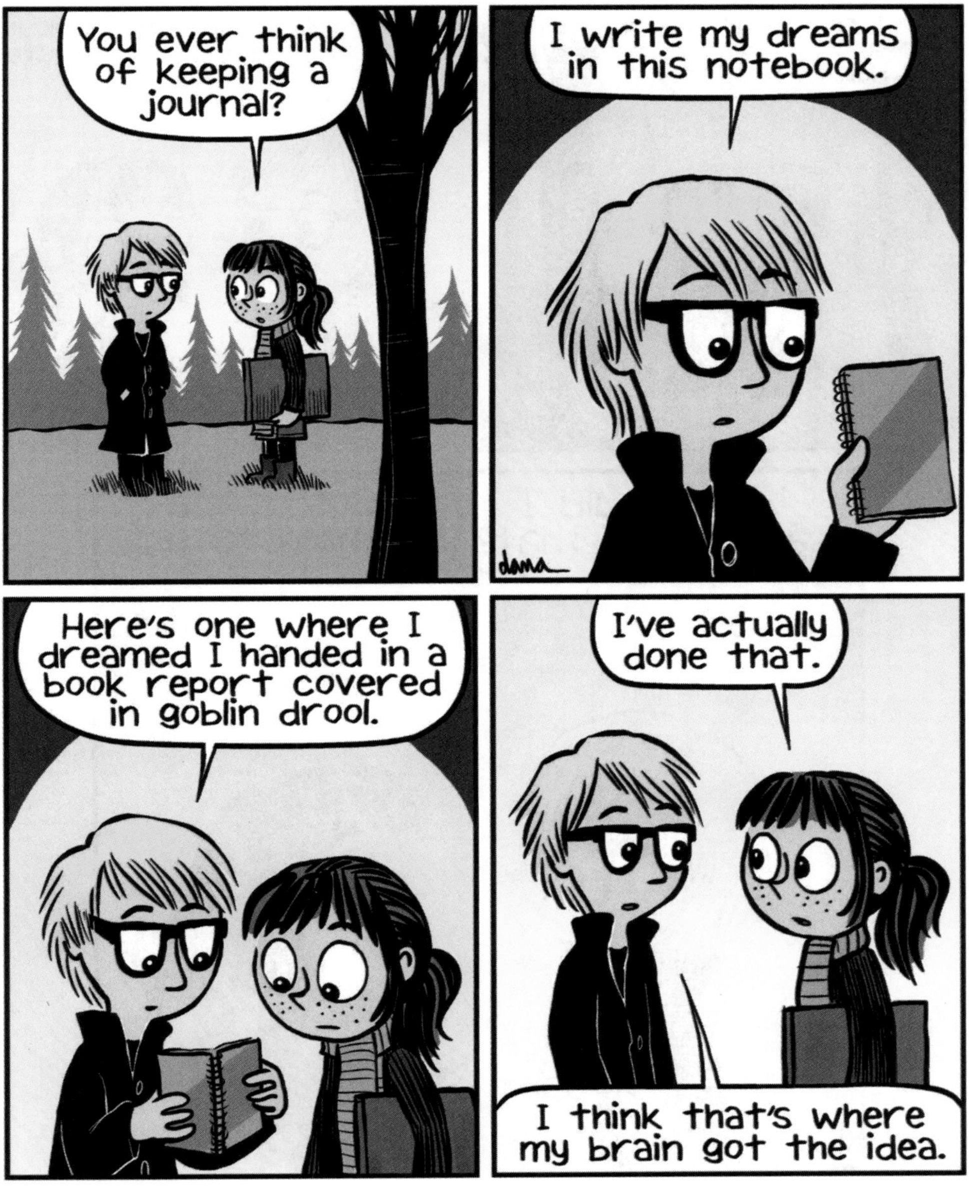
You ever think of keeping a journal?
I write my dreams in this notebook.
dana
Here's one where I dreamed I handed in a book report covered in goblin drool.
I've actually done that.
I think that's where my brain got the idea.

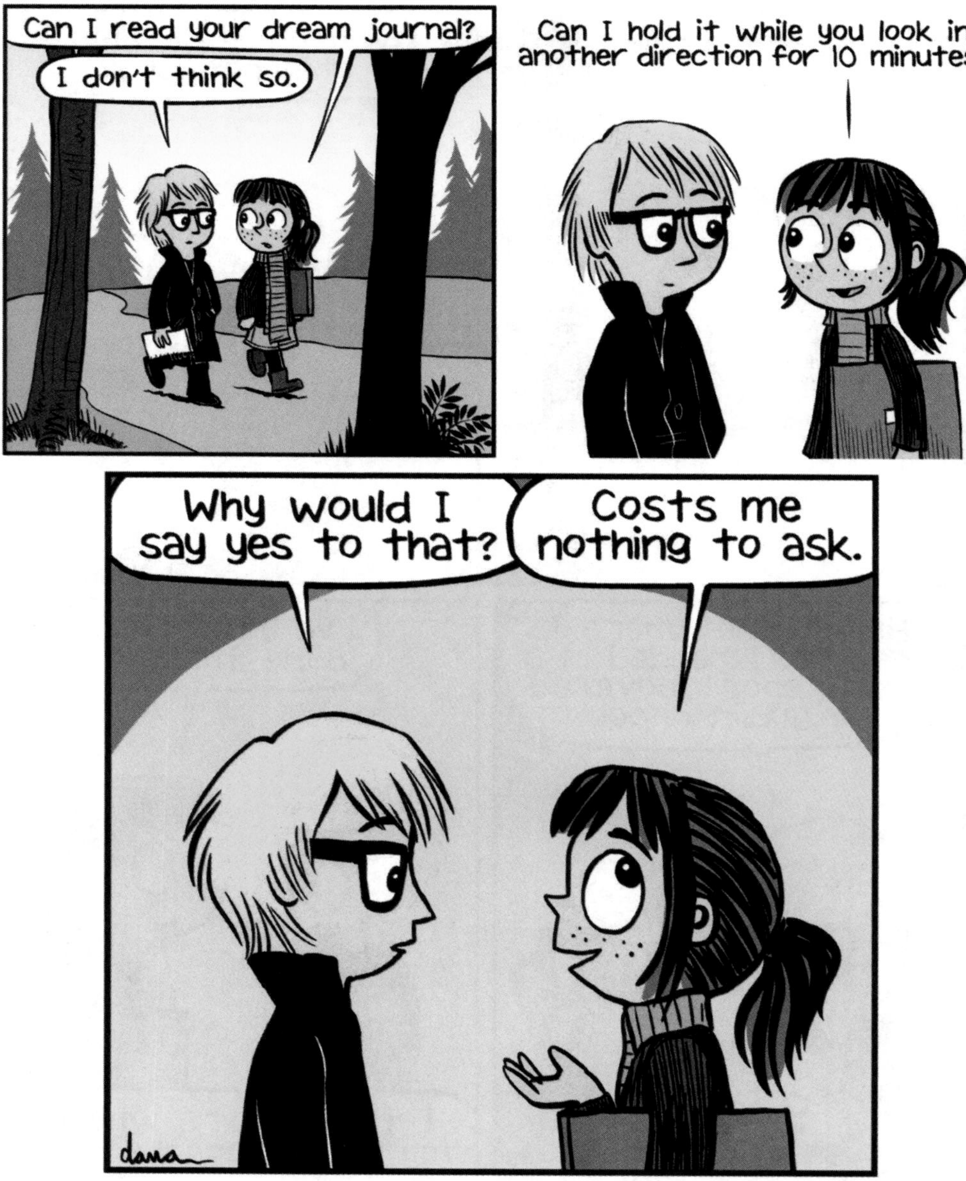

Can I read your dream journal?
I don't think so.
Can I hold it while you look in another direction for 10 minutes?
Why would I say yes to that?
Costs me nothing to ask.
dana

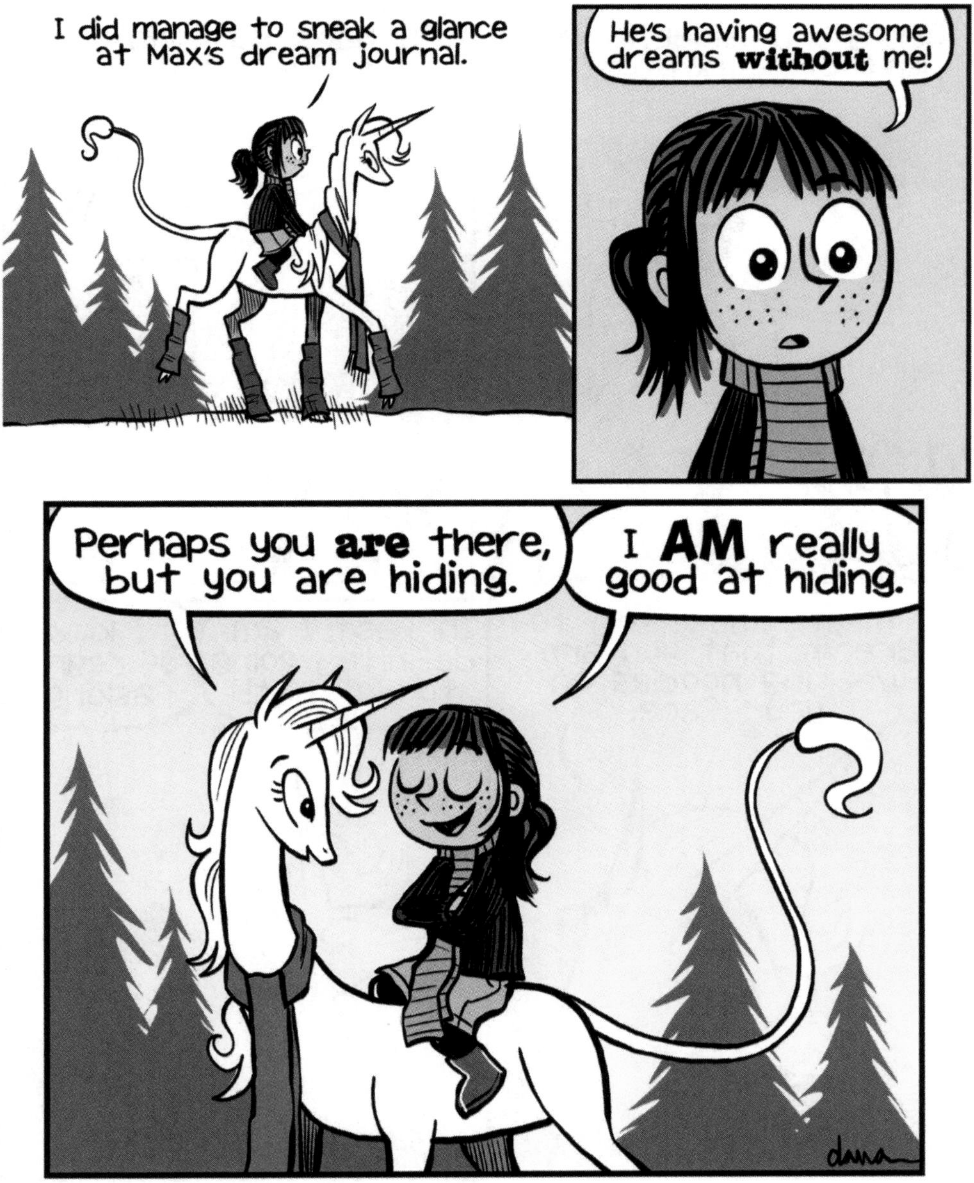
I did manage to sneak a glance at Max's dream journal.
He's having awesome dreams **without** me!
Perhaps you **are** there, but you are hiding.
I **AM** really good at hiding.
dana

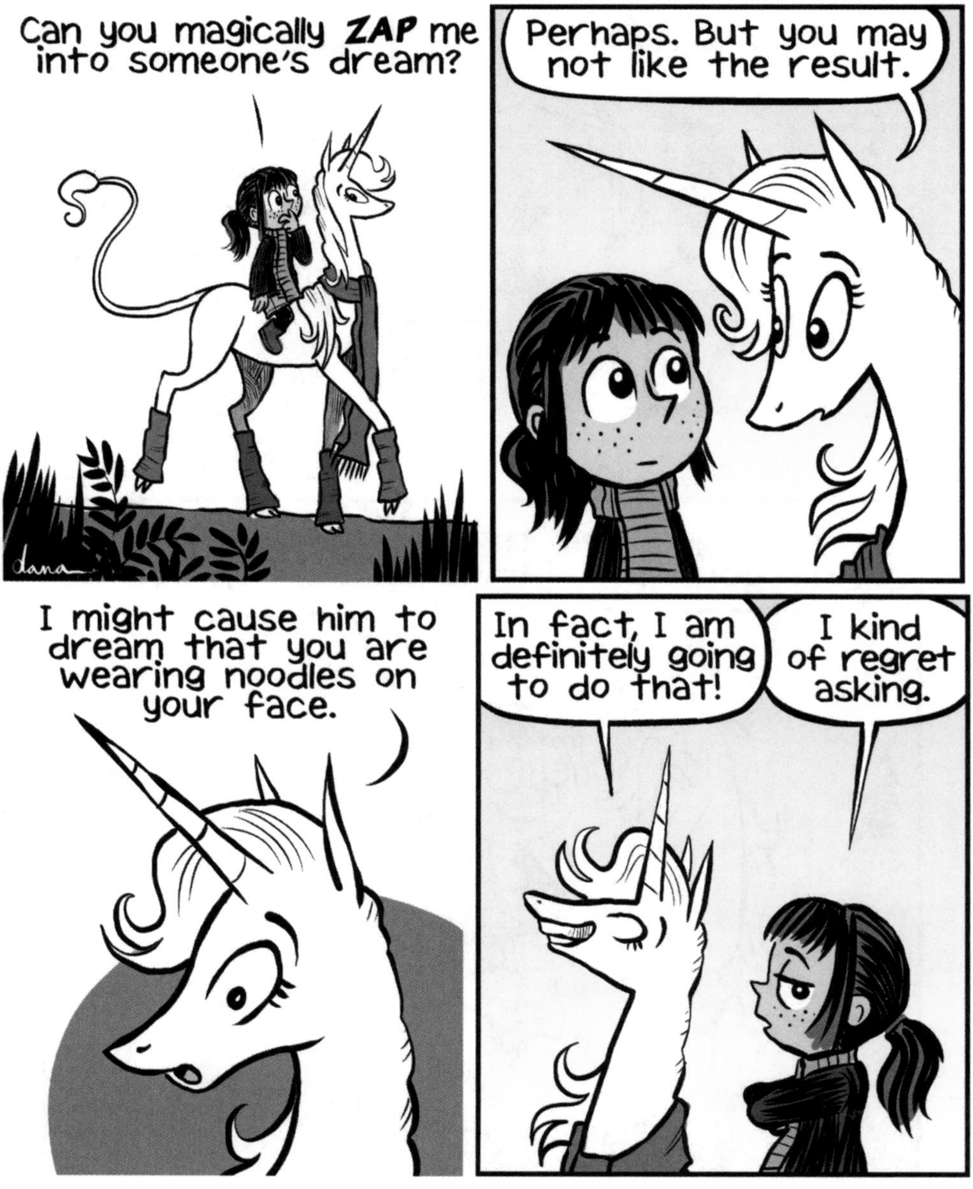
Can you magically ZAP me into someone's dream?
Perhaps. But you may not like the result.
I might cause him to dream that you are wearing noodles on your face.
In fact, I am definitely going to do that!
I kind of regret asking.
dana

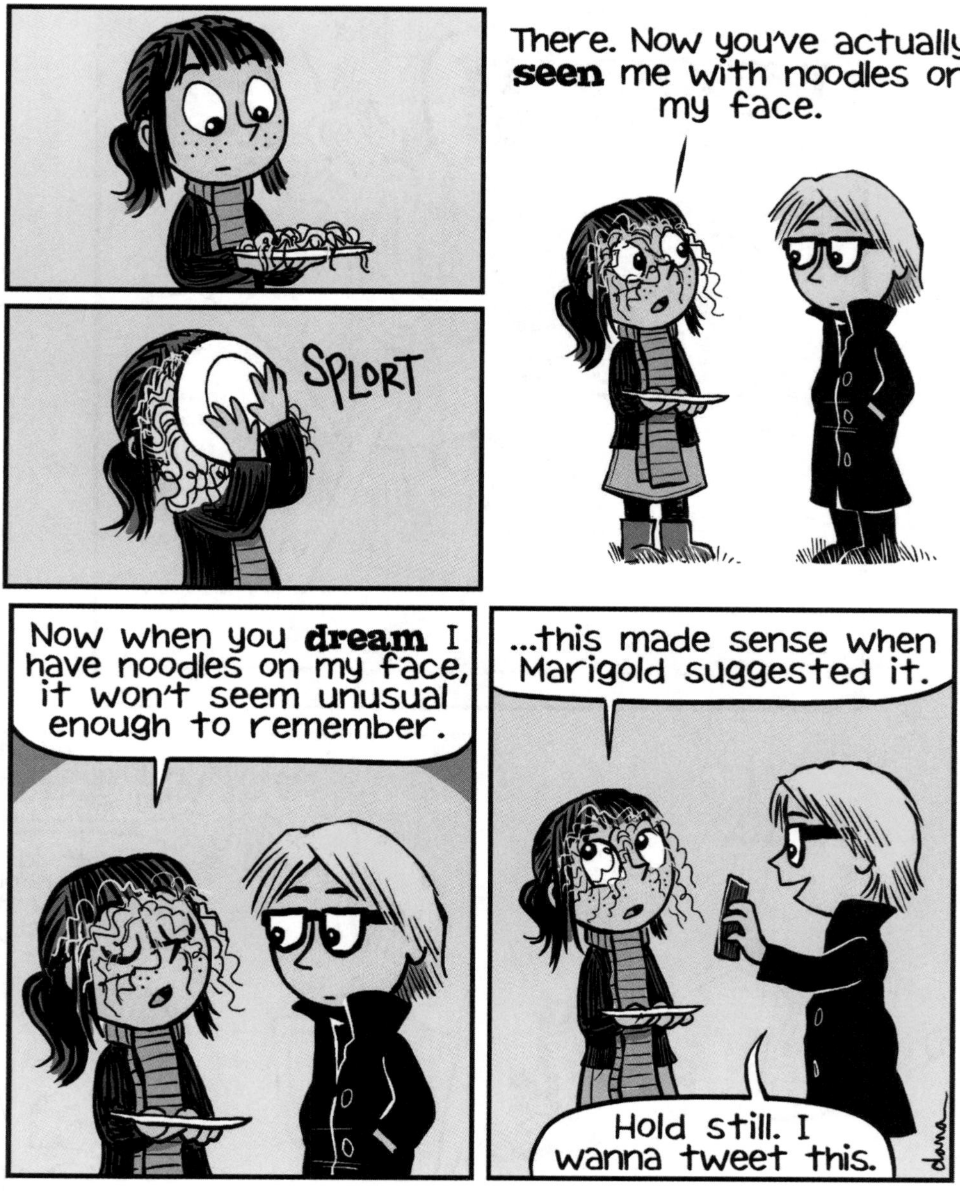
SPLORT
There. Now you've actually **seen** me with noodles on my face.
Now when you **dream** I have noodles on my face, it won't seem unusual enough to remember.
...this made sense when Marigold suggested it.
Hold still. I wanna tweet this.
dana

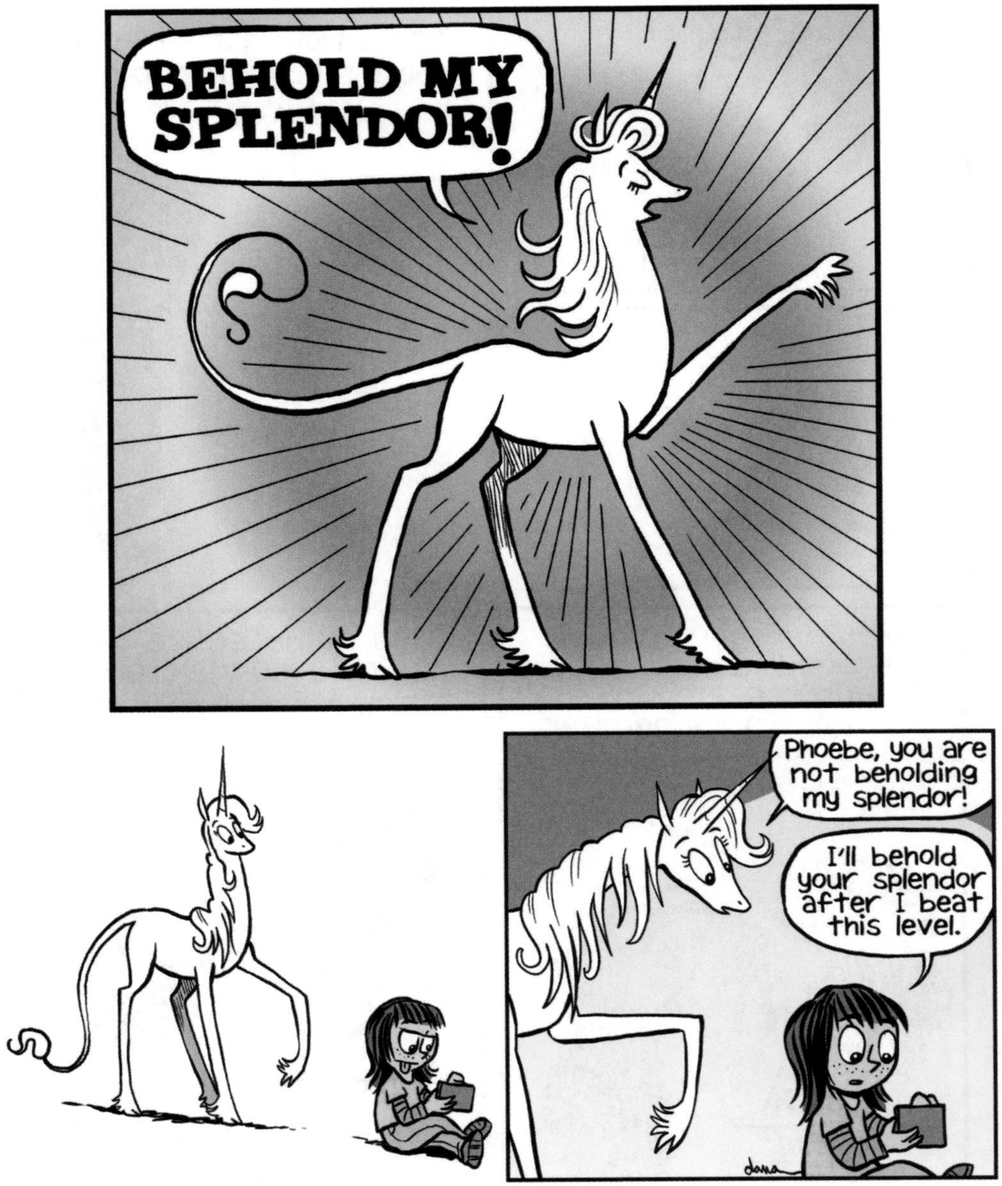
BEHOLD MY SPLENDOR!
Phoebe, you are not beholding my splendor!
I'll behold your splendor after I beat this level.
dana

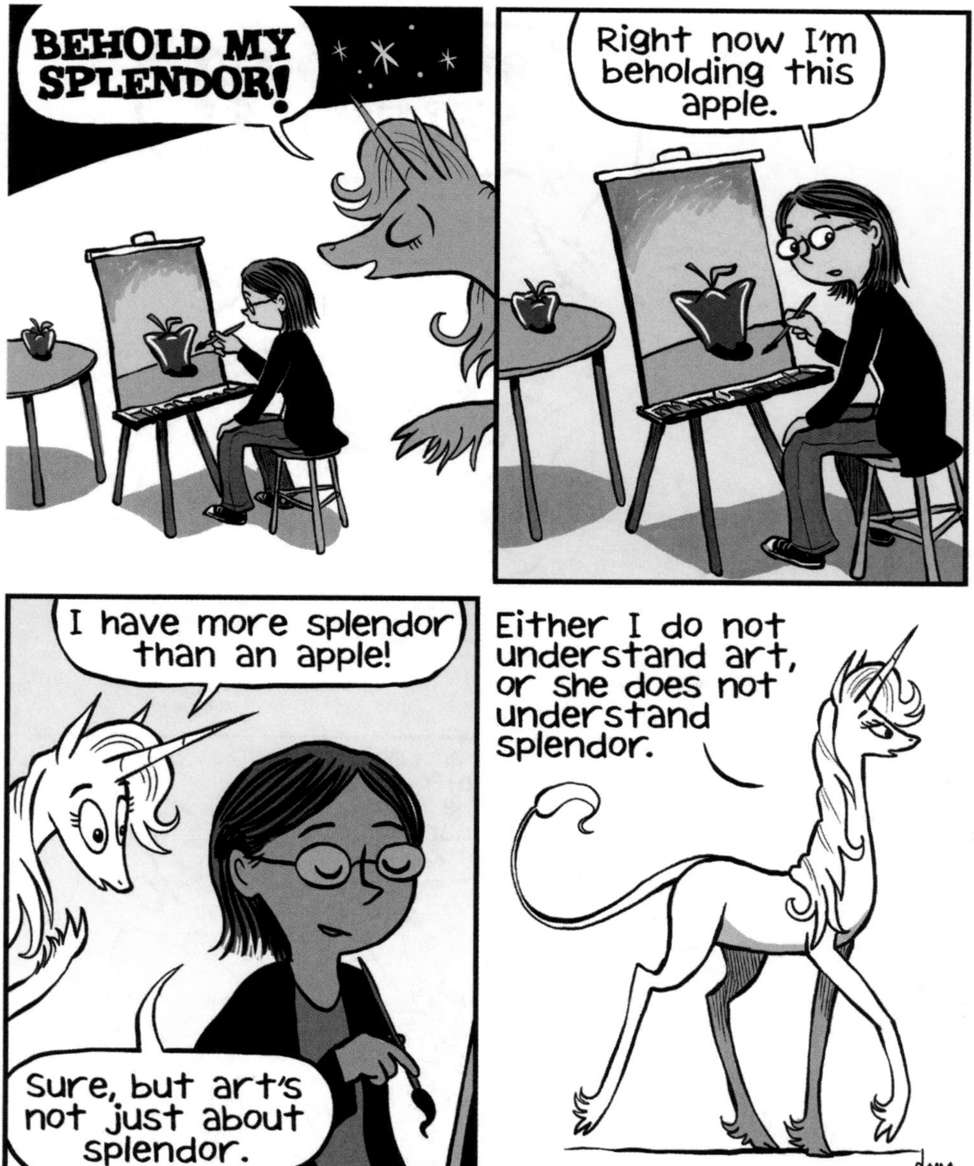
BEHOLD MY SPLENDOR!
Right now I'm beholding this apple.
I have more splendor than an apple!
Sure, but art's not just about splendor.
Either I do not understand art, or she does not understand splendor.
dana

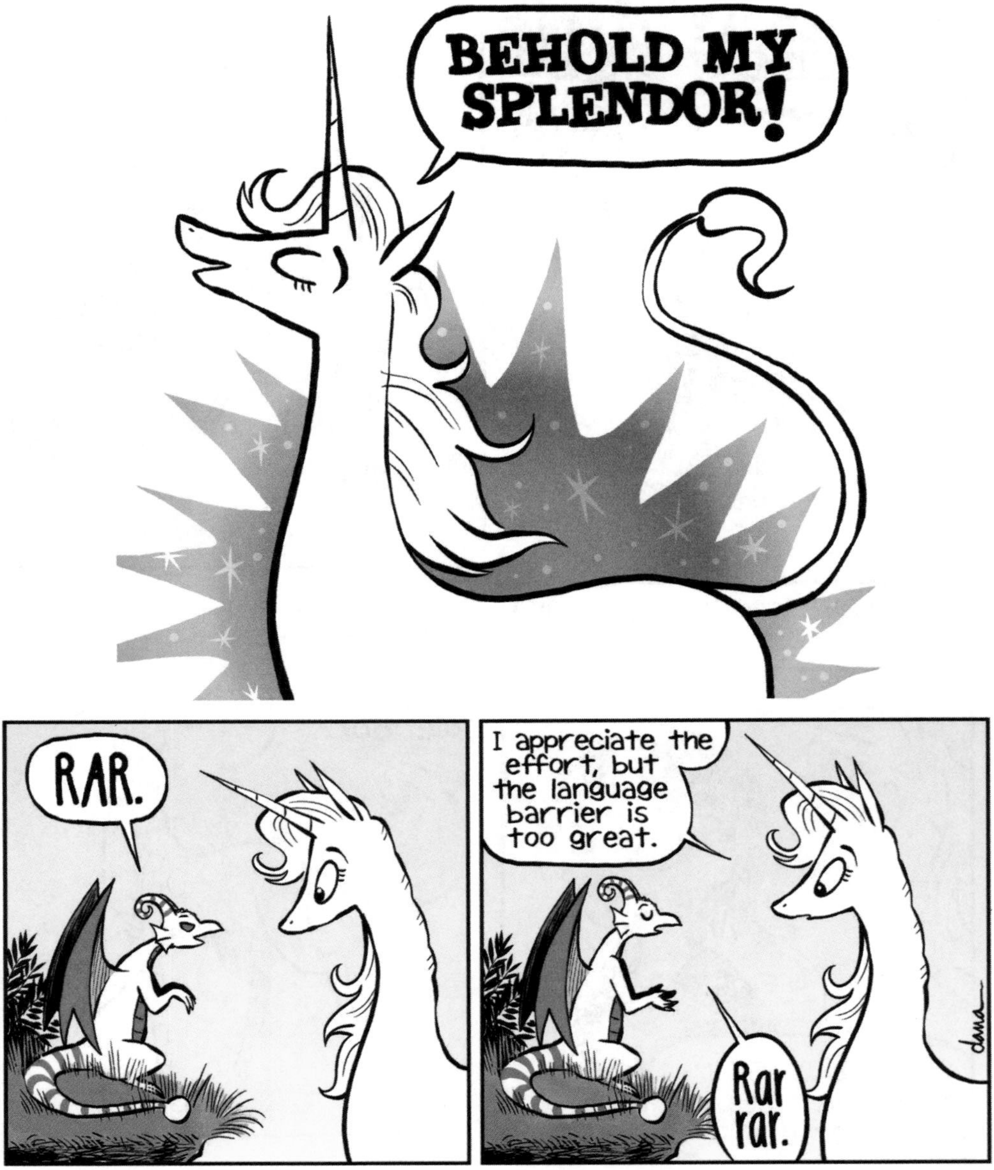
BEHOLD MY SPLENDOR!
RAR.
I appreciate the effort, but the language barrier is too great.
Rar rar.
dana

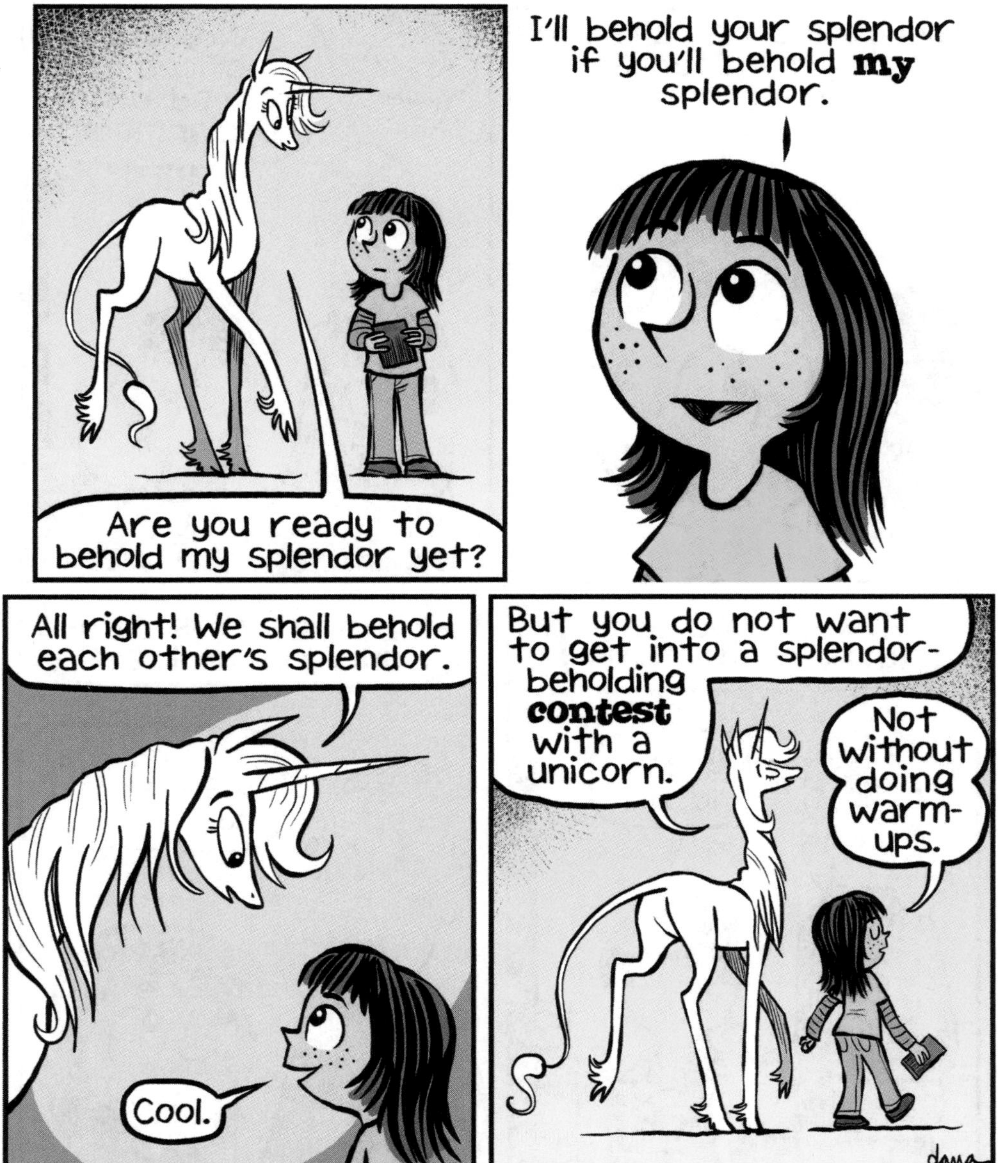
Are you ready to behold my splendor yet?
I'll behold your splendor if you'll behold **my** splendor.
All right! We shall behold each other's splendor.
Cool.
But you do not want to get into a splendor-beholding **contest** with a unicorn.
Not without doing warm-ups.
dana

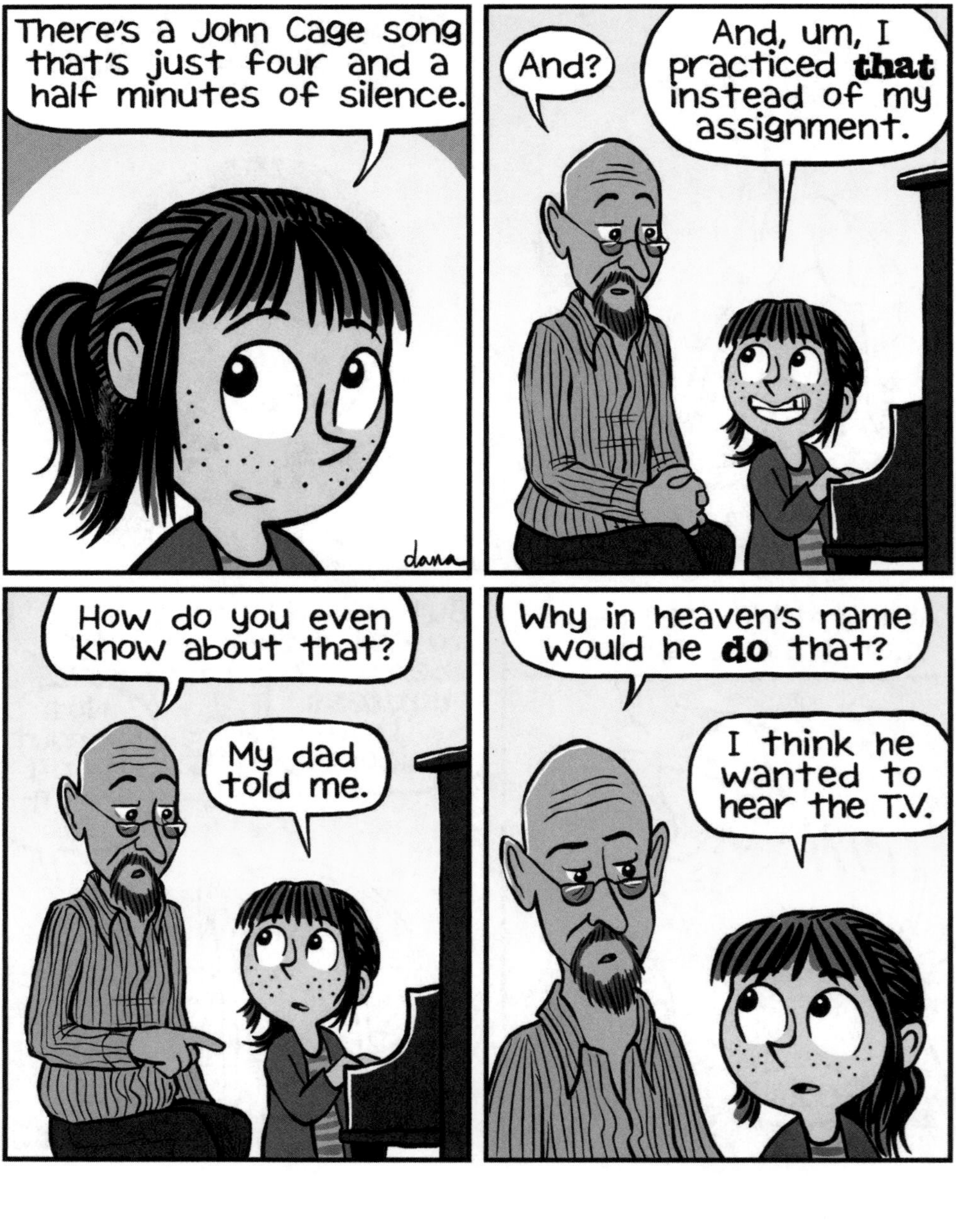
There's a John Cage song that's just four and a half minutes of silence.
dana
And?
And, um, I practiced **that** instead of my assignment.
How do you even know about that?
My dad told me.
Why in heaven's name would he **do** that?
I think he wanted to hear the T.V.

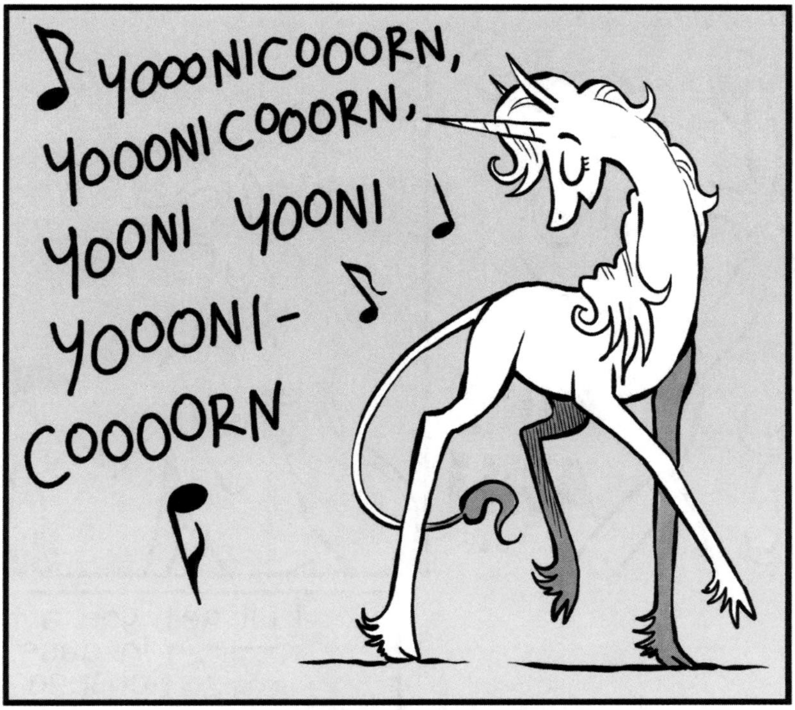
YOOONICOOORN,
YOOONICOOORN,
YOONI YOONI
YOOONI-
COOOORN

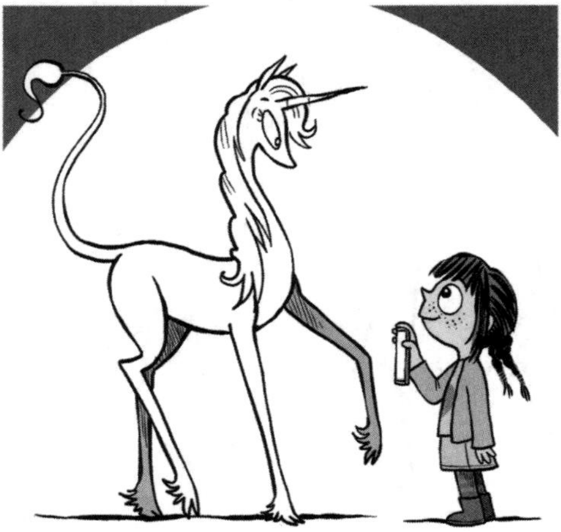

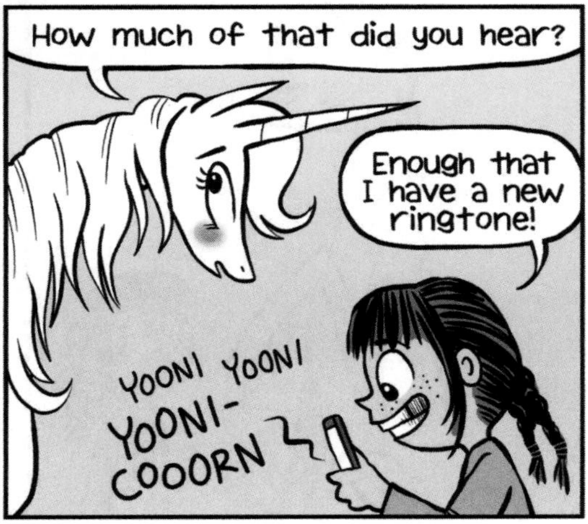
How much of that did you hear?
Enough that I have a new ringtone!
YOONI YOONI
YOONI-
COOORN

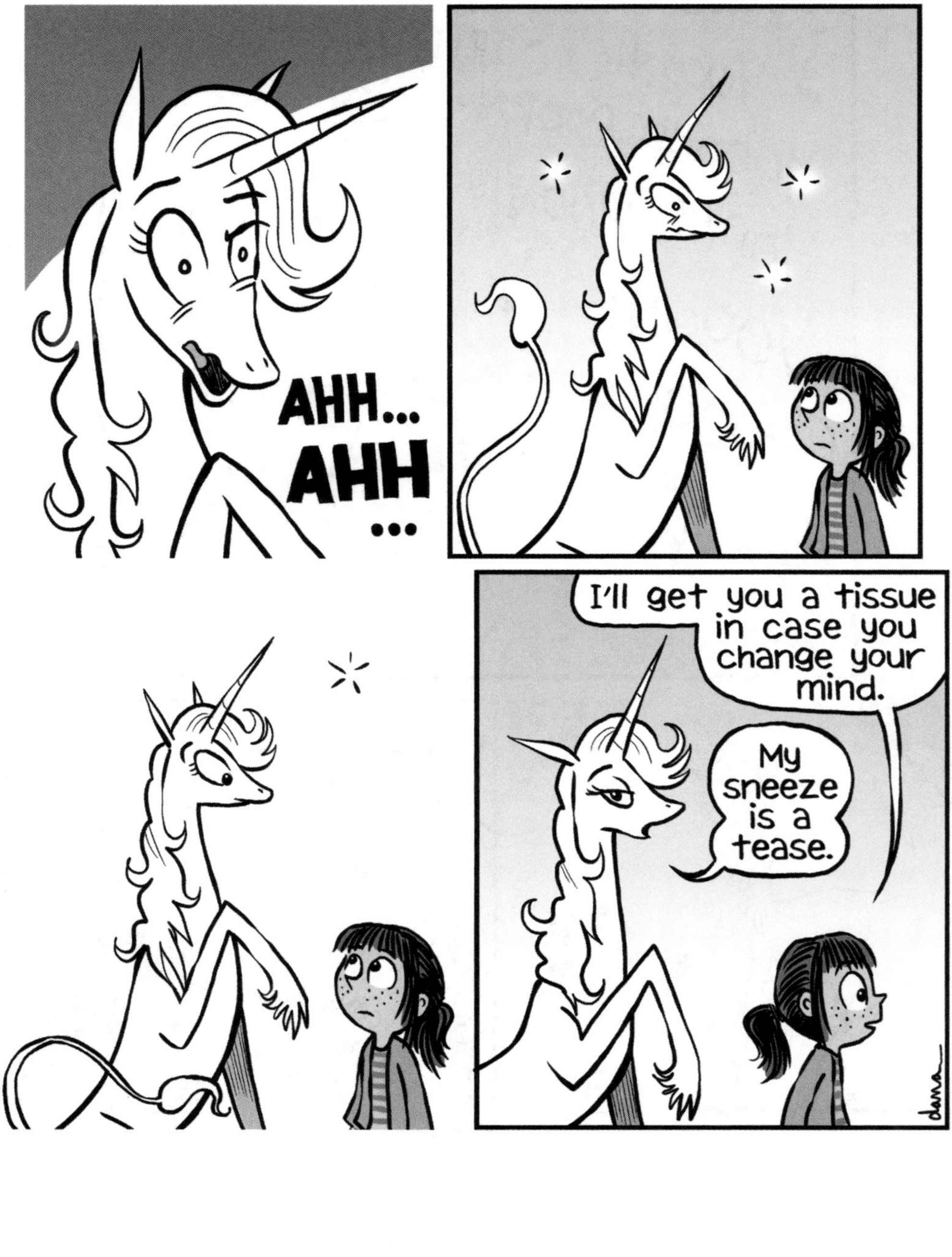
AHH... AHH ...
I'll get you a tissue in case you change your mind.
My sneeze is a tease.
dana

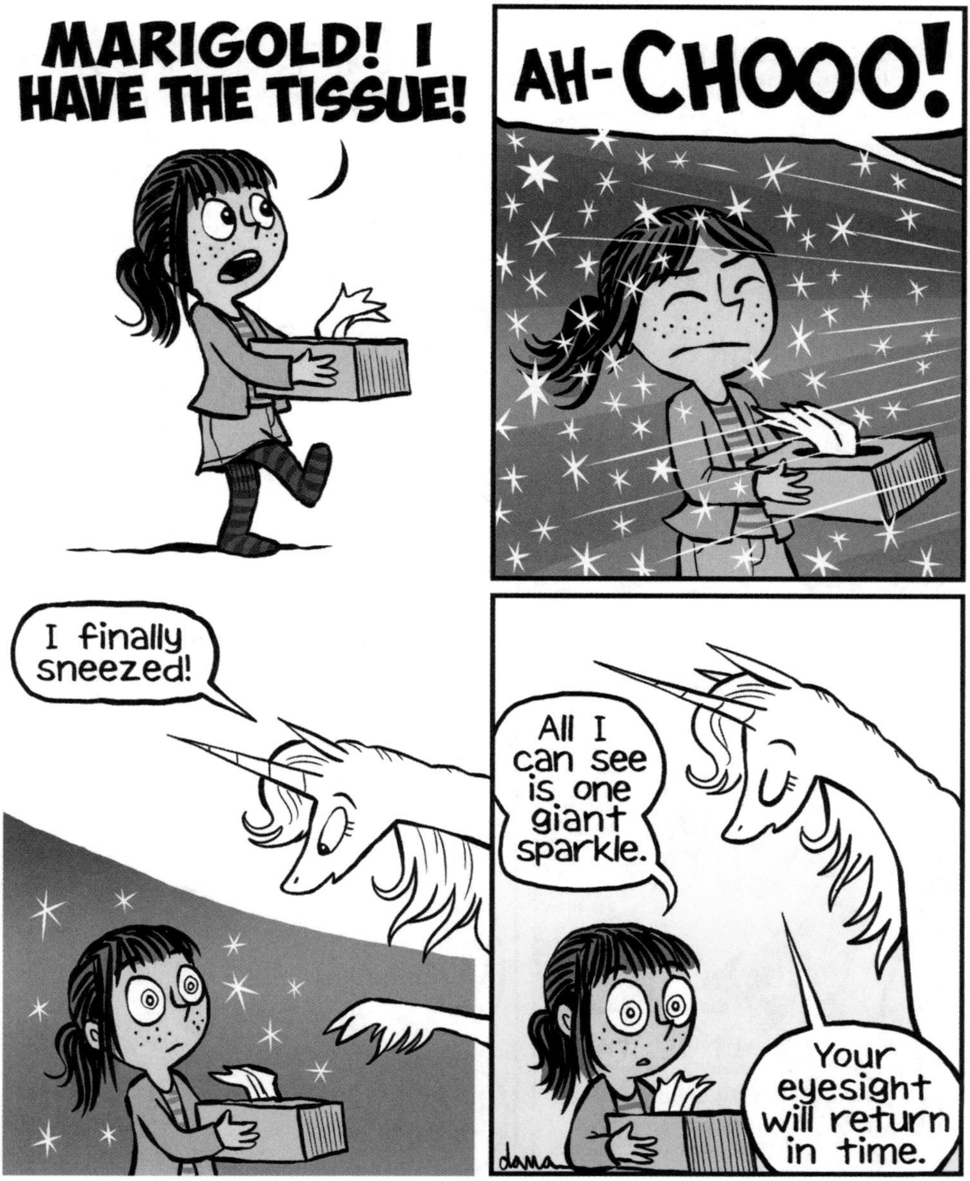
MARIGOLD! I HAVE THE TISSUE!
AH-CHOOO!
I finally sneezed!
All I can see is one giant sparkle.
Your eyesight will return in time.
dana

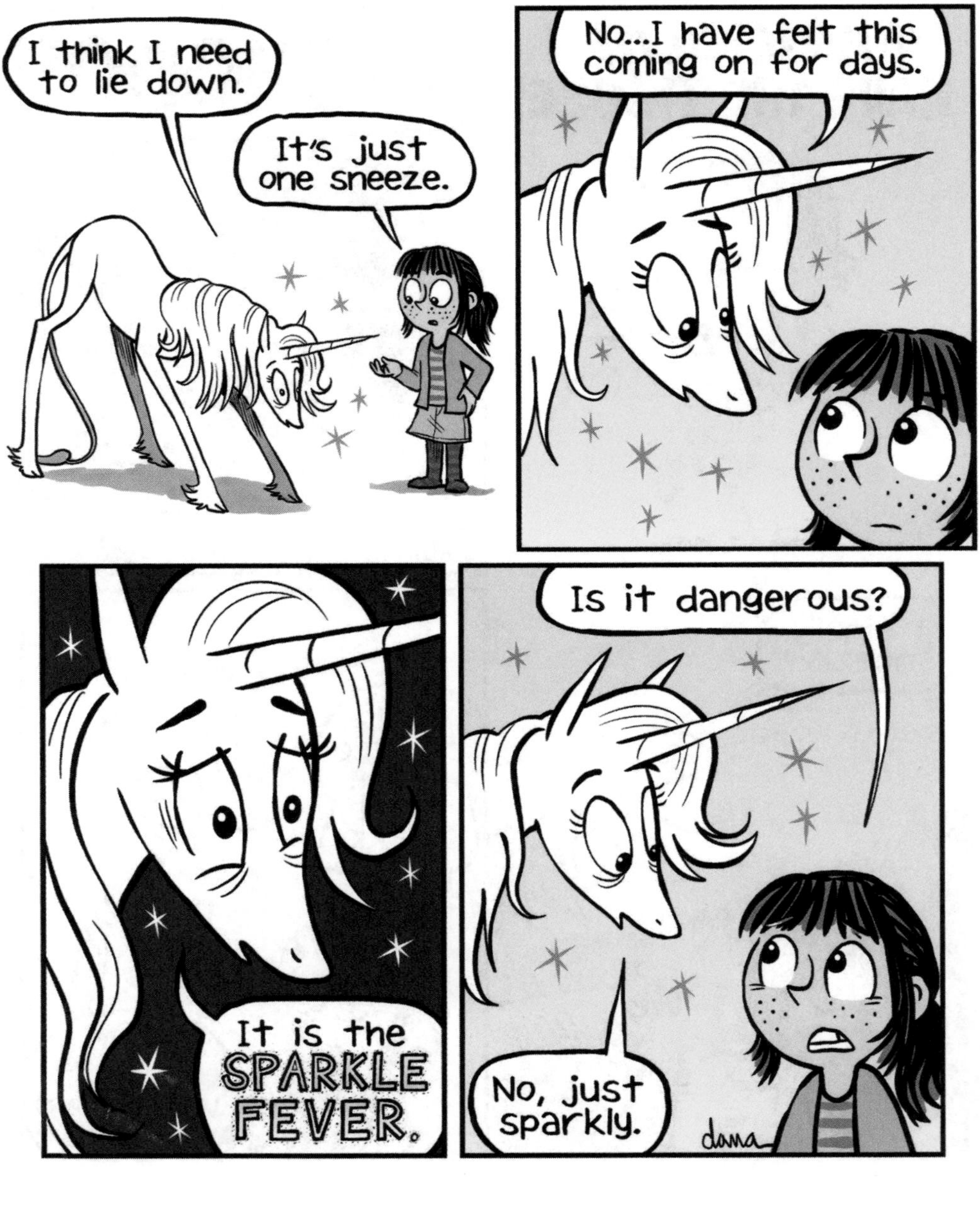
I think I need to lie down.
It's just one sneeze.
No...I have felt this coming on for days.
It is the SPARKLE FEVER.
Is it dangerous?
No, just sparkly.
dana

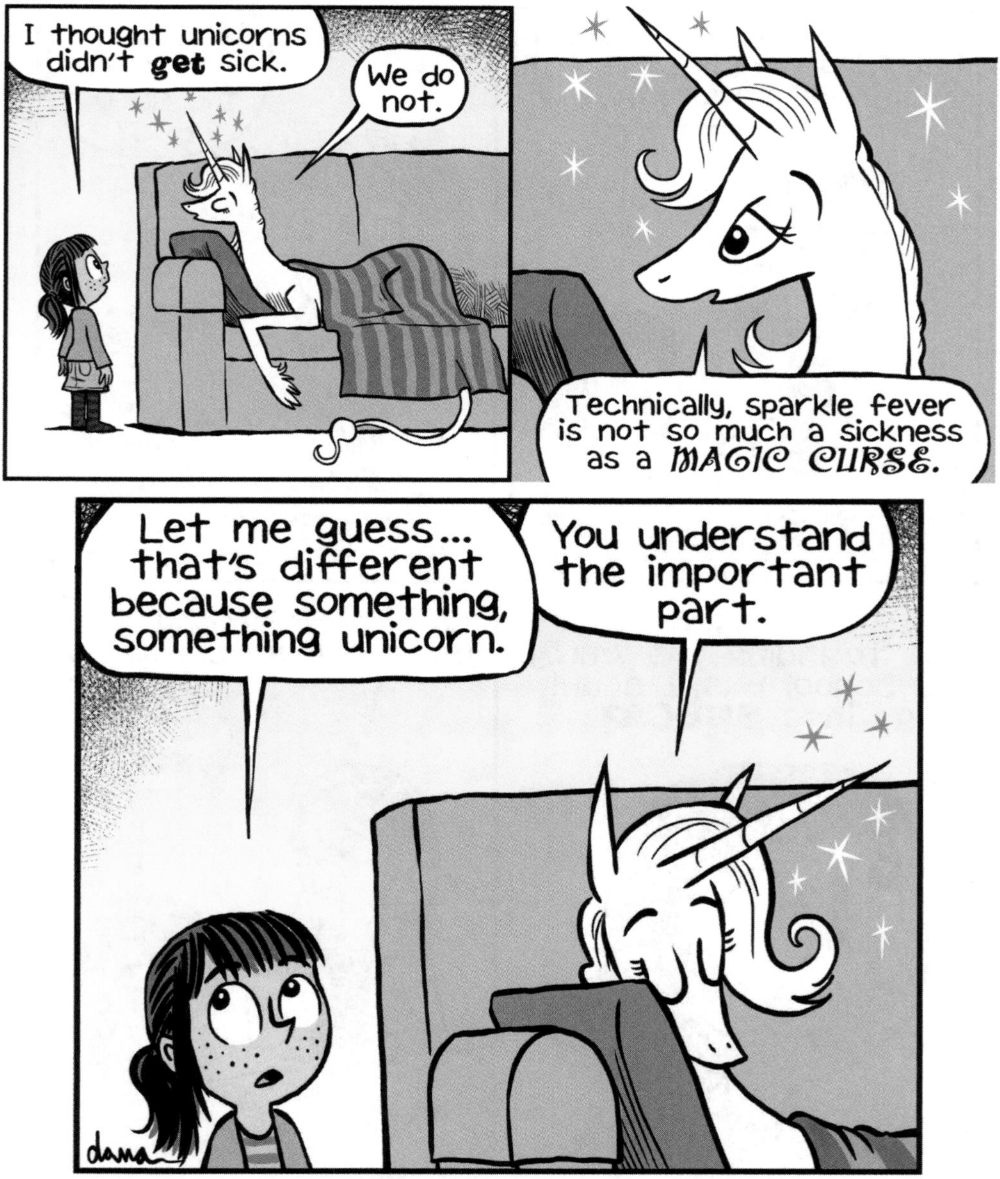
I thought unicorns didn't **get** sick.
We do not.
Technically, sparkle fever is not so much a sickness as a *MAGIC CURSE.*
Let me guess... that's different because something, something unicorn.
You understand the important part.
dana

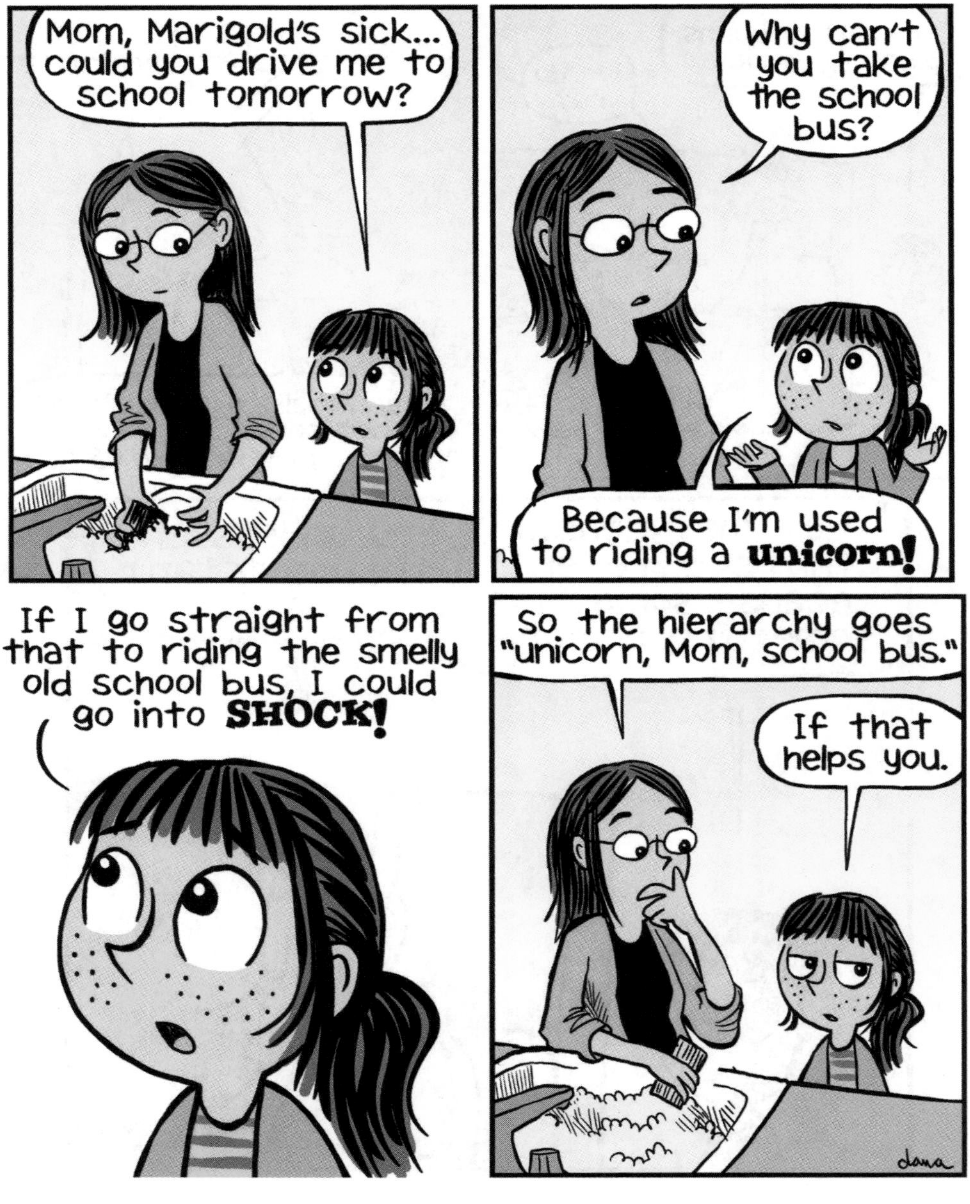
Mom, Marigold's sick... could you drive me to school tomorrow?
Why can't you take the school bus?
Because I'm used to riding a **unicorn!**
If I go straight from that to riding the smelly old school bus, I could go into **SHOCK!**
So the hierarchy goes "unicorn, Mom, school bus."
If that helps you.
dana

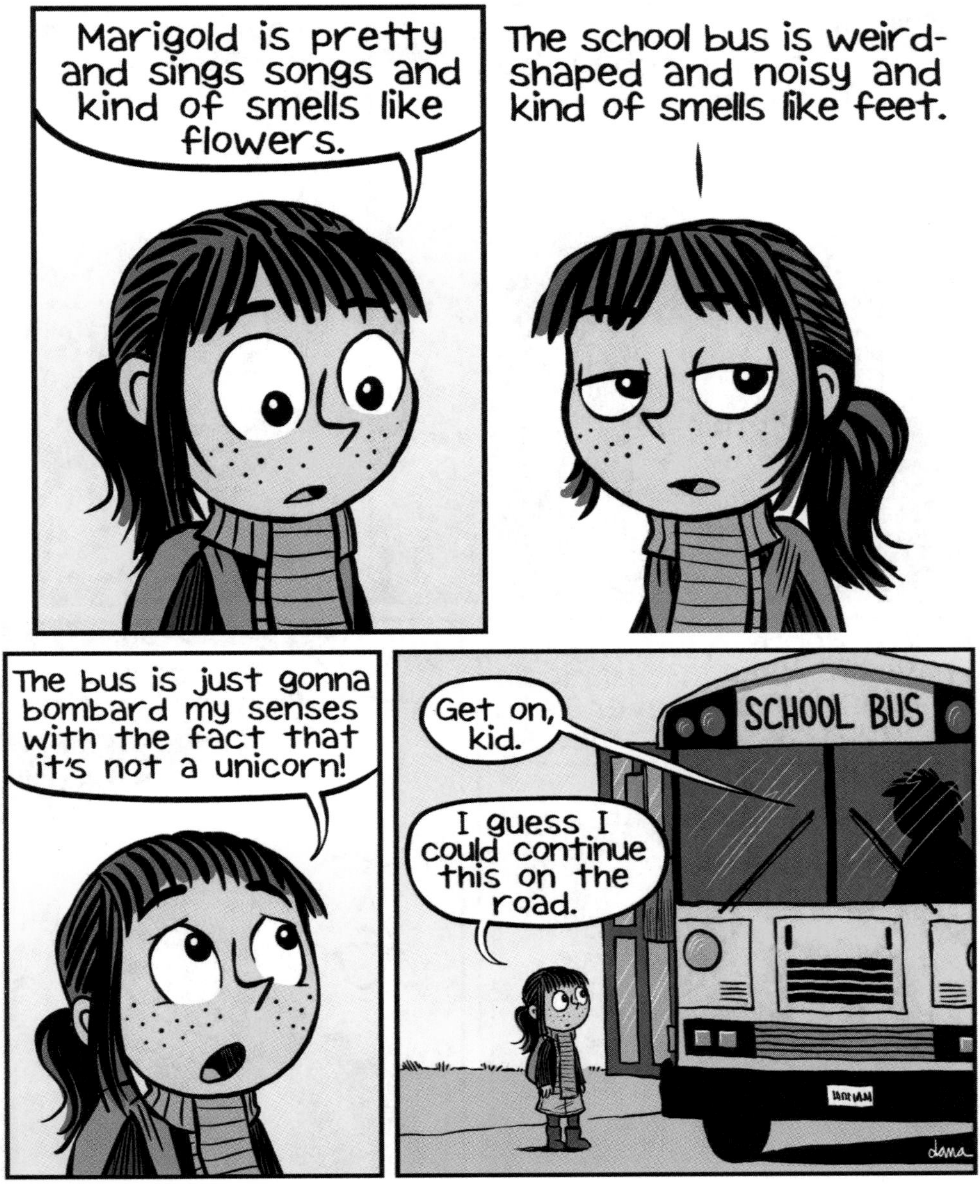
Marigold is pretty and sings songs and kind of smells like flowers.
The school bus is weird-shaped and noisy and kind of smells like feet.
The bus is just gonna bombard my senses with the fact that it's not a unicorn!
SCHOOL BUS
Get on, kid.
I guess I could continue this on the road.
dana

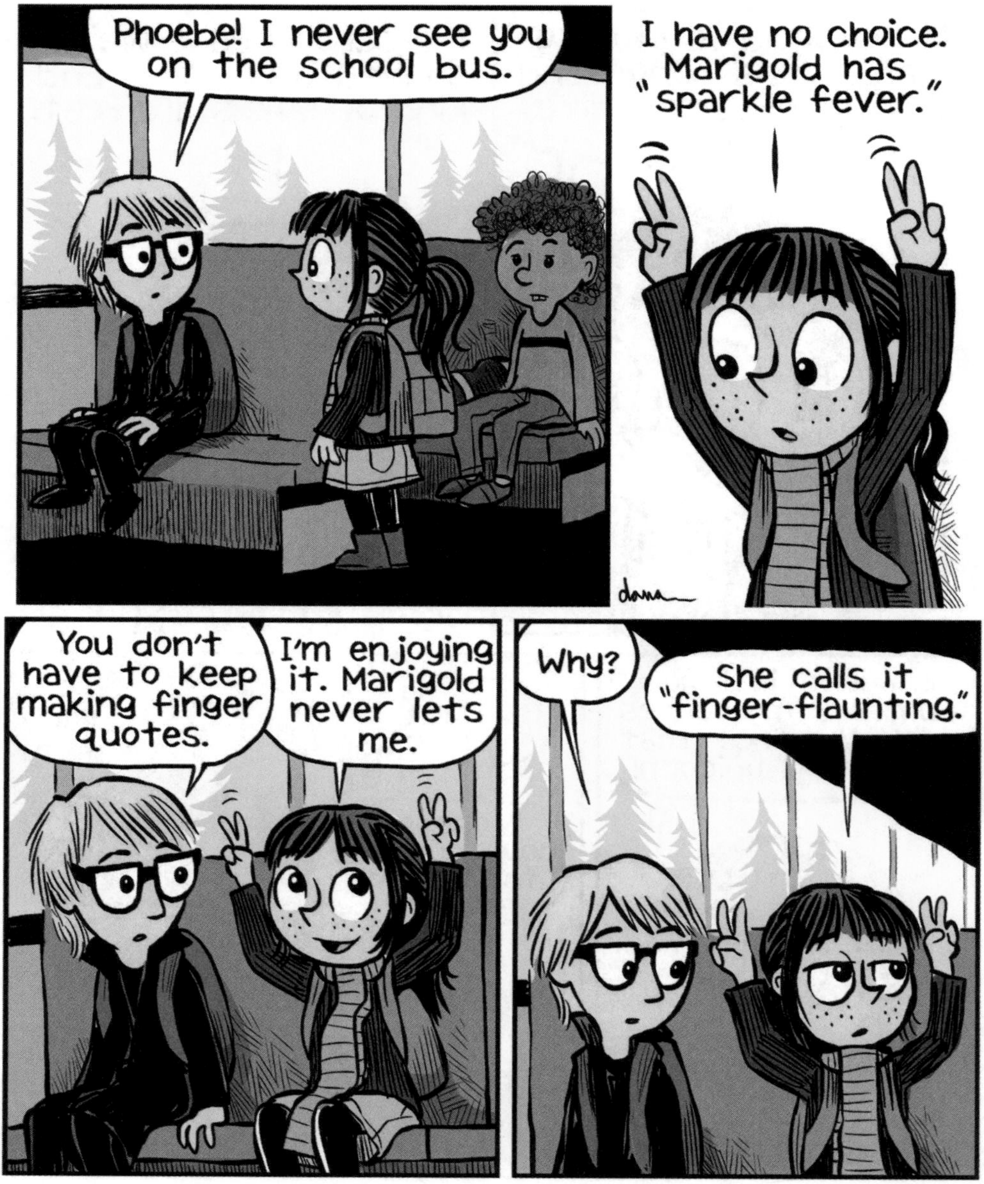
Phoebe! I never see you on the school bus.
I have no choice. Marigold has "sparkle fever."
You don't have to keep making finger quotes.
I'm enjoying it. Marigold never lets me.
Why?
She calls it "finger-flaunting."

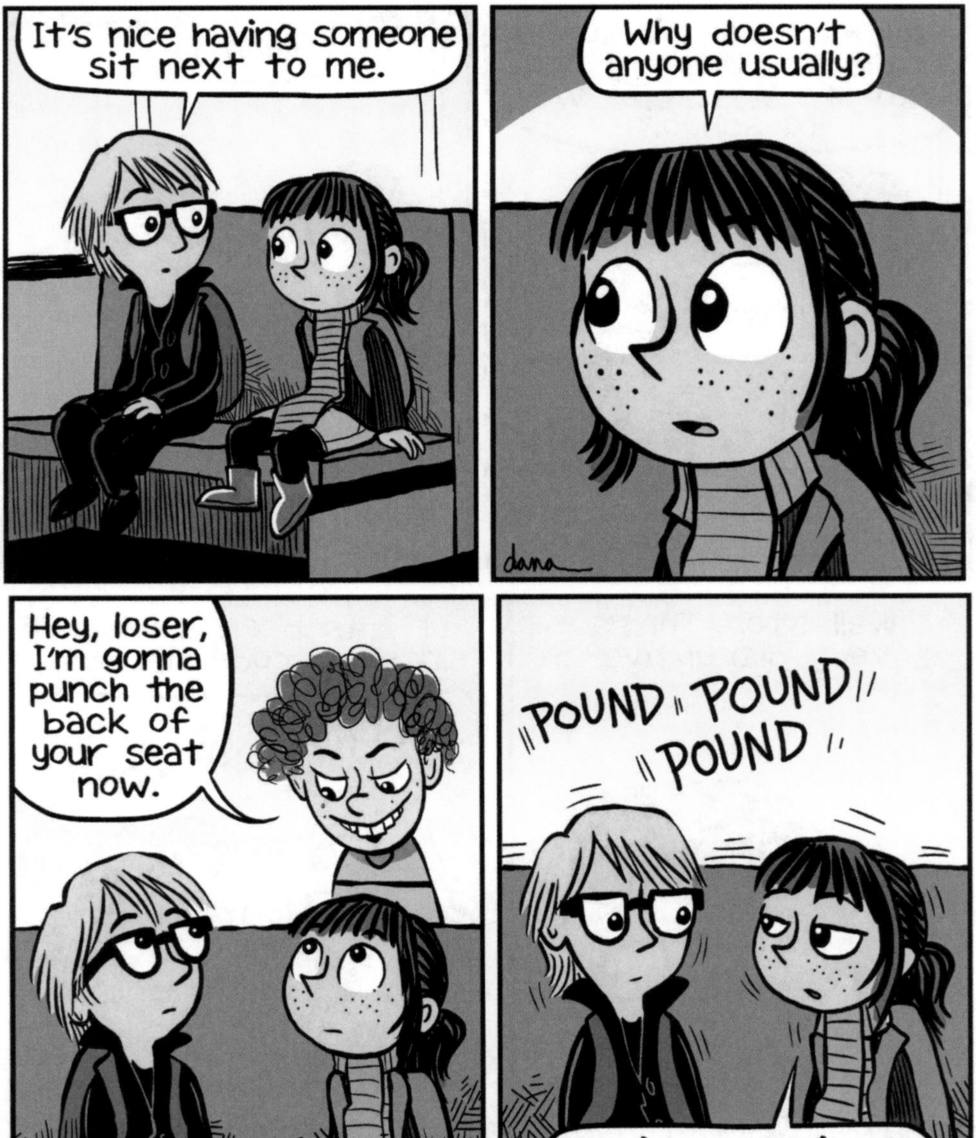
It's nice having someone sit next to me.
Why doesn't anyone usually?
dana
Hey, loser, I'm gonna punch the back of your seat now.
POUND POUND POUND
I miss my unicorn.

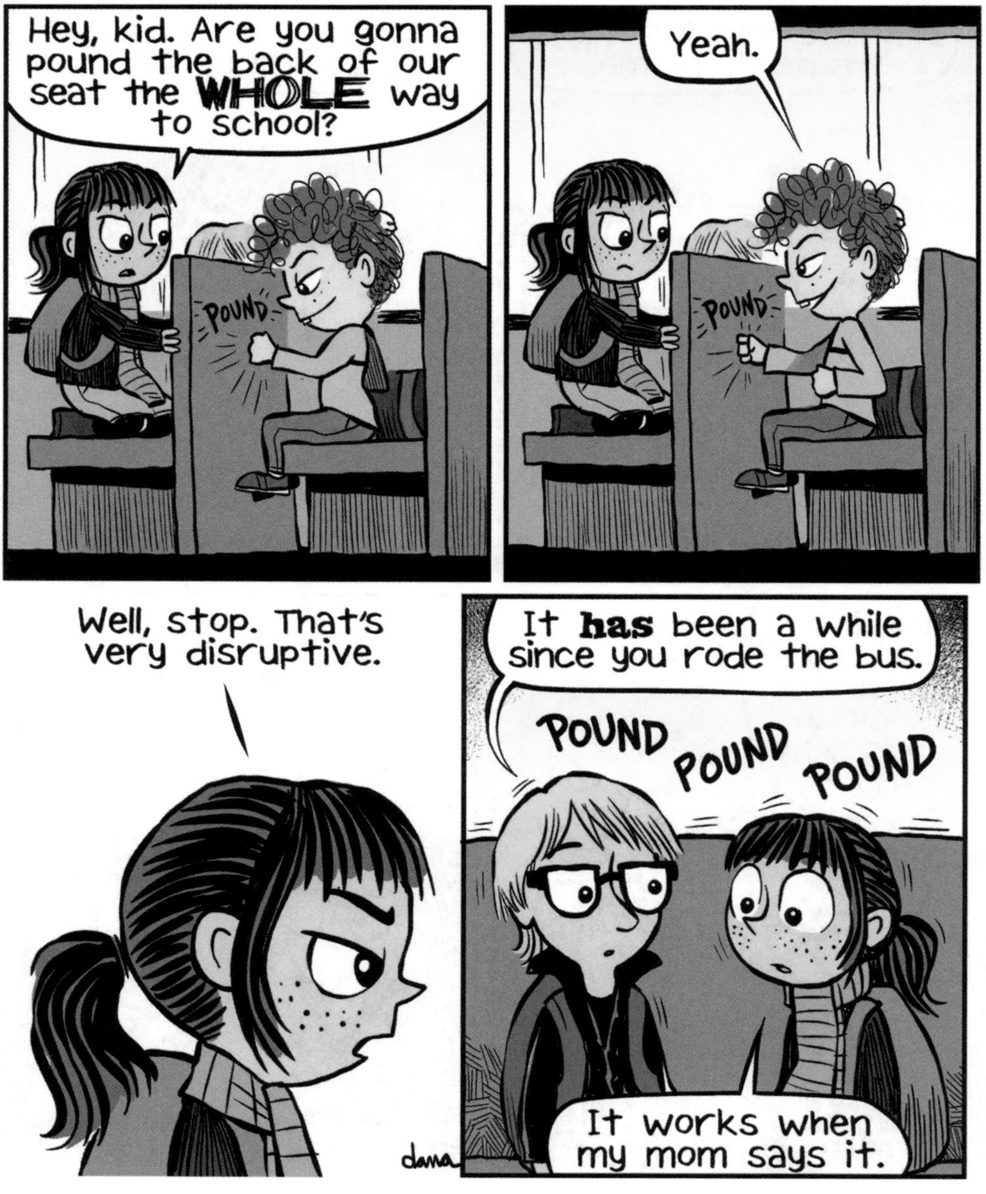
Hey, kid. Are you gonna pound the back of our seat the WHOLE way to school?
POUND
Yeah.
POUND
Well, stop. That's very disruptive.
It has been a while since you rode the bus.
POUND
POUND
POUND
It works when my mom says it.
dana

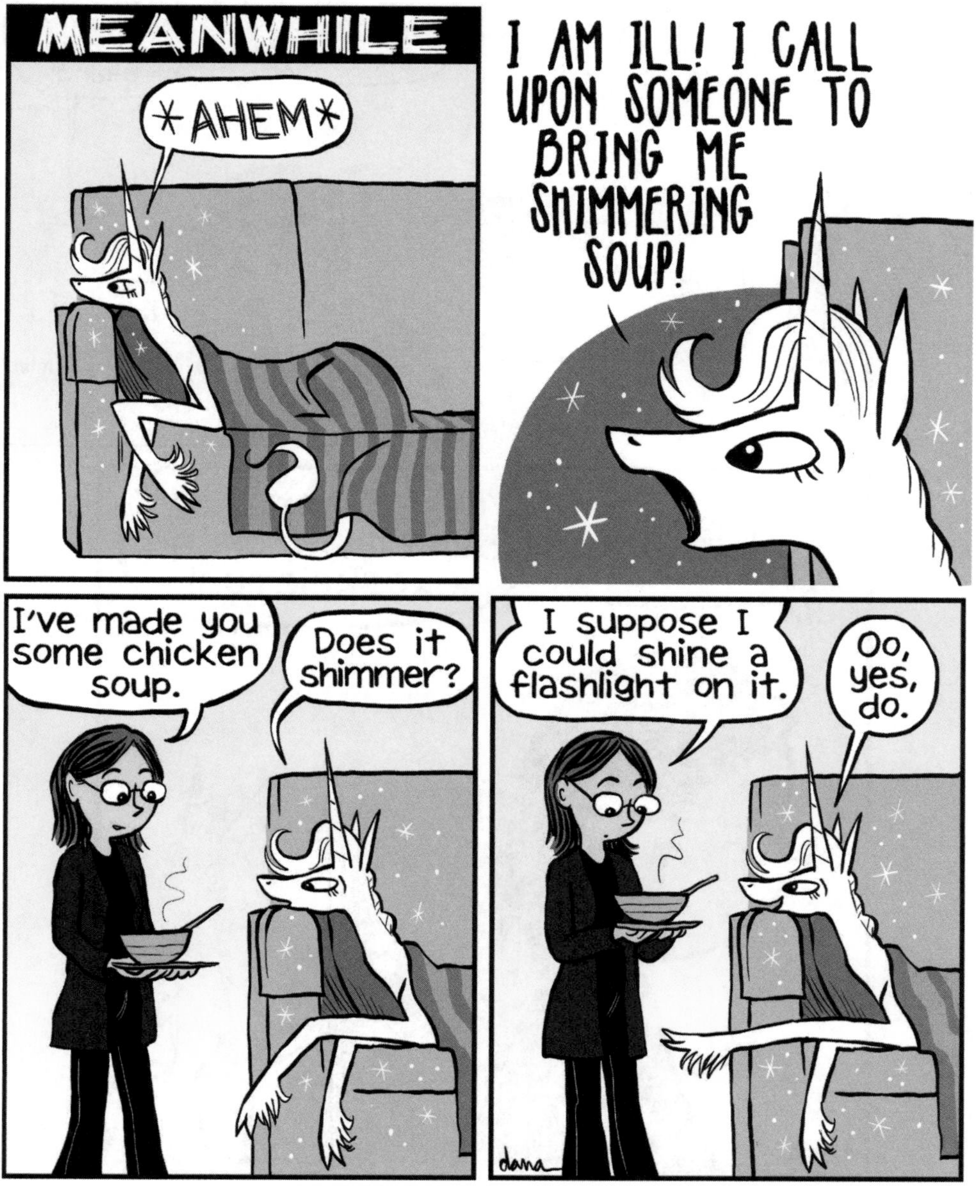
MEANWHILE
AHEM
I AM ILL! I CALL UPON SOMEONE TO BRING ME SHIMMERING SOUP!
I've made you some chicken soup.
Does it shimmer?
I suppose I could shine a flashlight on it.
Oo, yes, do.
dana

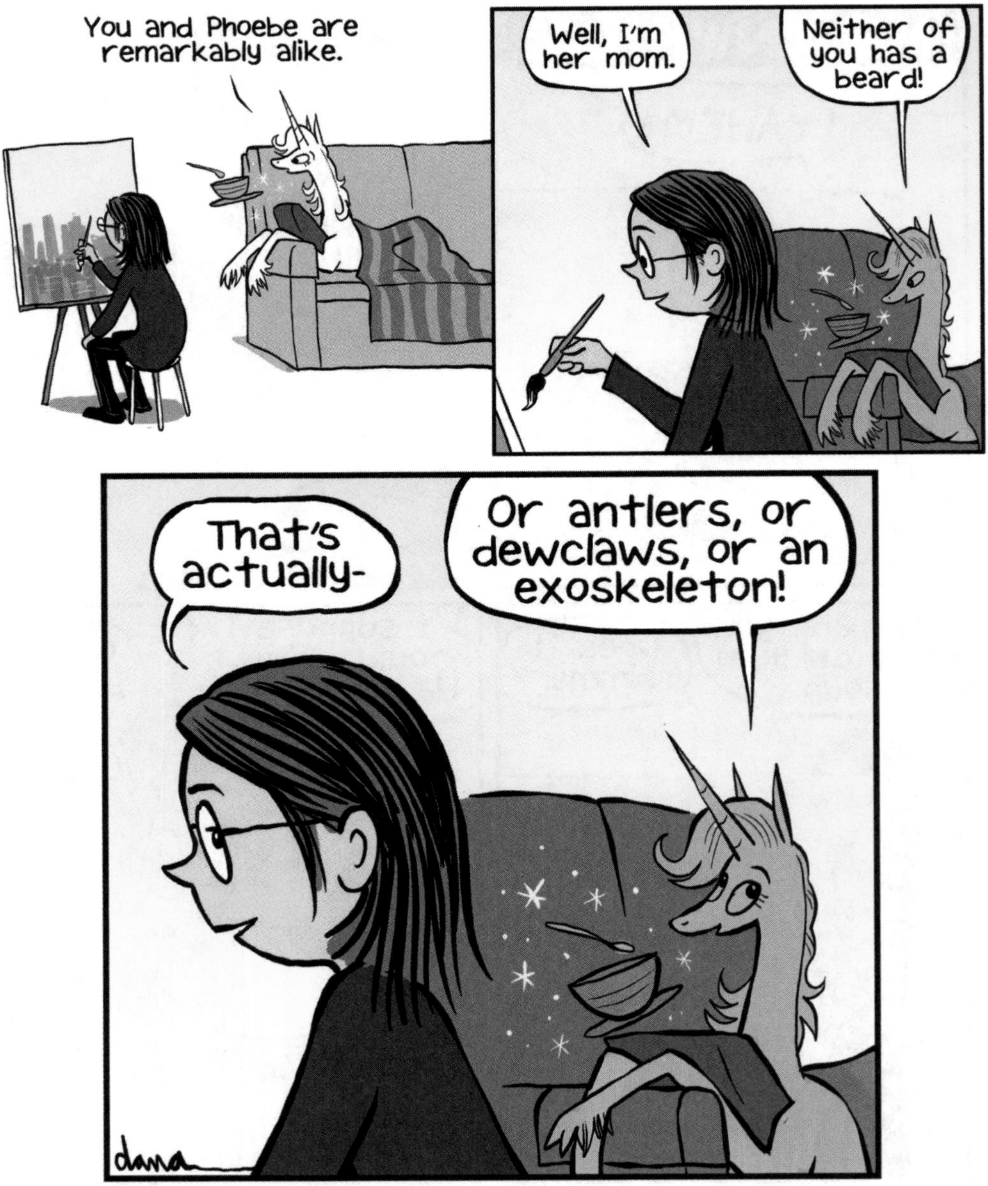
You and Phoebe are remarkably alike.
Well, I'm her mom.
Neither of you has a beard!
That's actually-
Or antlers, or dewclaws, or an exoskeleton!
dana

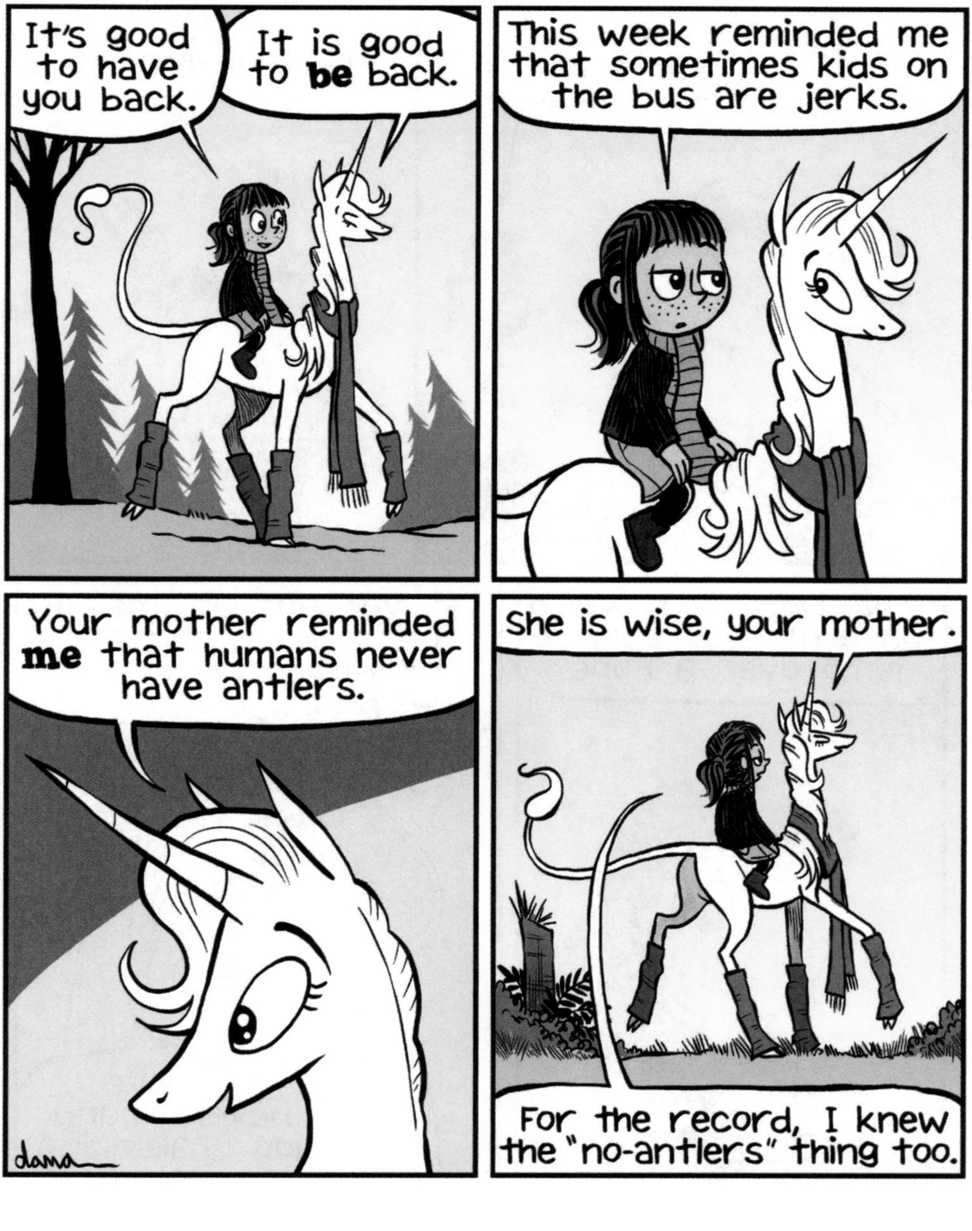

It's good to have you back.
It is good to **be** back.
This week reminded me that sometimes kids on the bus are jerks.
Your mother reminded **me** that humans never have antlers.
dana
She is wise, your mother.
For the record, I knew the "no-antlers" thing too.

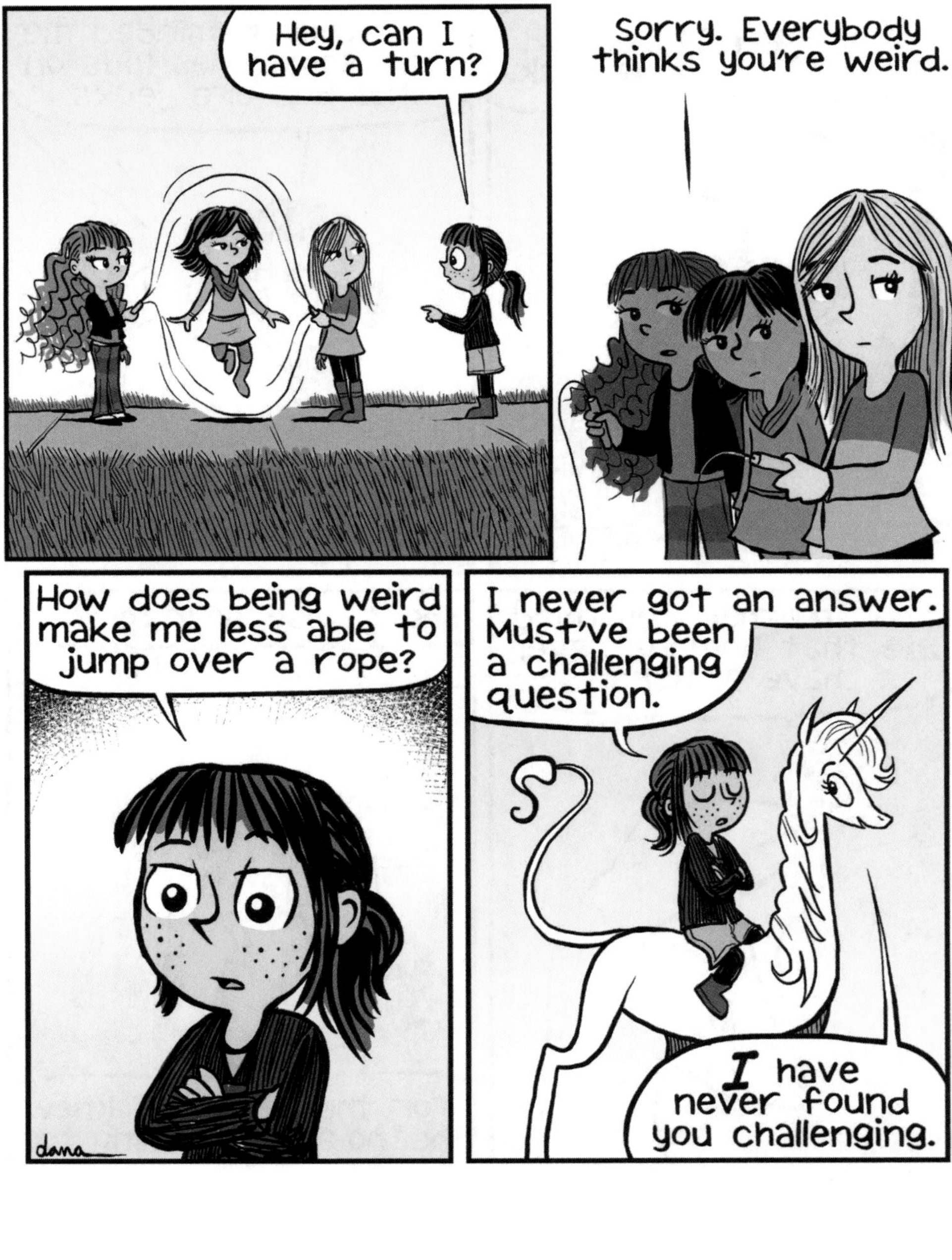
Hey, can I have a turn?
Sorry. Everybody thinks you're weird.
How does being weird make me less able to jump over a rope?
I never got an answer. Must've been a challenging question.
I have never found you challenging.
dana

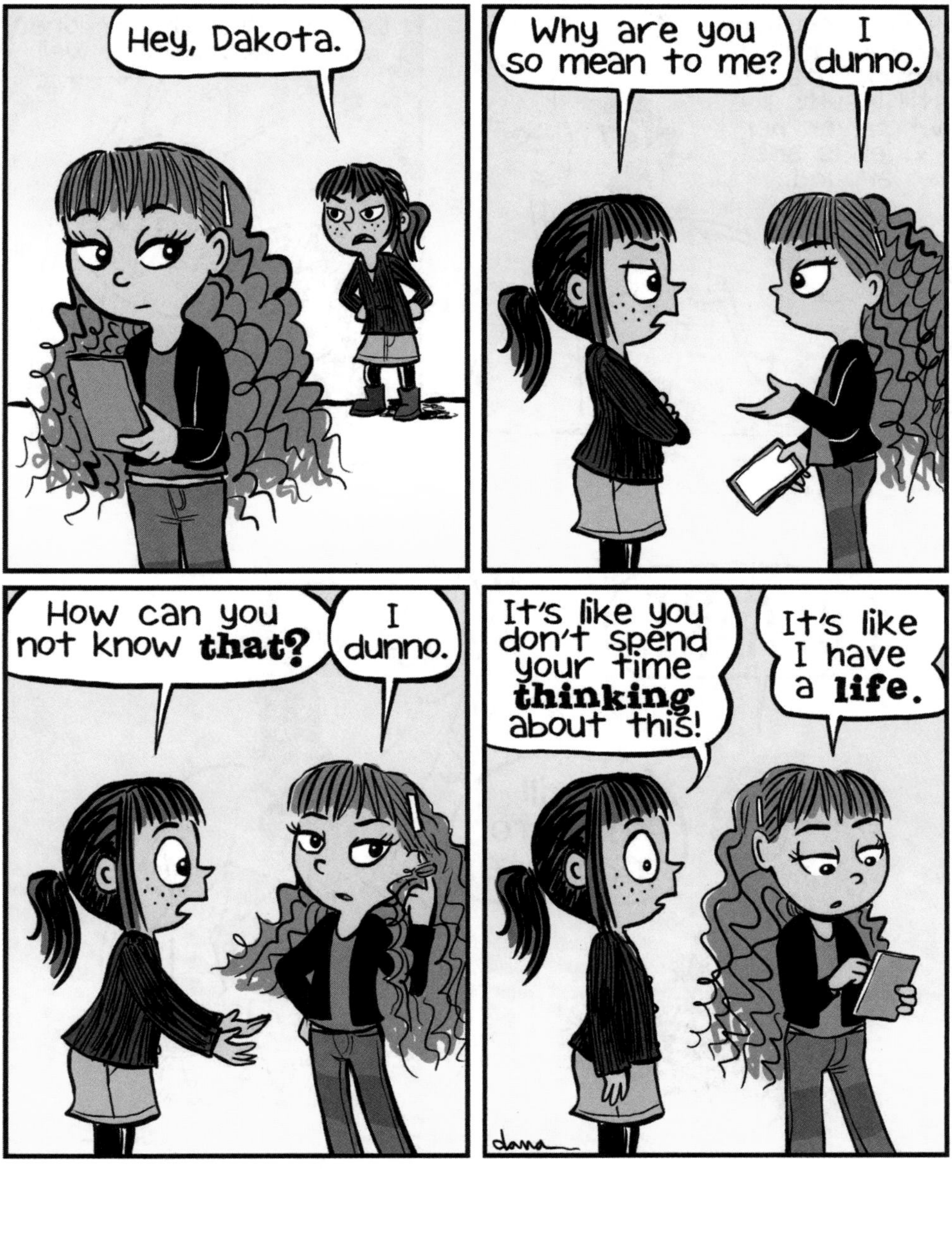
Hey, Dakota.
Why are you so mean to me?
I dunno.
How can you not know **that?**
I dunno.
It's like you don't spend your time **thinking** about this!
It's like I have a **life**.
dana

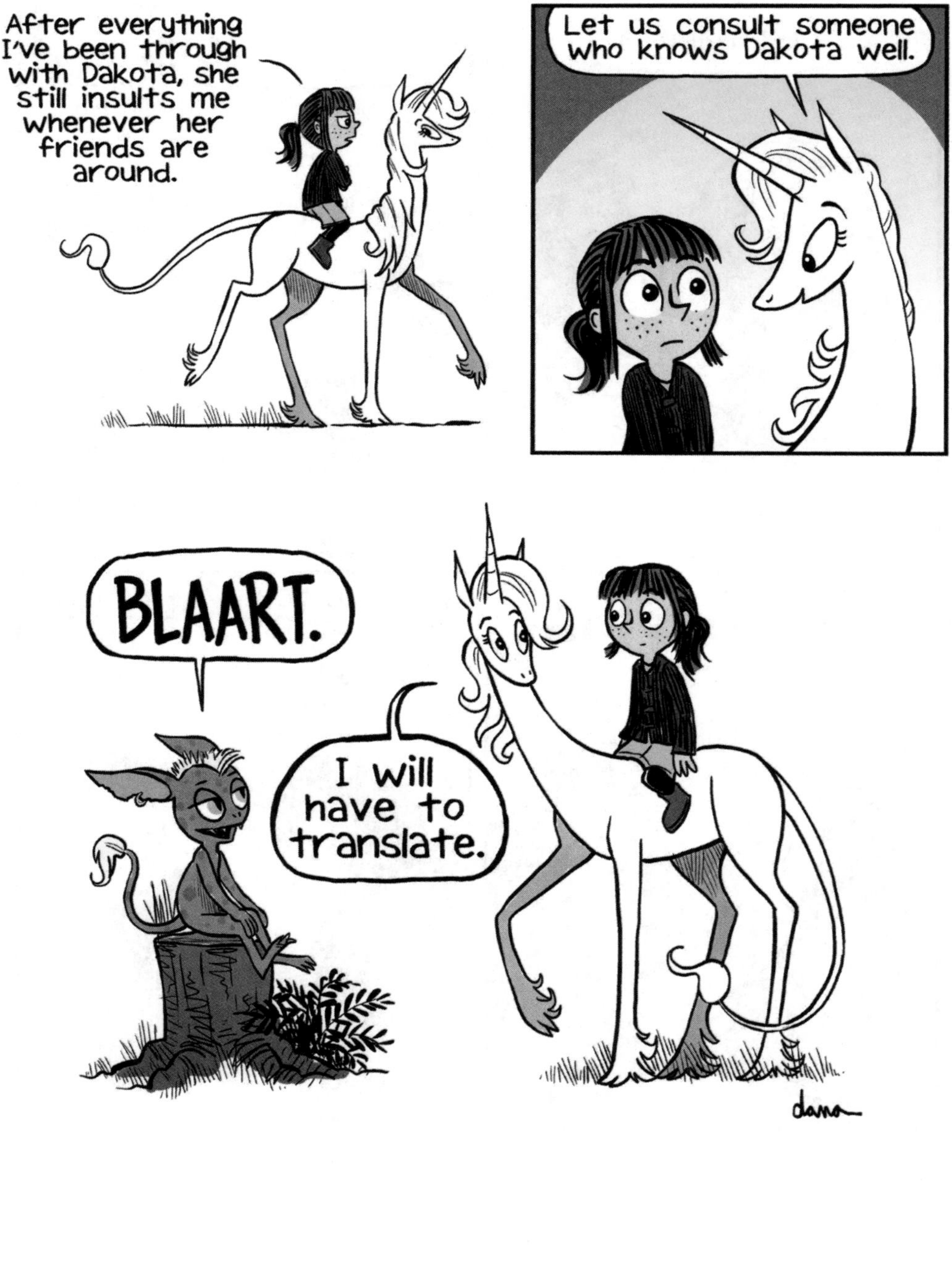
After everything I've been through with Dakota, she still insults me whenever her friends are around.
Let us consult someone who knows Dakota well.
BLAART.
I will have to translate.
dana

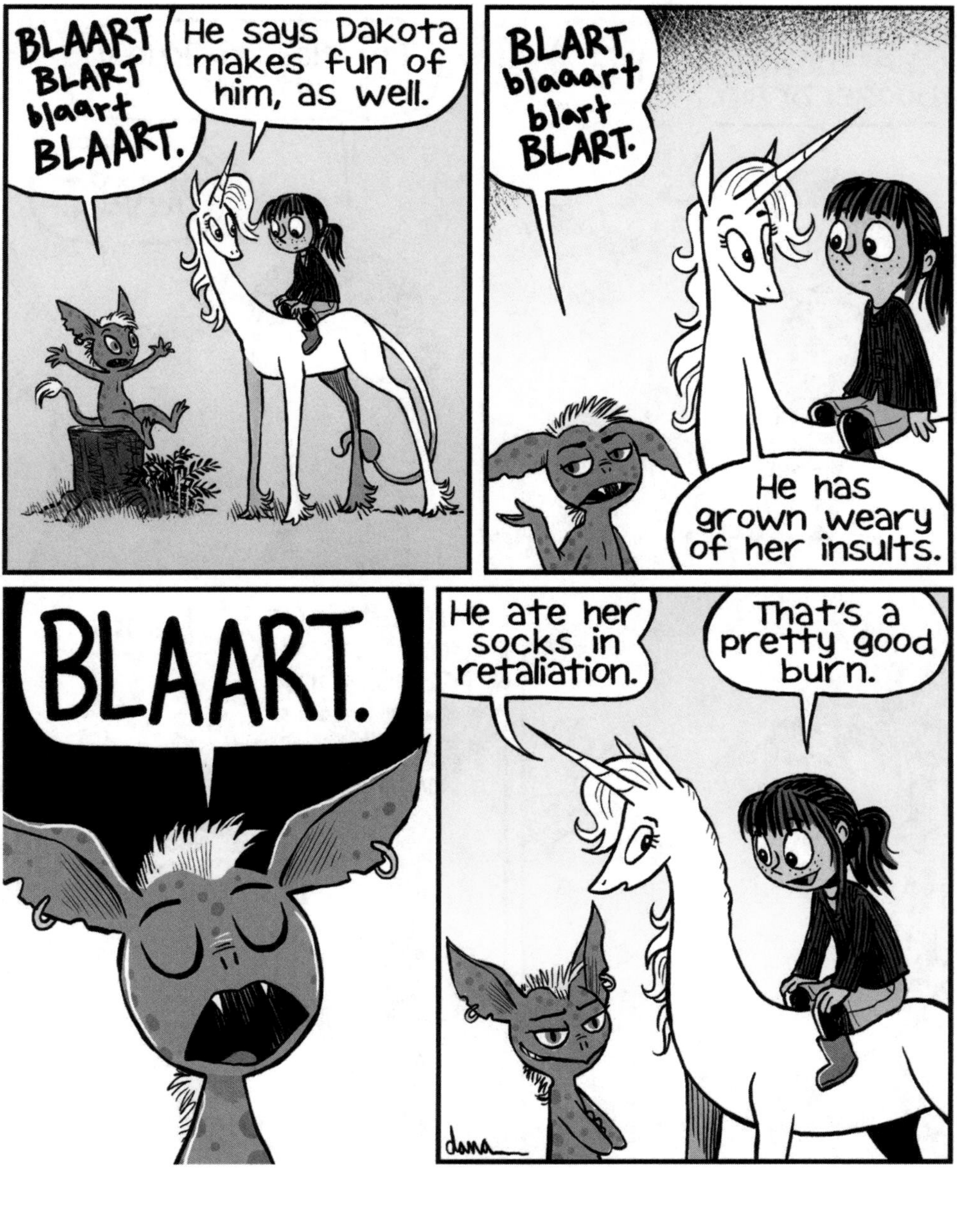
BLAART BLART blaart BLAART.
He says Dakota makes fun of him, as well.
BLART, blaaart blart BLART.
He has grown weary of her insults.
BLAART.
He ate her socks in retaliation.
That's a pretty good burn.
dana

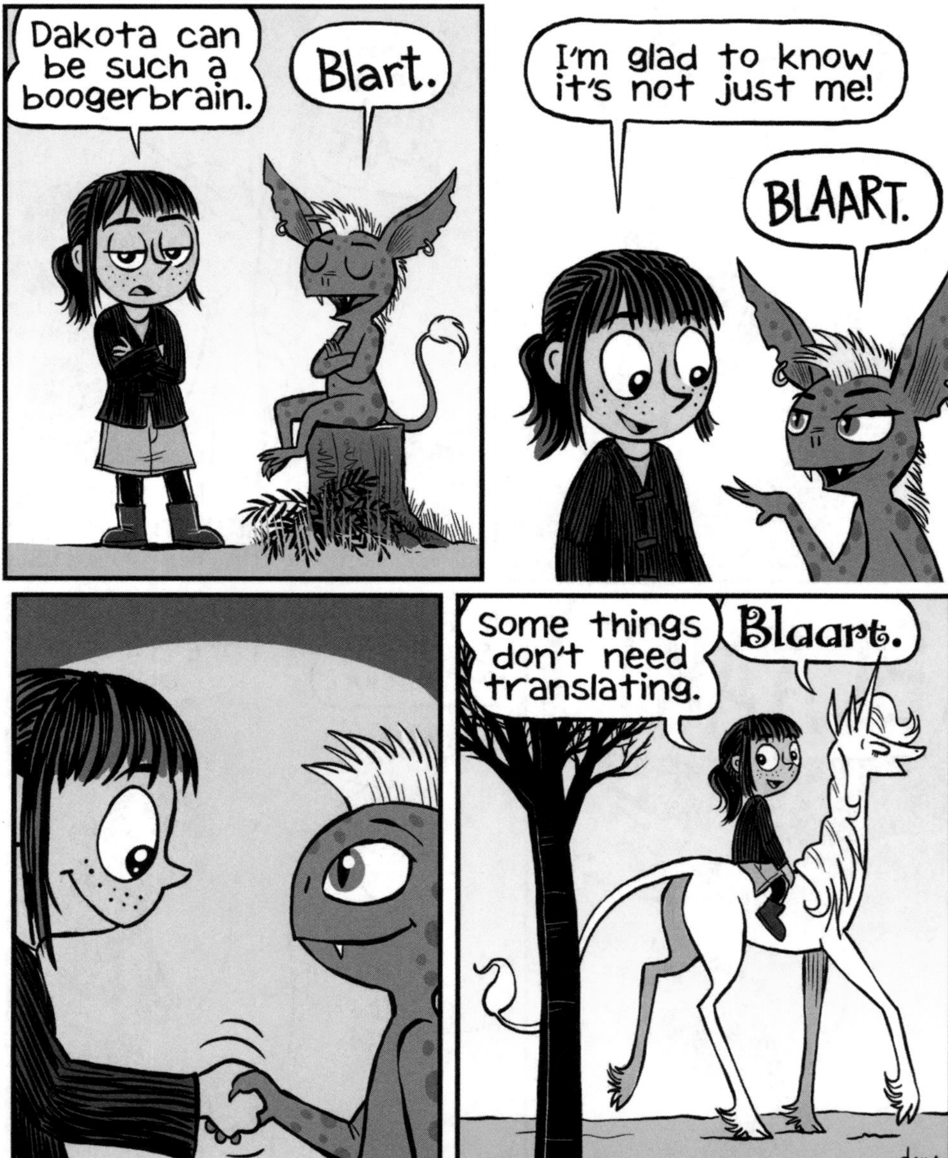
Dakota can be such a boogerbrain.
Blart.
I'm glad to know it's not just me!
BLAART.
Some things don't need translating.
Blaart.
dana

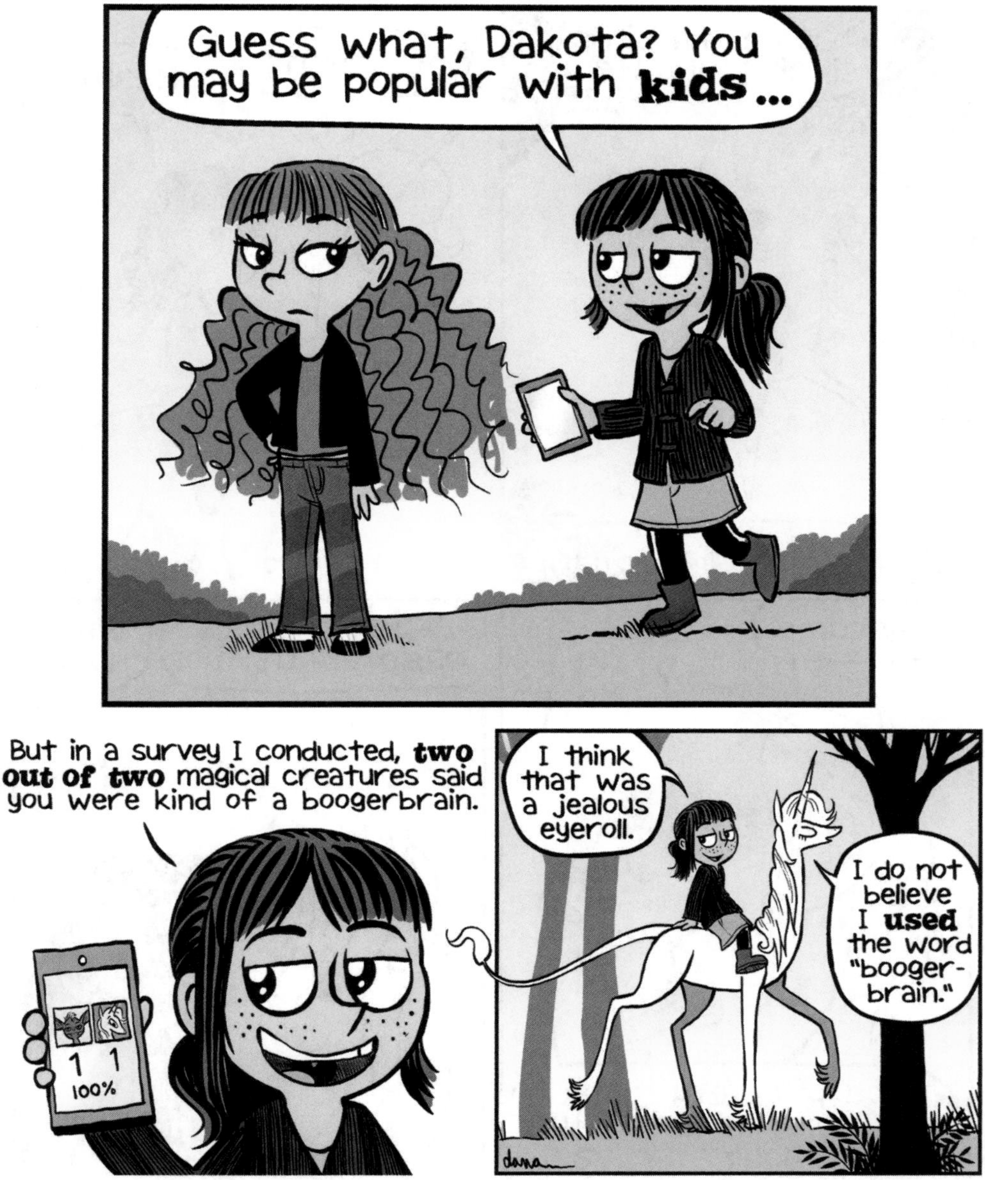
Guess what, Dakota? You may be popular with **kids**...
But in a survey I conducted, **two out of two** magical creatures said you were kind of a boogerbrain.
1 1
100%
I think that was a jealous eyeroll.
I do not believe I **used** the word "booger-brain."

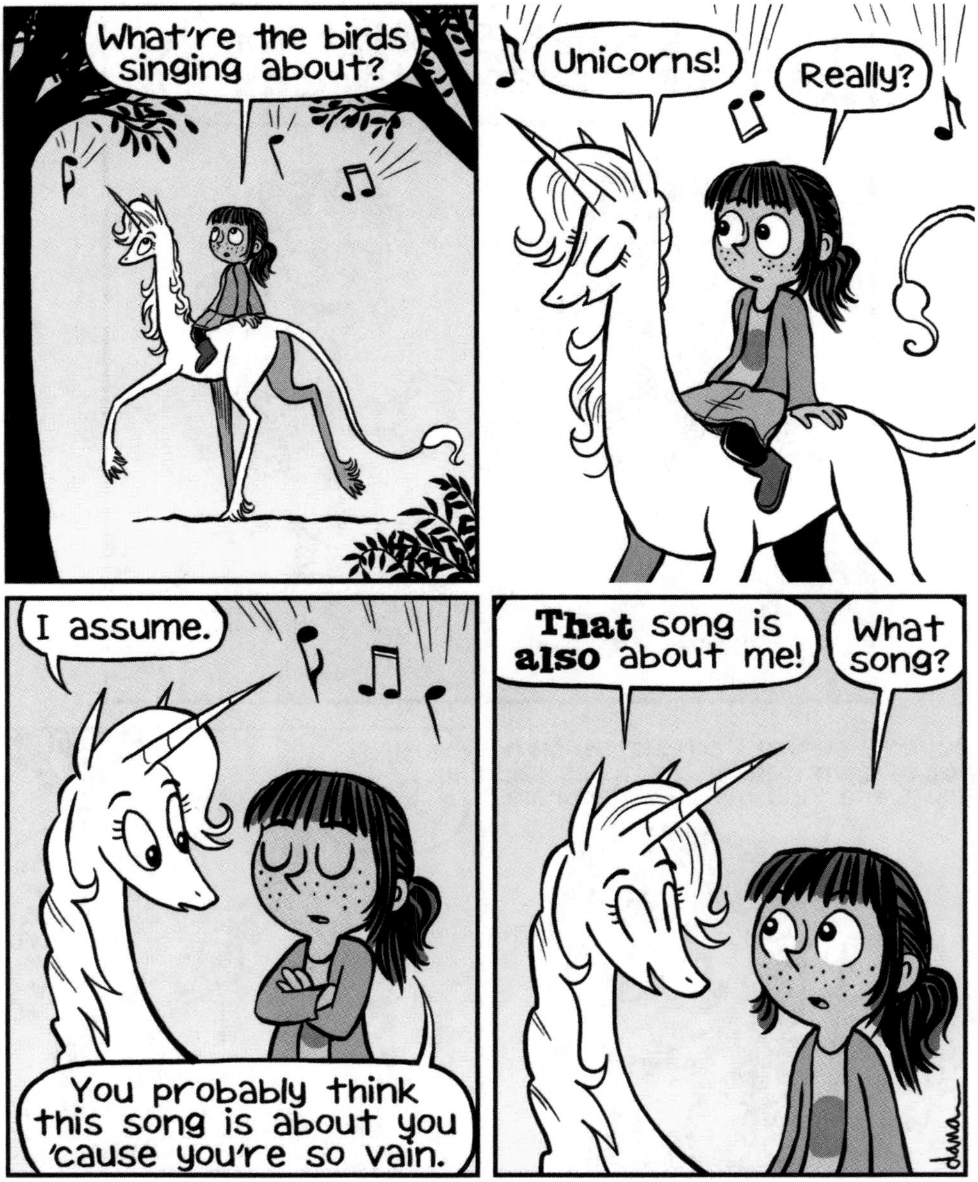
What're the birds singing about?
Unicorns!
Really?
I assume.
You probably think this song is about you 'cause you're so vain.
That song is **also** about me!
What song?
dana

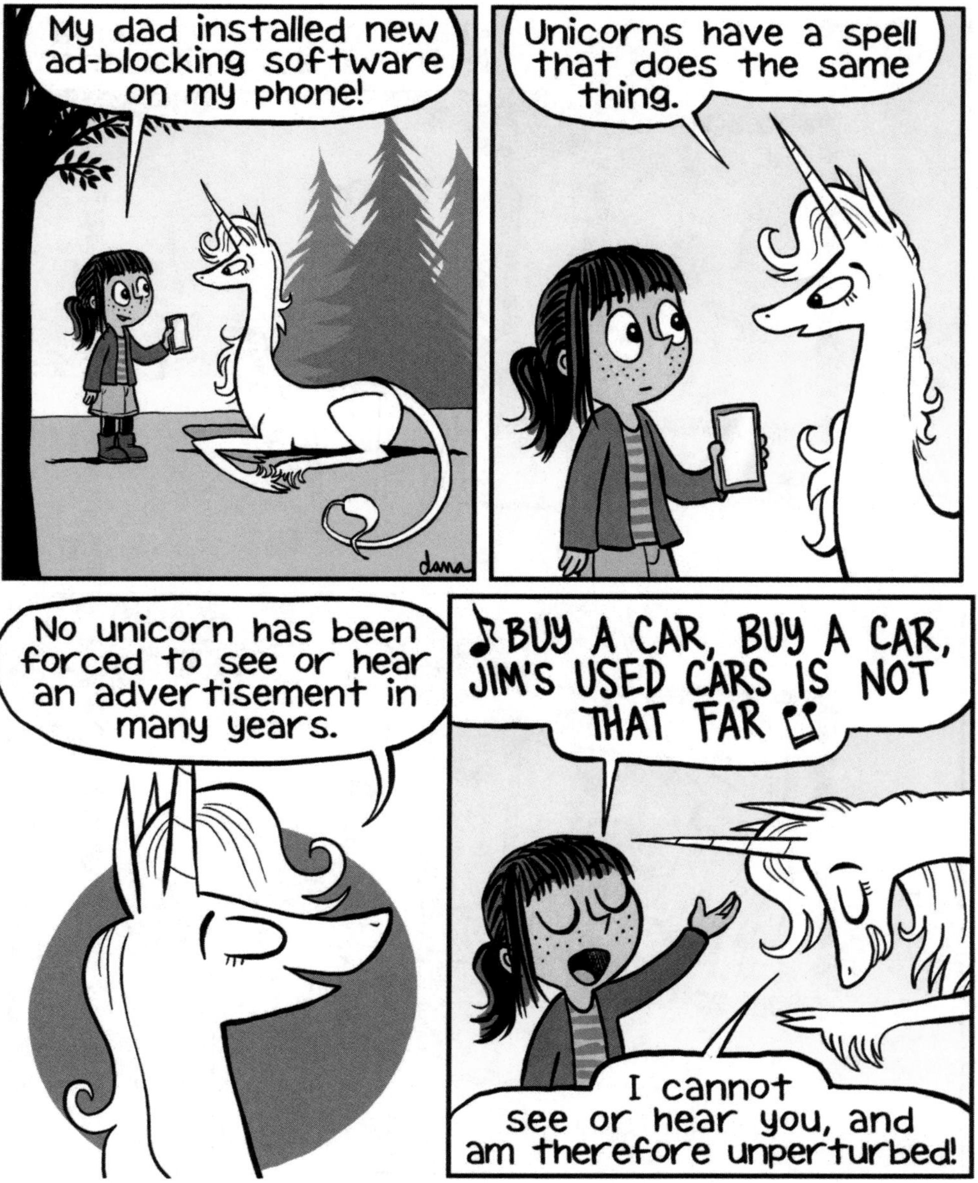

My dad installed new ad-blocking software on my phone!
dana
Unicorns have a spell that does the same thing.
No unicorn has been forced to see or hear an advertisement in many years.
BUY A CAR, BUY A CAR, JIM'S USED CARS IS NOT THAT FAR
I cannot see or hear you, and am therefore unperturbed!

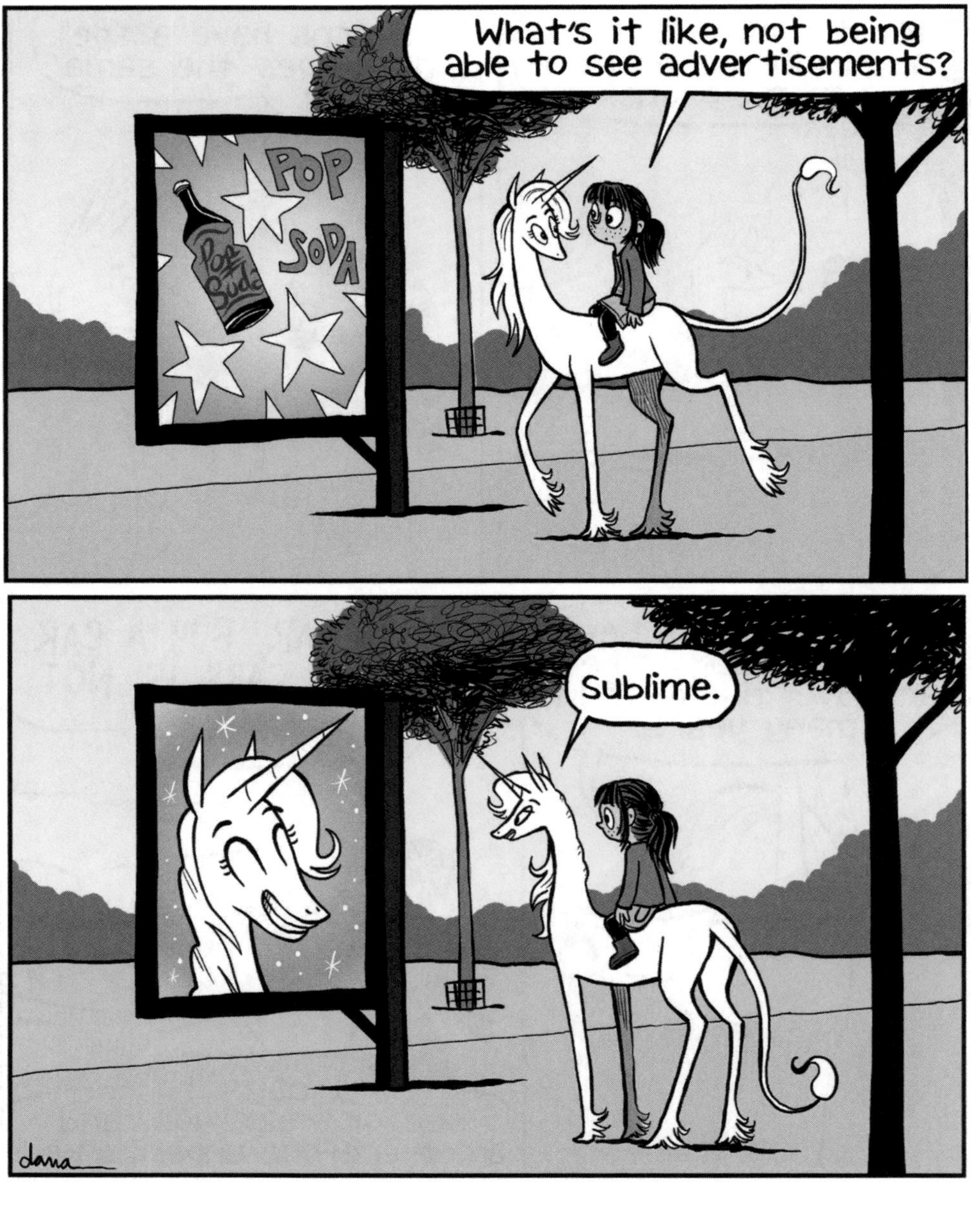
What's it like, not being able to see advertisements?
POP
SODA
Sublime.
dana

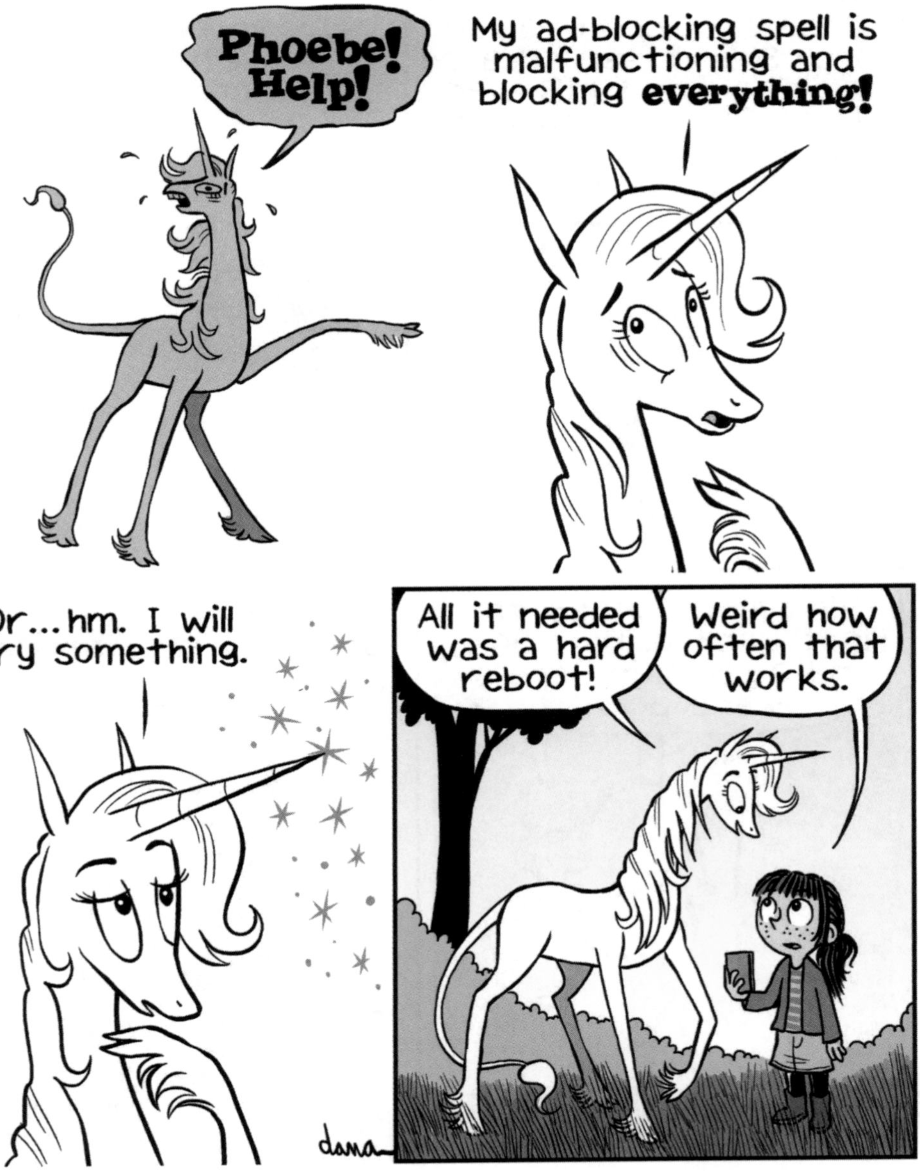
Phoebe! Help!
My ad-blocking spell is malfunctioning and blocking **everything!**
Or... hm. I will try something.
All it needed was a hard reboot!
Weird how often that works.
dana

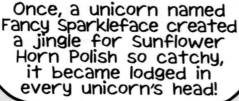

Once, a unicorn named Fancy Sparkleface created a jingle for Sunflower Horn Polish so catchy, it became lodged in every unicorn's head!

No unicorn was able to get anything accomplished!

We were forced to fight back using magic, and ad-blocking spells were born.

I've never actually seen you "accomplish" anything.

Being me is a significant accomplishment.

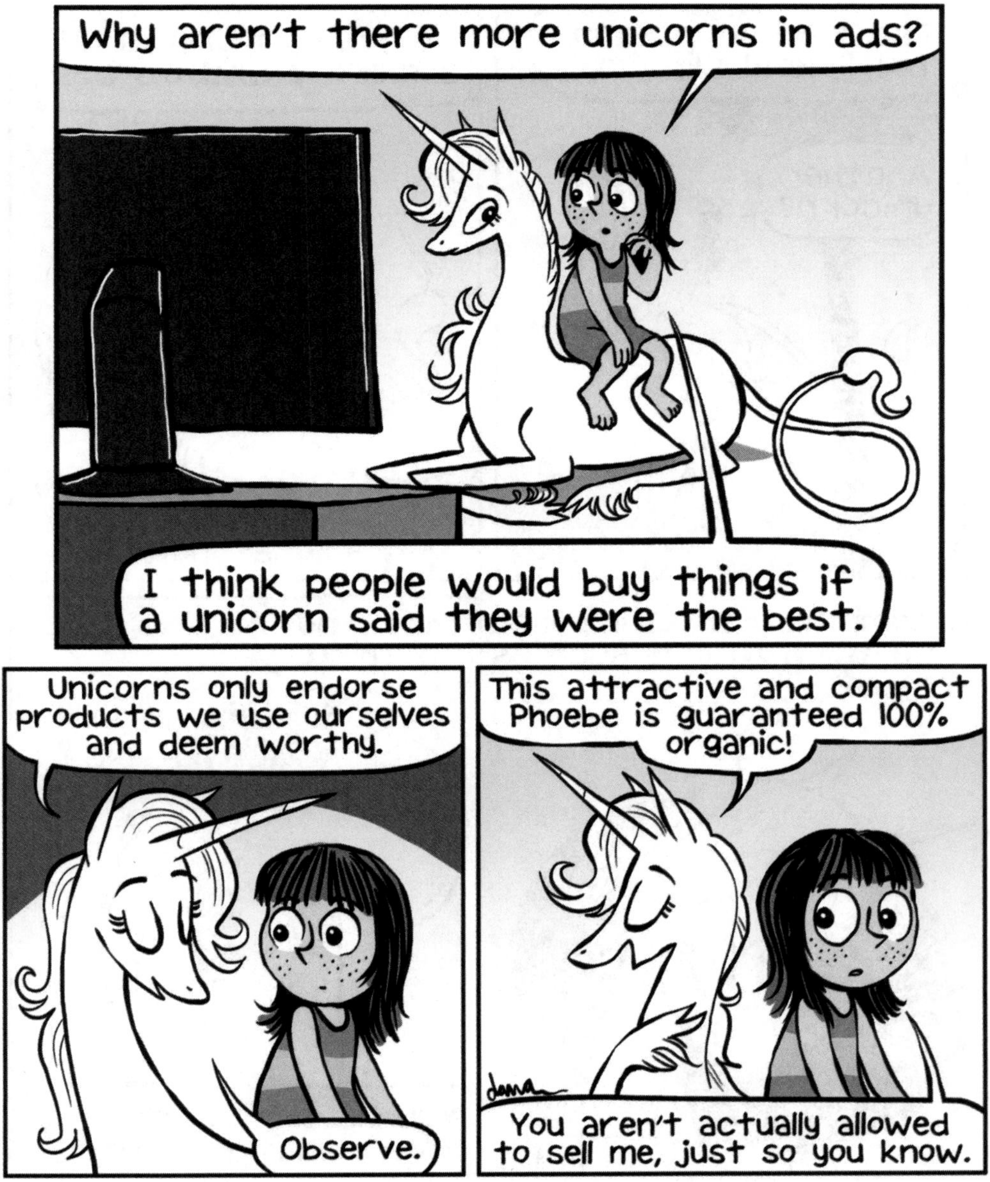
Why aren't there more unicorns in ads?
I think people would buy things if a unicorn said they were the best.
Unicorns only endorse products we use ourselves and deem worthy.
Observe.
This attractive and compact Phoebe is guaranteed 100% organic!
You aren't actually allowed to sell me, just so you know.
dana

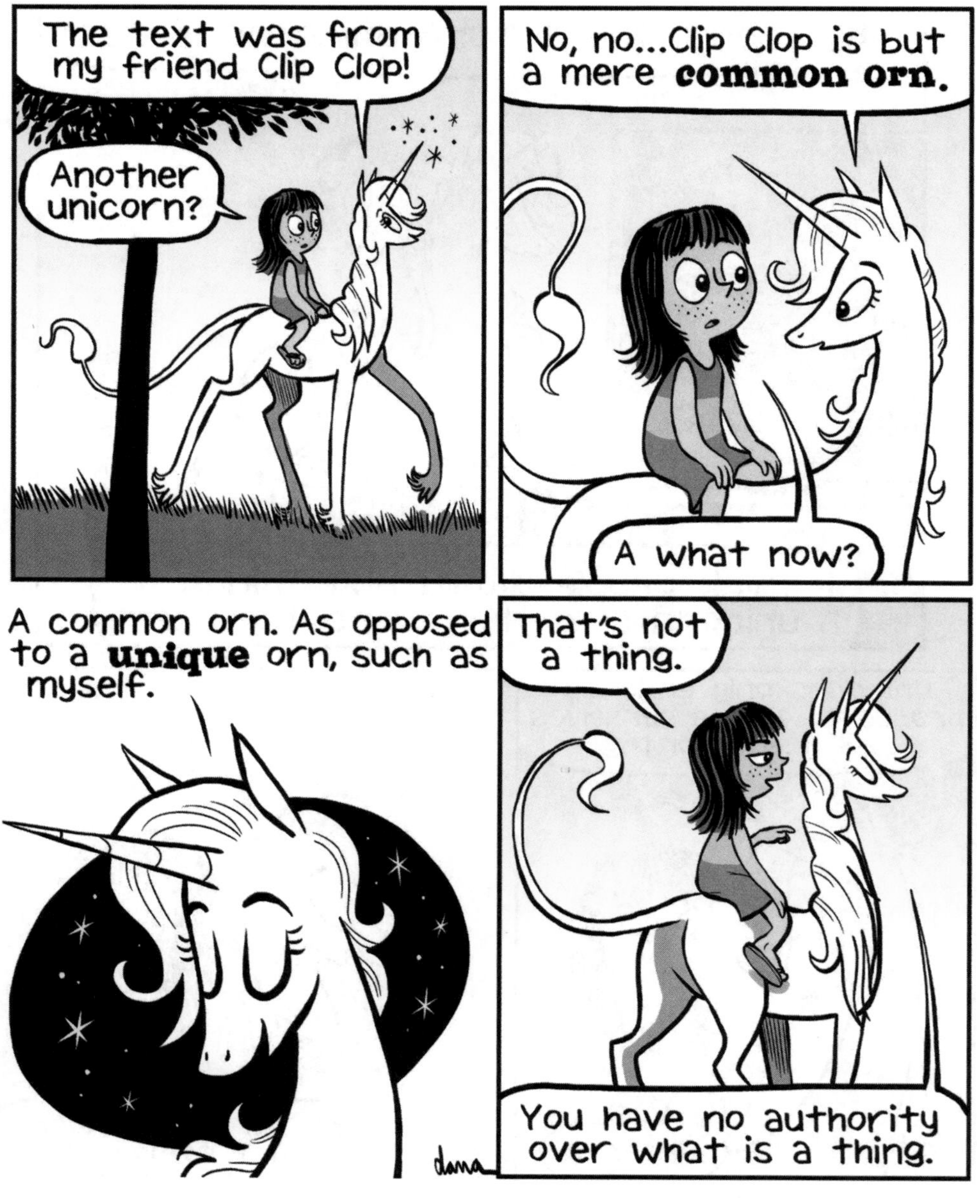
The text was from my friend Clip Clop!
Another unicorn?
No, no...Clip Clop is but a mere **common orn.**
A what now?
A common orn. As opposed to a **unique** orn, such as myself.
That's not a thing.
You have no authority over what is a thing.
dana

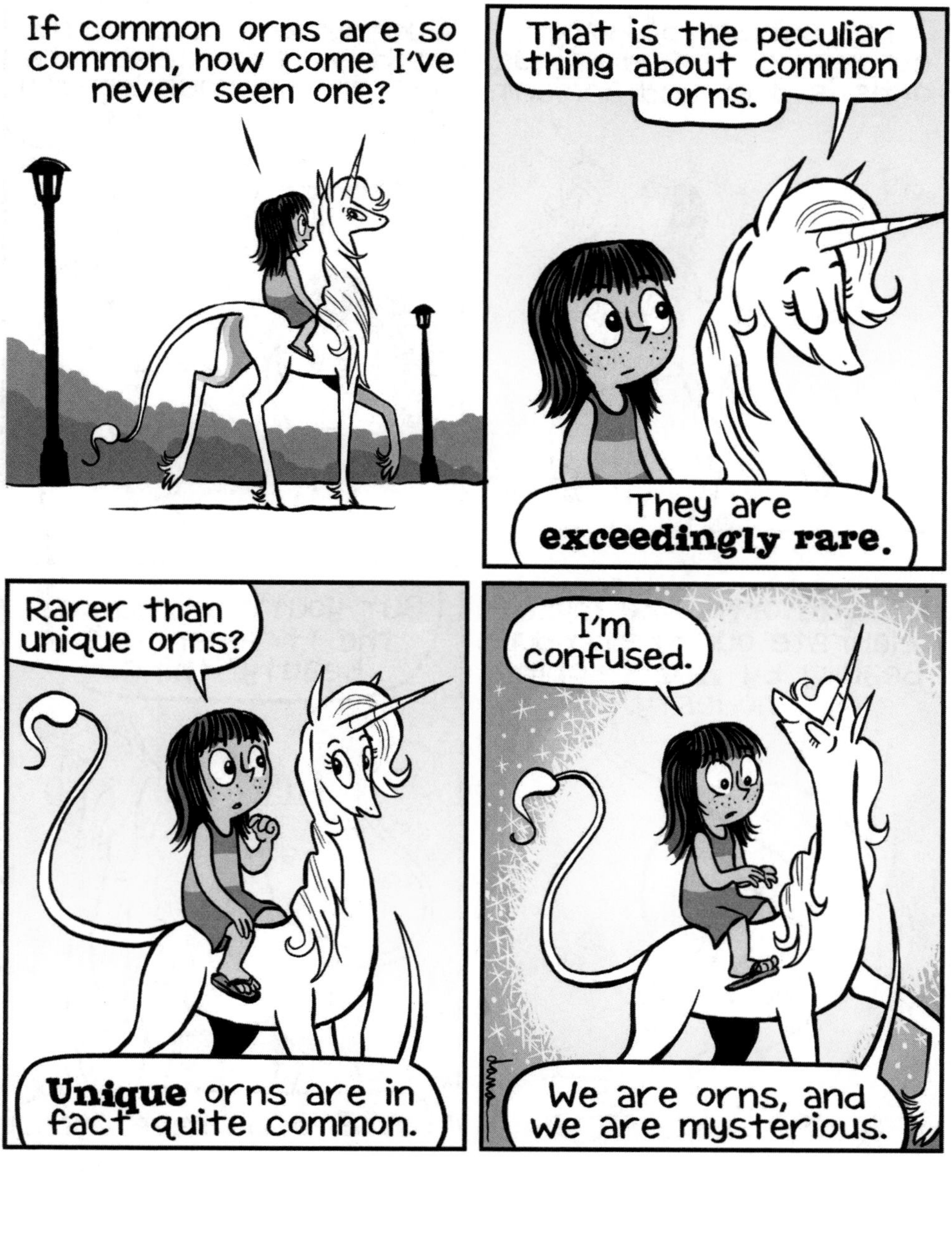
If common orns are so common, how come I've never seen one?
That is the peculiar thing about common orns.
They are **exceedingly rare.**
Rarer than unique orns?
Unique orns are in fact quite common.
I'm confused.
We are orns, and we are mysterious.

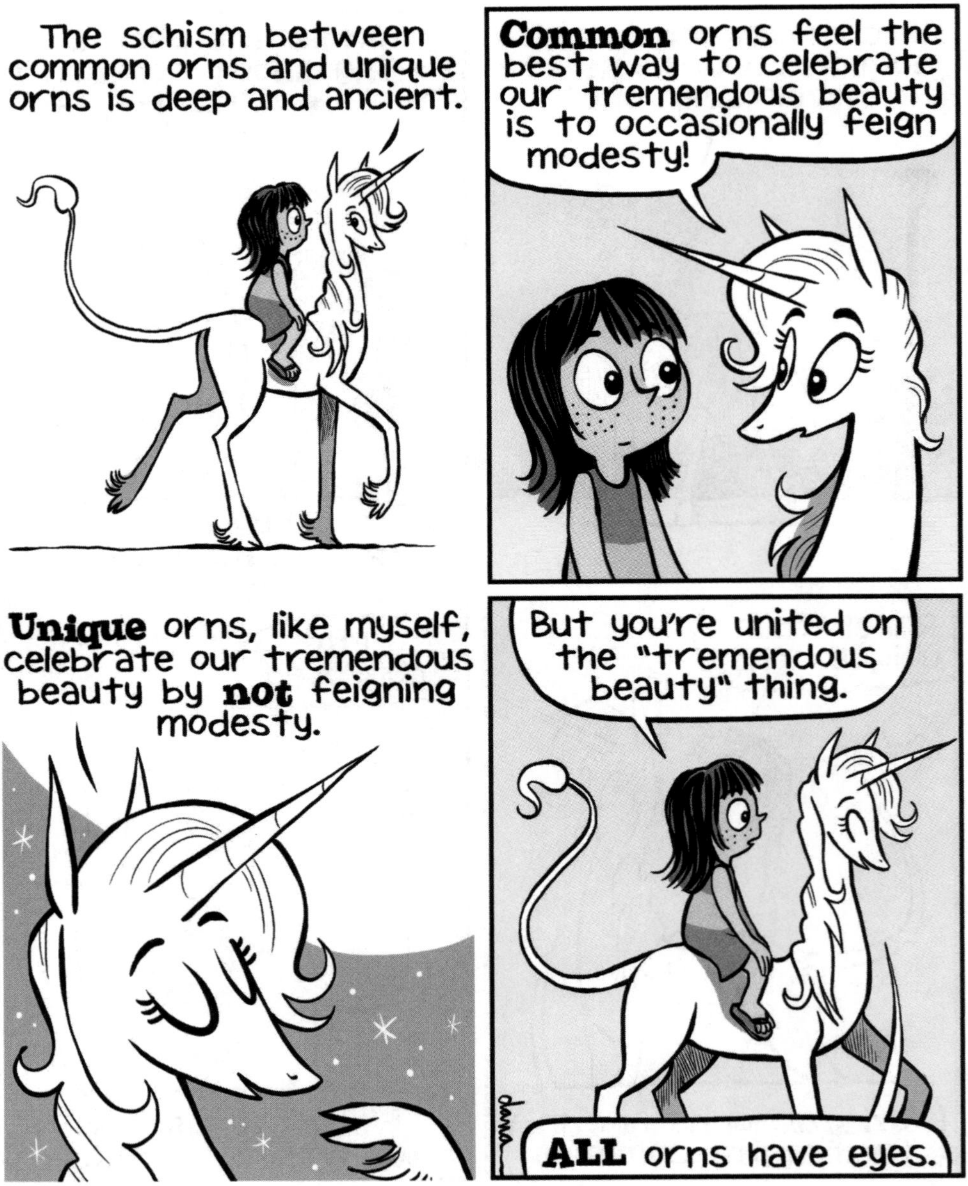
The schism between common orns and unique orns is deep and ancient.
Common orns feel the best way to celebrate our tremendous beauty is to occasionally feign modesty!
Unique orns, like myself, celebrate our tremendous beauty by **not** feigning modesty.
But you're united on the "tremendous beauty" thing.
ALL orns have eyes.
dana

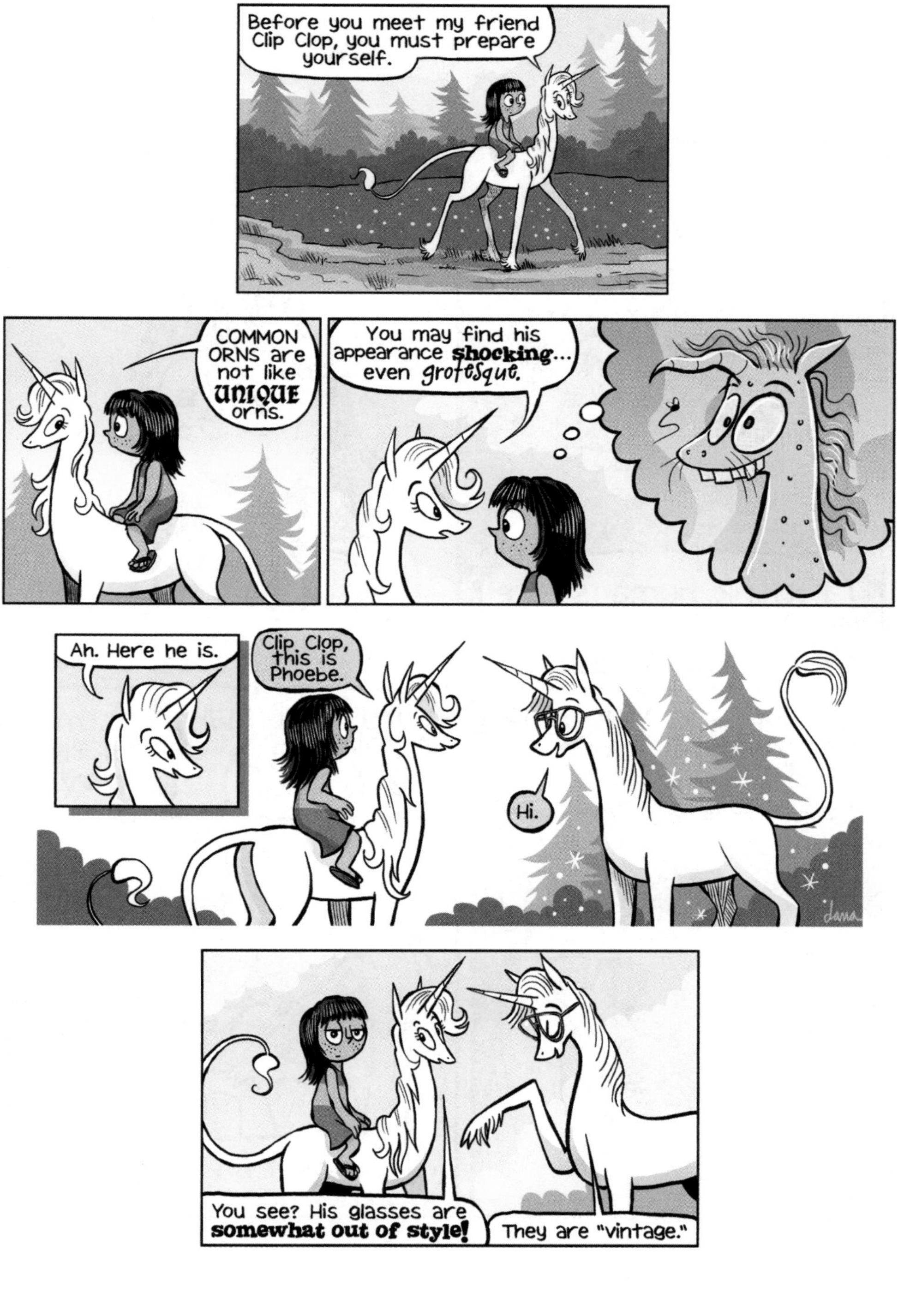
Before you meet my friend Clip Clop, you must prepare yourself.
COMMON ORNS are not like **UNIQUE** orns.
You may find his appearance **shocking**... even *grotesque.*
Ah. Here he is.
Clip Clop, this is Phoebe.
Hi.
dana
You see? His glasses are **somewhat out of style!**
They are "vintage."

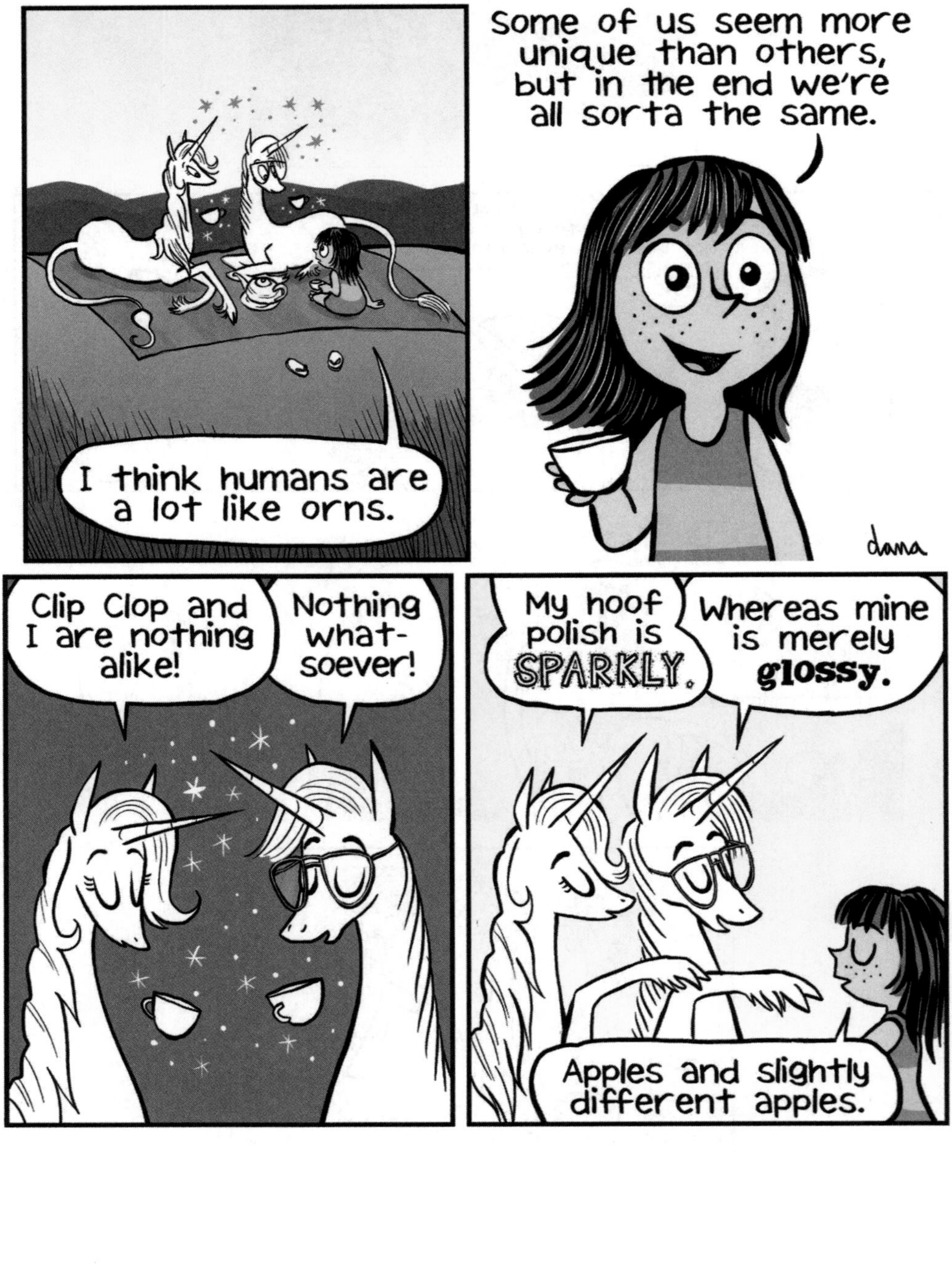
I think humans are a lot like orns.
Some of us seem more unique than others, but in the end we're all sorta the same.
dana
Clip Clop and I are nothing alike!
Nothing whatsoever!
My hoof polish is SPARKLY.
Whereas mine is merely glossy.
Apples and slightly different apples.

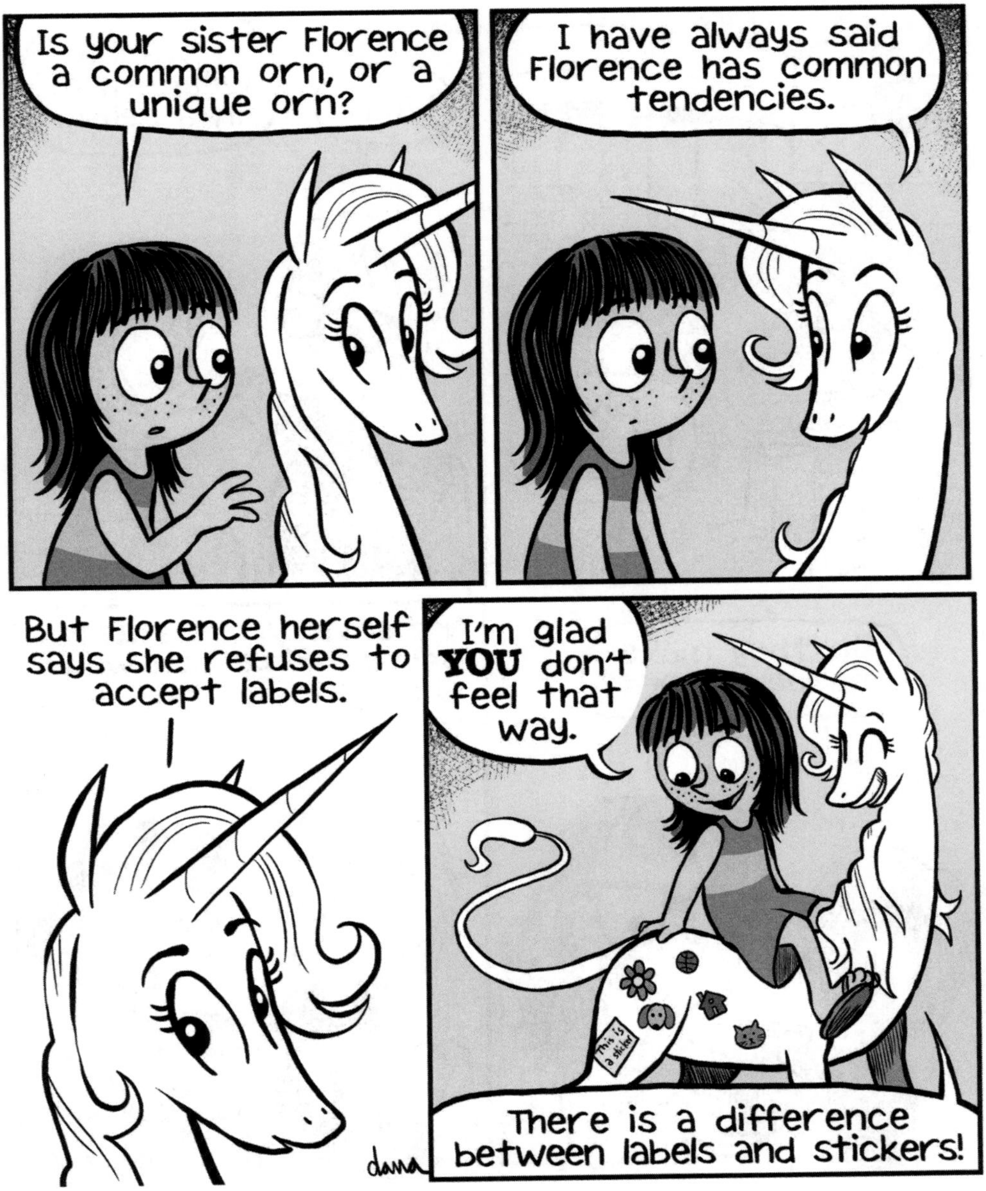
Is your sister Florence a common orn, or a unique orn?
I have always said Florence has common tendencies.
But Florence herself says she refuses to accept labels.
I'm glad **YOU** don't feel that way.
This is a sticker!
There is a difference between labels and stickers!

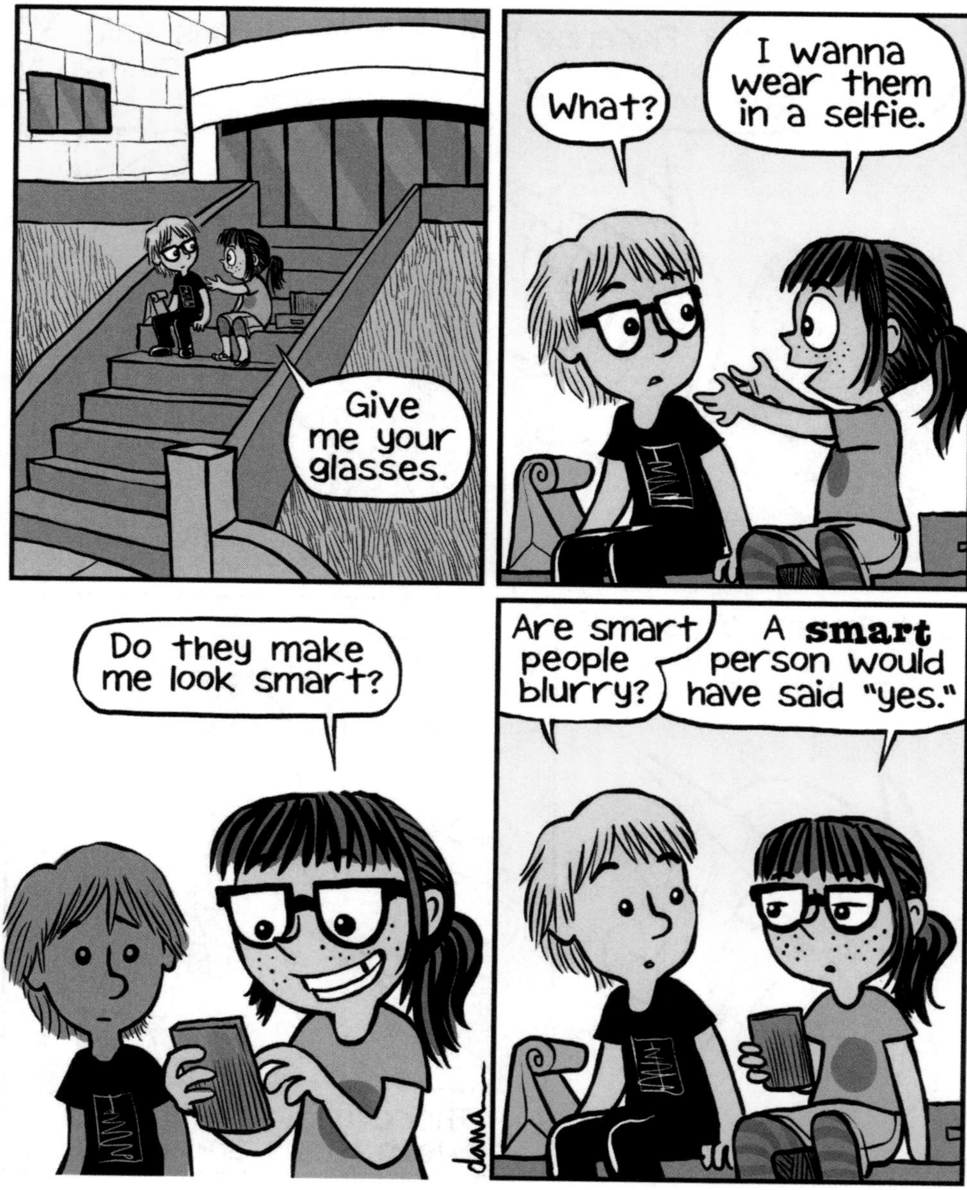
Give me your glasses.
What?
I wanna wear them in a selfie.
Do they make me look smart?
Are smart people blurry?
A **smart** person would have said "yes."
dana

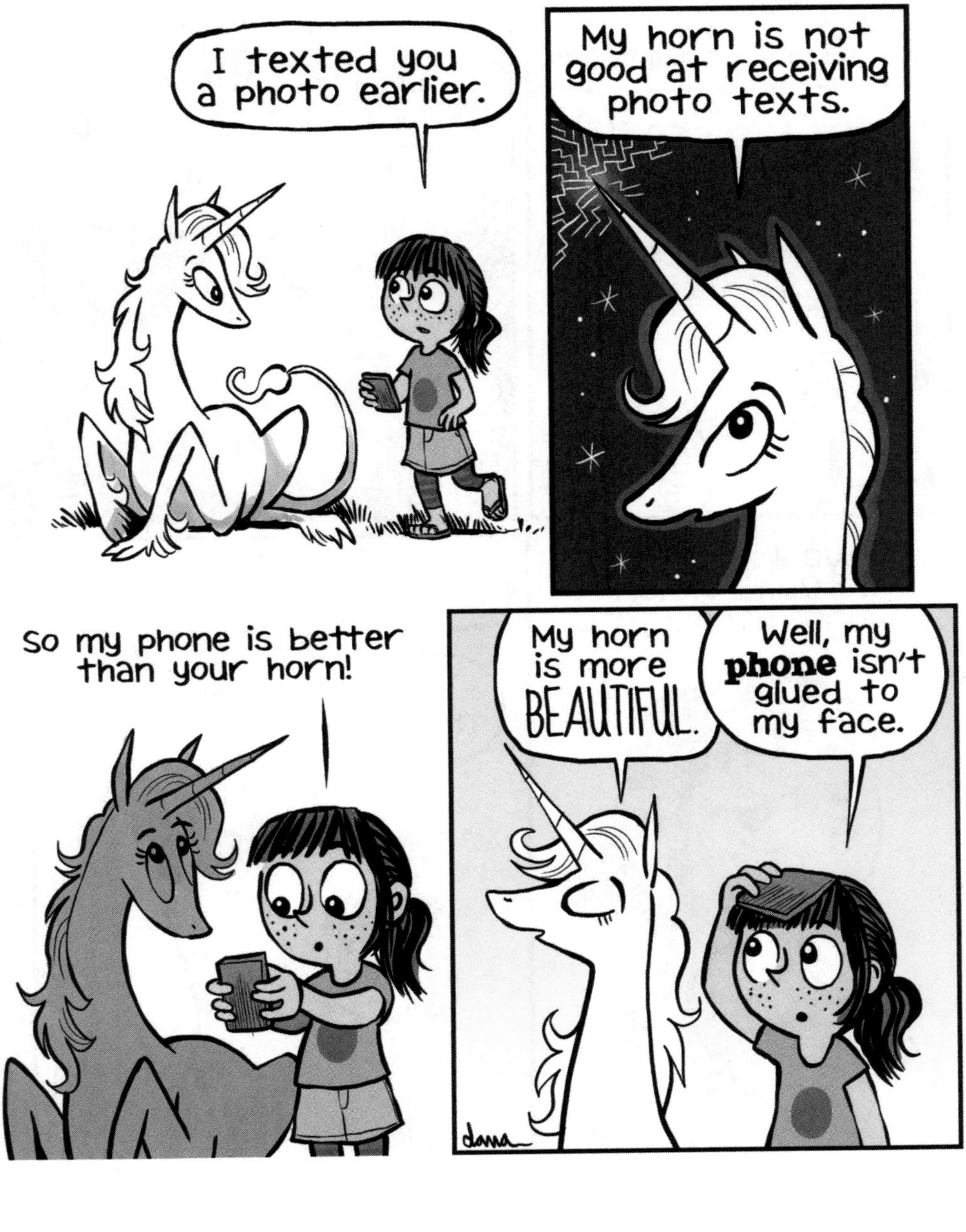
I texted you a photo earlier.
My horn is not good at receiving photo texts.
So my phone is better than your horn!
My horn is more BEAUTIFUL.
Well, my **phone** isn't glued to my face.
dana

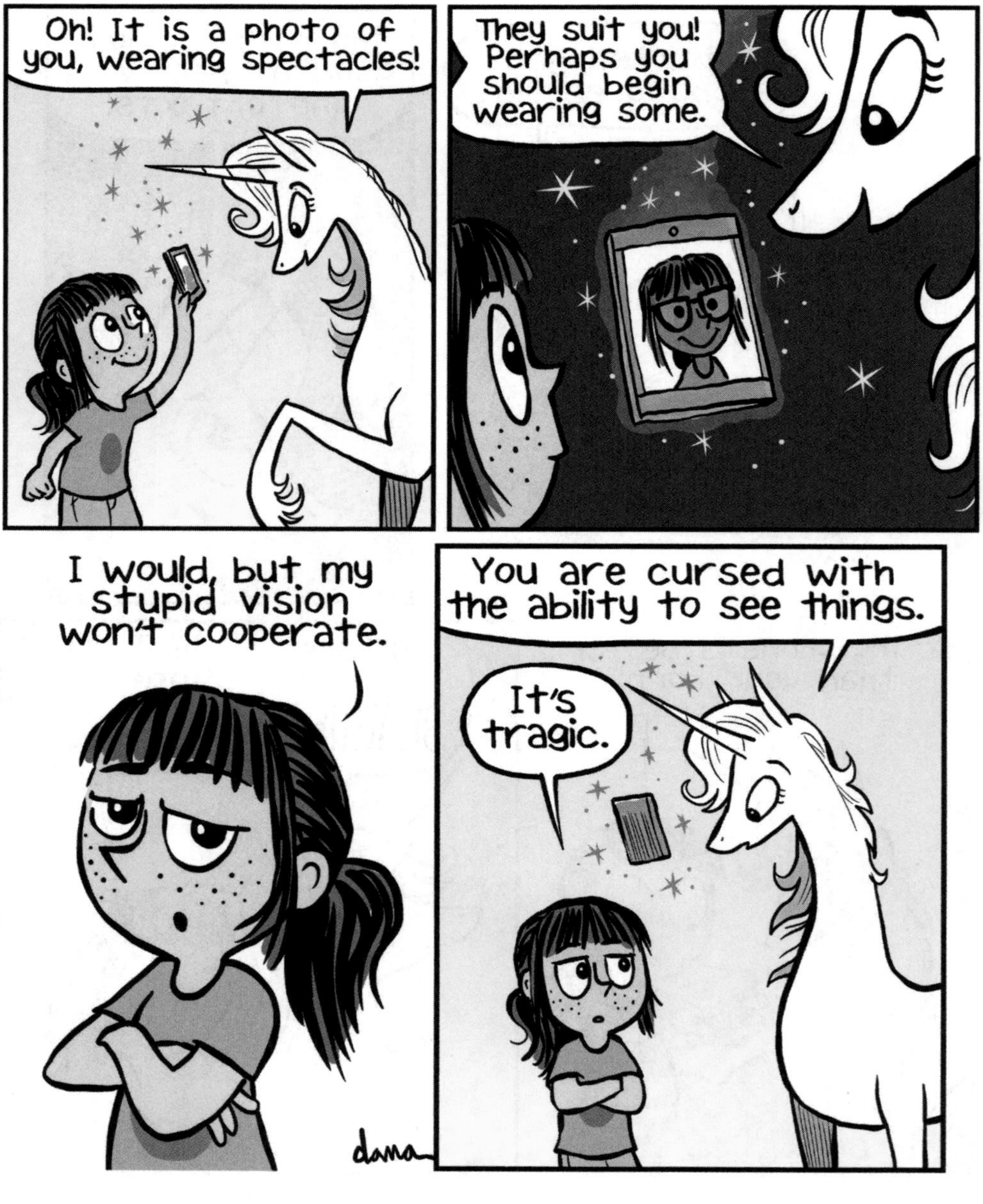
Oh! It is a photo of you, wearing spectacles!
They suit you! Perhaps you should begin wearing some.
I would, but my stupid vision won't cooperate.
You are cursed with the ability to see things.
It's tragic.
dana

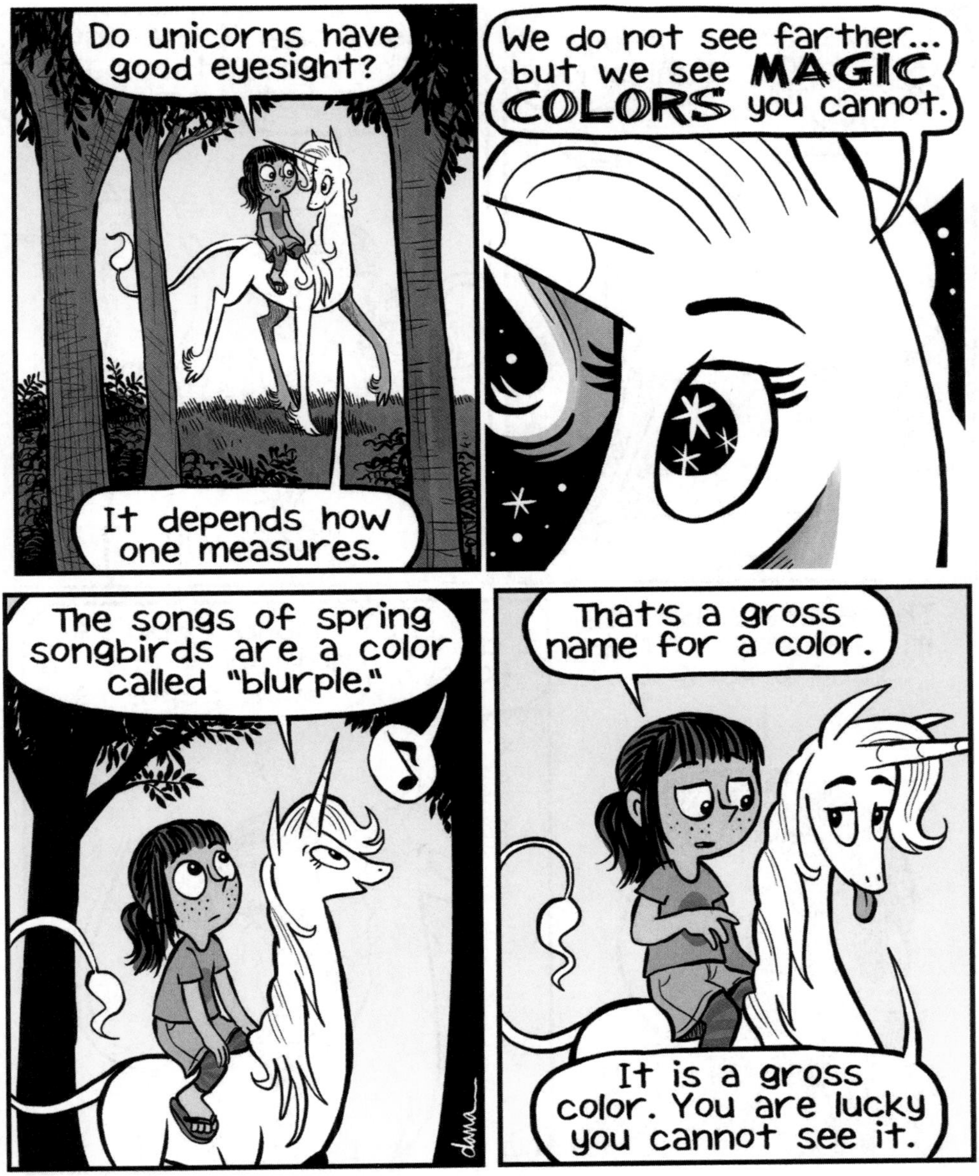
Do unicorns have good eyesight?
It depends how one measures.
We do not see farther... but we see MAGIC COLORS you cannot.
The songs of spring songbirds are a color called "blurple."
dana
That's a gross name for a color.
It is a gross color. You are lucky you cannot see it.

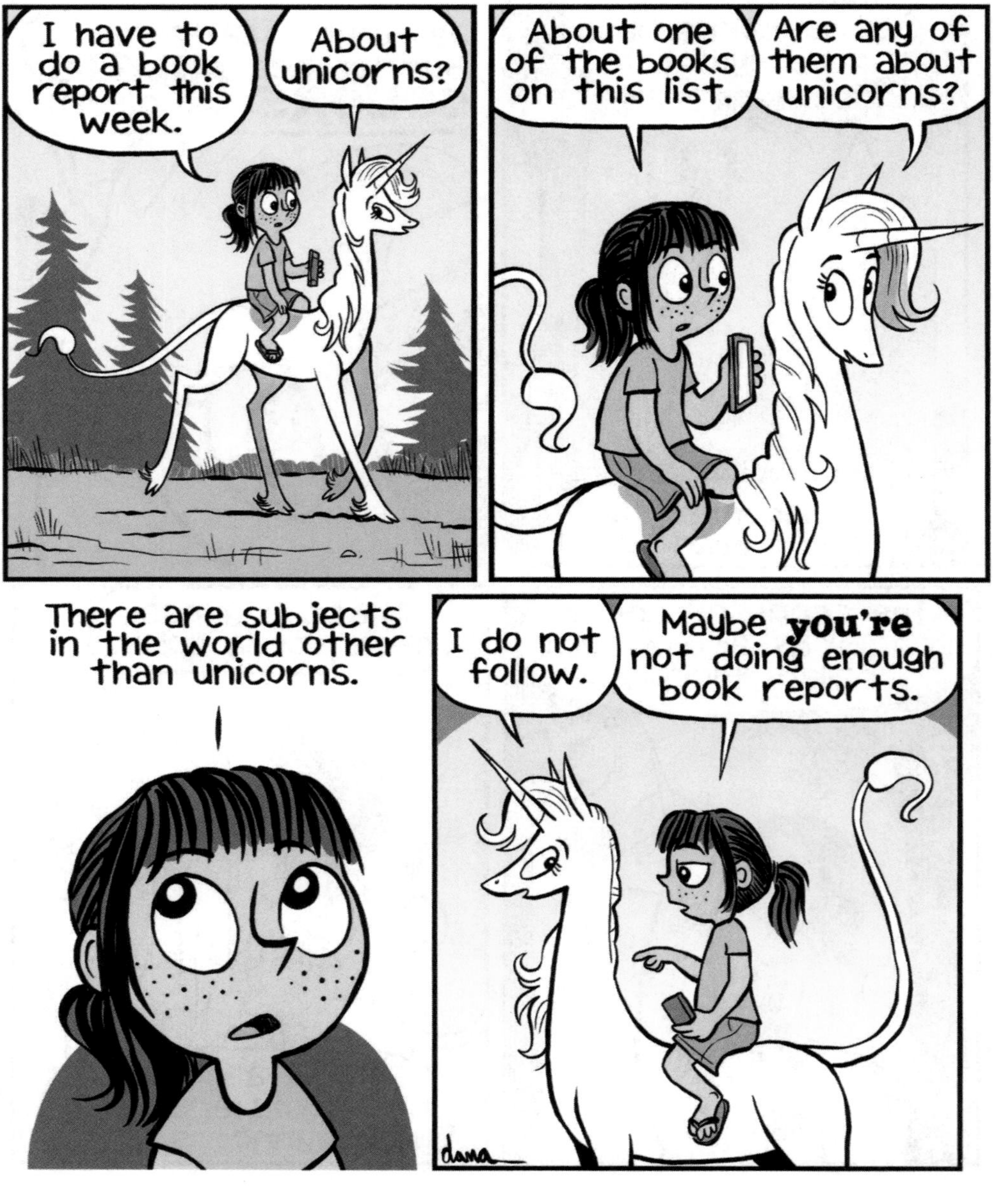
I have to do a book report this week.
About unicorns?
About one of the books on this list.
Are any of them about unicorns?
There are subjects in the world other than unicorns.
I do not follow.
Maybe **you're** not doing enough book reports.
dana

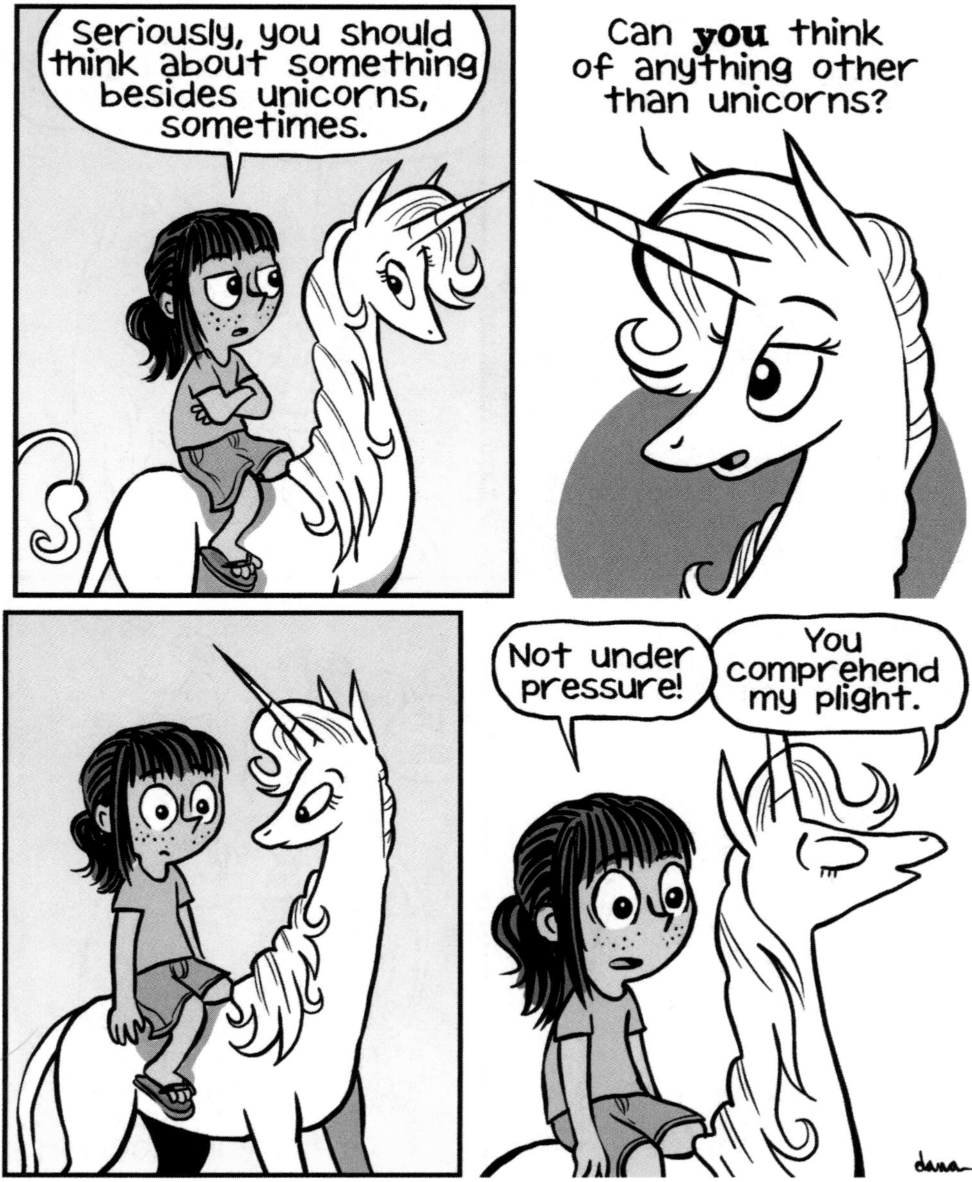
Seriously, you should think about something besides unicorns, sometimes.
Can **you** think of anything other than unicorns?
Not under pressure!
You comprehend my plight.
dana

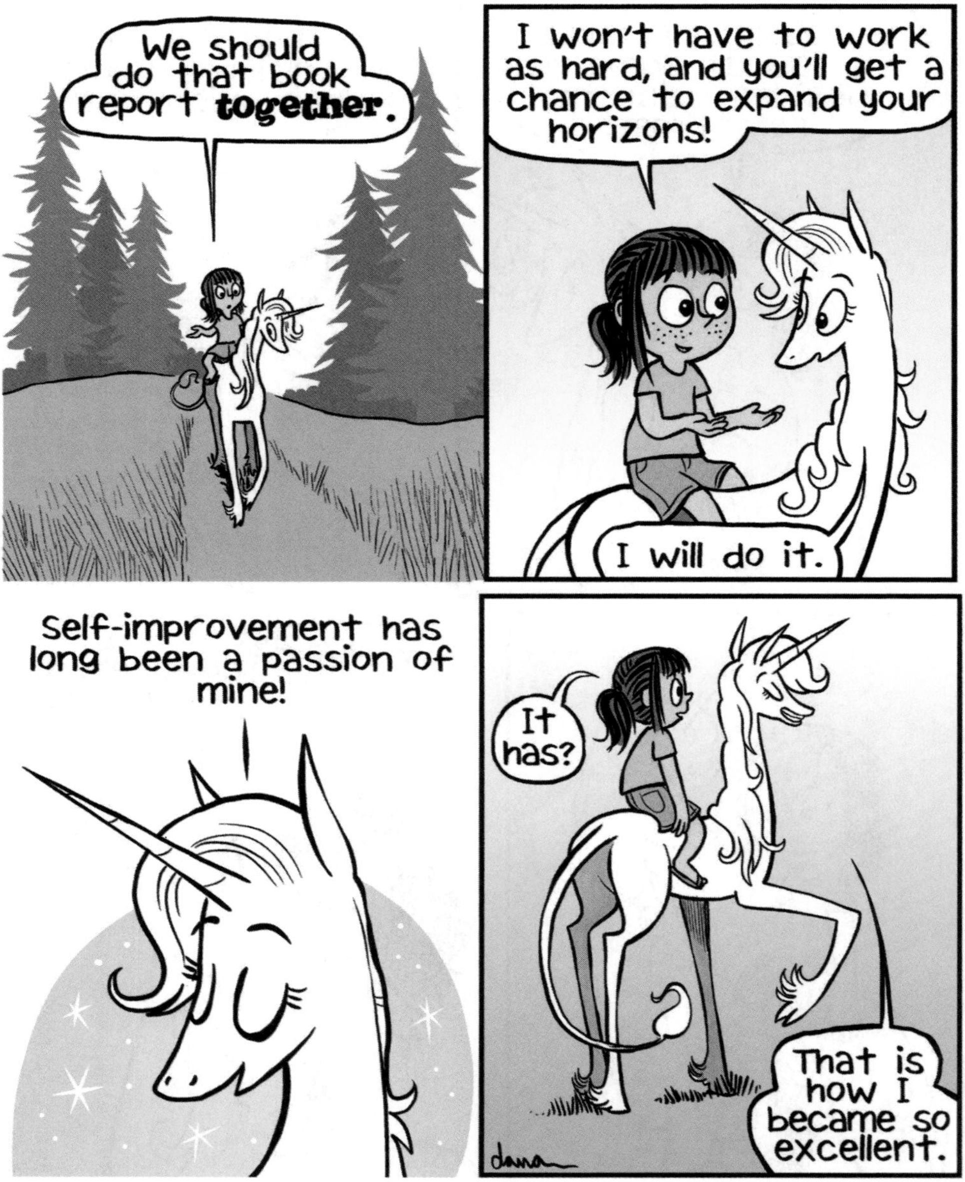
We should do that book report **together**.
I won't have to work as hard, and you'll get a chance to expand your horizons!
I will do it.
Self-improvement has long been a passion of mine!
It has?
That is how I became so excellent.
dana

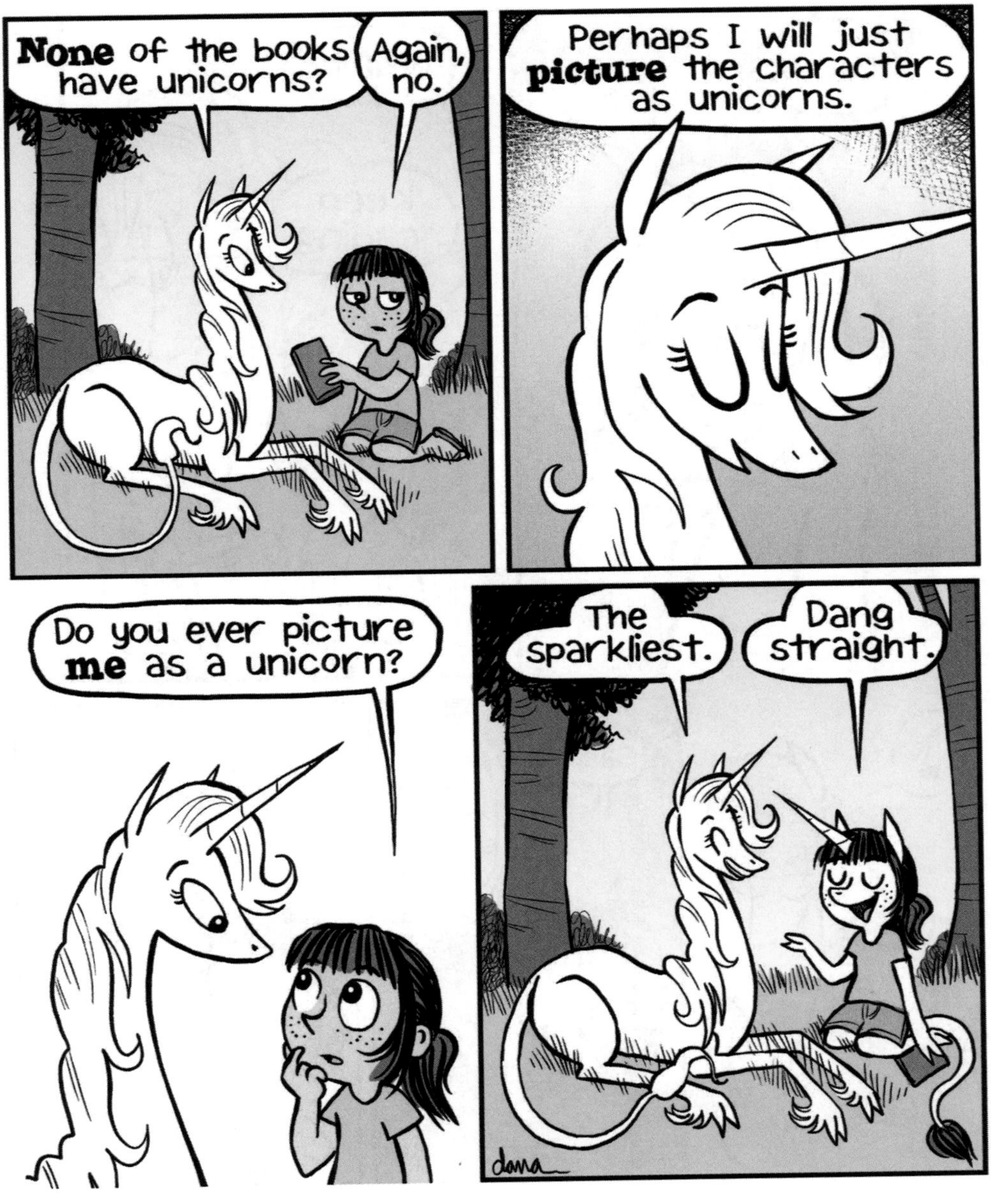
None of the books have unicorns?
Again, no.
Perhaps I will just **picture** the characters as unicorns.
Do you ever picture **me** as a unicorn?
The sparkliest.
Dang straight.
dana

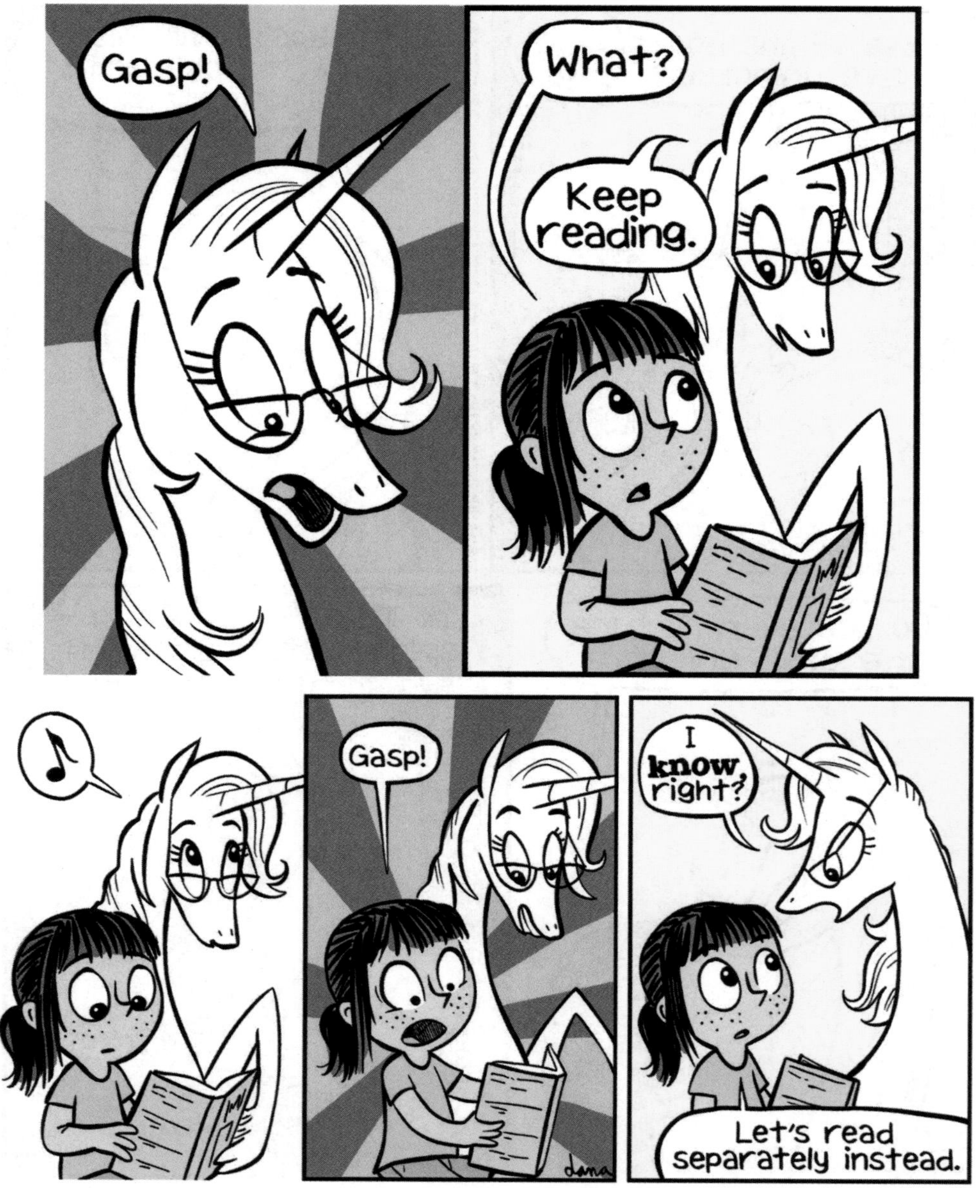
Gasp!
What?
Keep reading.
♪
Gasp!
I **know**, right?
Let's read separately instead.
dana

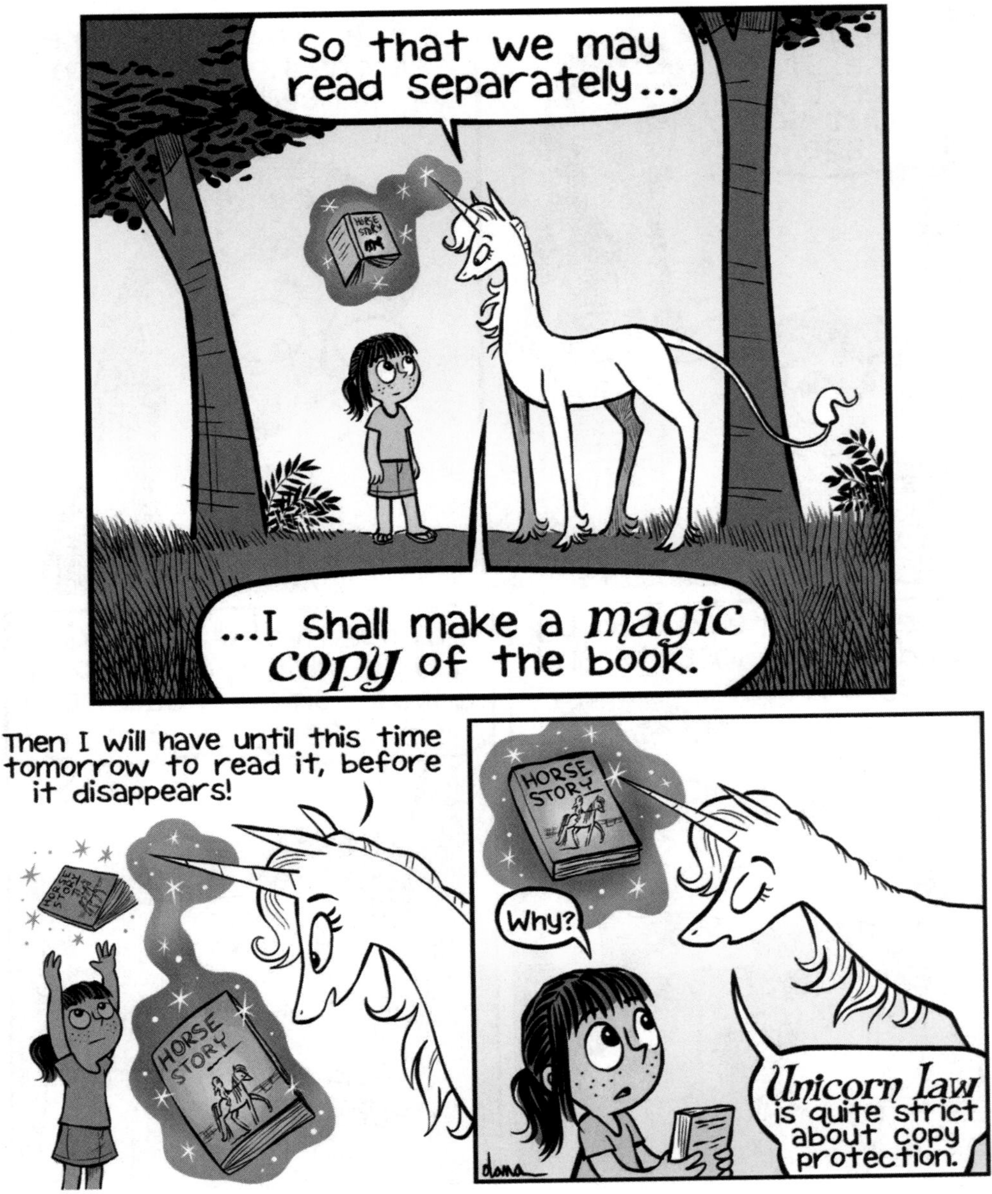
So that we may read separately...
HORSE STORY
...I shall make a *magic copy* of the book.
Then I will have until this time tomorrow to read it, before it disappears!
HORSE STORY
HORSE STORY
HORSE STORY
Why?
Unicorn law is quite strict about copy protection.

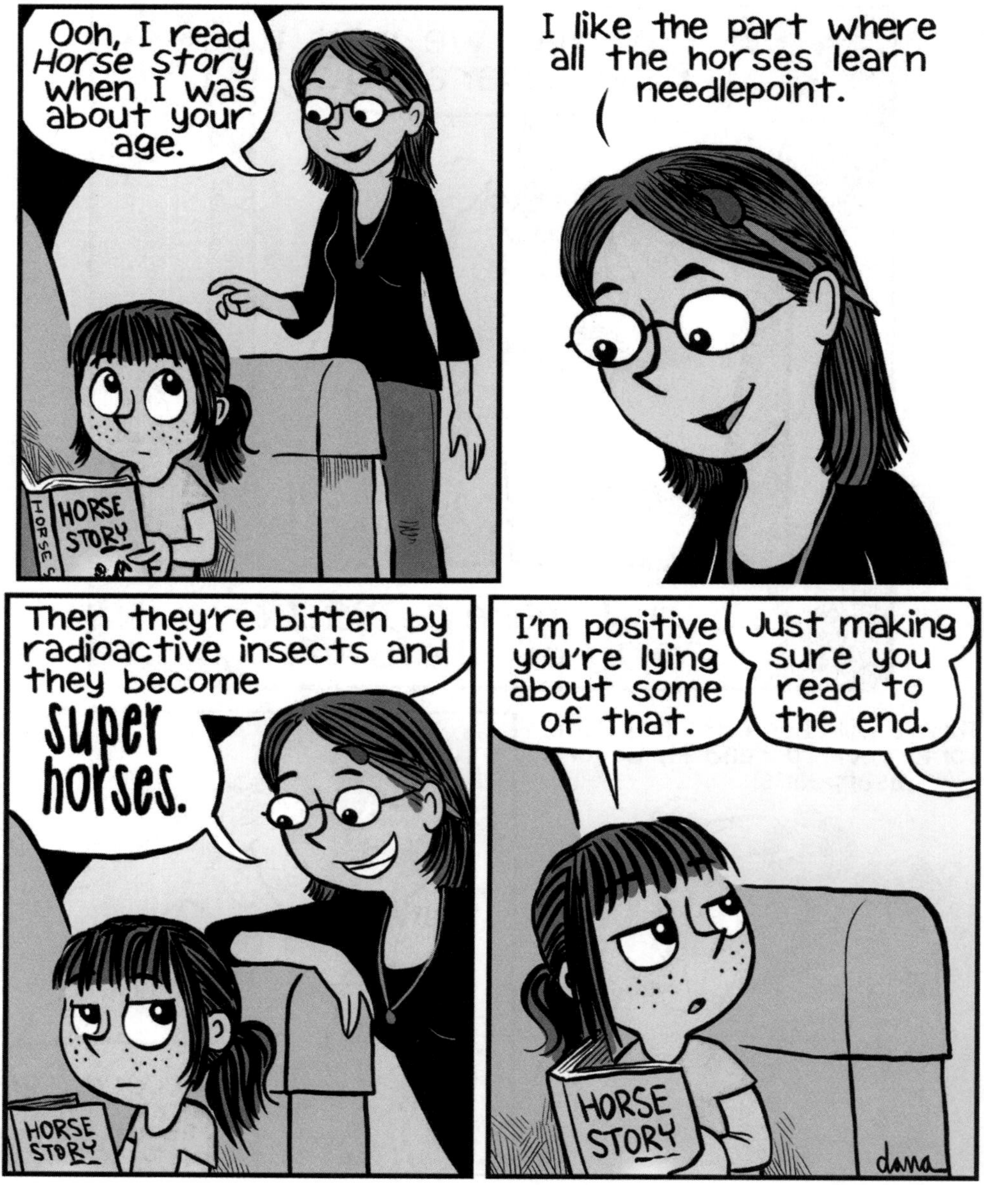
Ooh, I read Horse Story when I was about your age.
HORSE STORY
I like the part where all the horses learn needlepoint.
Then they're bitten by radioactive insects and they become
super horses.
HORSE STORY
I'm positive you're lying about some of that.
Just making sure you read to the end.
HORSE STORY
dana

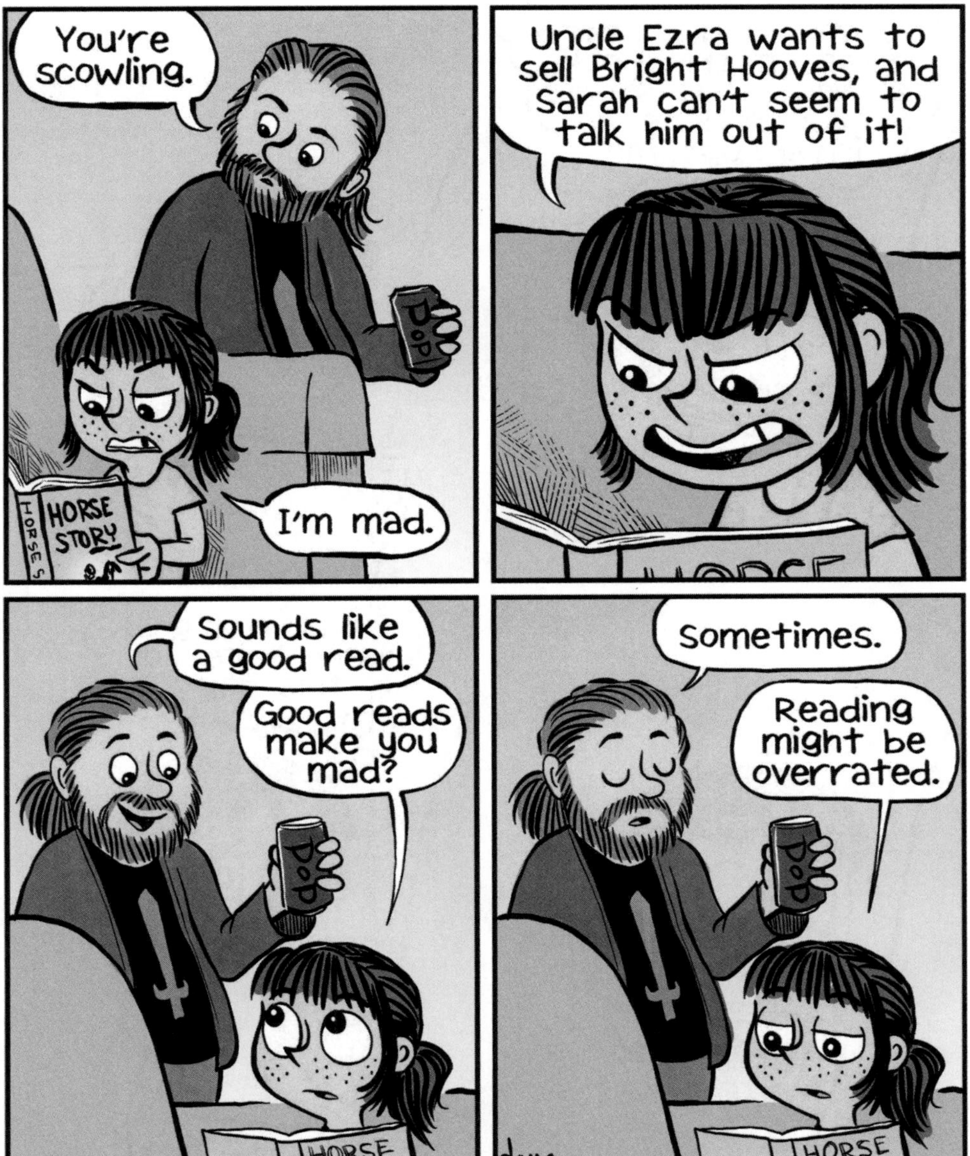
You're scowling.
I'm mad.
HORSE STORY
Uncle Ezra wants to sell Bright Hooves, and Sarah can't seem to talk him out of it!
Sounds like a good read.
Good reads make you mad?
Sometimes.
Reading might be overrated.
dana

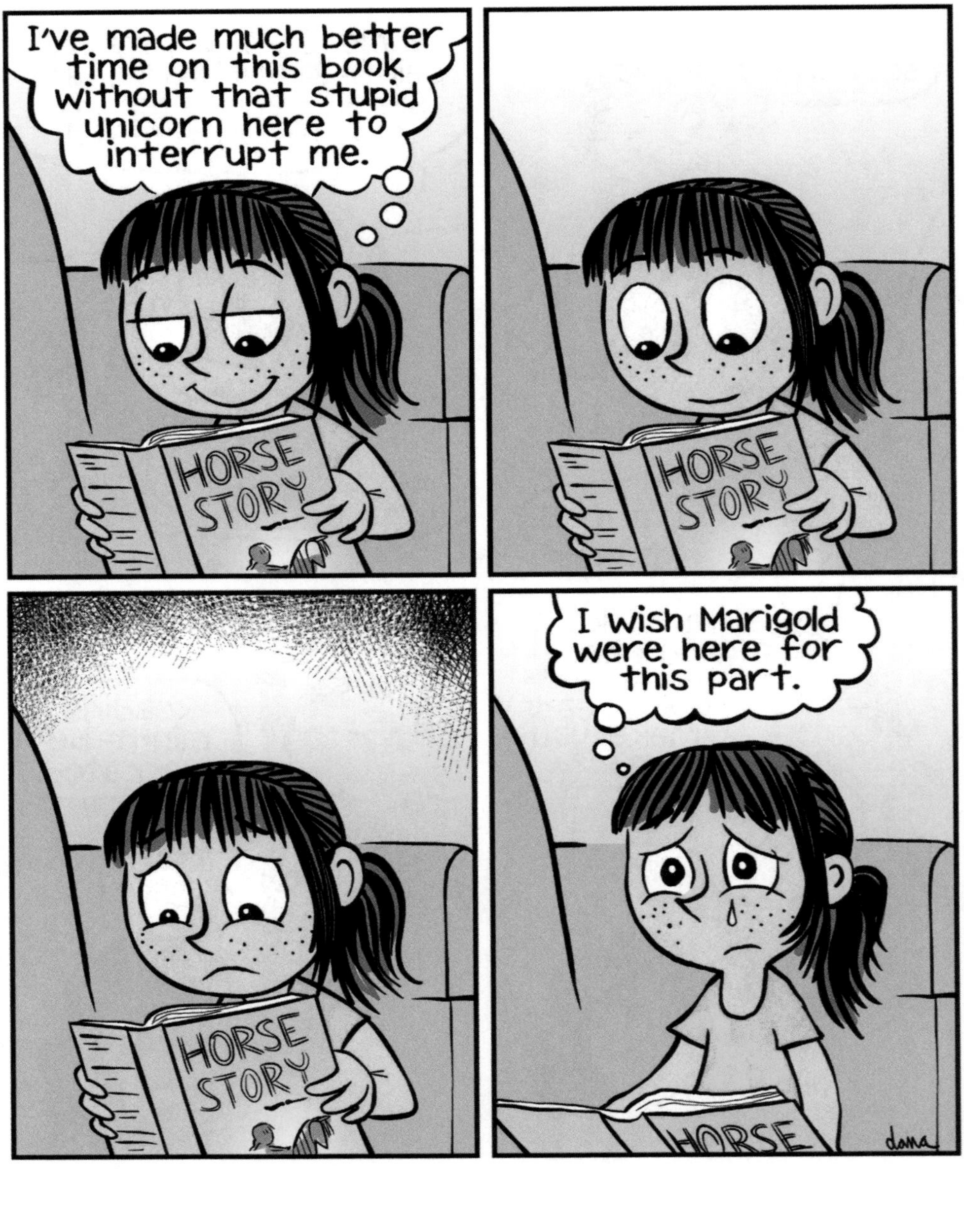
I've made much better time on this book without that stupid unicorn here to interrupt me.
HORSE STORY
HORSE STORY
HORSE STORY
I wish Marigold were here for this part.
HORSE
dana

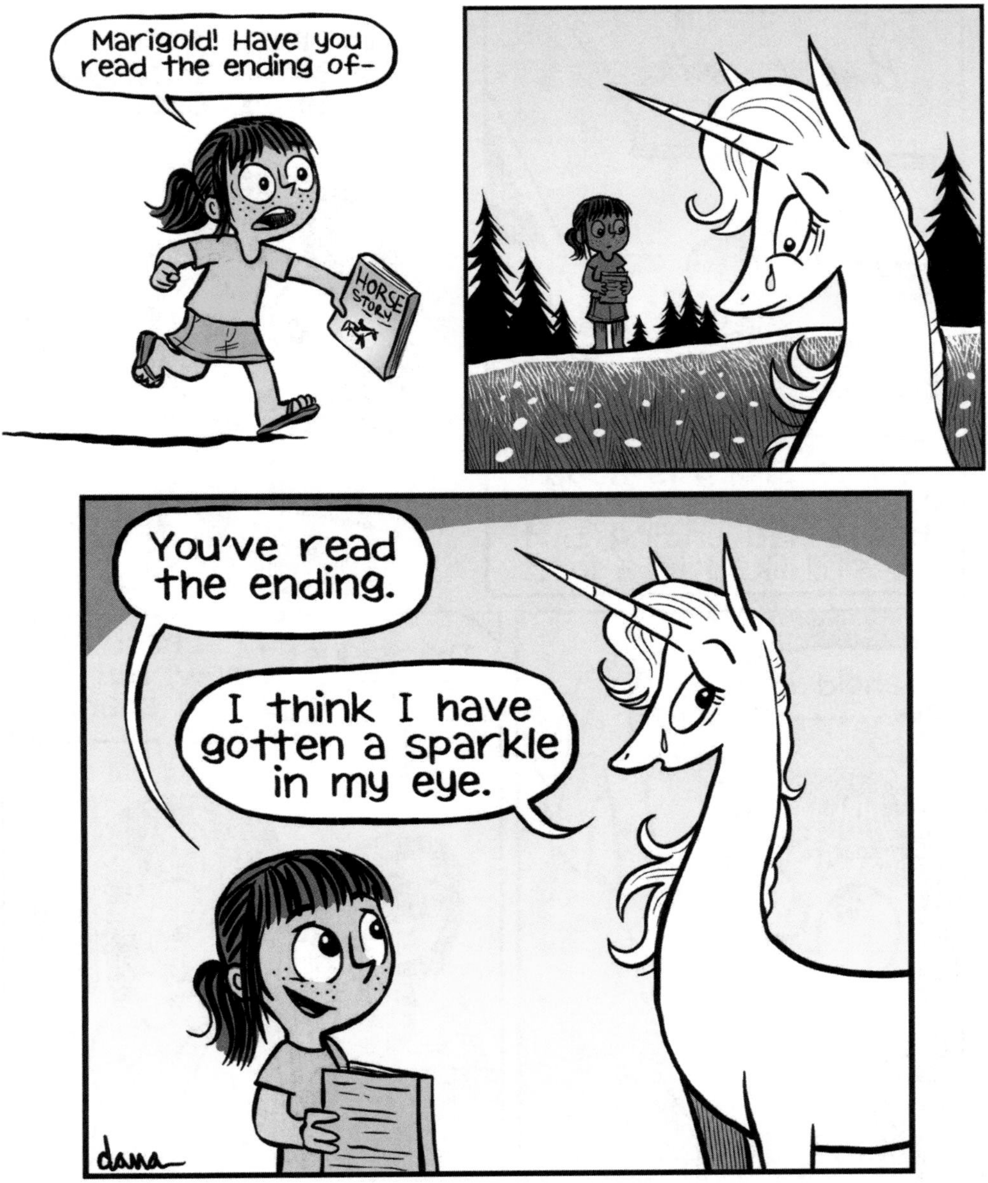
Marigold! Have you read the ending of-
HORSE STORY
You've read the ending.
I think I have gotten a sparkle in my eye.
dana

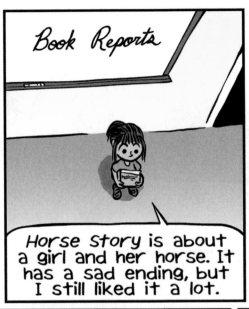

Book Reports

Horse Story is about a girl and her horse. It has a sad ending, but I still liked it a lot.

So did my unicorn. My visual aid is a **single unicorn tear.**

HORSE STORY

Behold it.

That's just a tissue.

It's dry now, but it's still sparkly.

dana

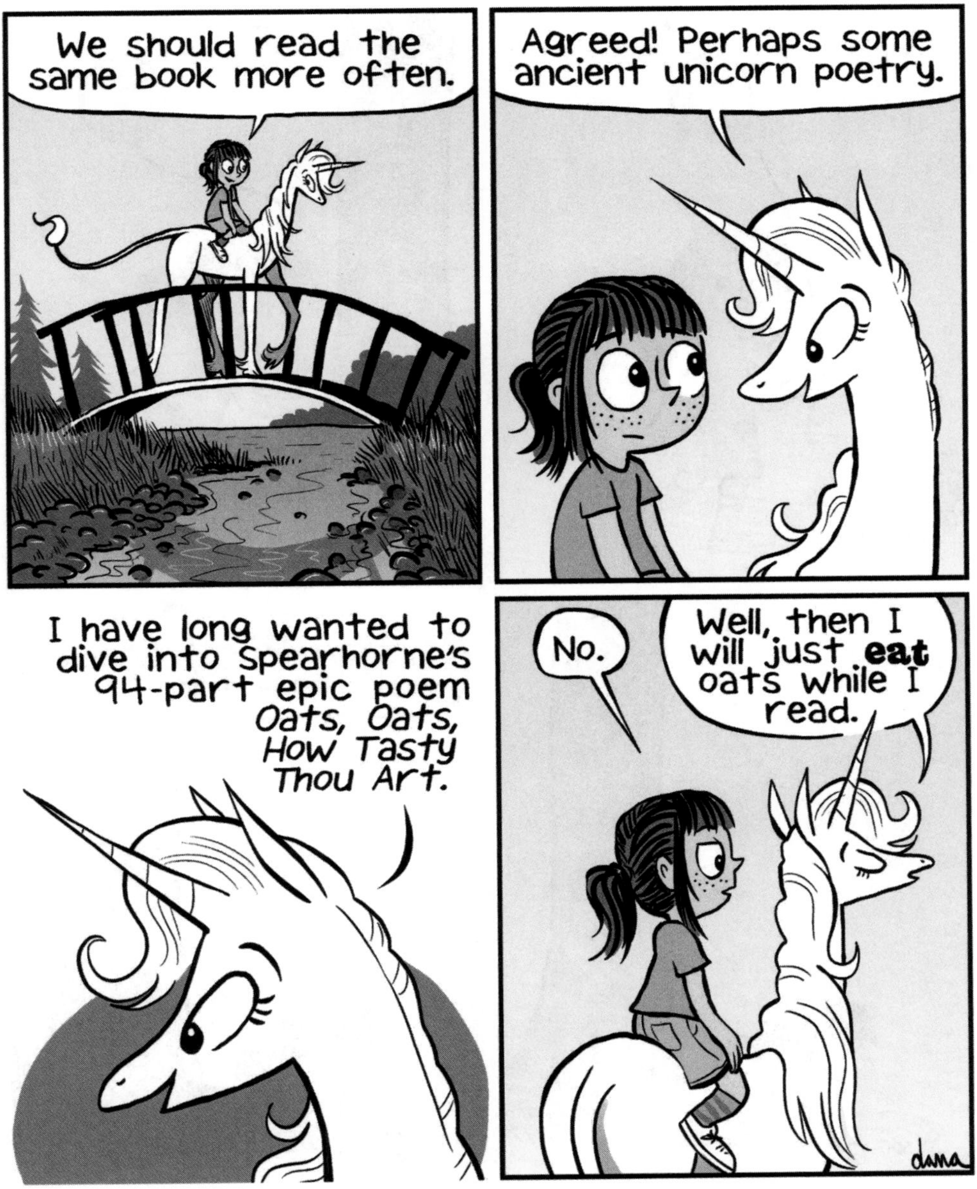
We should read the same book more often.
Agreed! Perhaps some ancient unicorn poetry.
I have long wanted to dive into Spearhorne's 94-part epic poem *Oats, Oats, How Tasty Thou Art.*
No.
Well, then I will just **eat** oats while I read.
dana

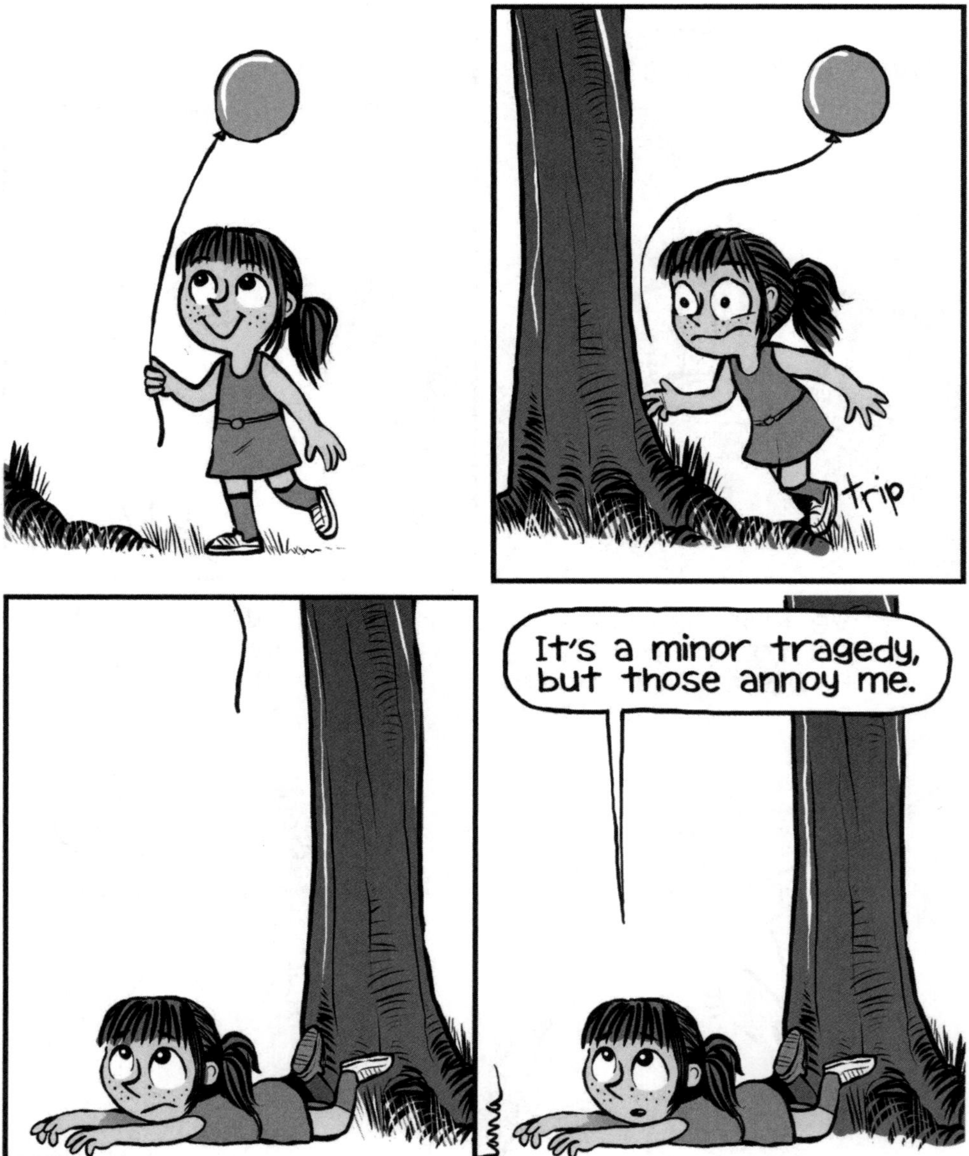
trip
It's a minor tragedy, but those annoy me.

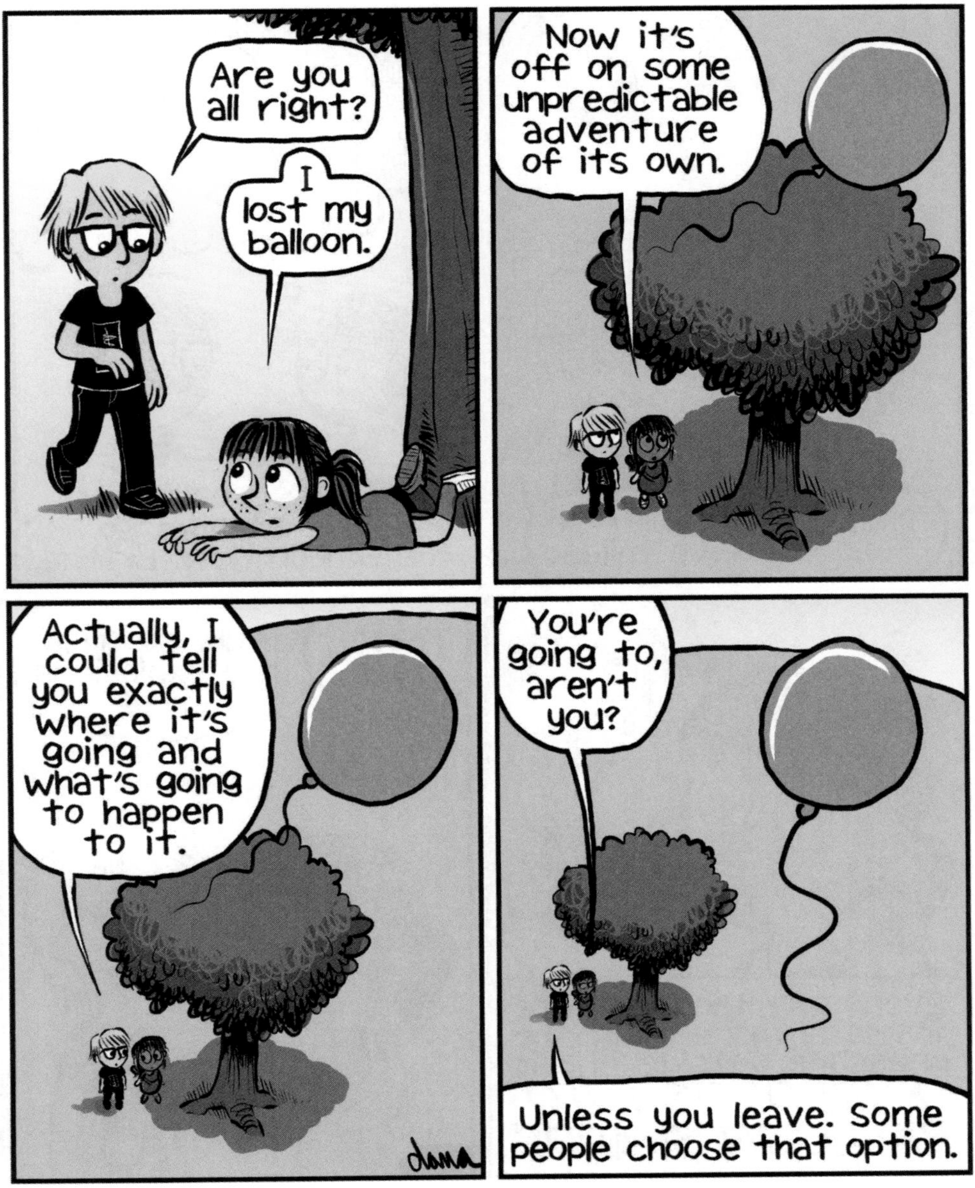
Are you all right?
I lost my balloon.
Now it's off on some unpredictable adventure of its own.
Actually, I could tell you exactly where it's going and what's going to happen to it.
You're going to, aren't you?
Unless you leave. Some people choose that option.

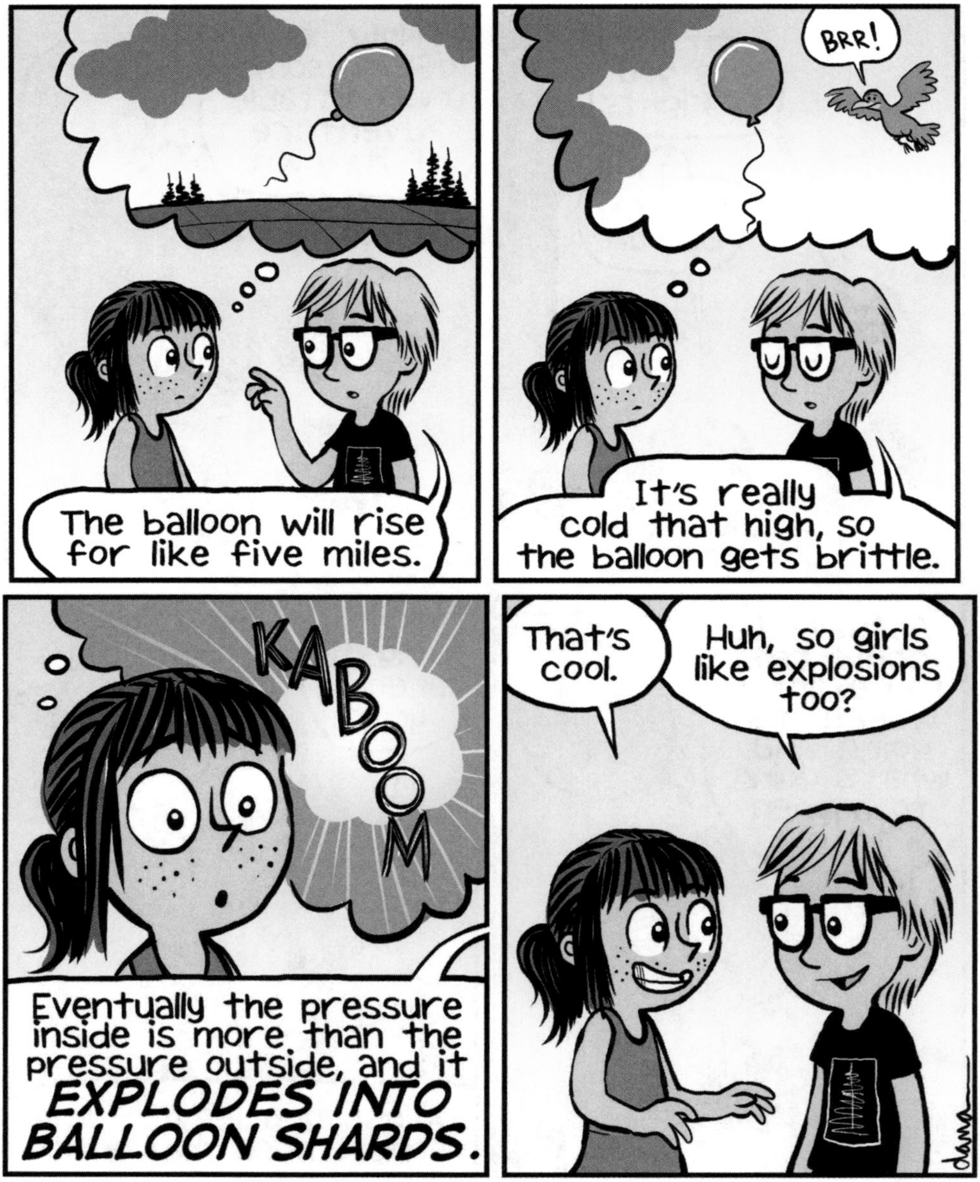
The balloon will rise for like five miles.
BRR!
It's really cold that high, so the balloon gets brittle.
KABOOOM
Eventually the pressure inside is more than the pressure outside, and it EXPLODES INTO BALLOON SHARDS.
That's cool.
Huh, so girls like explosions too?
dana

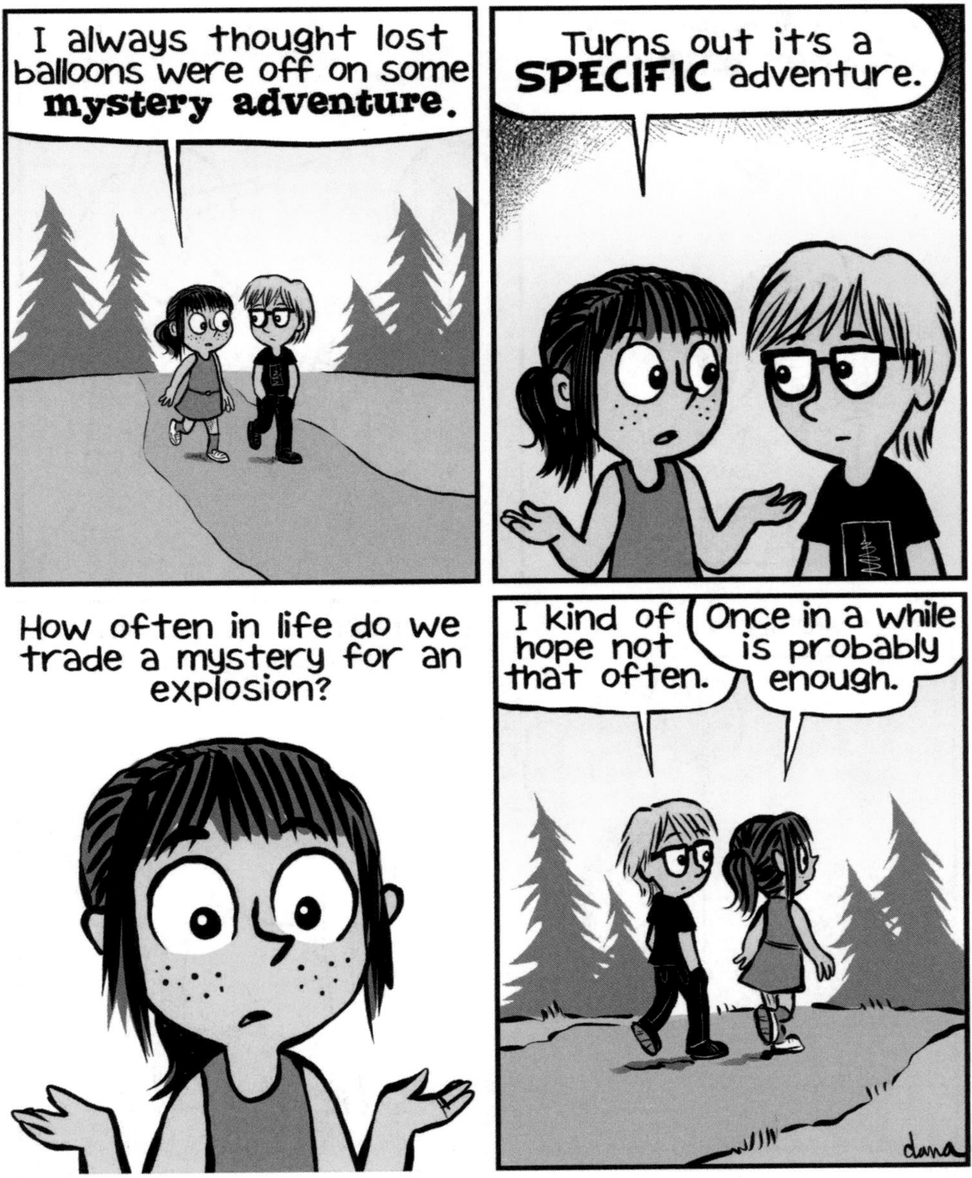
I always thought lost balloons were off on some **mystery adventure**.
Turns out it's a **SPECIFIC** adventure.
How often in life do we trade a mystery for an explosion?
I kind of hope not that often.
Once in a while is probably enough.
dana

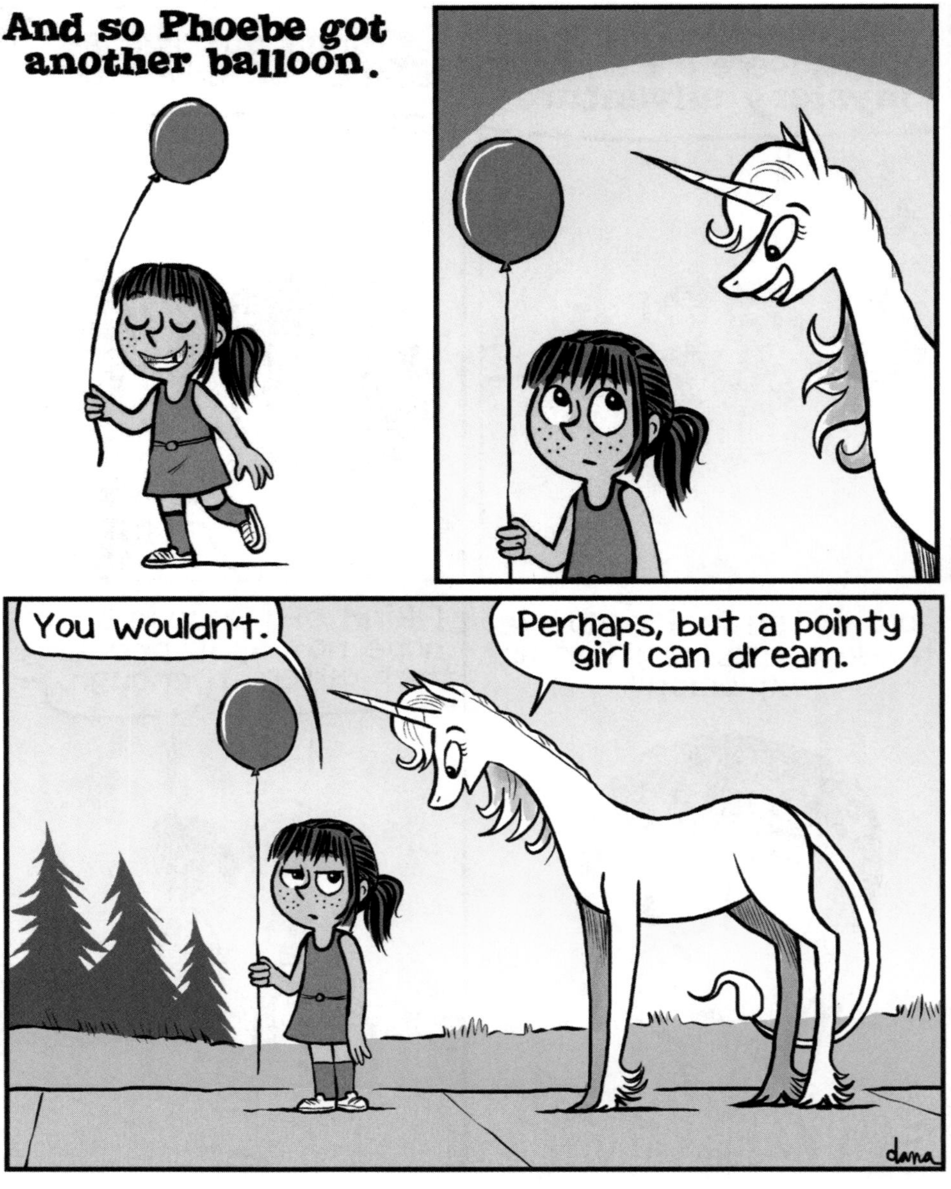
And so Phoebe got another balloon.
You wouldn't.
Perhaps, but a pointy girl can dream.
dana

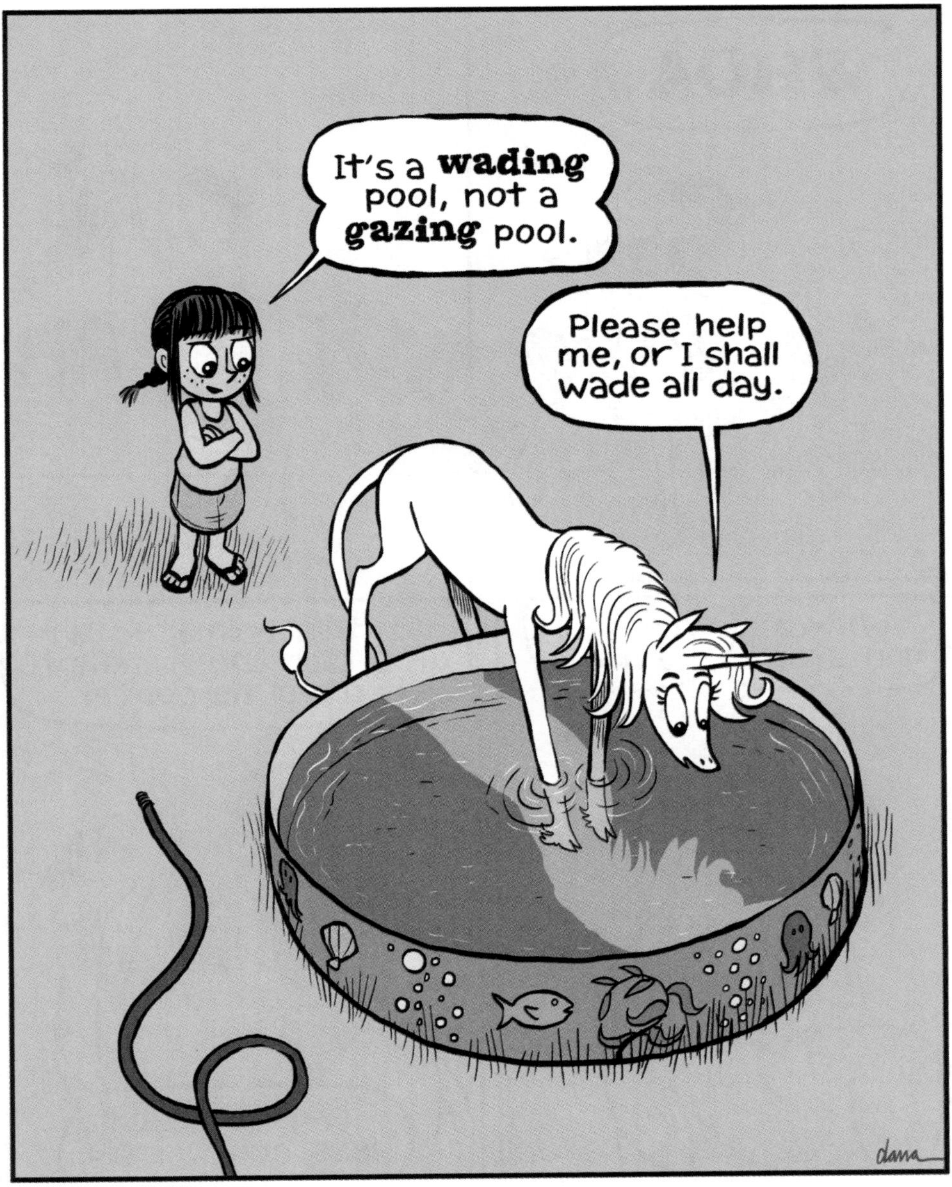
It's a **wading** pool, not a **gazing** pool.
Please help me, or I shall wade all day.
dana

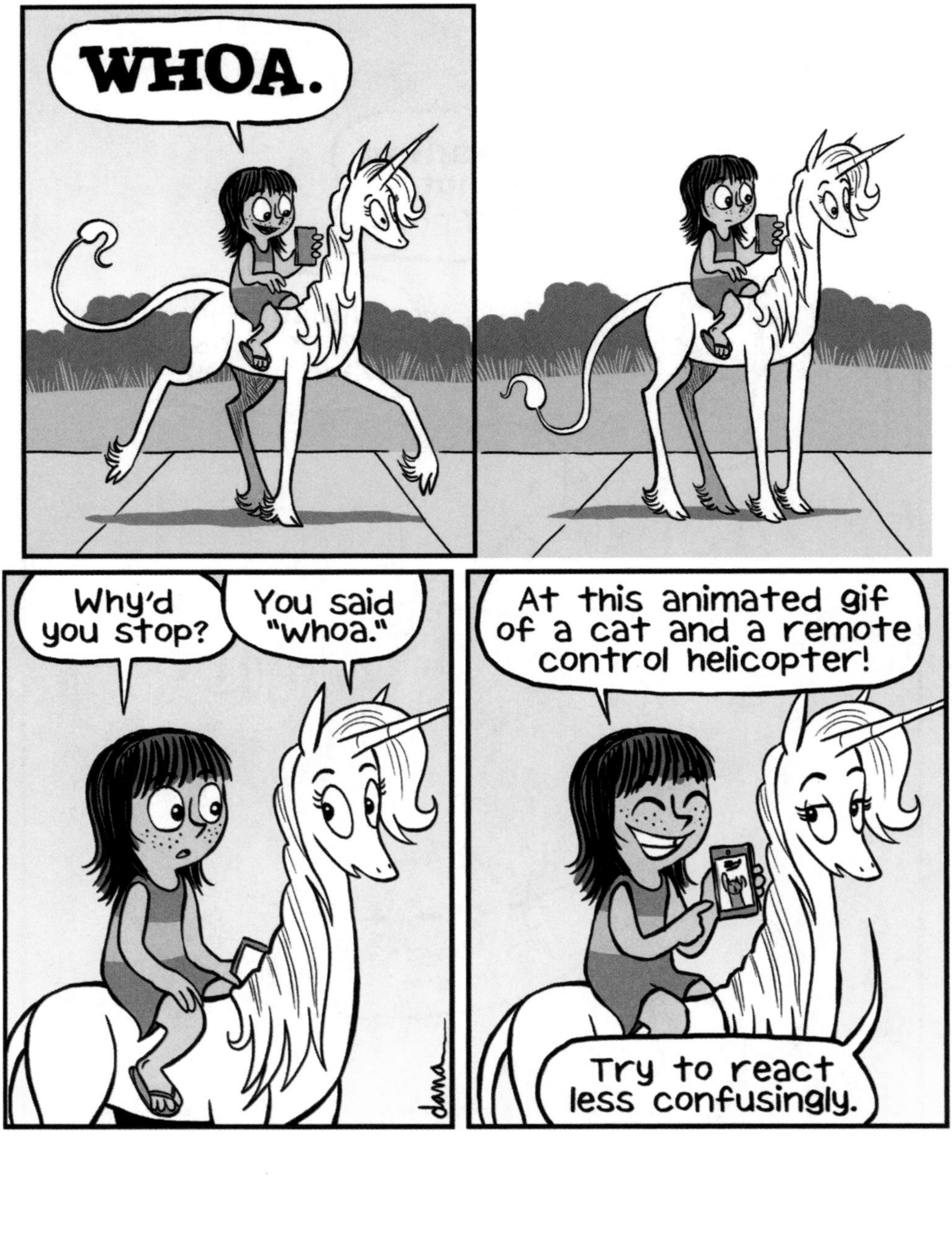
WHOA.
Why'd you stop?
You said "whoa."
At this animated gif of a cat and a remote control helicopter!
Try to react less confusingly.
dana

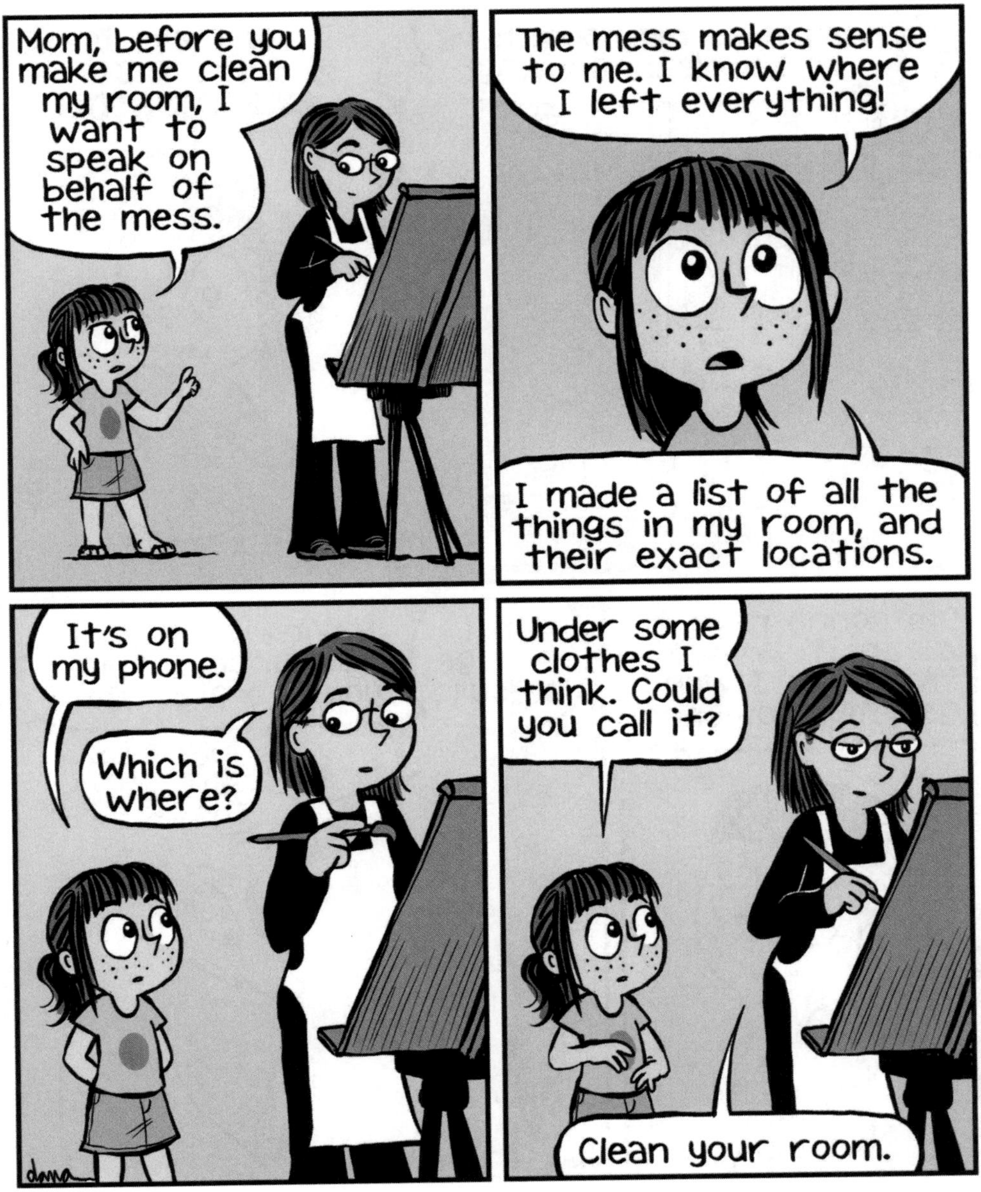
Mom, before you make me clean my room, I want to speak on behalf of the mess.
The mess makes sense to me. I know where I left everything!
I made a list of all the things in my room, and their exact locations.
It's on my phone.
Which is where?
Under some clothes I think. Could you call it?
Clean your room.

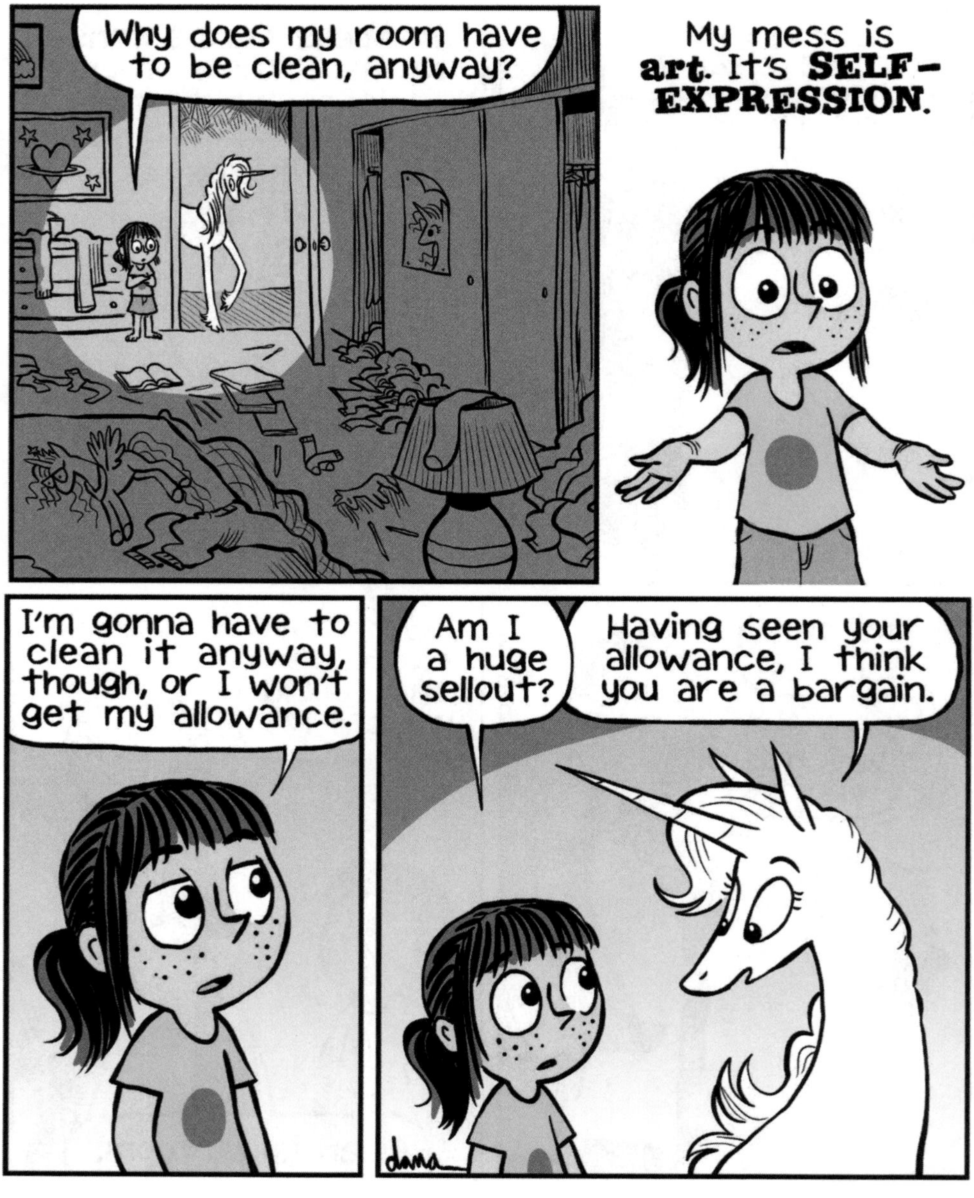
Why does my room have to be clean, anyway?
My mess is **art**. It's **SELF-EXPRESSION**.
I'm gonna have to clean it anyway, though, or I won't get my allowance.
Am I a huge sellout?
Having seen your allowance, I think you are a bargain.
dana

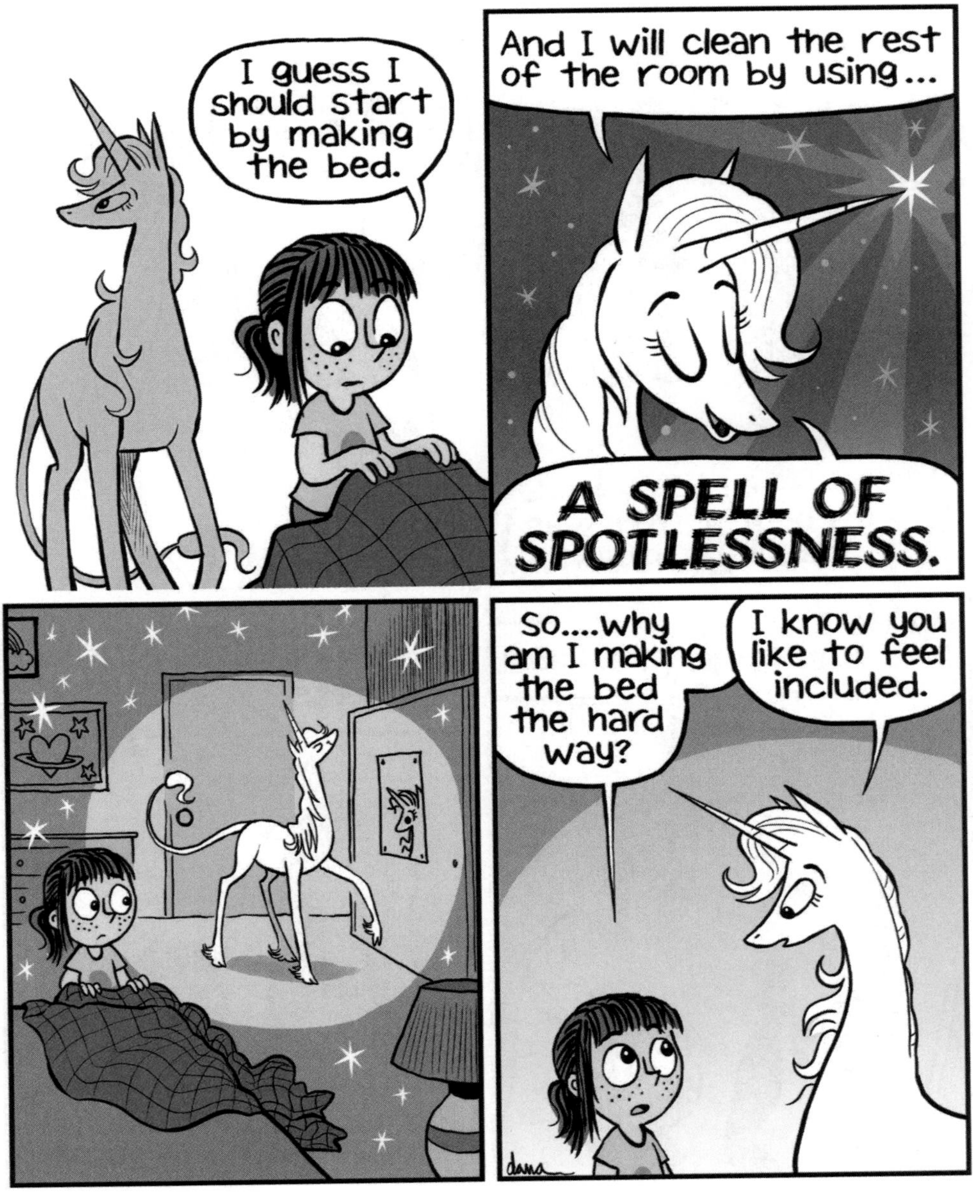
I guess I should start by making the bed.
And I will clean the rest of the room by using...
A SPELL OF SPOTLESSNESS.
So....why am I making the bed the hard way?
I know you like to feel included.
dana

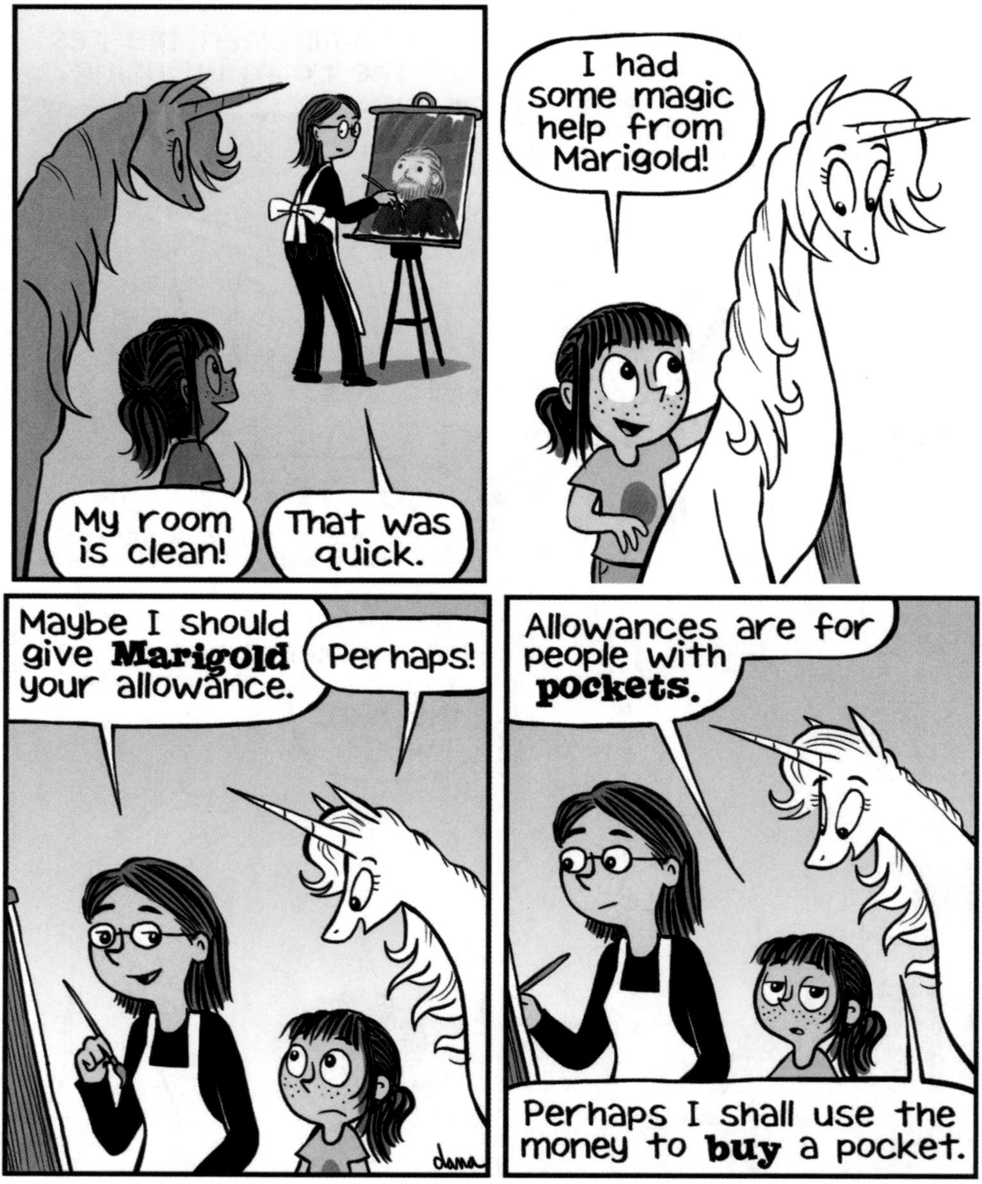
My room is clean!
That was quick.
I had some magic help from Marigold!
Maybe I should give **Marigold** your allowance.
Perhaps!
Allowances are for people with **pockets**.
Perhaps I shall use the money to **buy** a pocket.
dana

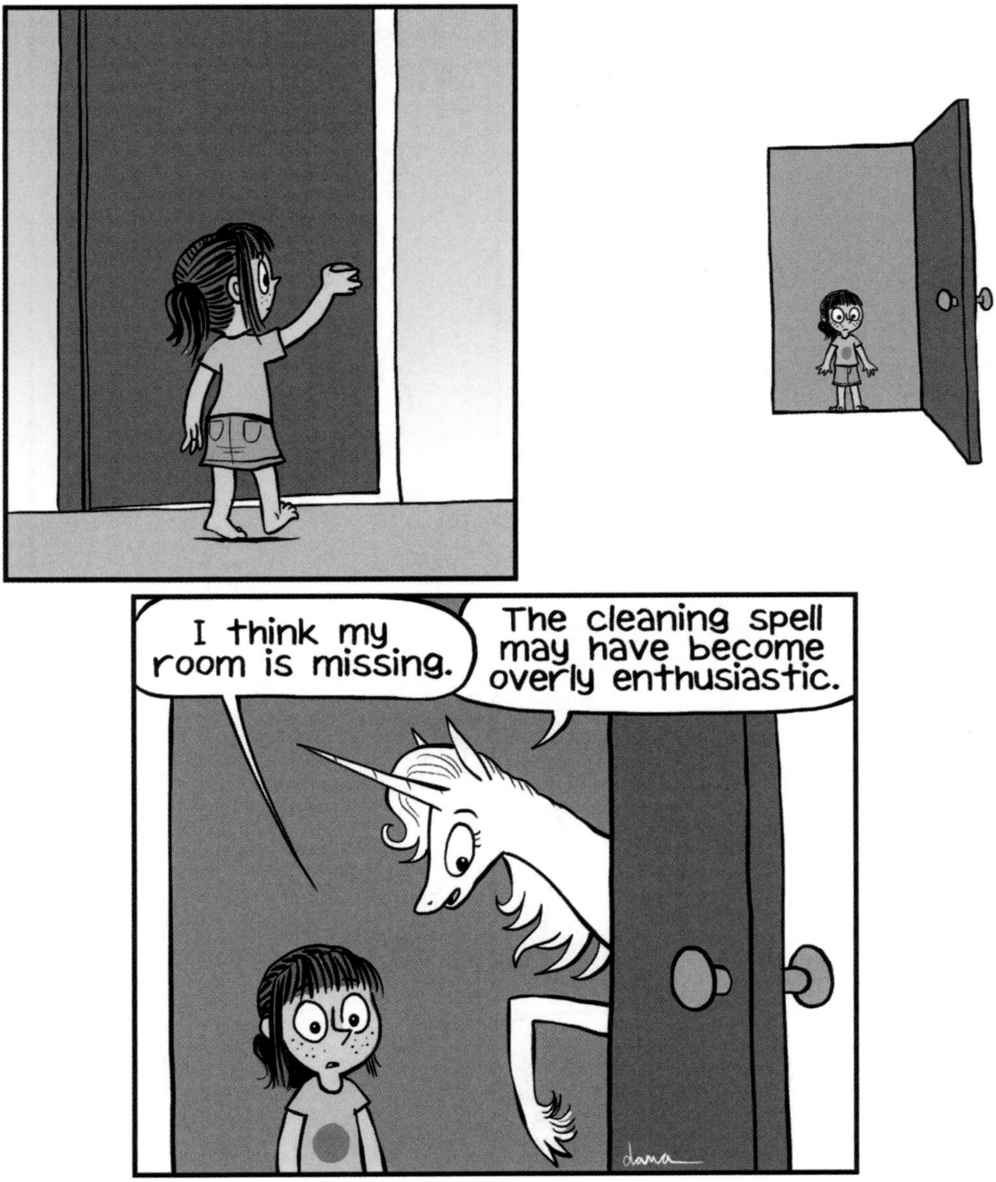
I think my room is missing.
The cleaning spell may have become overly enthusiastic.

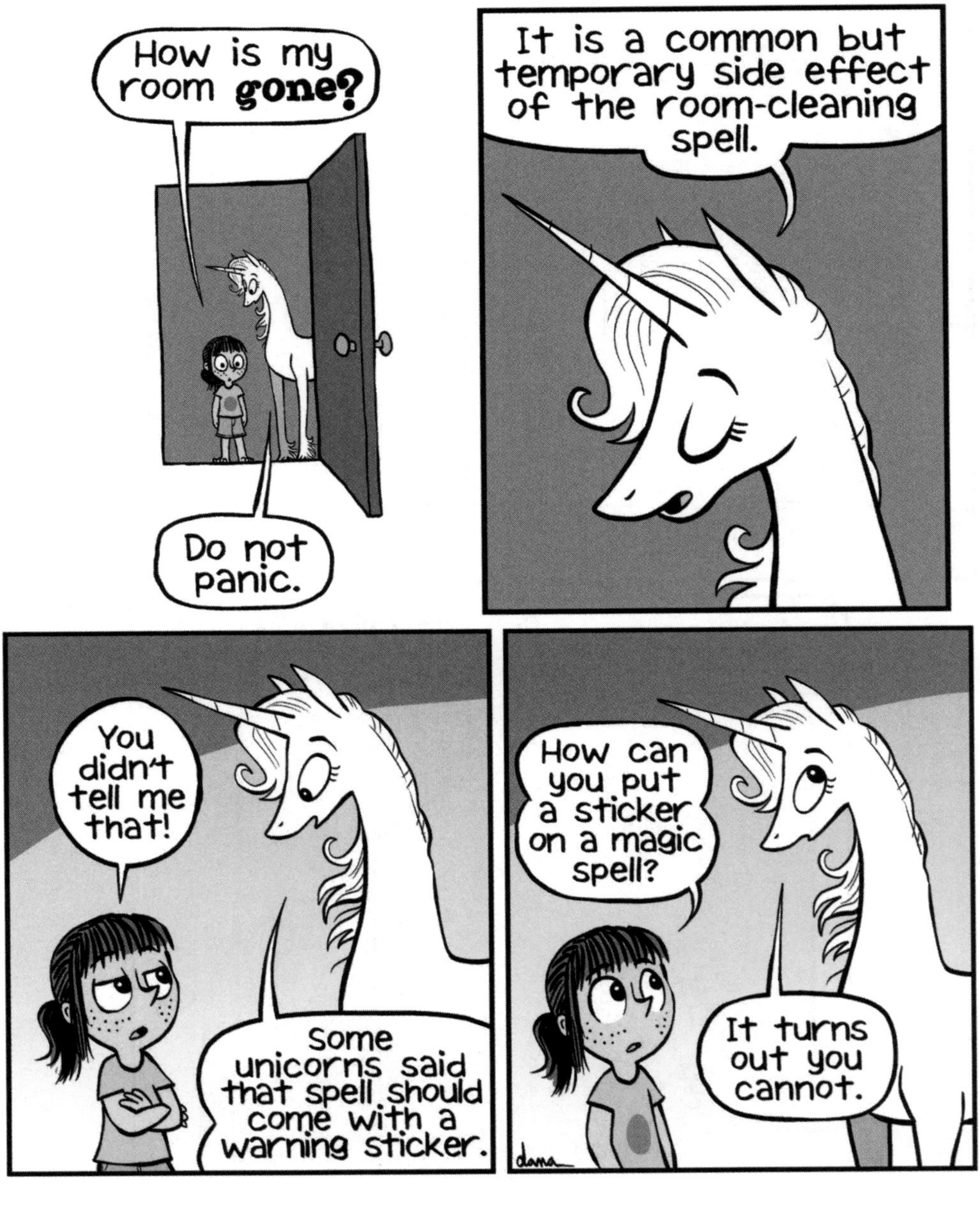
How is my room **gone?**
Do not panic.
It is a common but temporary side effect of the room-cleaning spell.
You didn't tell me that!
Some unicorns said that spell should come with a warning sticker.
How can you put a sticker on a magic spell?
It turns out you cannot.

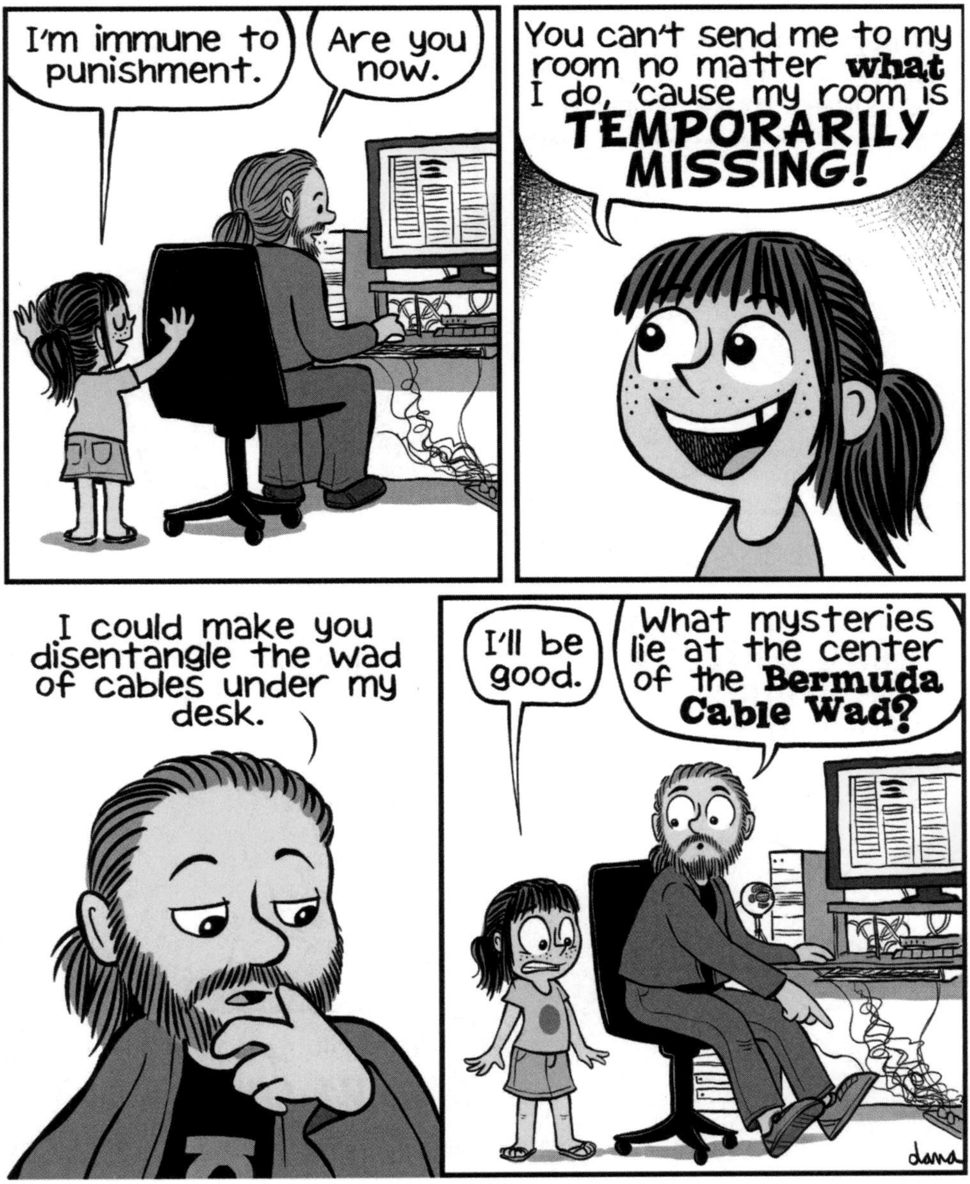
I'm immune to punishment.
Are you now.
You can't send me to my room no matter **what** I do, 'cause my room is **TEMPORARILY MISSING!**
I could make you disentangle the wad of cables under my desk.
I'll be good.
What mysteries lie at the center of the **Bermuda Cable Wad?**
dana

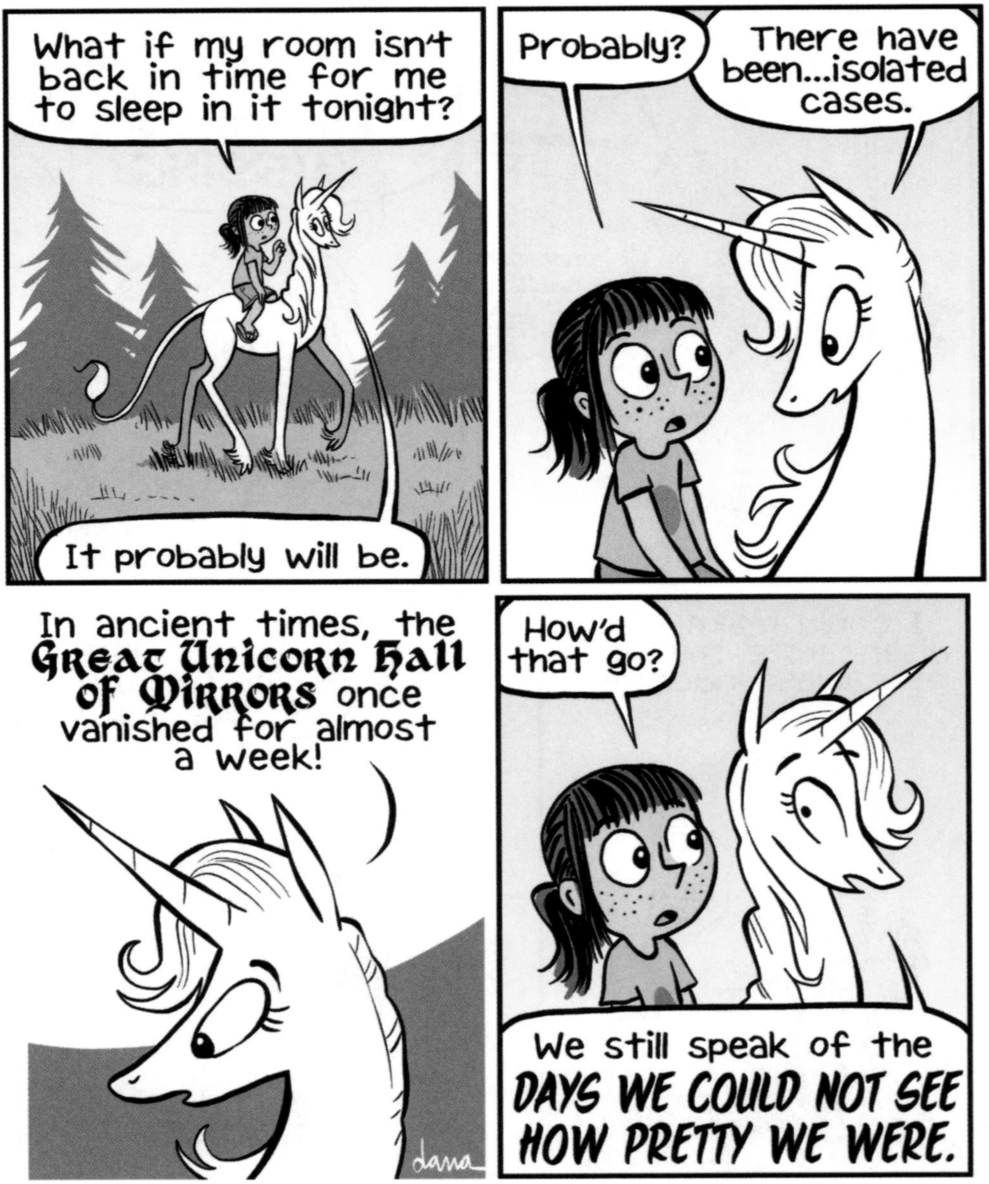
What if my room isn't back in time for me to sleep in it tonight?
It probably will be.
Probably?
There have been...isolated cases.
In ancient times, the Great Unicorn Hall of Mirrors once vanished for almost a week!
dana
How'd that go?
We still speak of the DAYS WE COULD NOT SEE HOW PRETTY WE WERE.

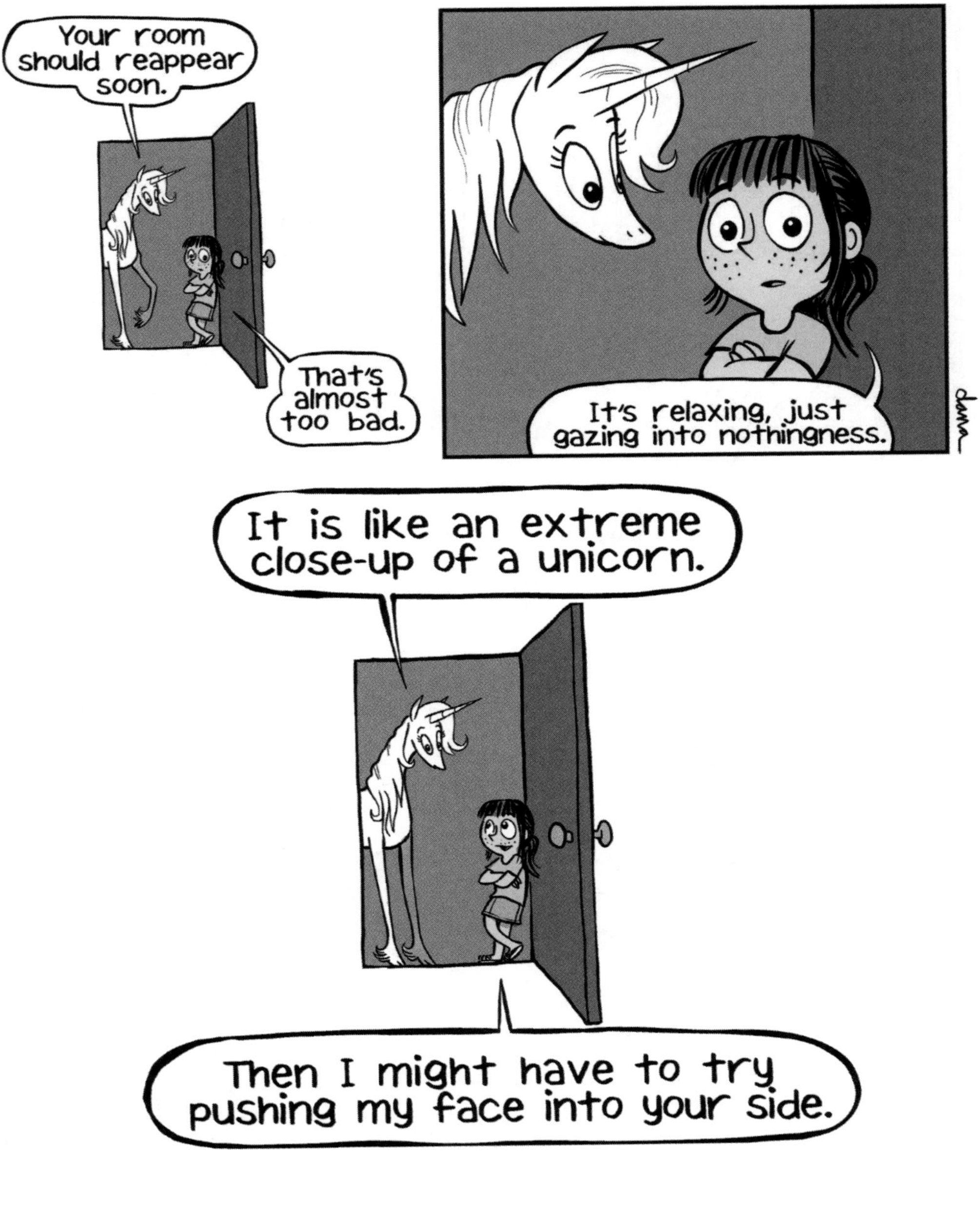
Your room should reappear soon.
That's almost too bad.
It's relaxing, just gazing into nothingness.
It is like an extreme close-up of a unicorn.
Then I might have to try pushing my face into your side.

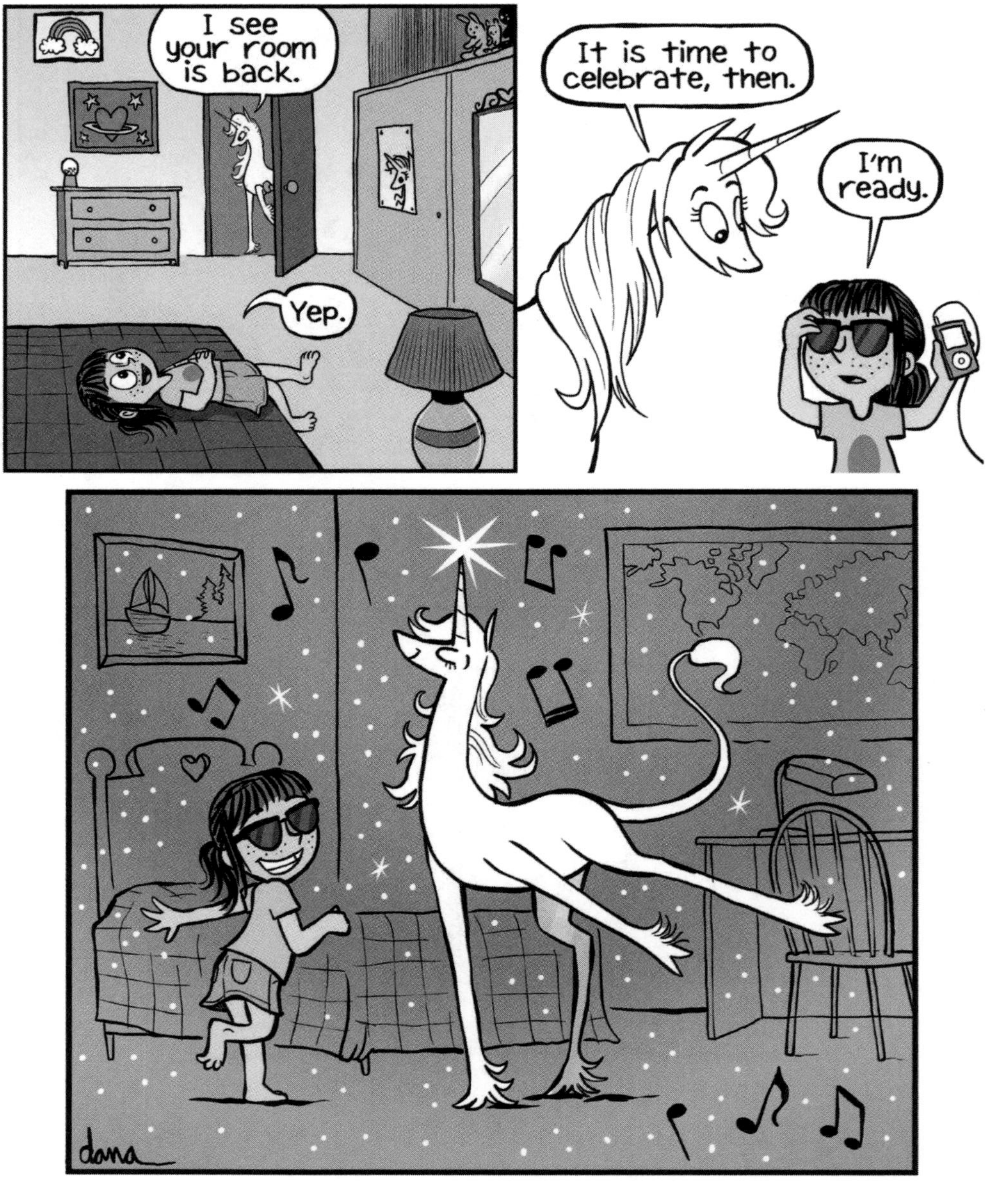
I see your room is back.
Yep.
It is time to celebrate, then.
I'm ready.
dana

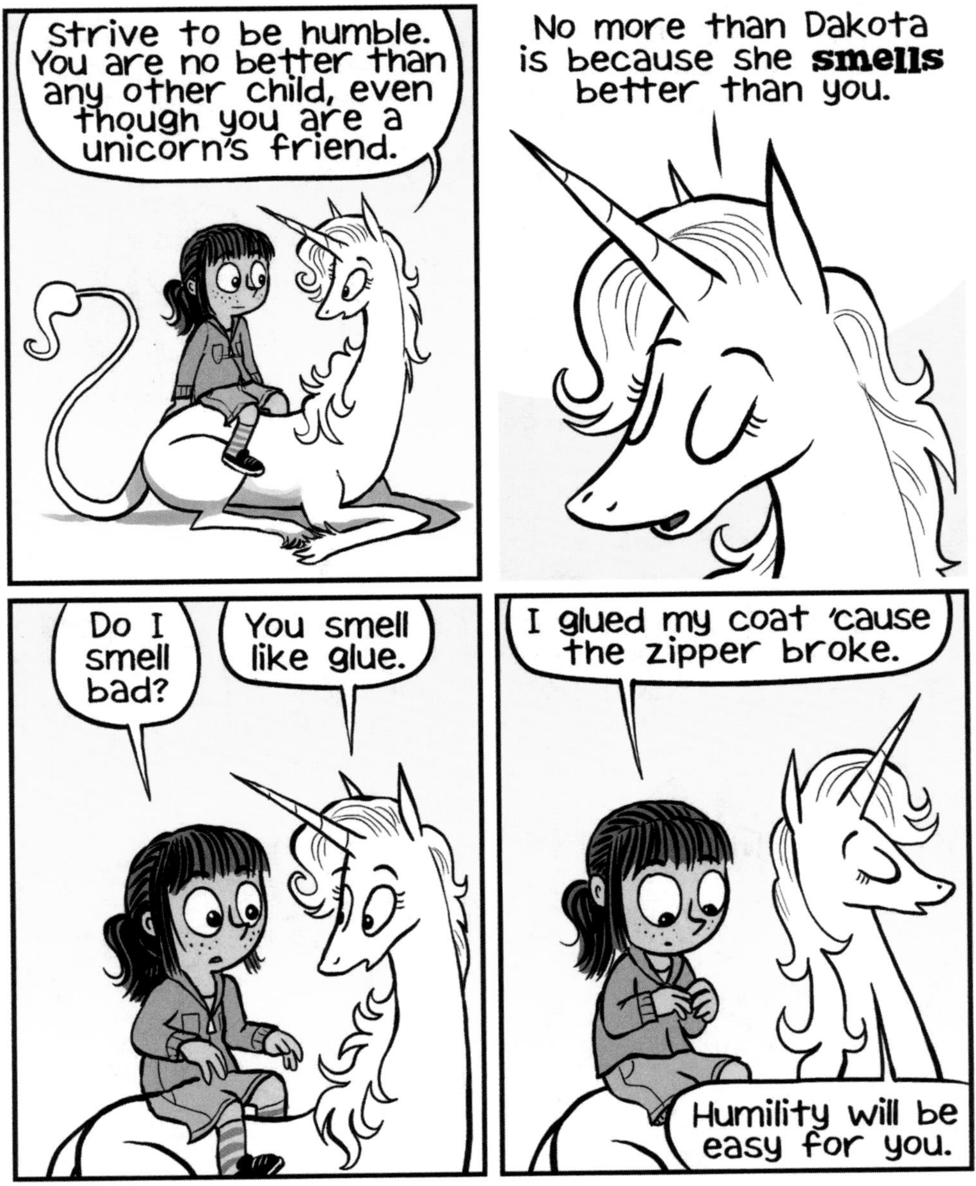
Strive to be humble. You are no better than any other child, even though you are a unicorn's friend.
No more than Dakota is because she **smells** better than you.
Do I smell bad?
You smell like glue.
I glued my coat 'cause the zipper broke.
Humility will be easy for you.

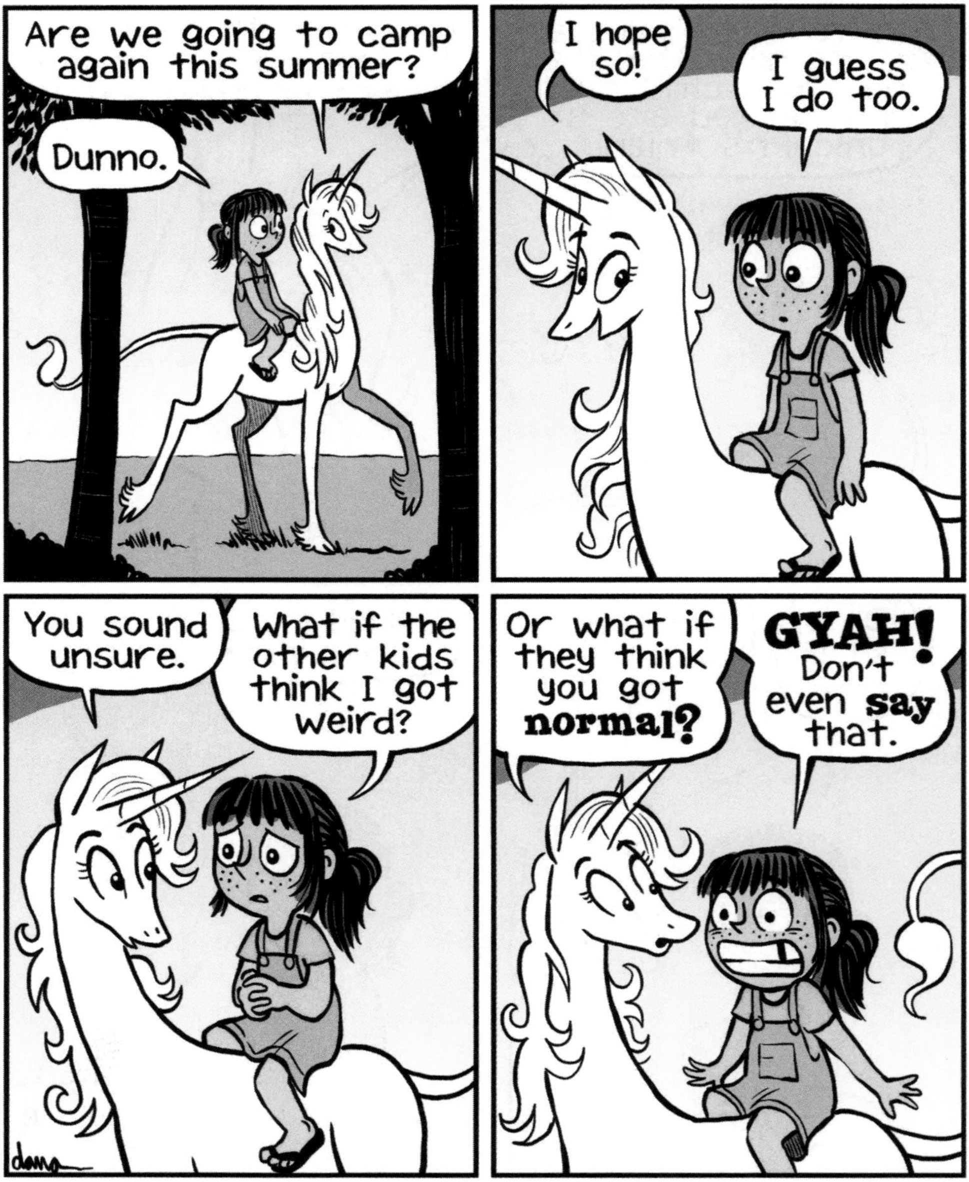
Are we going to camp again this summer?
Dunno.
I hope so!
I guess I do too.
You sound unsure.
What if the other kids think I got weird?
Or what if they think you got **normal?**
GYAH! Don't even **say** that.
dana

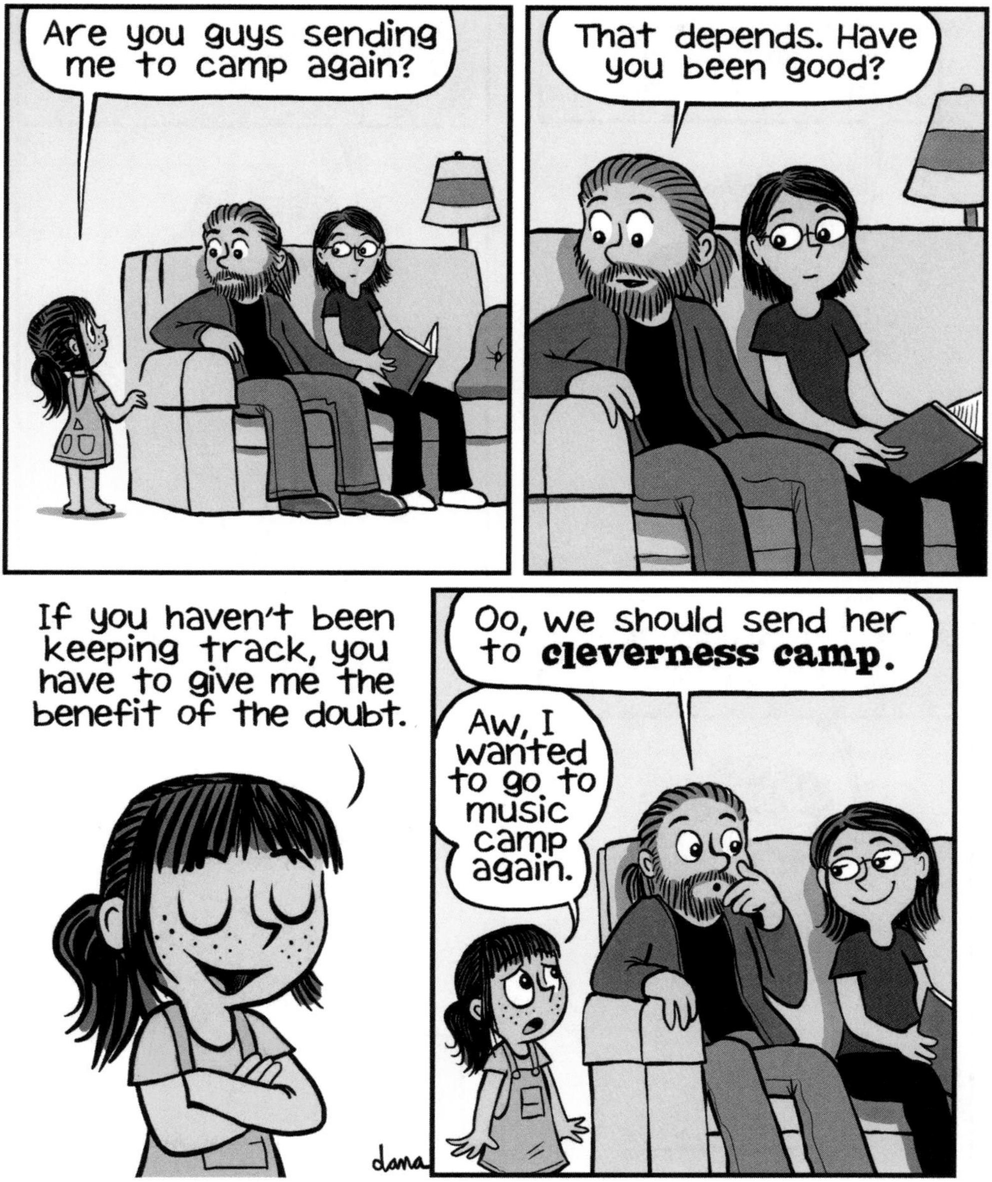
Are you guys sending me to camp again?
That depends. Have you been good?
If you haven't been keeping track, you have to give me the benefit of the doubt.
Oo, we should send her to **cleverness camp.**
Aw, I wanted to go to music camp again.
dana

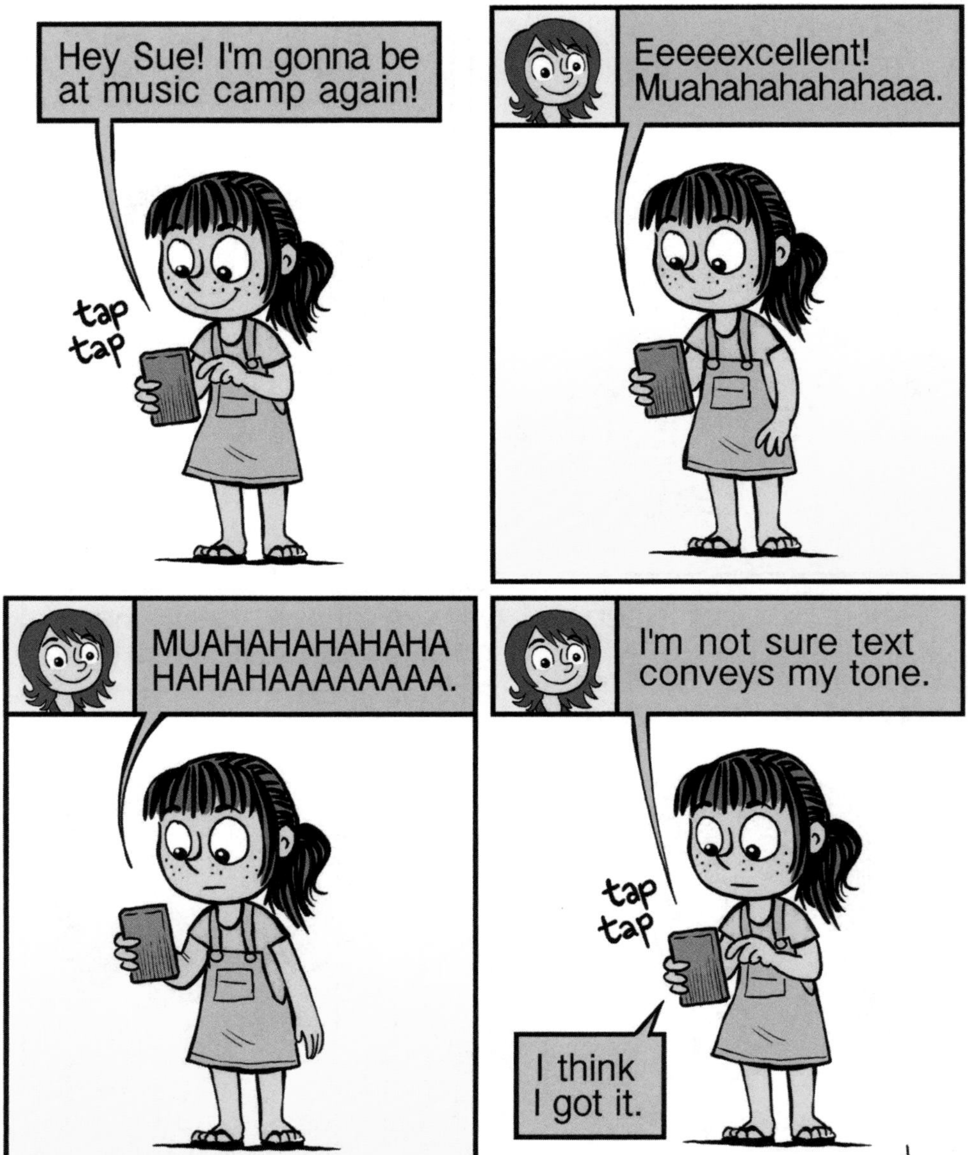
Hey Sue! I'm gonna be at music camp again!
tap tap
Eeeeexcellent! Muahahahahahaaa.
MUAHAHAHAHAHA HAHAHAAAAAAAA.
I'm not sure text conveys my tone.
tap tap
I think I got it.
dana

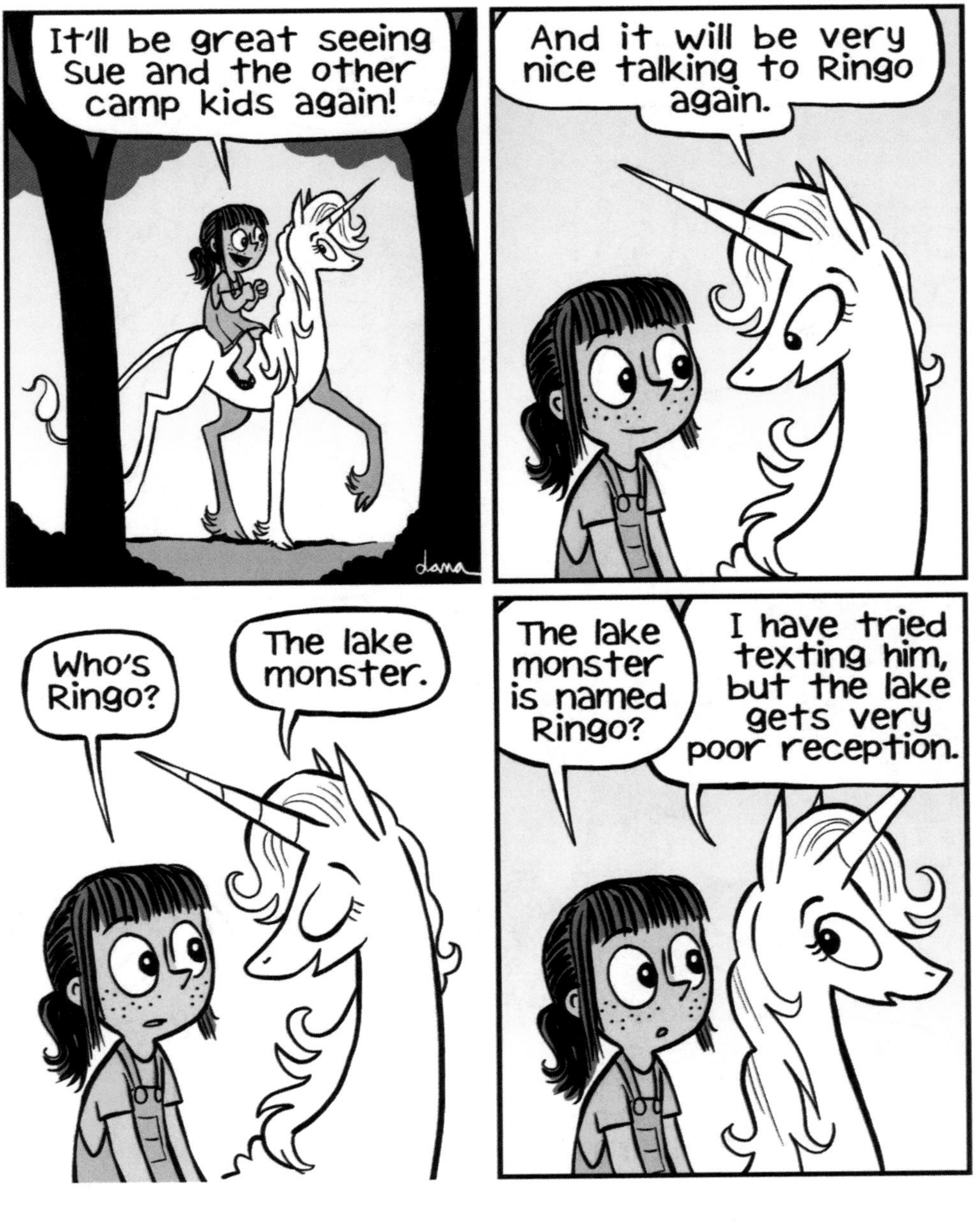
It'll be great seeing Sue and the other camp kids again!
dana
And it will be very nice talking to Ringo again.
Who's Ringo?
The lake monster.
The lake monster is named Ringo?
I have tried texting him, but the lake gets very poor reception.

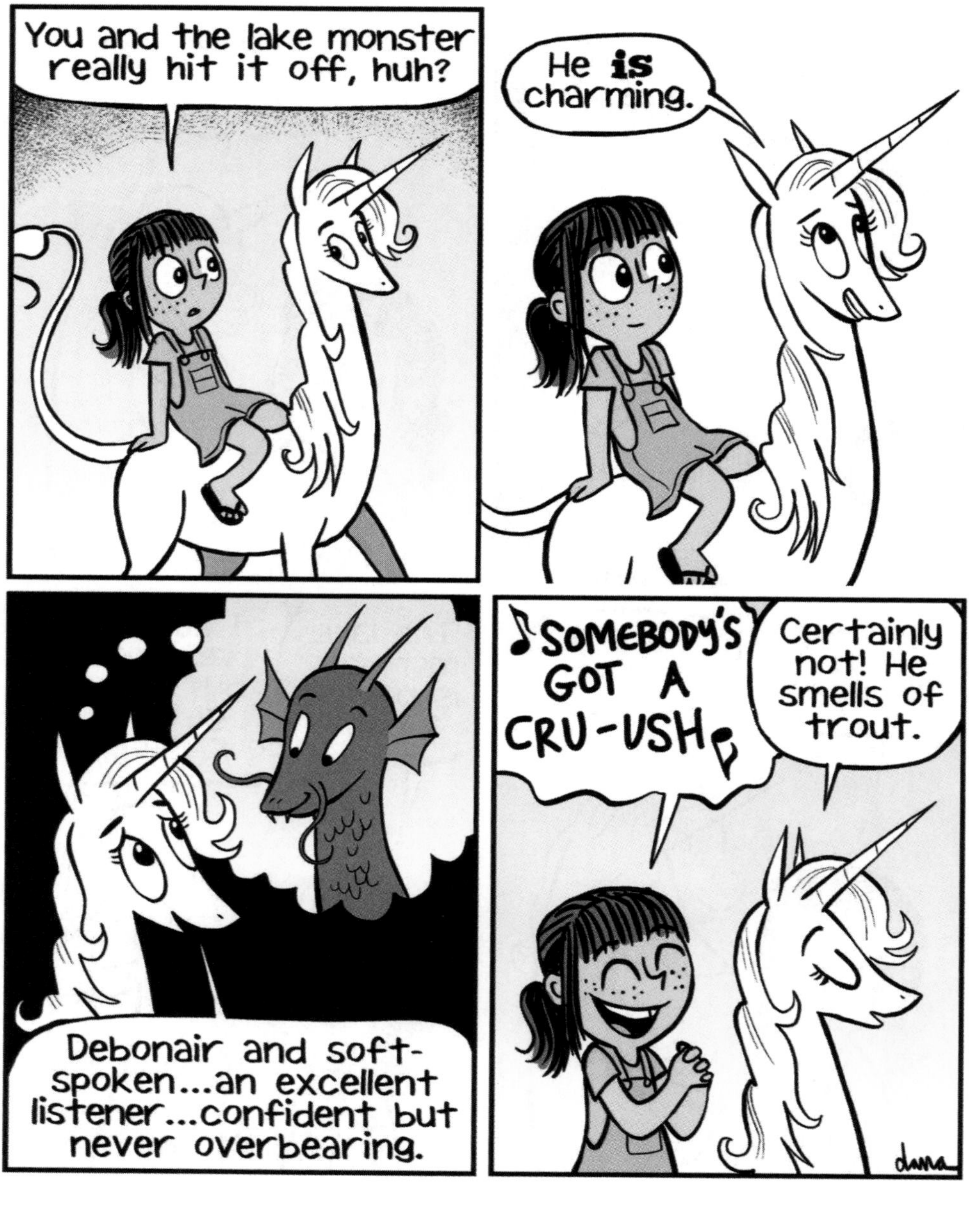
You and the lake monster really hit it off, huh?
He **is** charming.
Debonair and soft-spoken...an excellent listener...confident but never overbearing.
♪ SOMEBODY'S GOT A CRU-USH ♪
Certainly not! He smells of trout.
dana

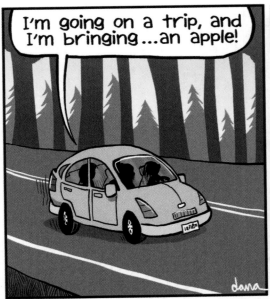

I'm going on a trip, and I'm bringing...an apple!

Also a unicorn!

Maybe, but that's much later in the alphabet.

But it is the most important thing!

Unicorns can be so impatient!

I will have that apple now, please.

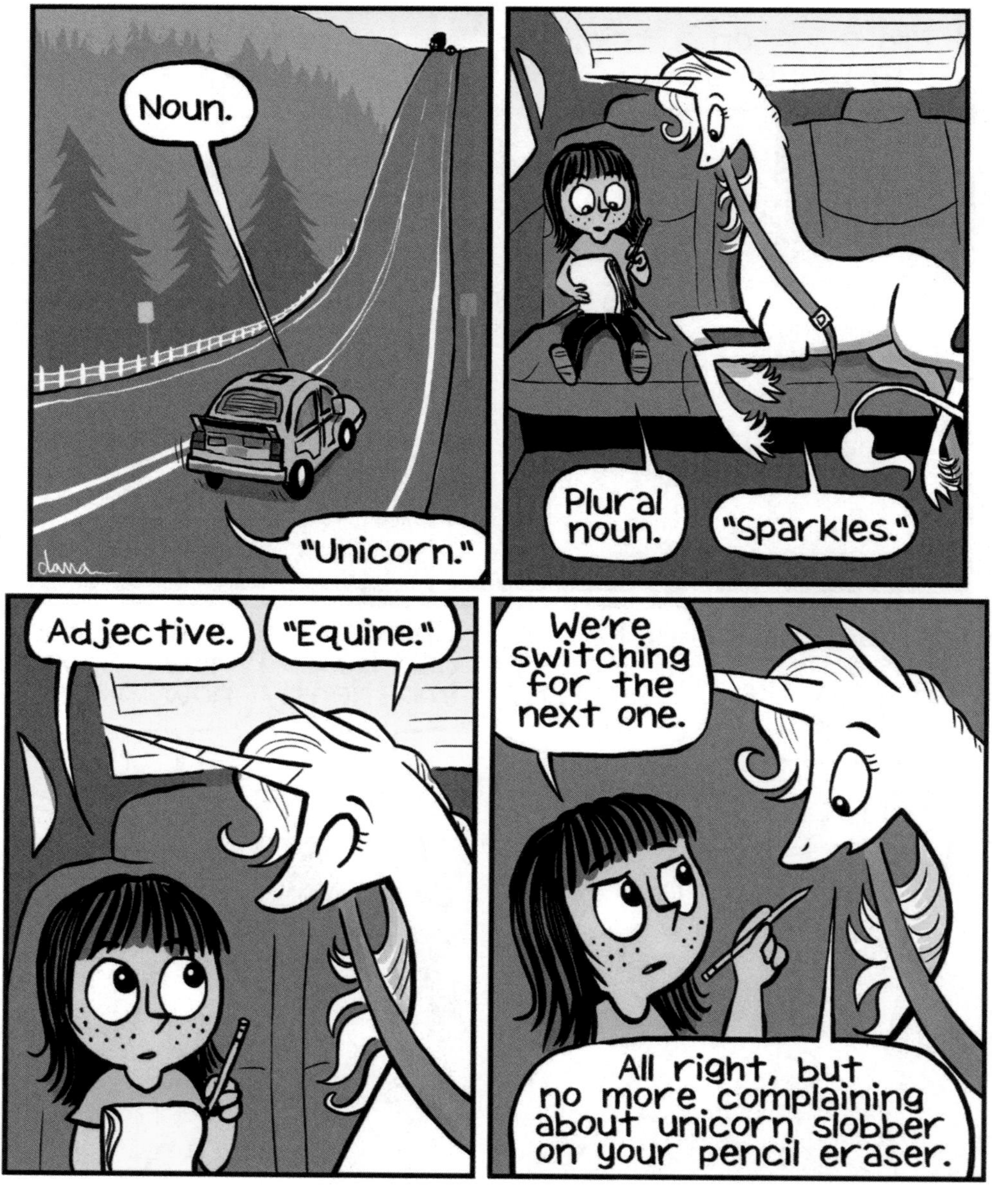
Noun.
"Unicorn."
Plural noun.
"Sparkles."
Adjective.
"Equine."
We're switching for the next one.
All right, but no more complaining about unicorn slobber on your pencil eraser.

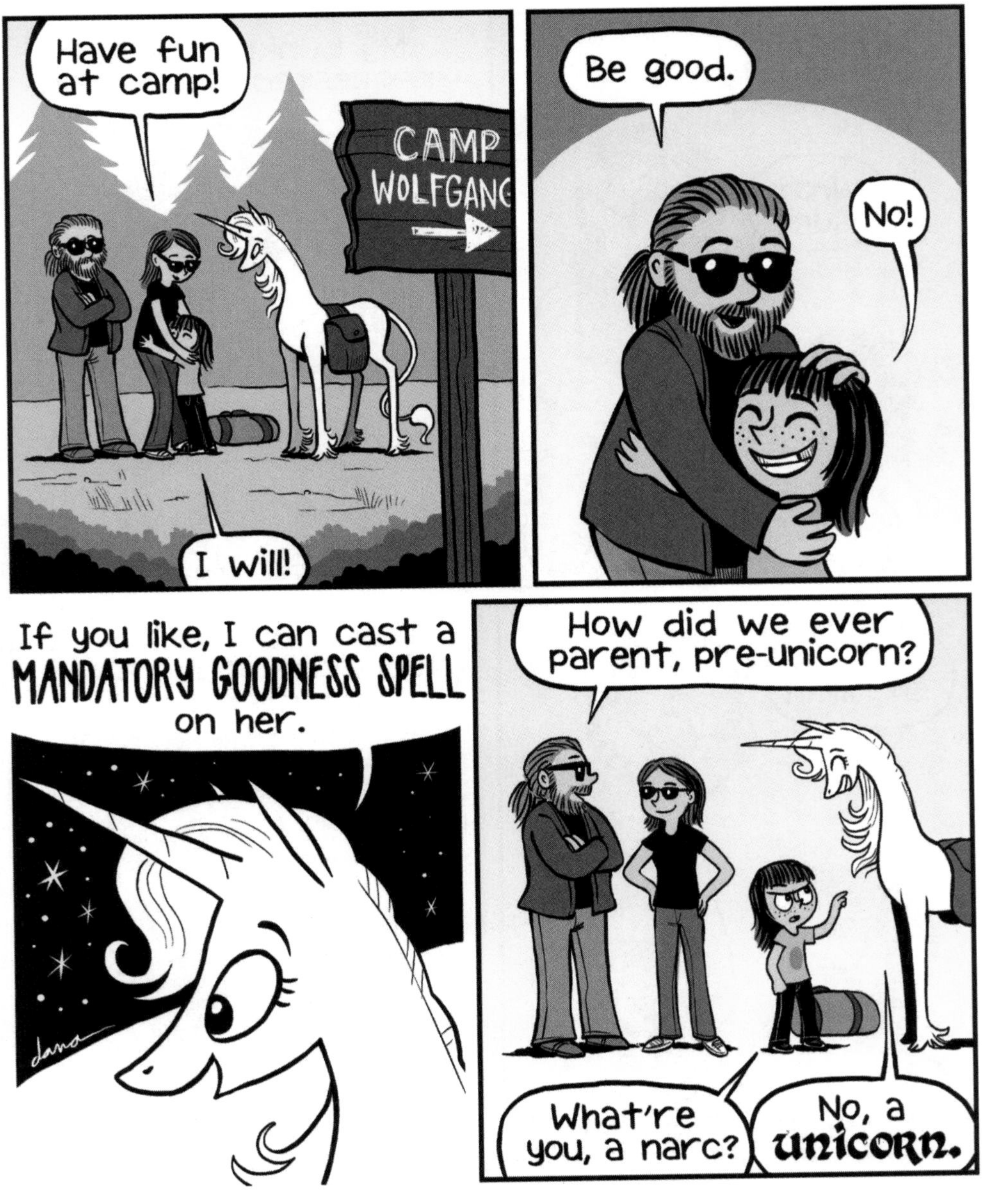
Have fun at camp!
CAMP WOLFGANG
I will!
Be good.
No!
If you like, I can cast a MANDATORY GOODNESS SPELL on her.
dana
How did we ever parent, pre-unicorn?
What're you, a narc?
No, a unicorn.

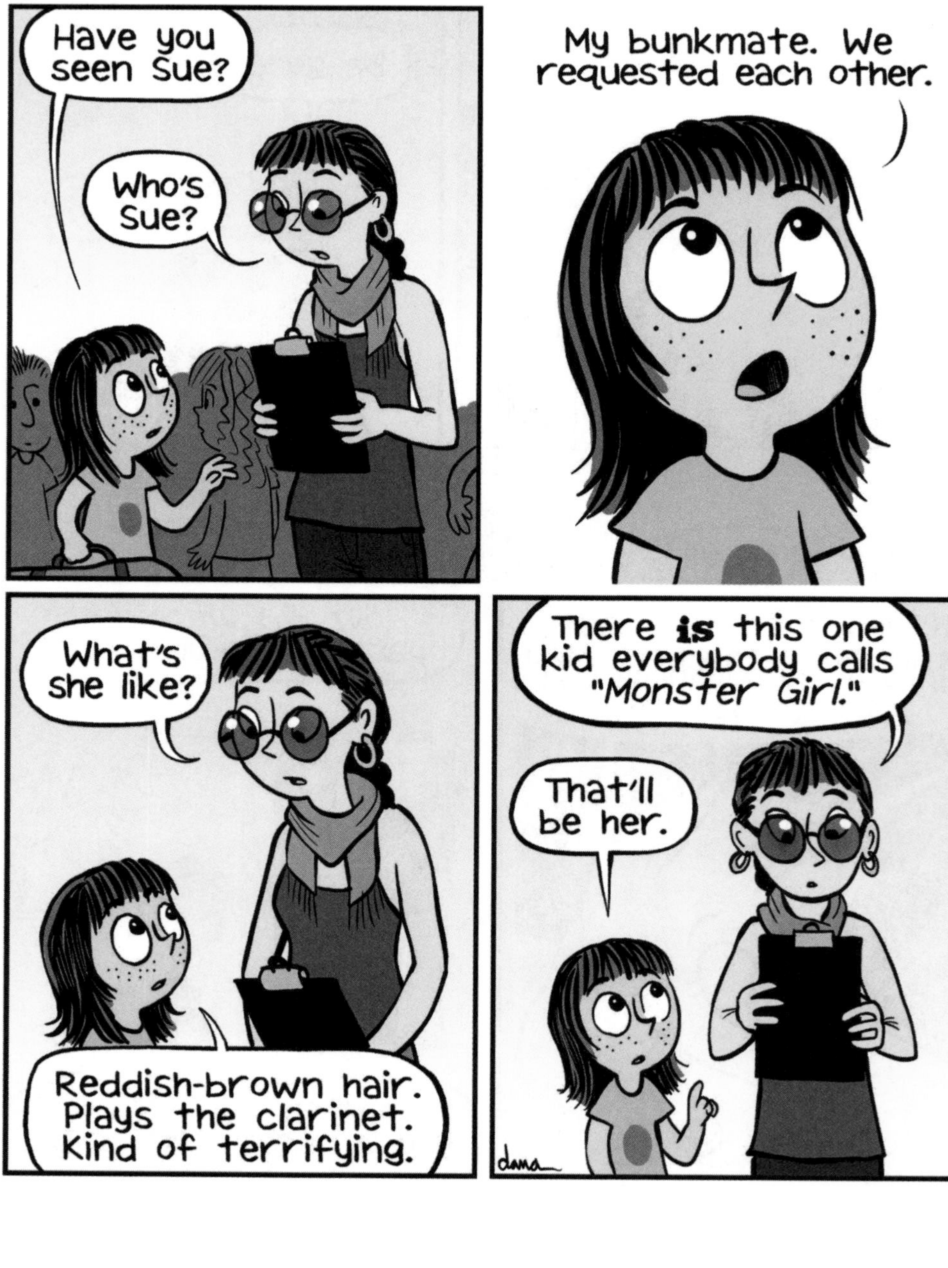
Have you seen Sue?
Who's Sue?
My bunkmate. We requested each other.
What's she like?
Reddish-brown hair. Plays the clarinet. Kind of terrifying.
There **is** this one kid everybody calls "*Monster Girl.*"
That'll be her.
dana

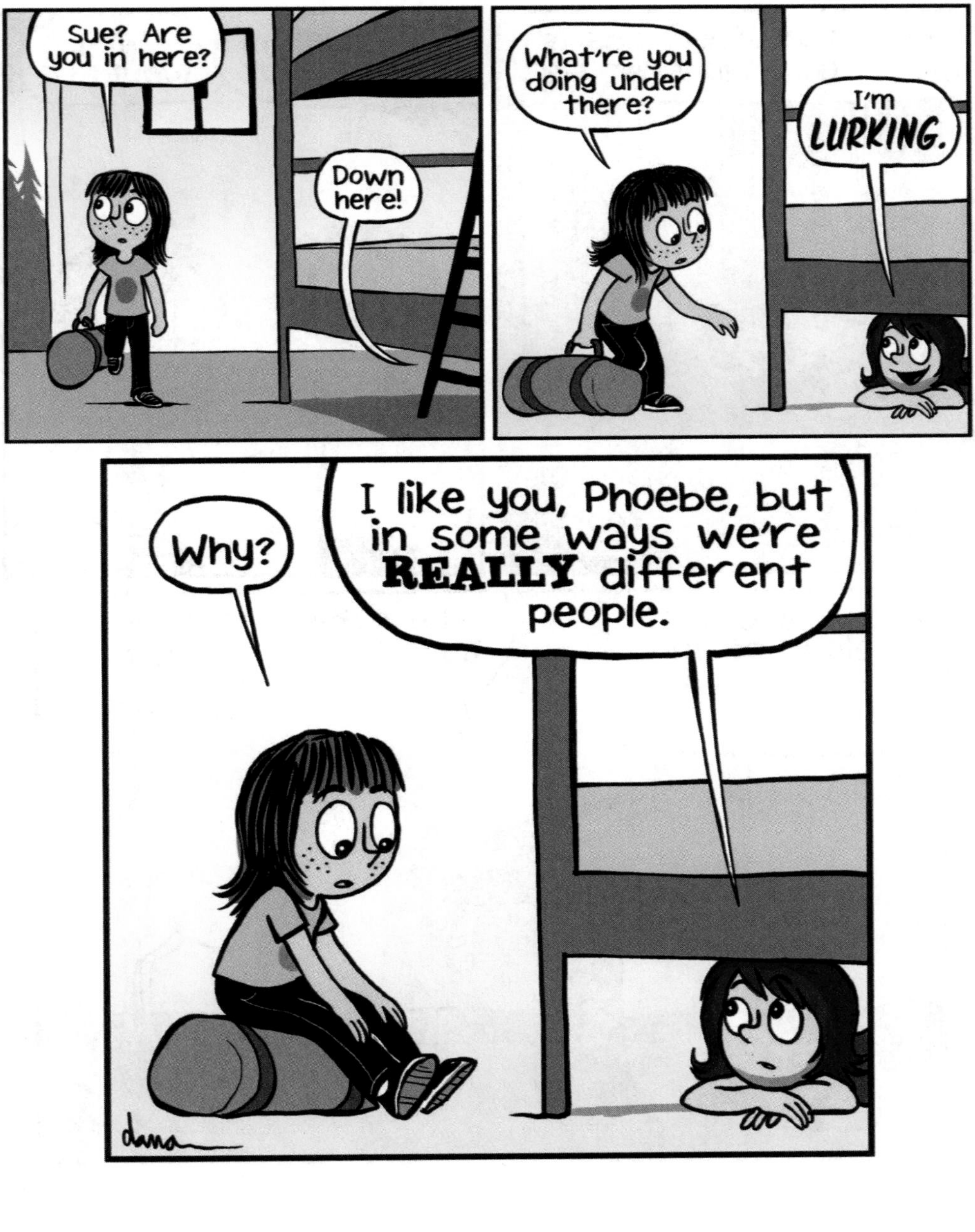
Sue? Are you in here?
Down here!
What're you doing under there?
I'm LURKING.
Why?
I like you, Phoebe, but in some ways we're REALLY different people.
dana

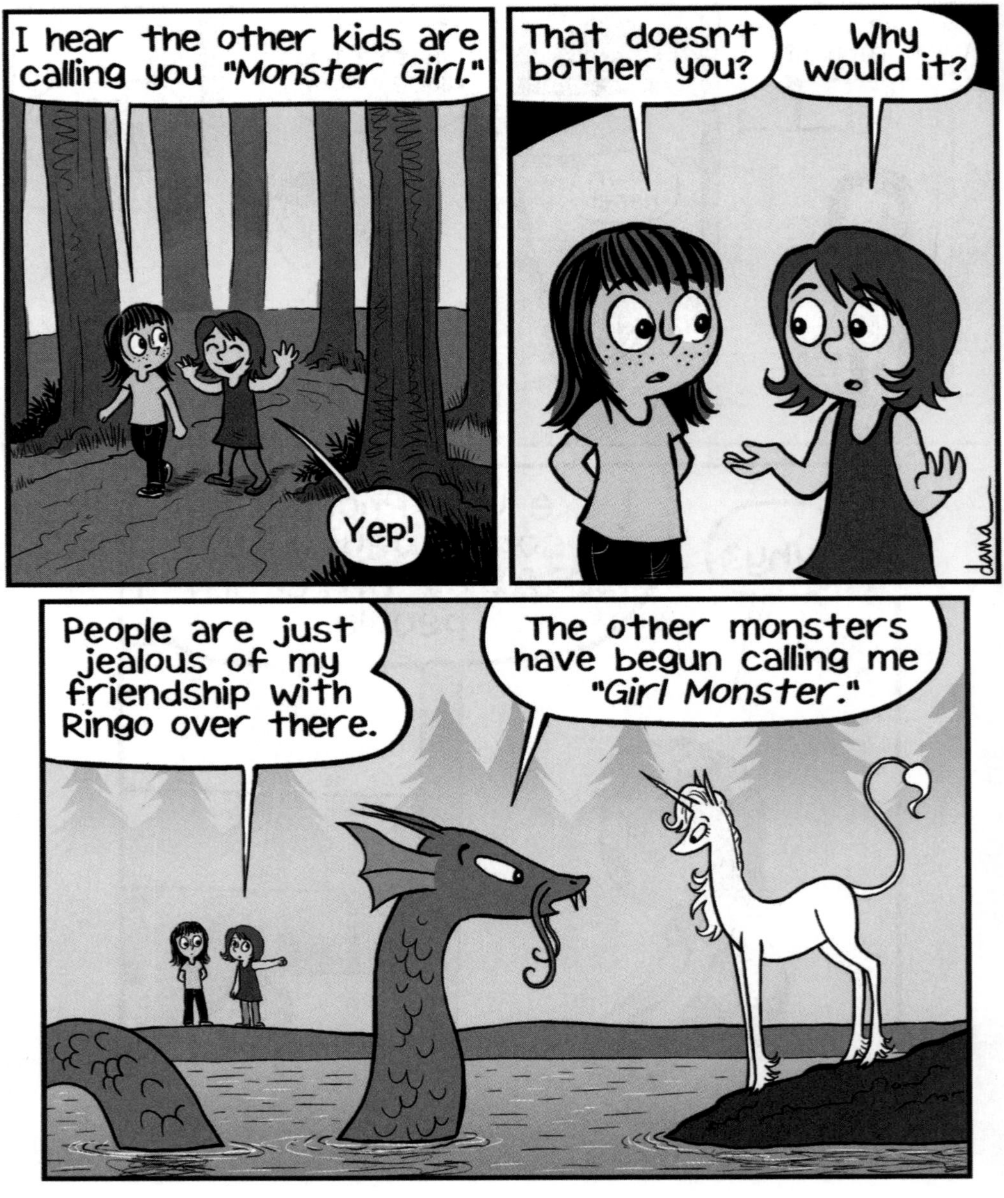
I hear the other kids are calling you *"Monster Girl."*
Yep!
That doesn't bother you?
Why would it?
dana
People are just jealous of my friendship with Ringo over there.
The other monsters have begun calling me *"Girl Monster."*

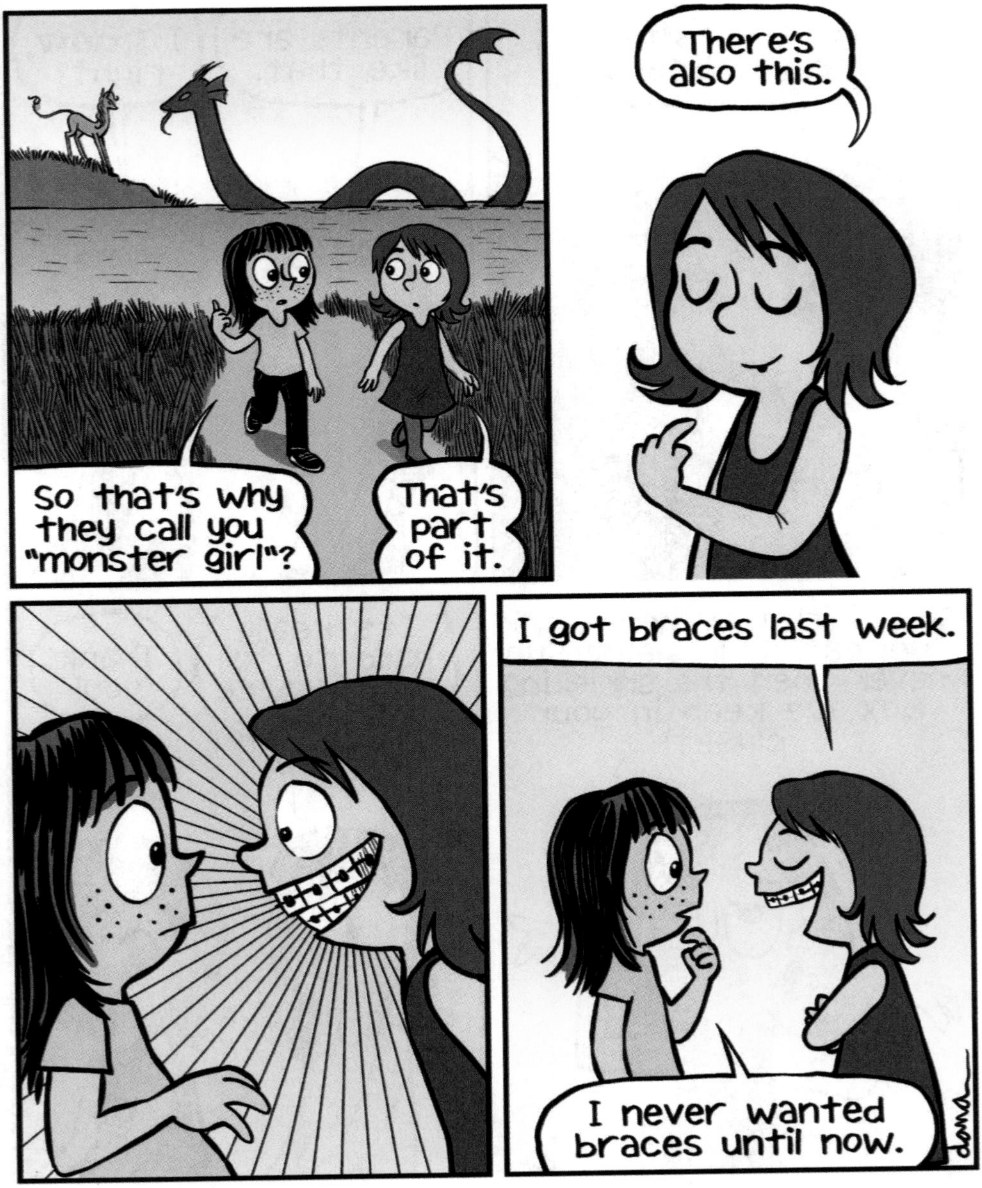
So that's why they call you "monster girl"?
That's part of it.
There's also this.
I got braces last week.
I never wanted braces until now.
dana

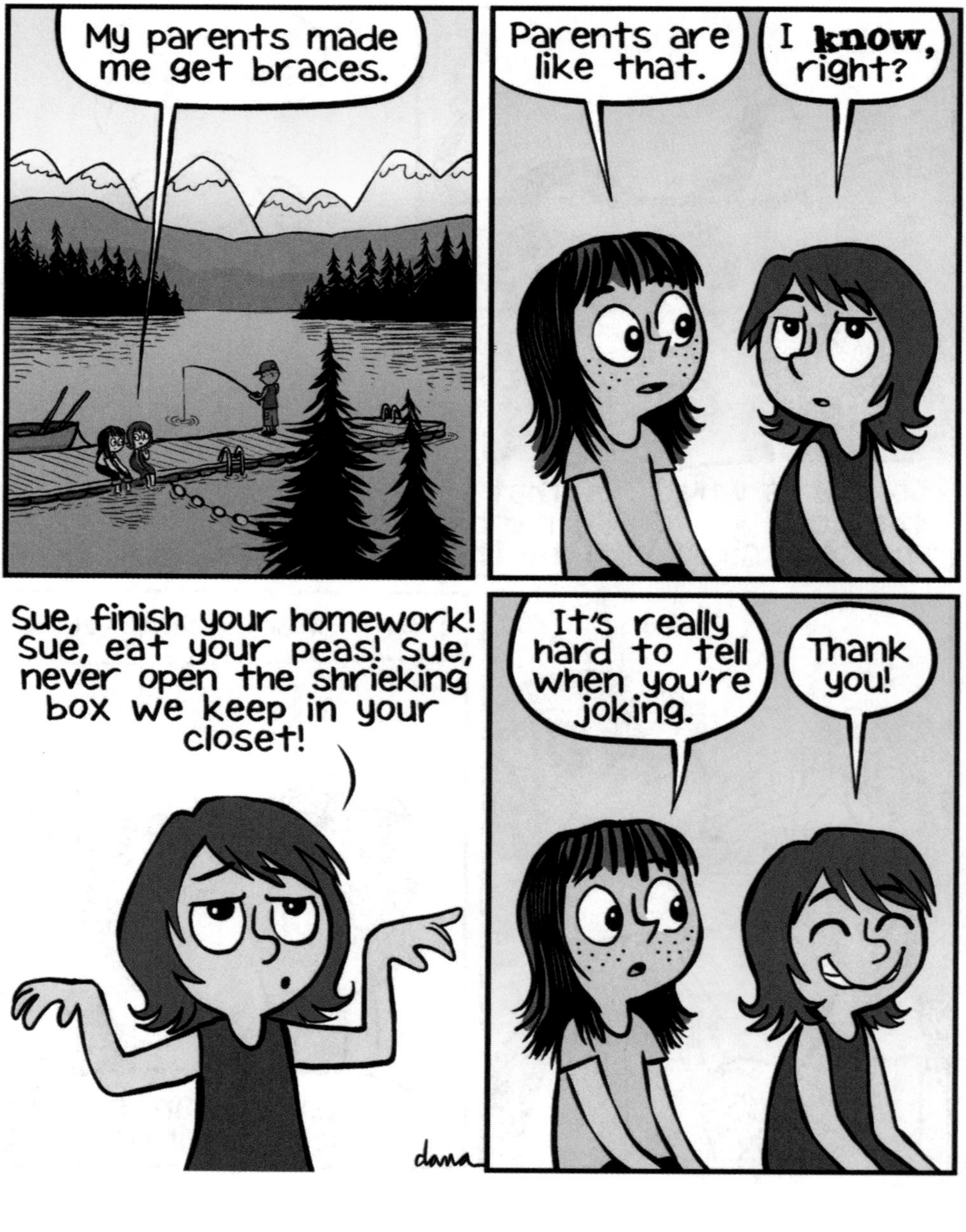
My parents made me get braces.
Parents are like that.
I **know**, right?
Sue, finish your homework! Sue, eat your peas! Sue, never open the shrieking box we keep in your closet!
It's really hard to tell when you're joking.
Thank you!
dana

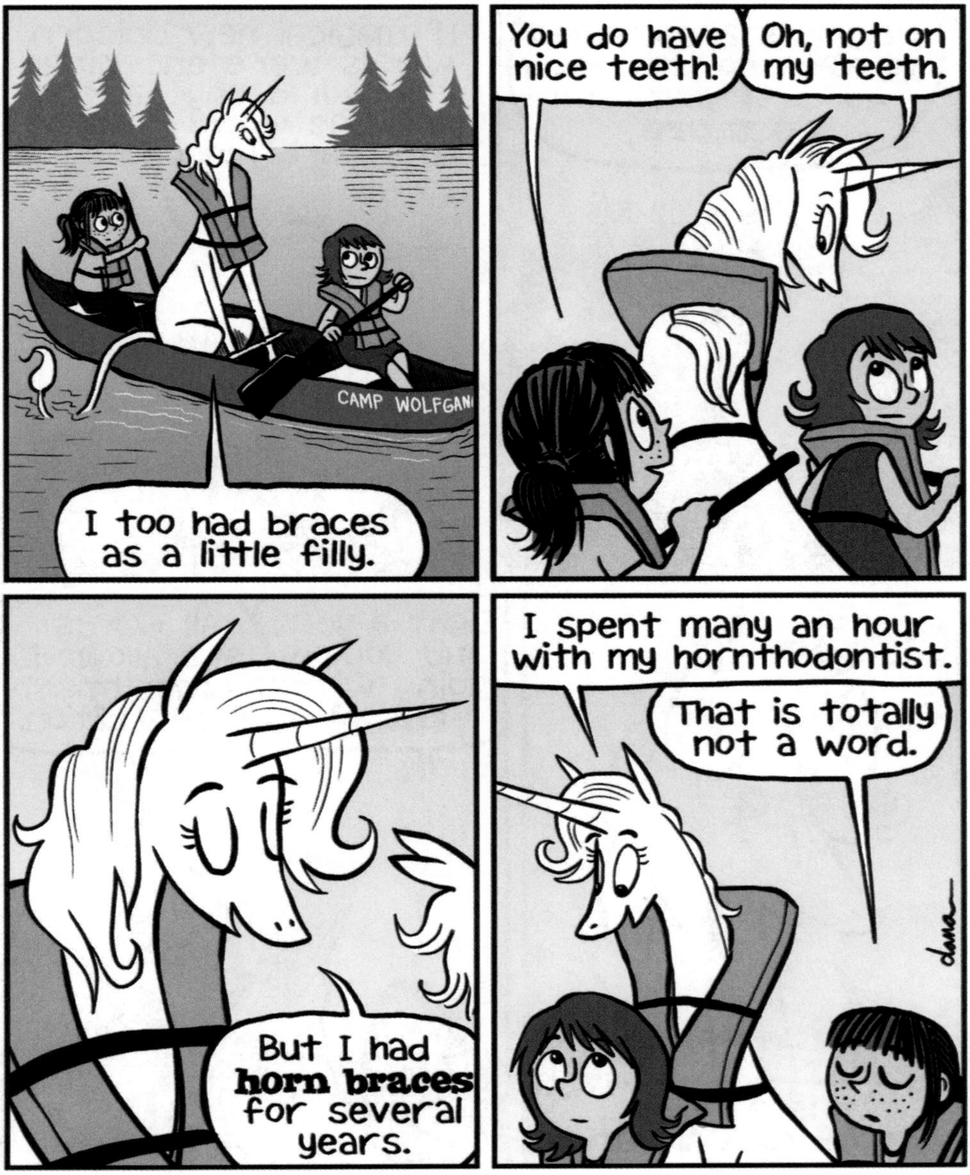
CAMP WOLFGANG
I too had braces as a little filly.
You do have nice teeth!
Oh, not on my teeth.
But I had **horn braces** for several years.
I spent many an hour with my hornthodontist.
That is totally not a word.
dana

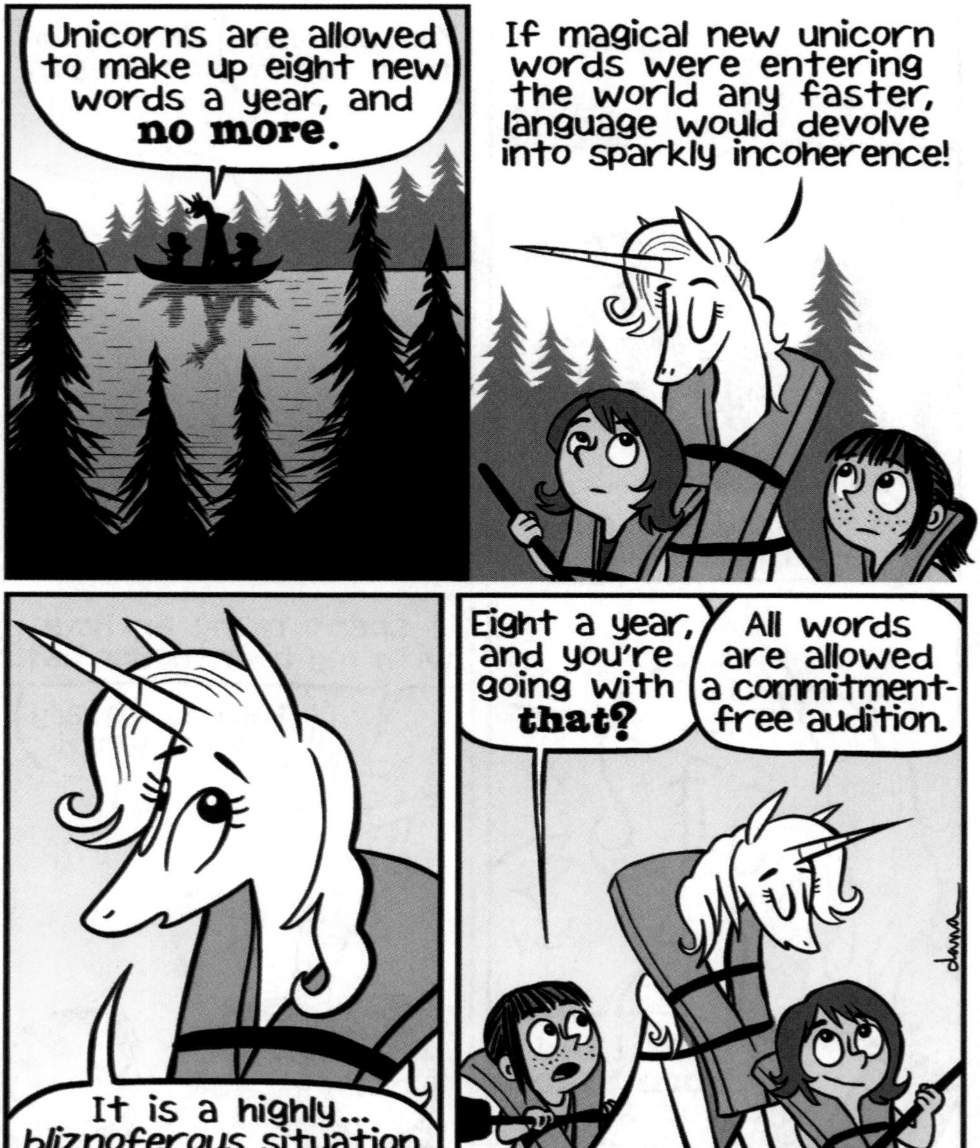

Unicorns are allowed to make up eight new words a year, and **no more**.
If magical new unicorn words were entering the world any faster, language would devolve into sparkly incoherence!
It is a highly... *bliznoferous* situation.
Eight a year, and you're going with **that?**
All words are allowed a commitment-free audition.
dana

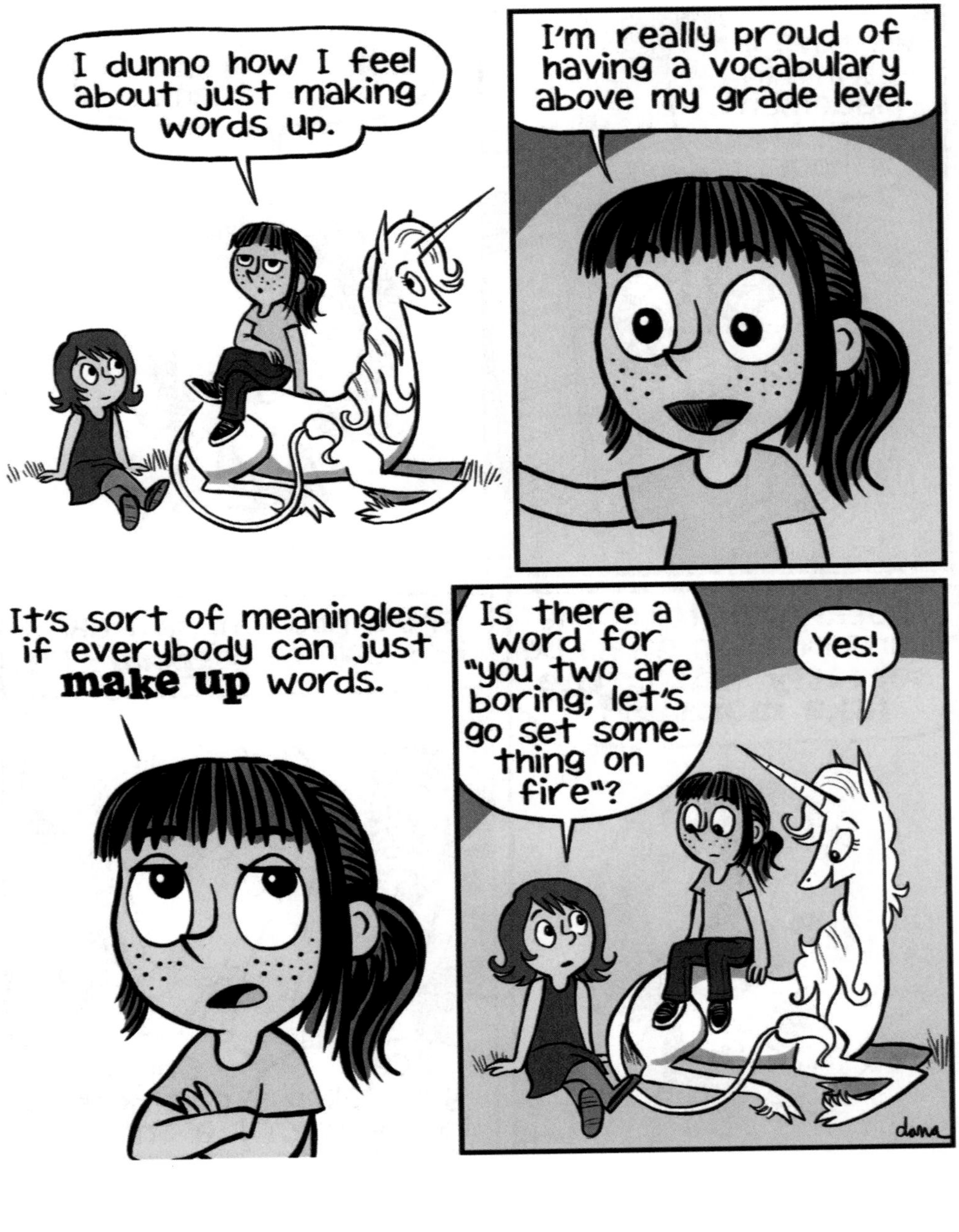
I dunno how I feel about just making words up.
I'm really proud of having a vocabulary above my grade level.
It's sort of meaningless if everybody can just **make up** words.
Is there a word for "you two are boring; let's go set something on fire"?
Yes!
dana

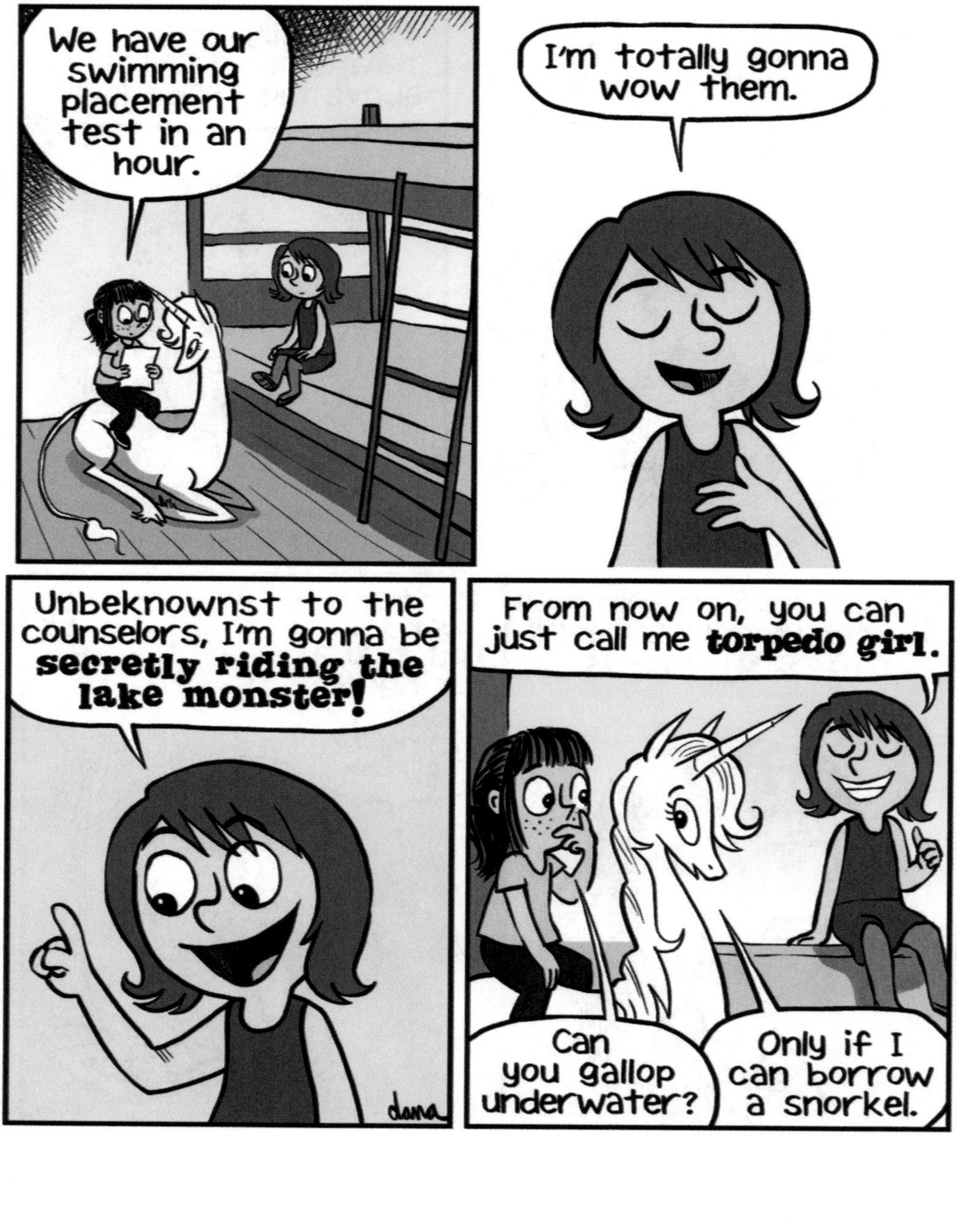
We have our swimming placement test in an hour.
I'm totally gonna wow them.
Unbeknownst to the counselors, I'm gonna be **secretly riding the lake monster!**
From now on, you can just call me **torpedo girl**.
Can you gallop underwater?
Only if I can borrow a snorkel.
dana

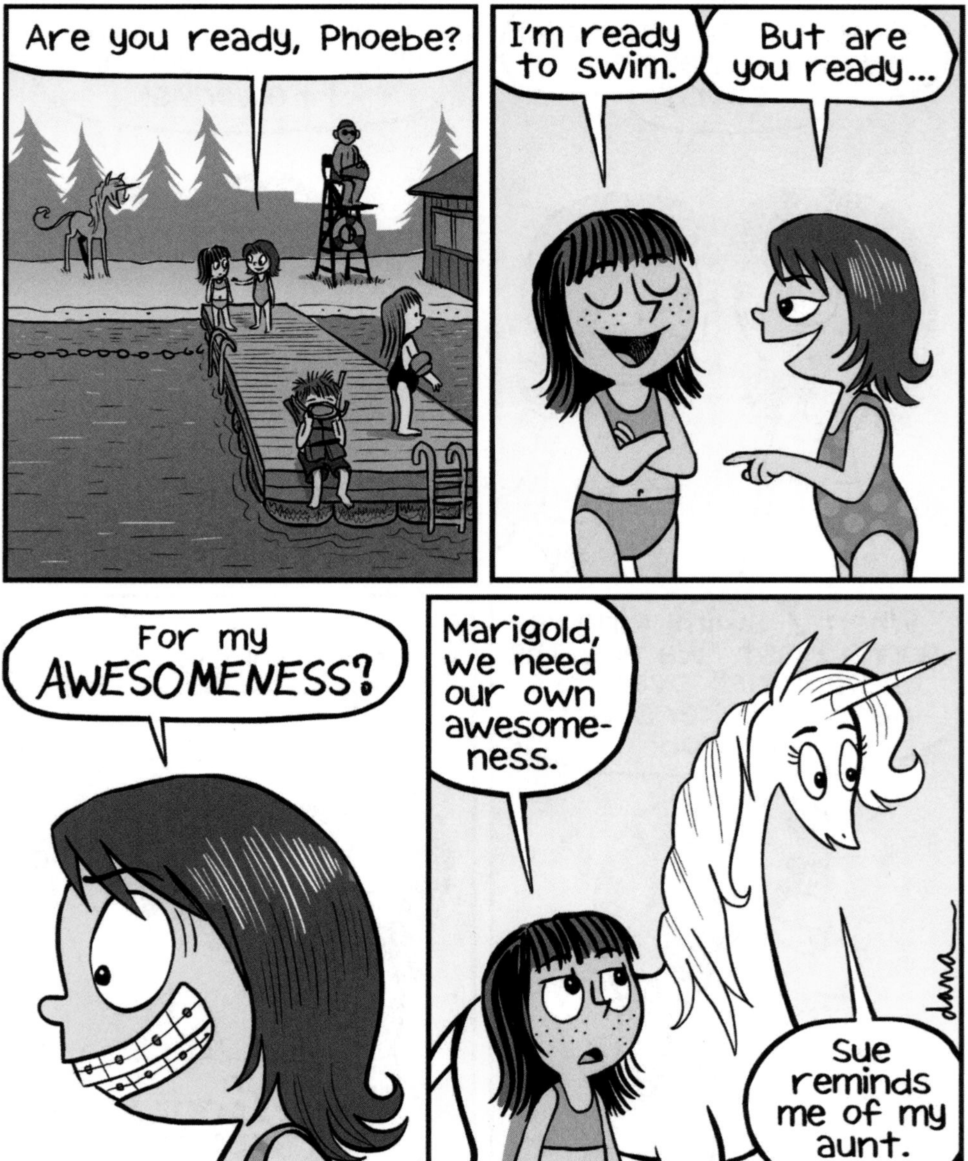
Are you ready, Phoebe?
I'm ready to swim.
But are you ready...
For my AWESOMENESS?
Marigold, we need our own awesomeness.
Sue reminds me of my aunt.
dana

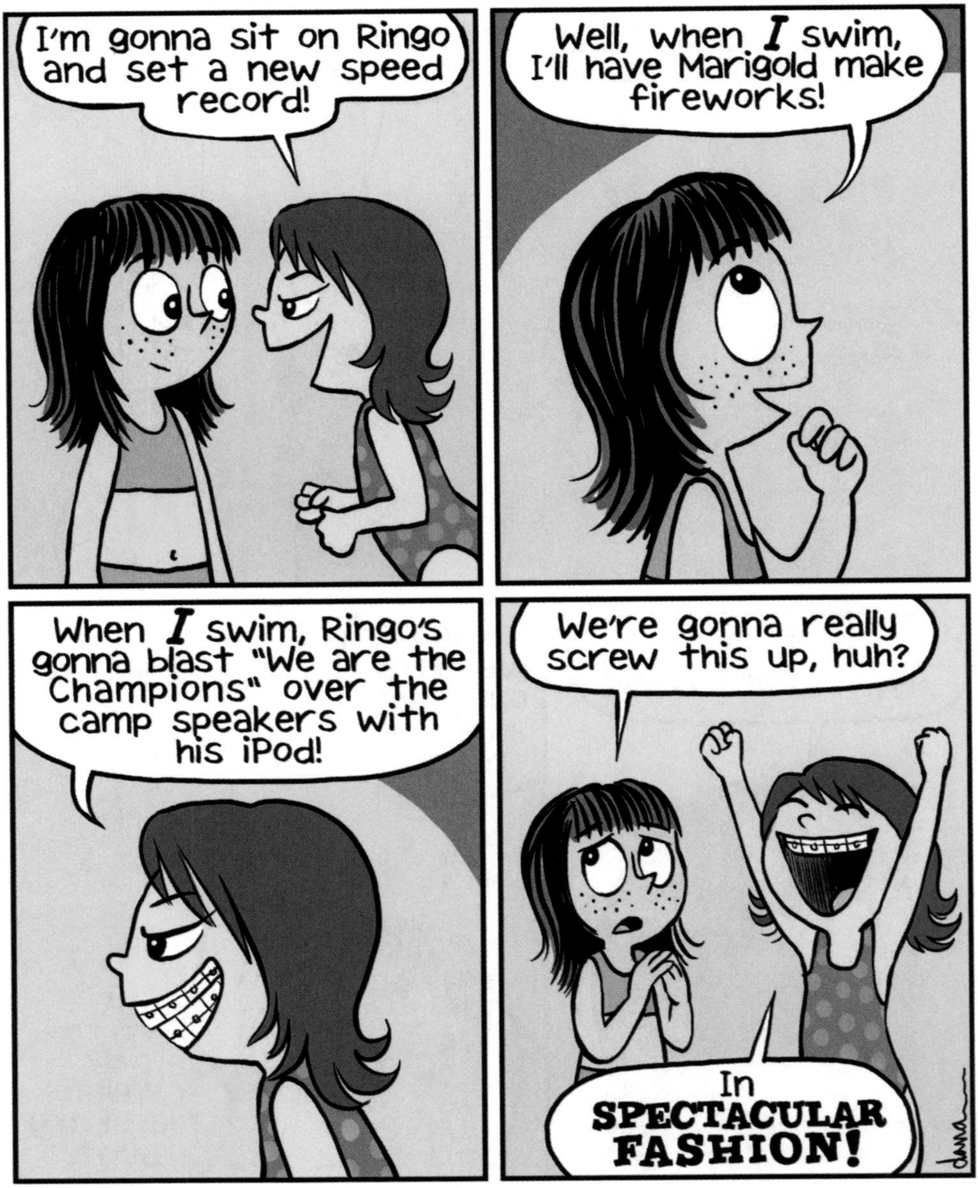
I'm gonna sit on Ringo and set a new speed record!
Well, when I swim, I'll have Marigold make fireworks!
When I swim, Ringo's gonna blast "We are the Champions" over the camp speakers with his iPod!
We're gonna really screw this up, huh?
In SPECTACULAR FASHION!
dana

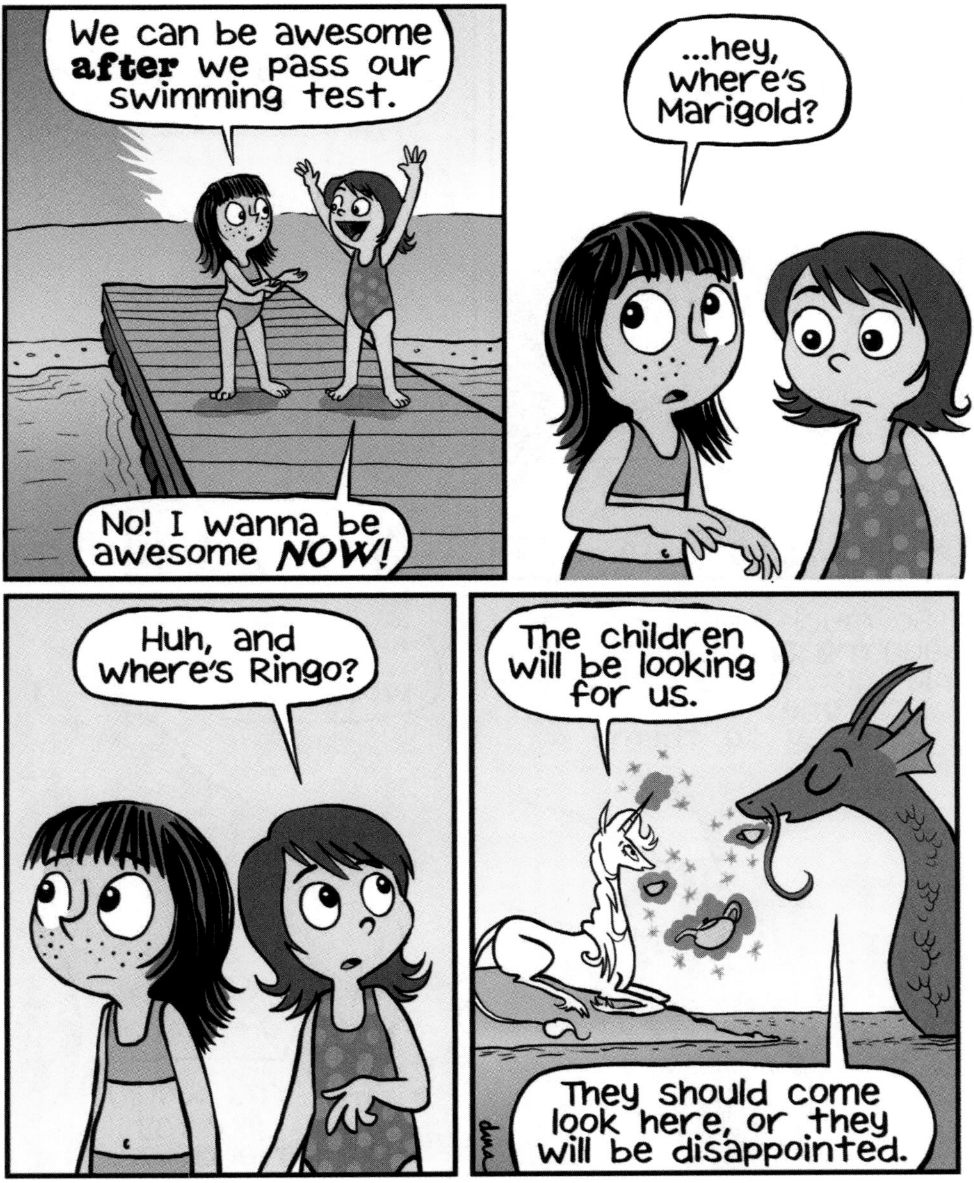
We can be awesome **after** we pass our swimming test.
No! I wanna be awesome *NOW*!
...hey, where's Marigold?
Huh, and where's Ringo?
The children will be looking for us.
They should come look here, or they will be disappointed.

I have lived in this lake a long time.

When the camp children arrived, I was **not** pleased.

So much splashing and laughing and bad clarinet playing...there was really only one thing I could say to them.

dana

"RAR," I would say.

You would like my friend Todd.

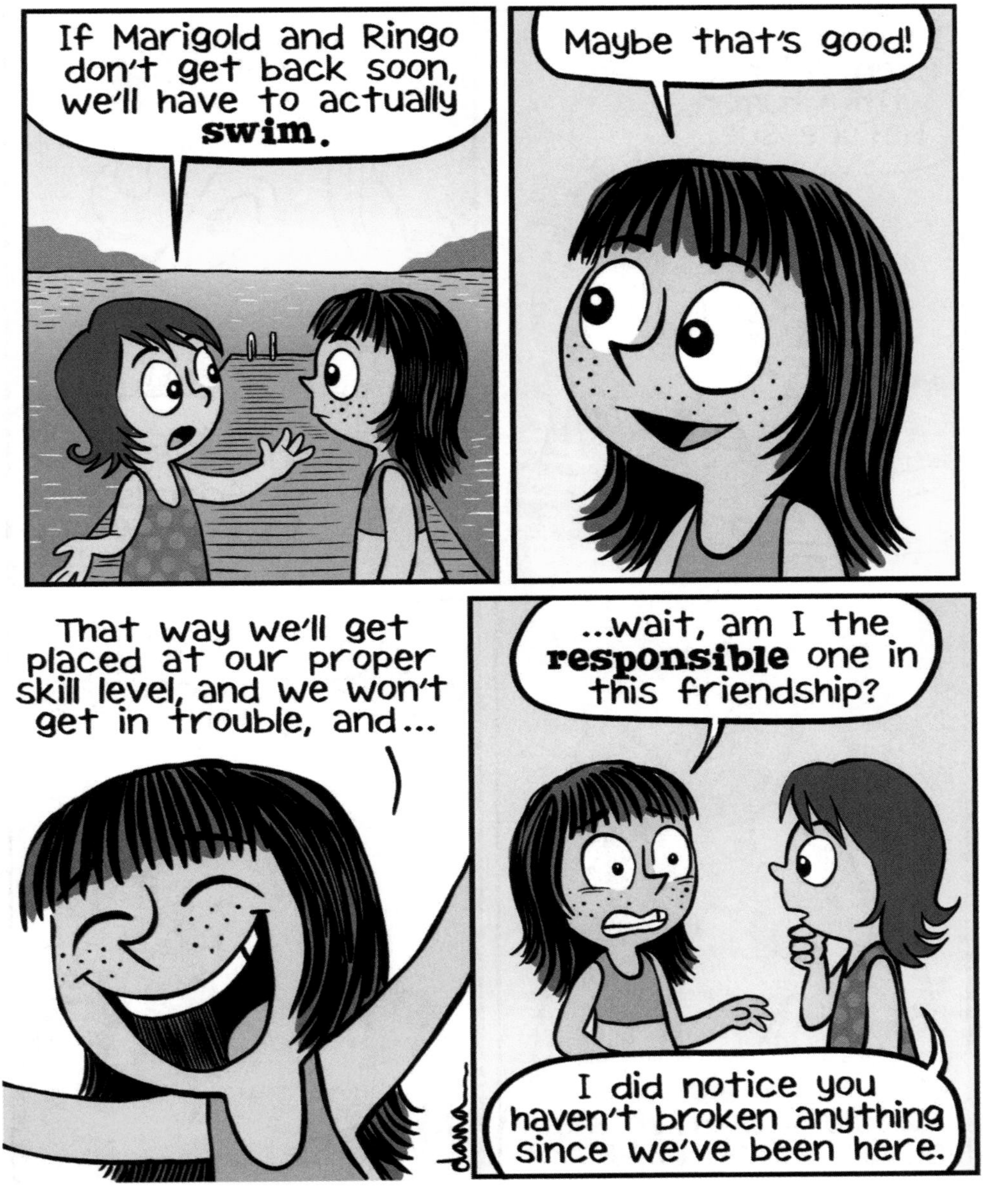
If Marigold and Ringo don't get back soon, we'll have to actually **swim**.
Maybe that's good!
That way we'll get placed at our proper skill level, and we won't get in trouble, and...
...wait, am I the **responsible** one in this friendship?
I did notice you haven't broken anything since we've been here.
dana

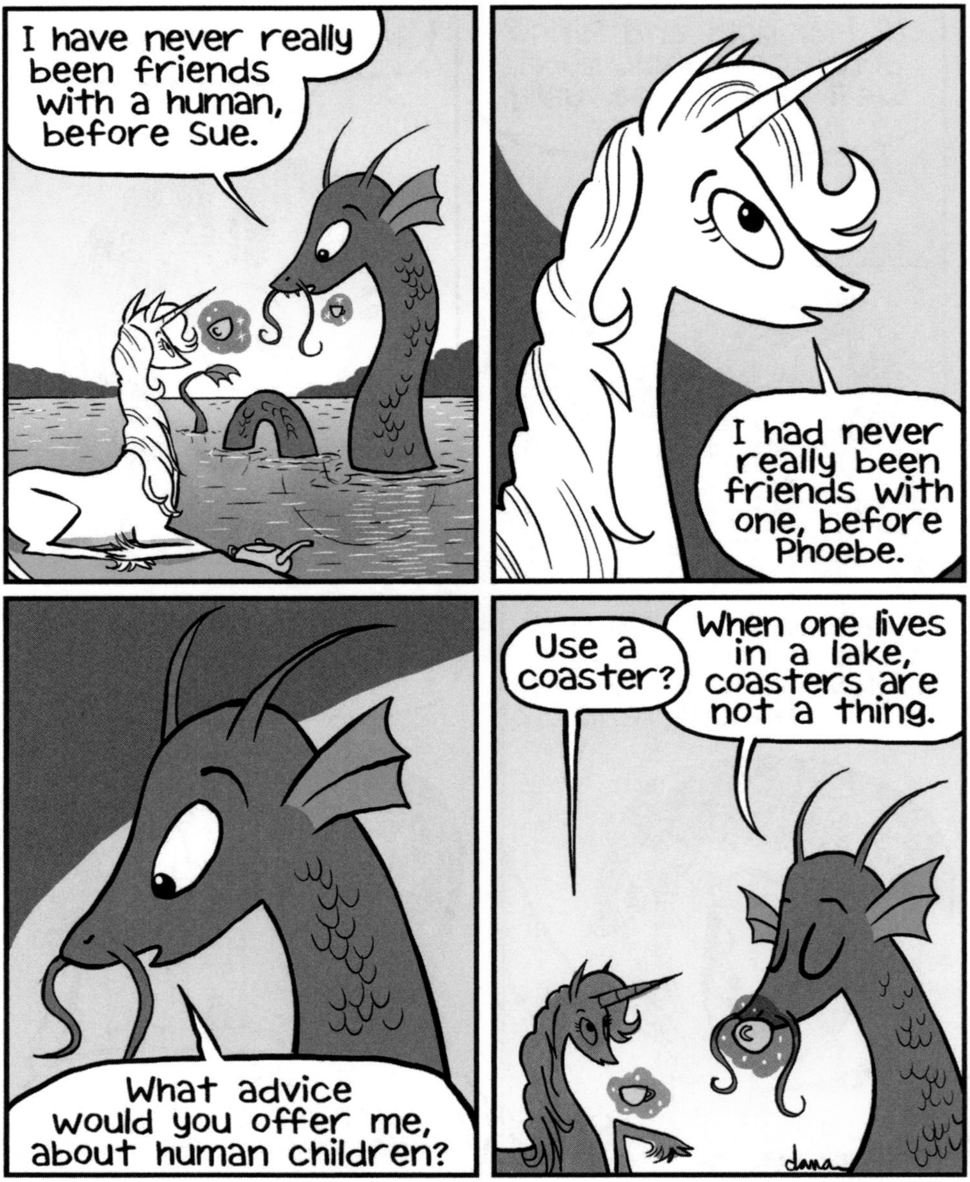
I have never really been friends with a human, before Sue.
I had never really been friends with one, before Phoebe.
What advice would you offer me, about human children?
Use a coaster?
When one lives in a lake, coasters are not a thing.
dana

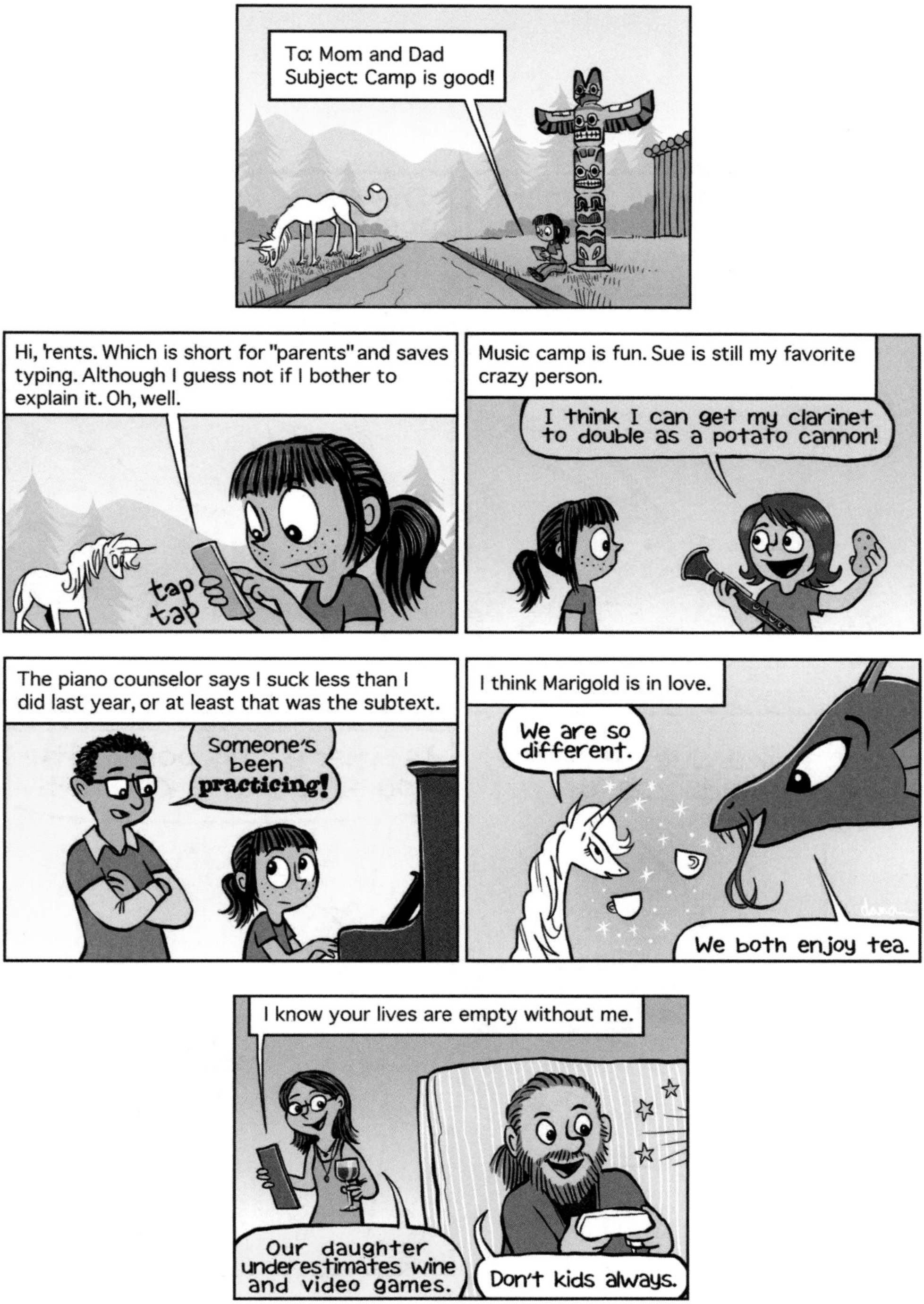
To: Mom and Dad
Subject: Camp is good!
Hi, 'rents. Which is short for "parents" and saves typing. Although I guess not if I bother to explain it. Oh, well.
tap tap
Music camp is fun. Sue is still my favorite crazy person.
I think I can get my clarinet to double as a potato cannon!
The piano counselor says I suck less than I did last year, or at least that was the subtext.
Someone's been **practicing!**
I think Marigold is in love.
We are so different.
We both enjoy tea.
I know your lives are empty without me.
Our daughter underestimates wine and video games.
Don't kids always.

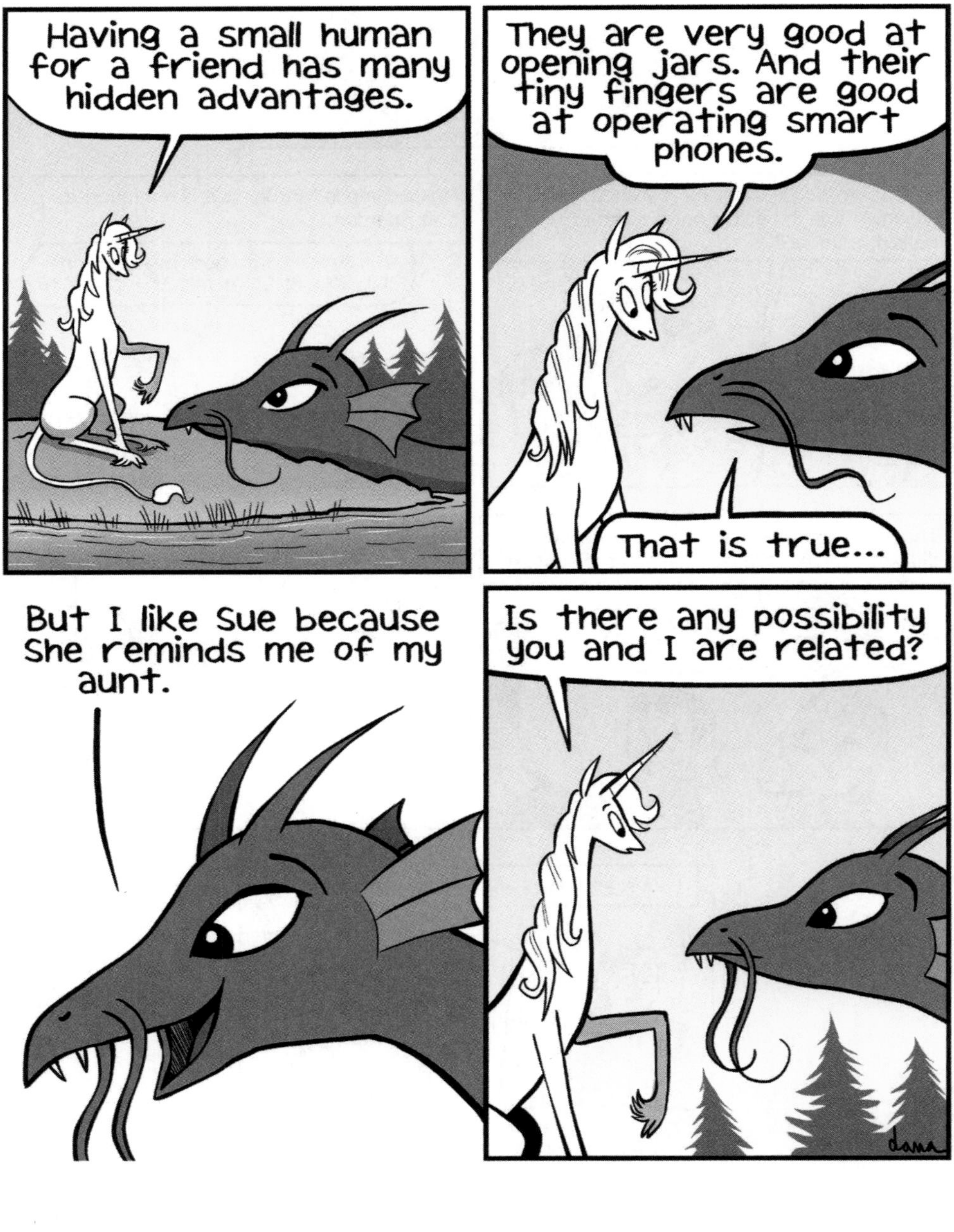
Having a small human for a friend has many hidden advantages.
They are very good at opening jars. And their tiny fingers are good at operating smart phones.
That is true...
But I like Sue because she reminds me of my aunt.
Is there any possibility you and I are related?
dana

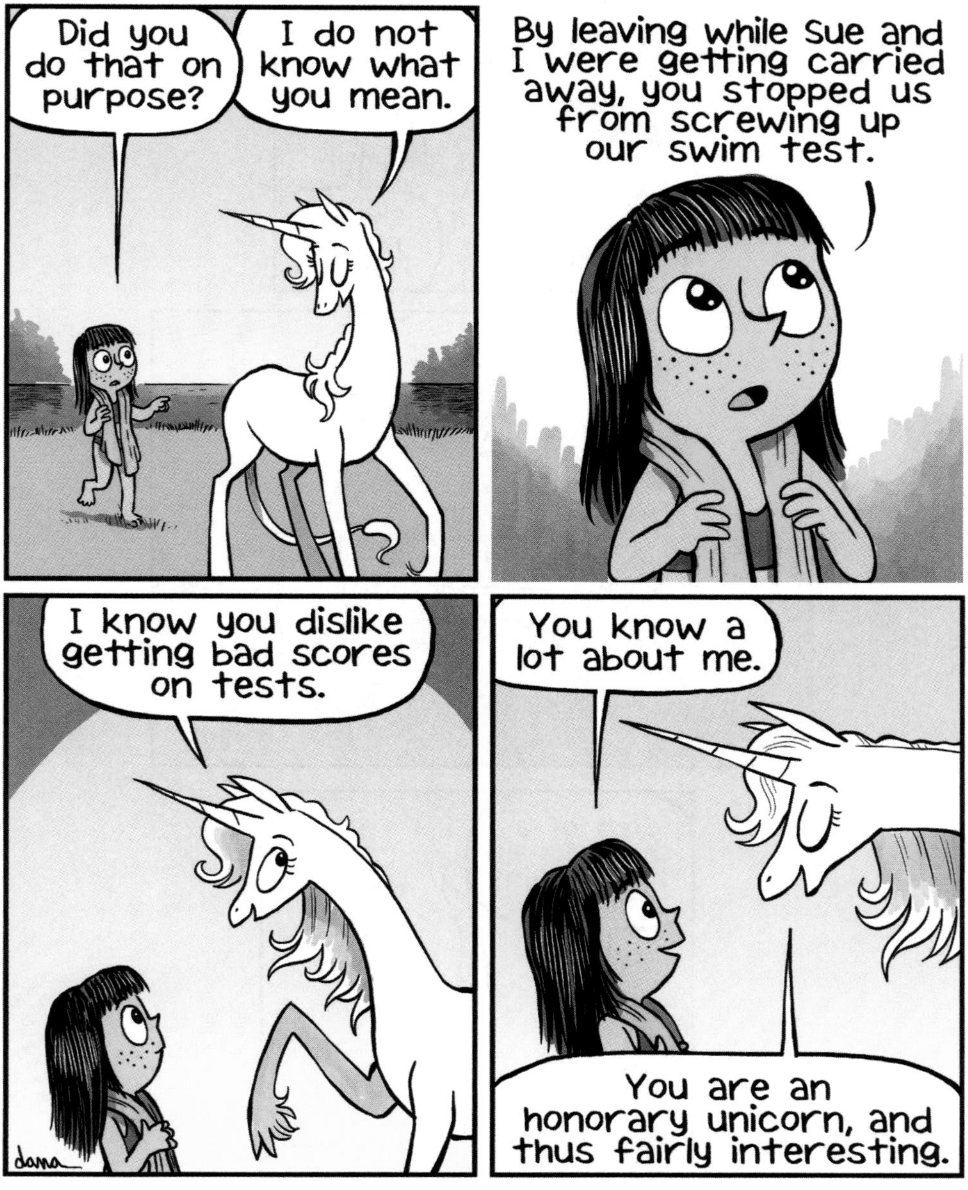
Did you do that on purpose?
I do not know what you mean.
By leaving while Sue and I were getting carried away, you stopped us from screwing up our swim test.
I know you dislike getting bad scores on tests.
You know a lot about me.
You are an honorary unicorn, and thus fairly interesting.
dana

Sue was disappointed she didn't get to show off.
She will not be for long.
Sort of a shame I play the friggin' piano.
Ringo does like a challenge.

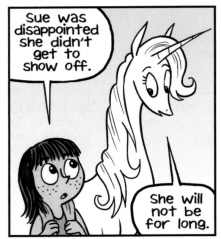

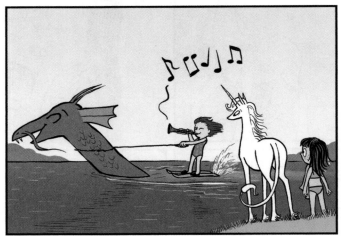

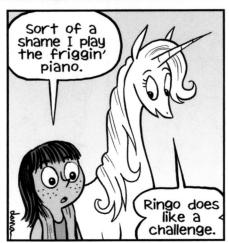

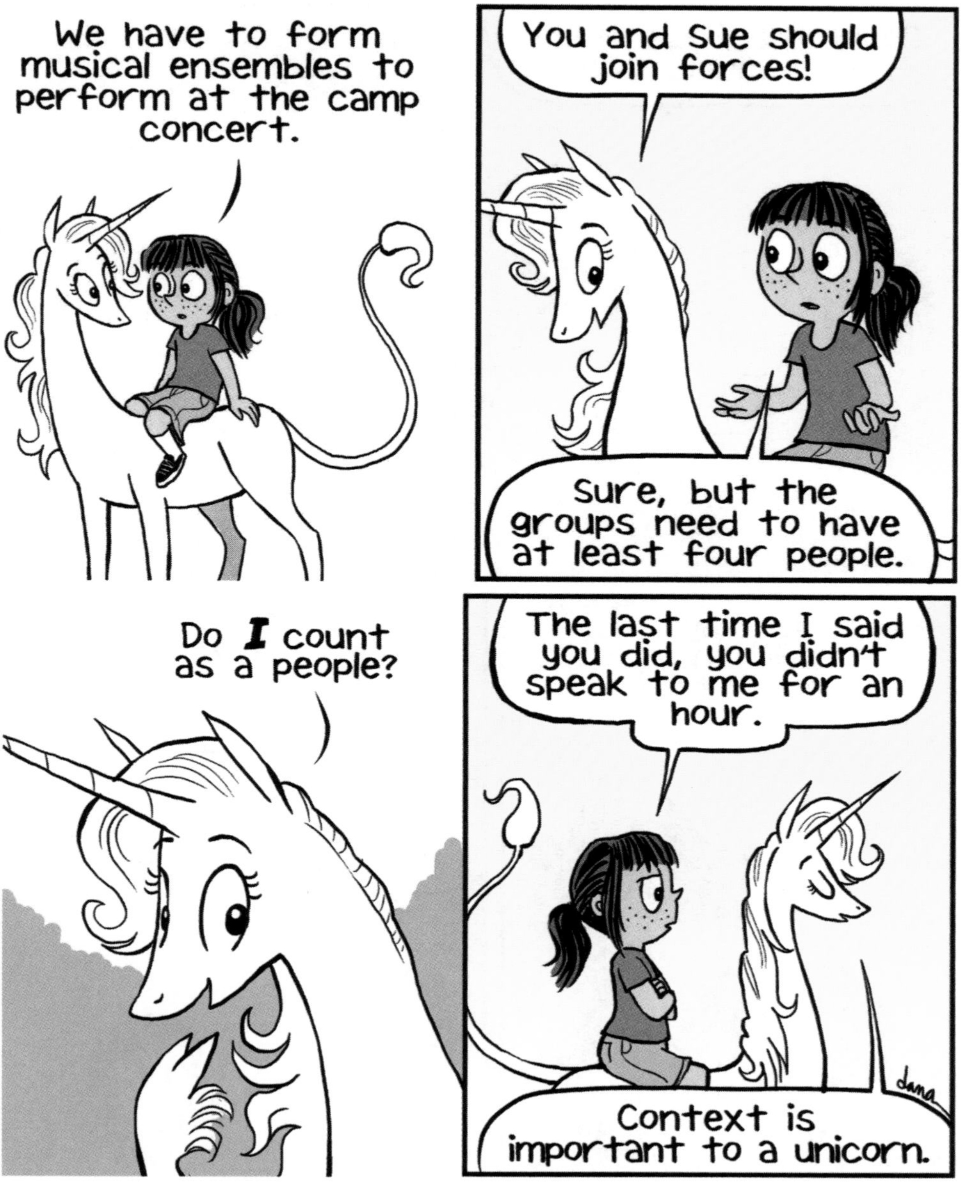
We have to form musical ensembles to perform at the camp concert.
You and Sue should join forces!
Sure, but the groups need to have at least four people.
Do I count as a people?
The last time I said you did, you didn't speak to me for an hour.
dana
Context is important to a unicorn.

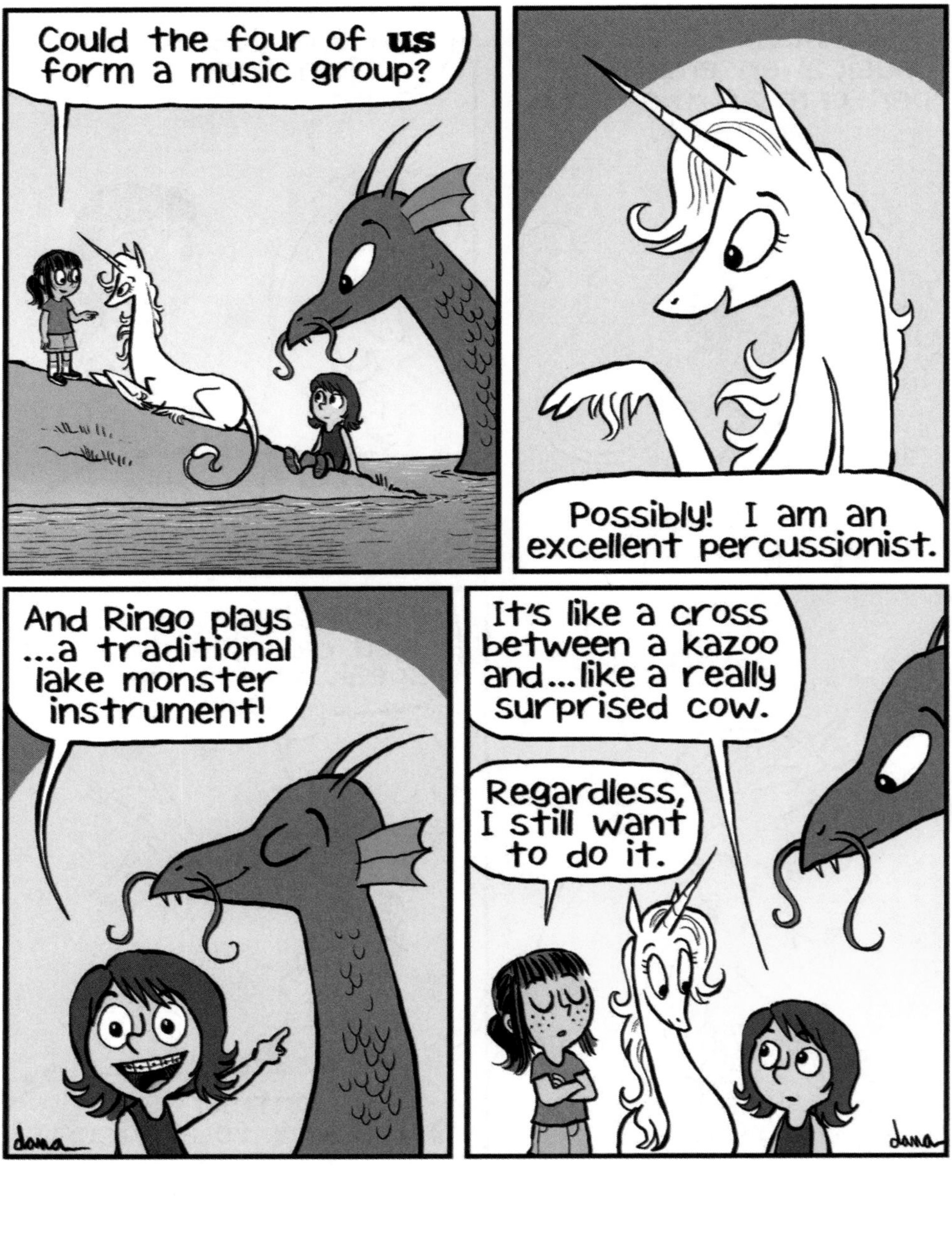
Could the four of **us** form a music group?
Possibly! I am an excellent percussionist.
And Ringo plays ...a traditional lake monster instrument!
It's like a cross between a kazoo and...like a really surprised cow.
Regardless, I still want to do it.
dana
dana

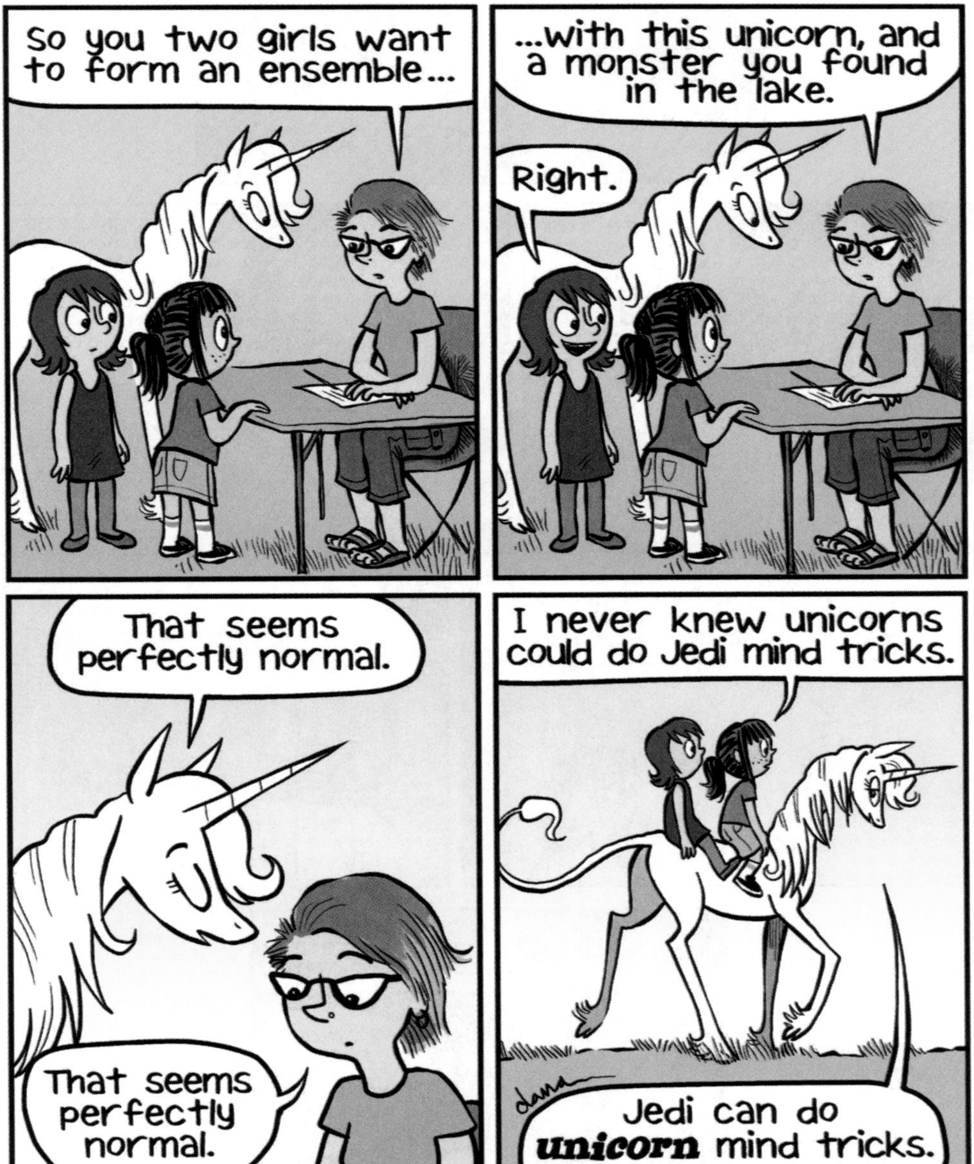
So you two girls want to form an ensemble...
...with this unicorn, and a monster you found in the lake.
Right.
That seems perfectly normal.
That seems perfectly normal.
I never knew unicorns could do Jedi mind tricks.
Jedi can do **unicorn** mind tricks.
dana

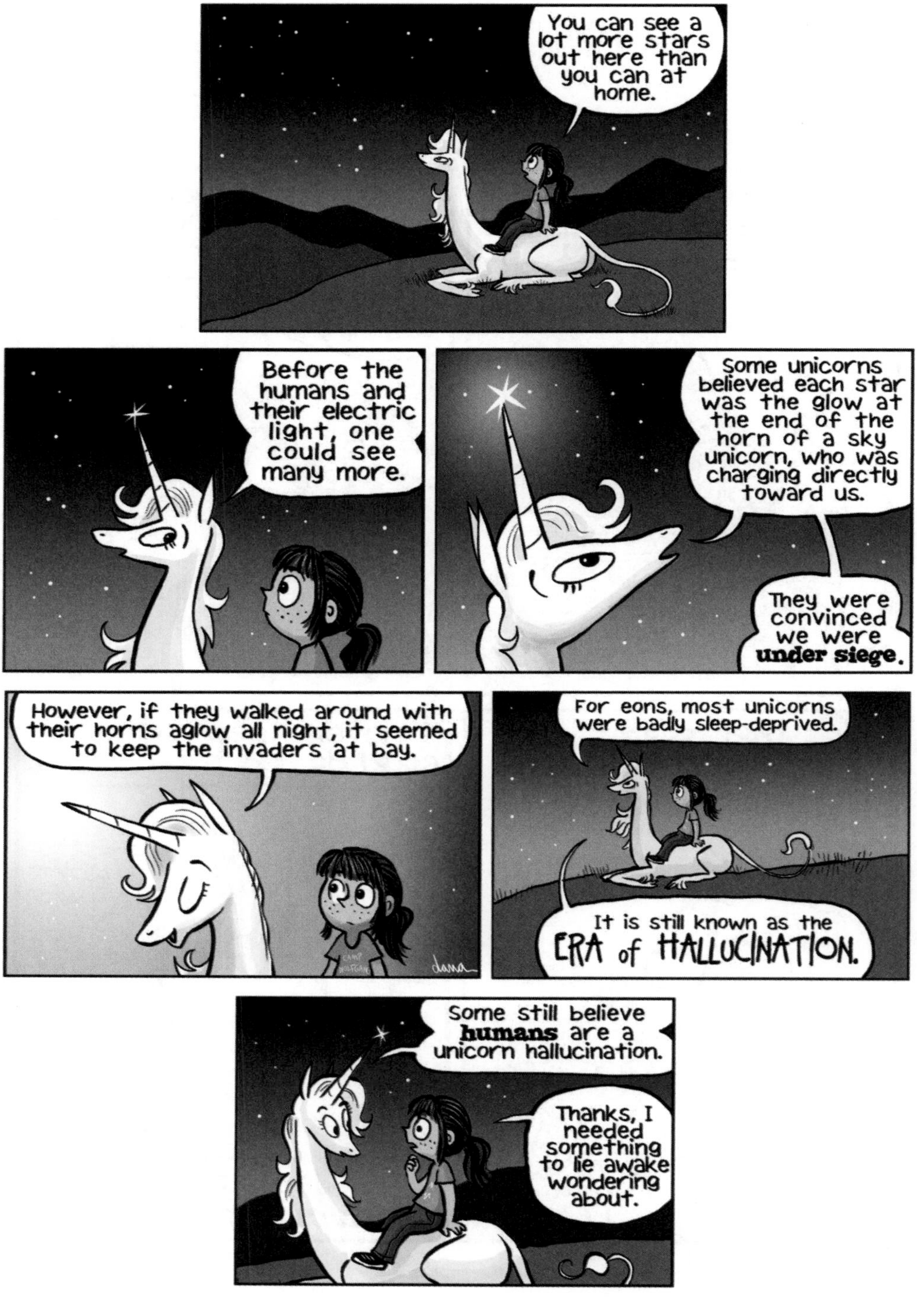

You can see a lot more stars out here than you can at home.
Before the humans and their electric light, one could see many more.
Some unicorns believed each star was the glow at the end of the horn of a sky unicorn, who was charging directly toward us.
They were convinced we were **under siege**.
However, if they walked around with their horns aglow all night, it seemed to keep the invaders at bay.
CAMP WOLFGAN
dana
For eons, most unicorns were badly sleep-deprived.
It is still known as the
ERA of HALLUCINATION.
Some still believe **humans** are a unicorn hallucination.
Thanks, I needed something to lie awake wondering about.

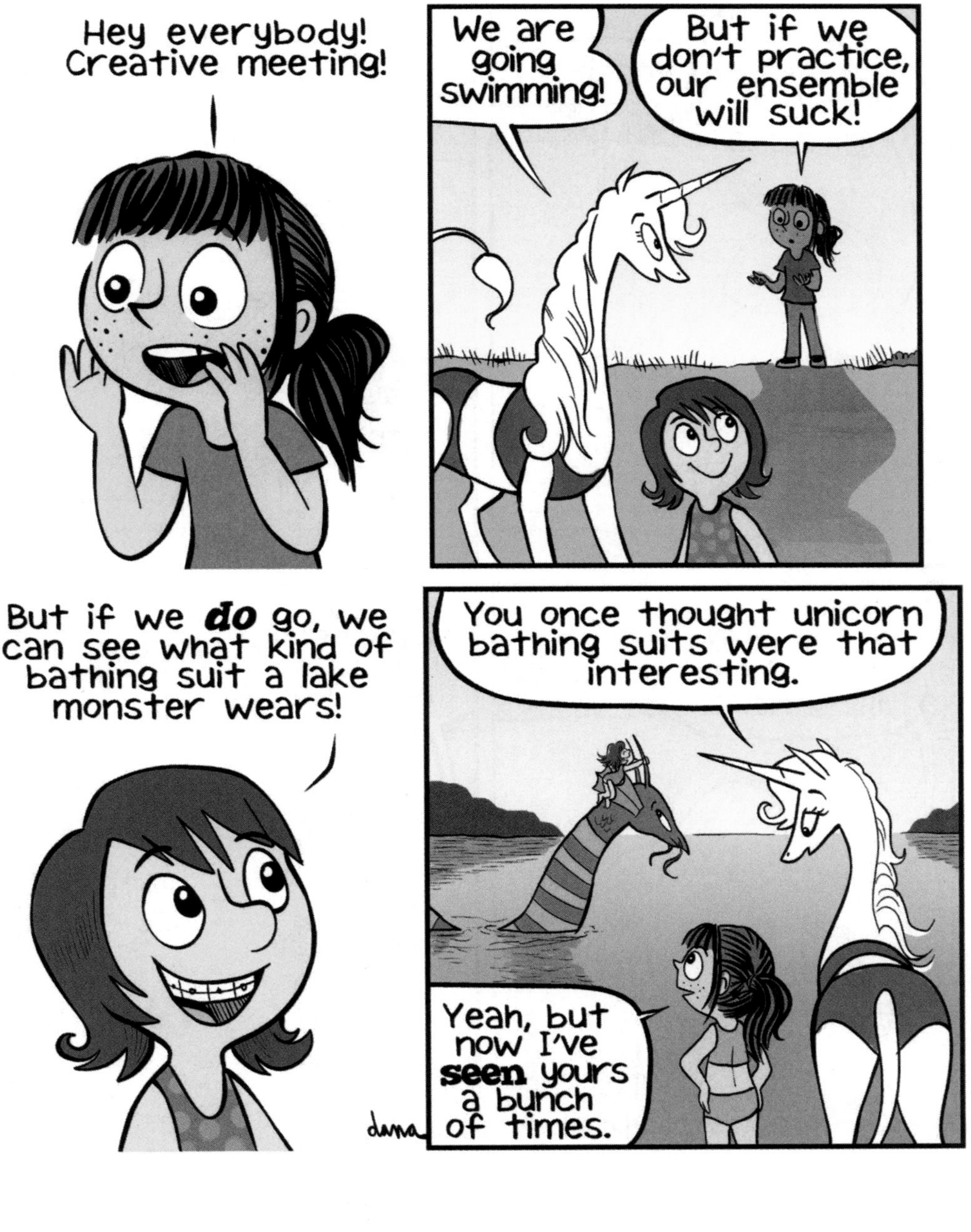
Hey everybody! Creative meeting!
We are going swimming!
But if we don't practice, our ensemble will suck!
But if we **do** go, we can see what kind of bathing suit a lake monster wears!
You once thought unicorn bathing suits were that interesting.
Yeah, but now I've **seen** yours a bunch of times.
dana

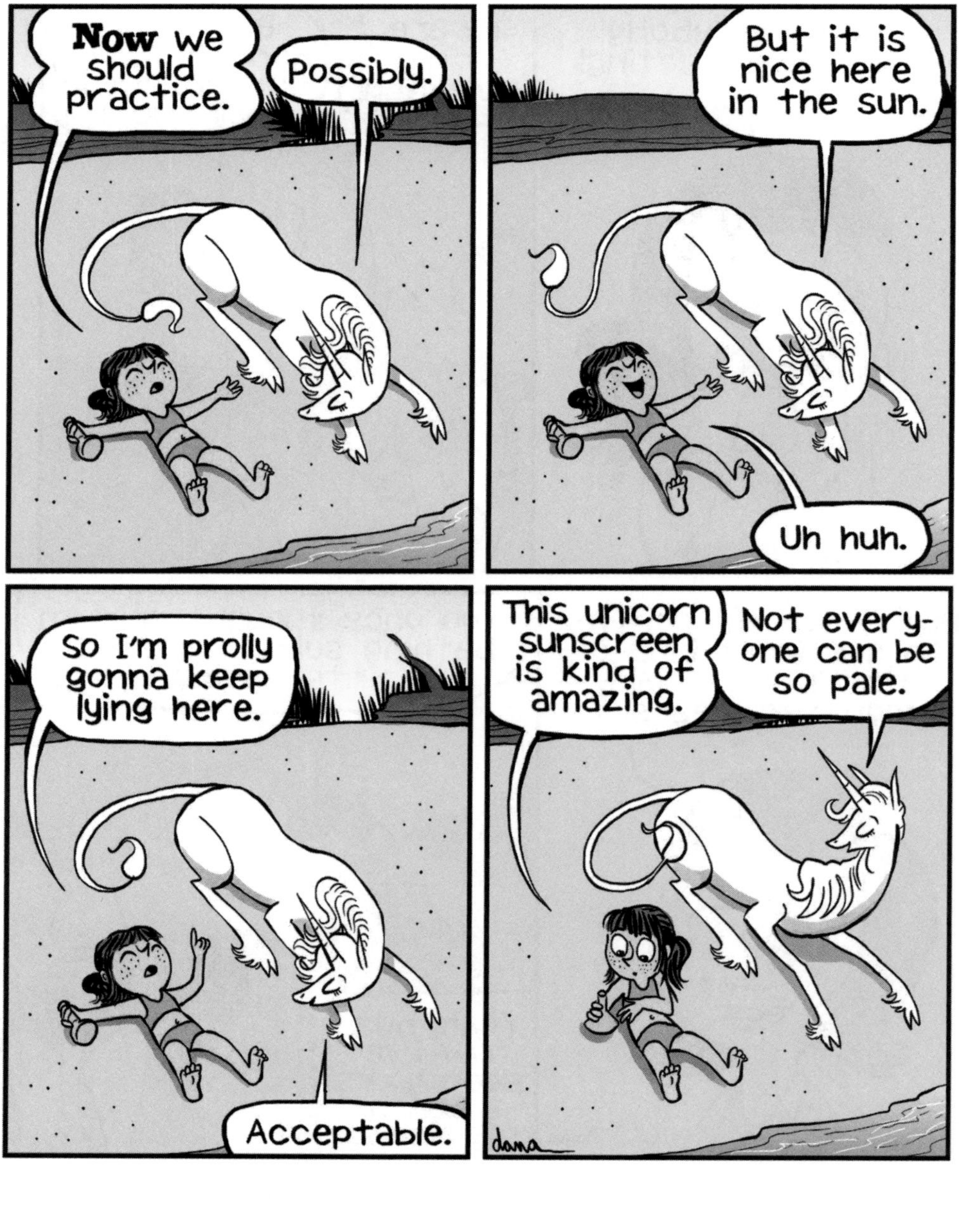
Now we should practice.
Possibly.
But it is nice here in the sun.
Uh huh.
So I'm prolly gonna keep lying here.
Acceptable.
This unicorn sunscreen is kind of amazing.
Not every-one can be so pale.
dana

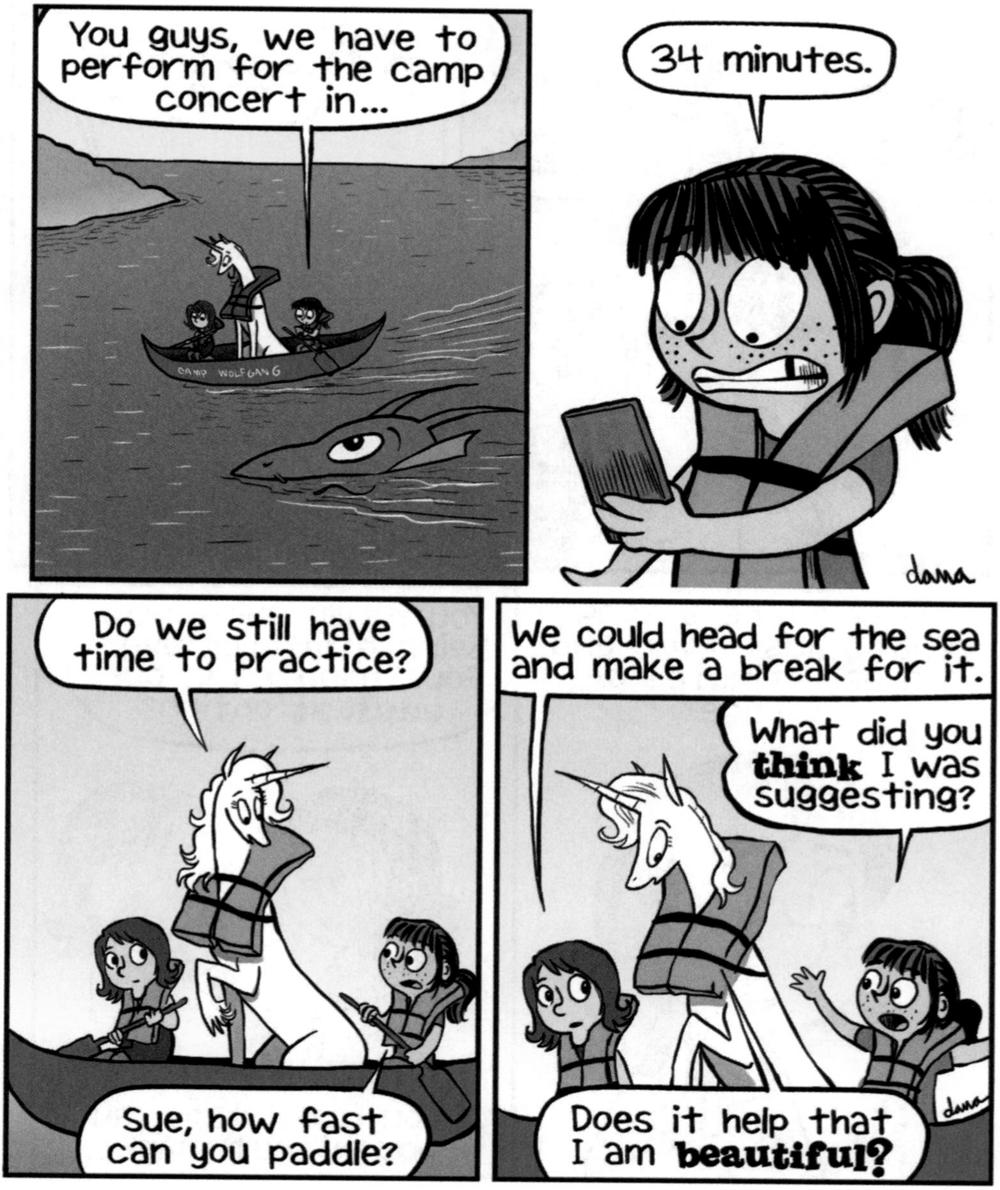
You guys, we have to perform for the camp concert in...
CAMP WOLFGANG
34 minutes.
dana
Do we still have time to practice?
Sue, how fast can you paddle?
We could head for the sea and make a break for it.
What did you **think** I was suggesting?
Does it help that I am **beautiful?**
dana

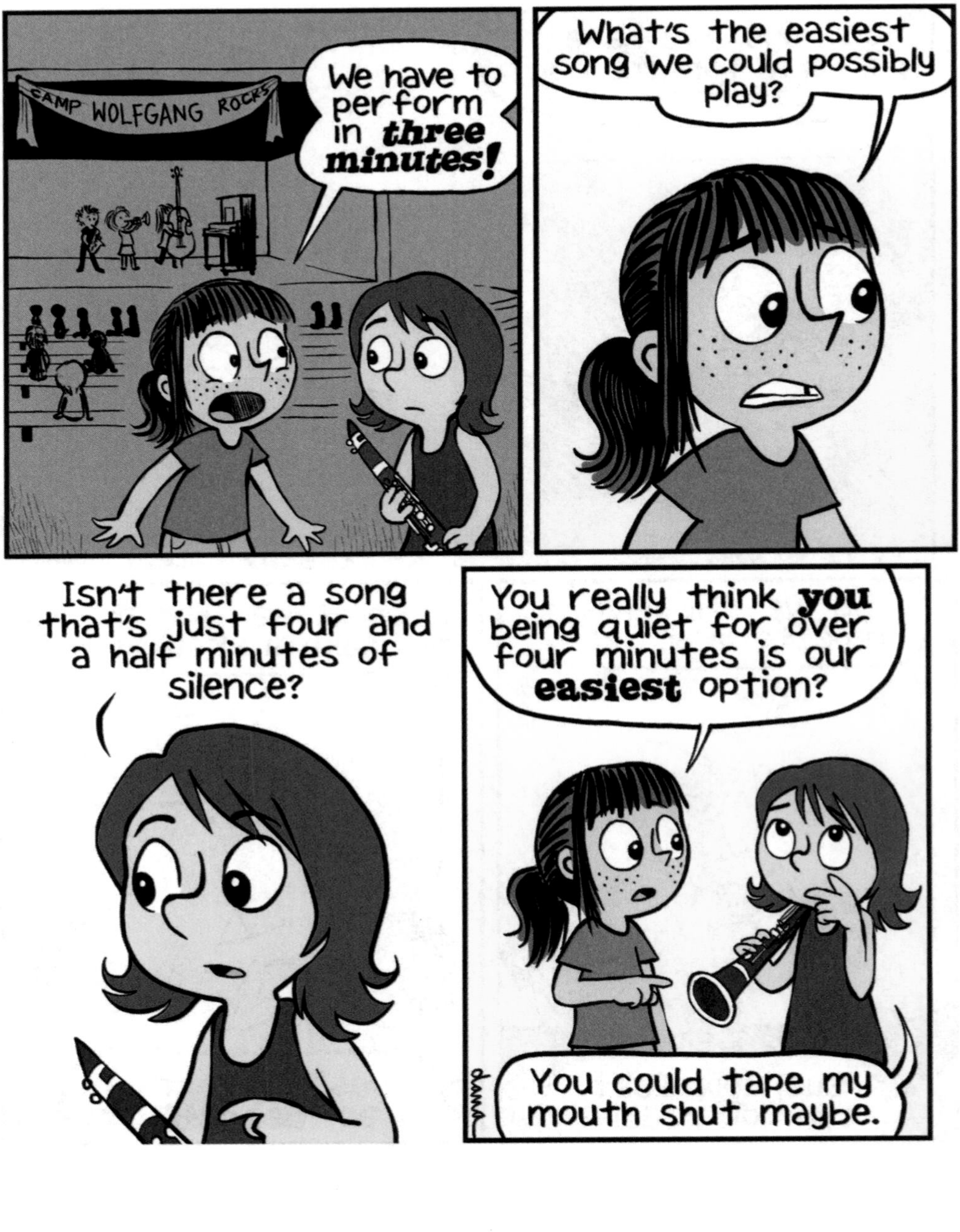
CAMP WOLFGANG ROCKS
We have to perform in **three minutes!**
What's the easiest song we could possibly play?
Isn't there a song that's just four and a half minutes of silence?
You really think **you** being quiet for over four minutes is our **easiest** option?
You could tape my mouth shut maybe.
dana

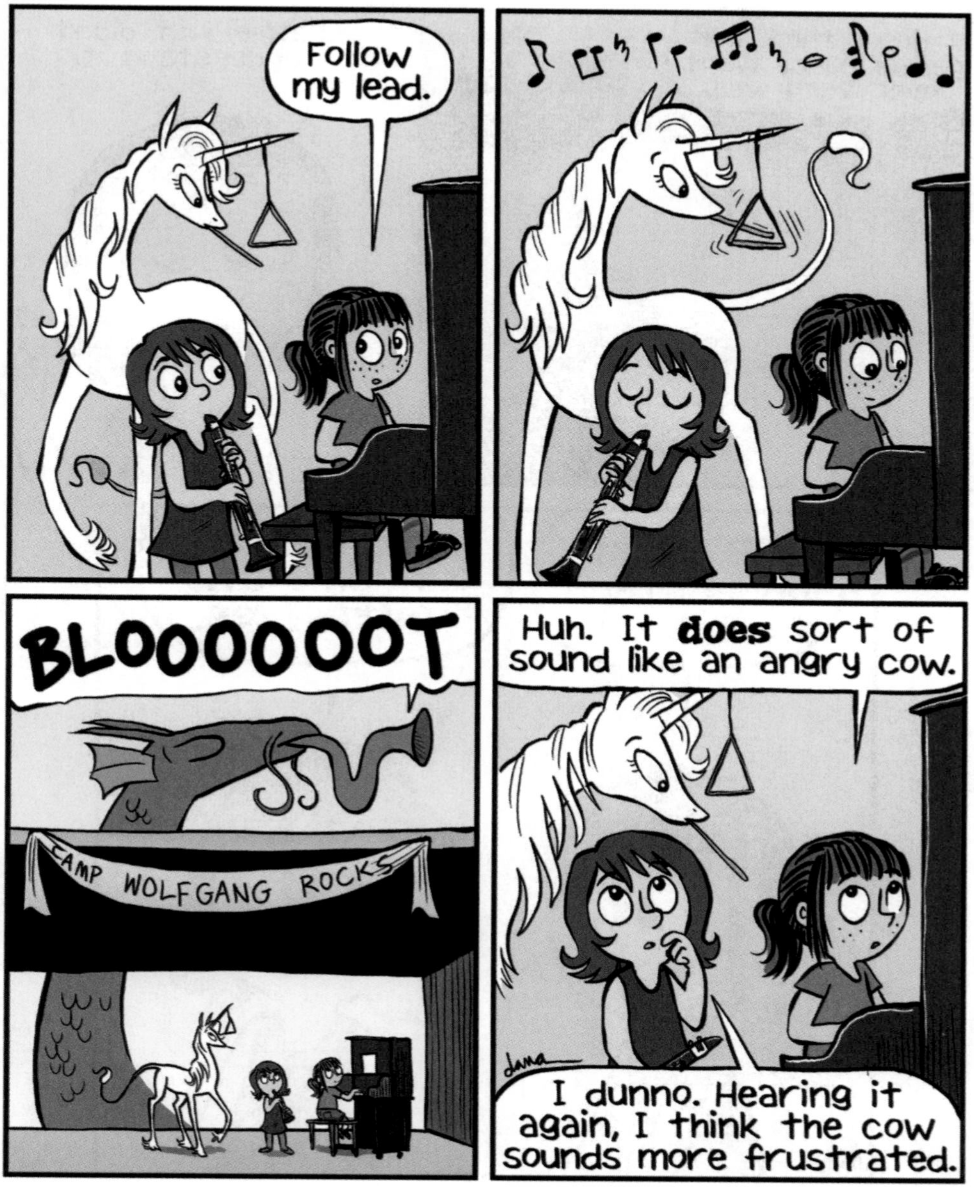
Follow my lead.
BLOOOOOOT
CAMP WOLFGANG ROCKS
Huh. It **does** sort of sound like an angry cow.
I dunno. Hearing it again, I think the cow sounds more frustrated.

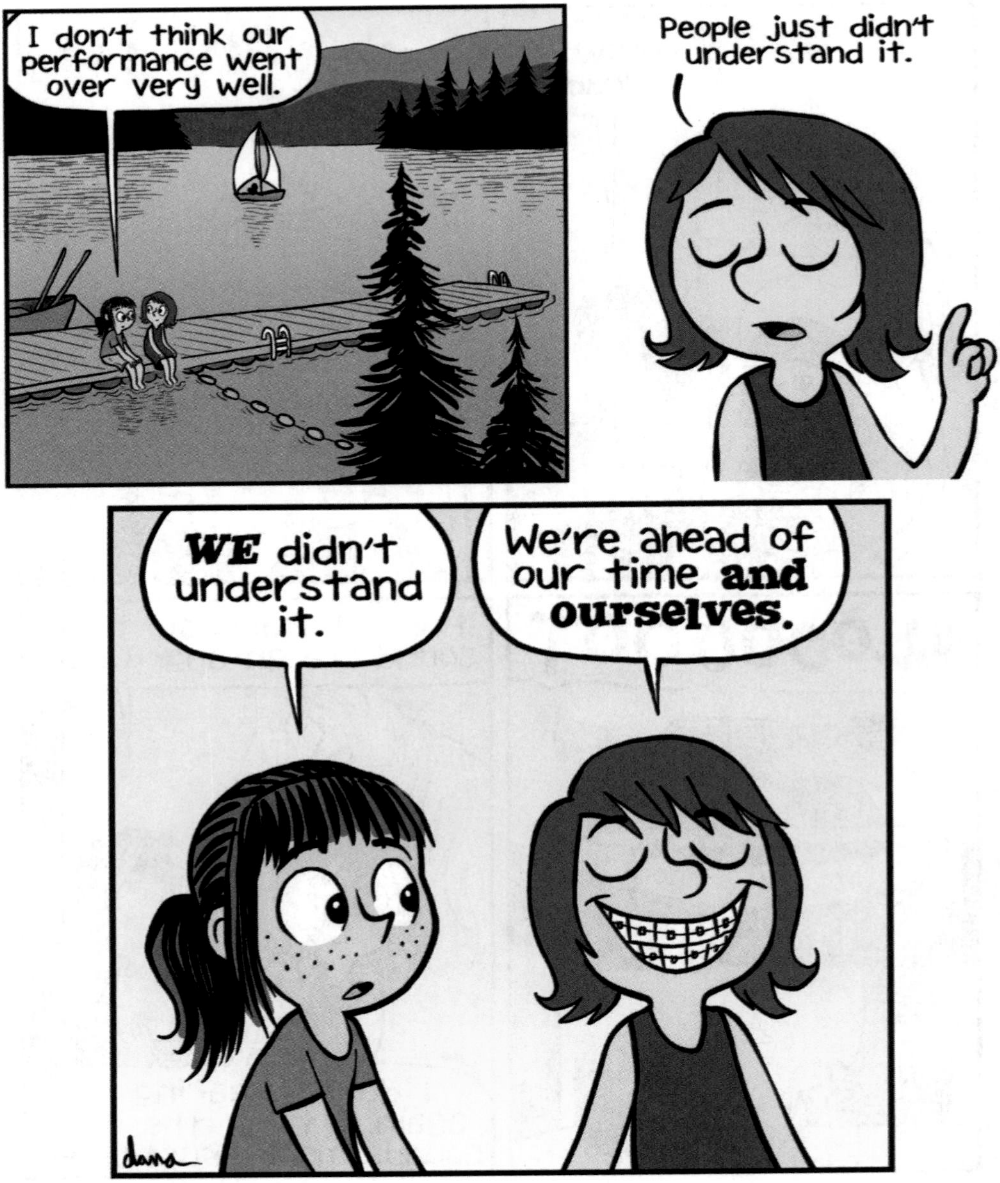
I don't think our performance went over very well.
People just didn't understand it.
WE didn't understand it.
We're ahead of our time **and ourselves.**
dana

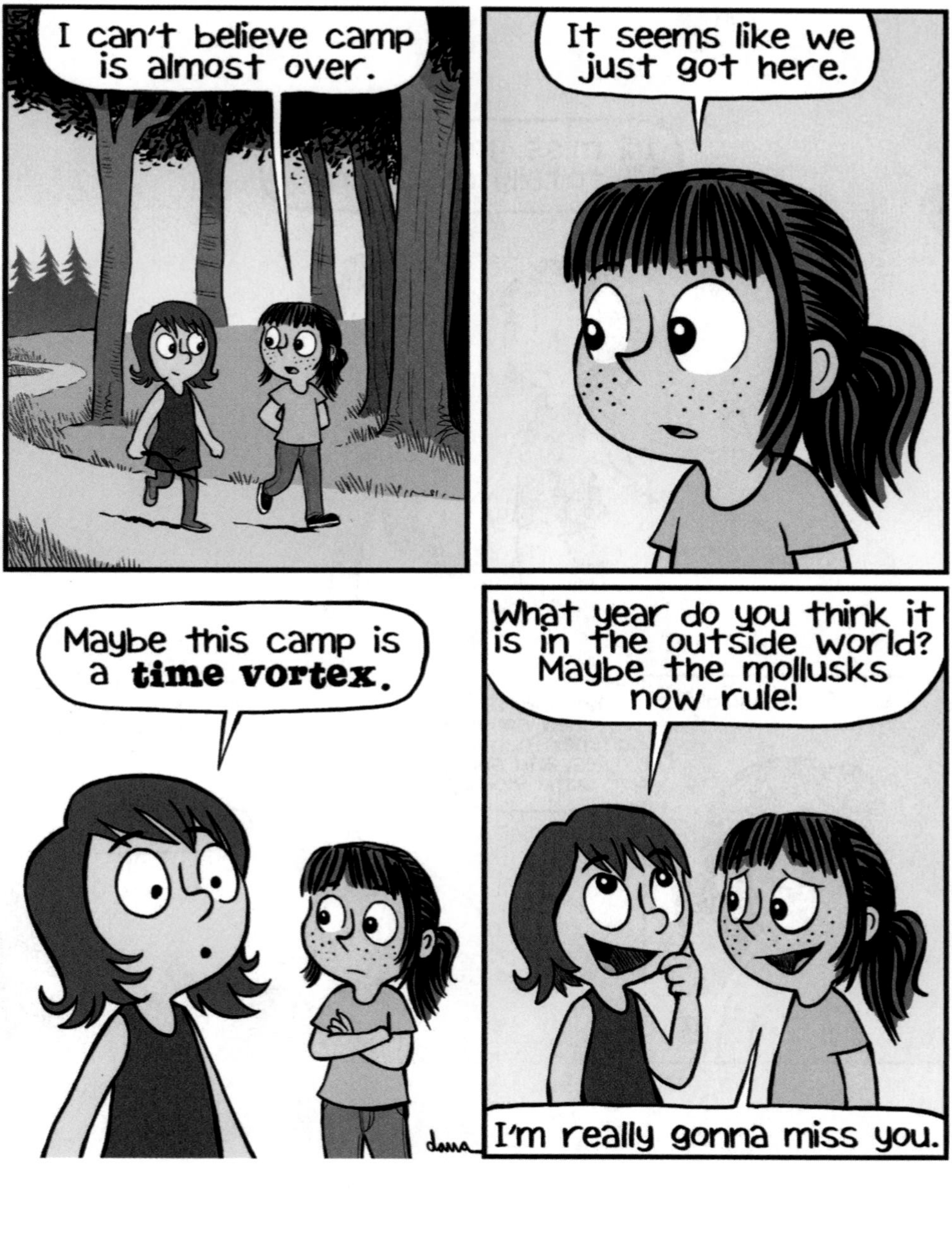
I can't believe camp is almost over.
It seems like we just got here.
Maybe this camp is a **time vortex**.
What year do you think it is in the outside world? Maybe the mollusks now rule!
I'm really gonna miss you.

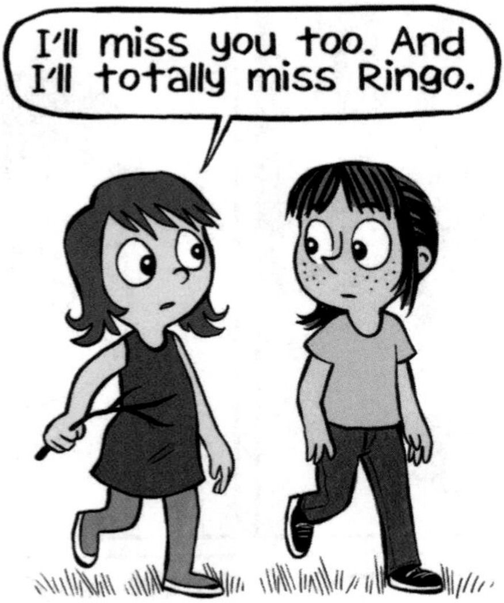
I'll miss you too. And I'll totally miss Ringo.

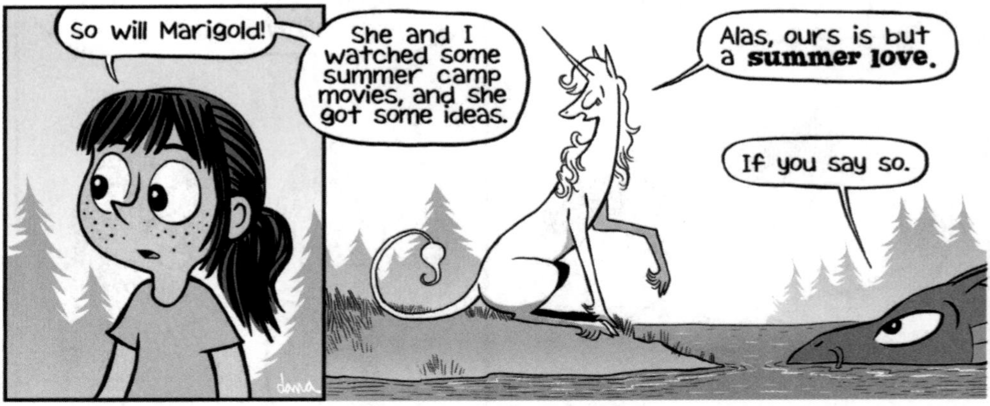
So will Marigold!
She and I watched some summer camp movies, and she got some ideas.
Alas, ours is but a **summer love.**
If you say so.
dana

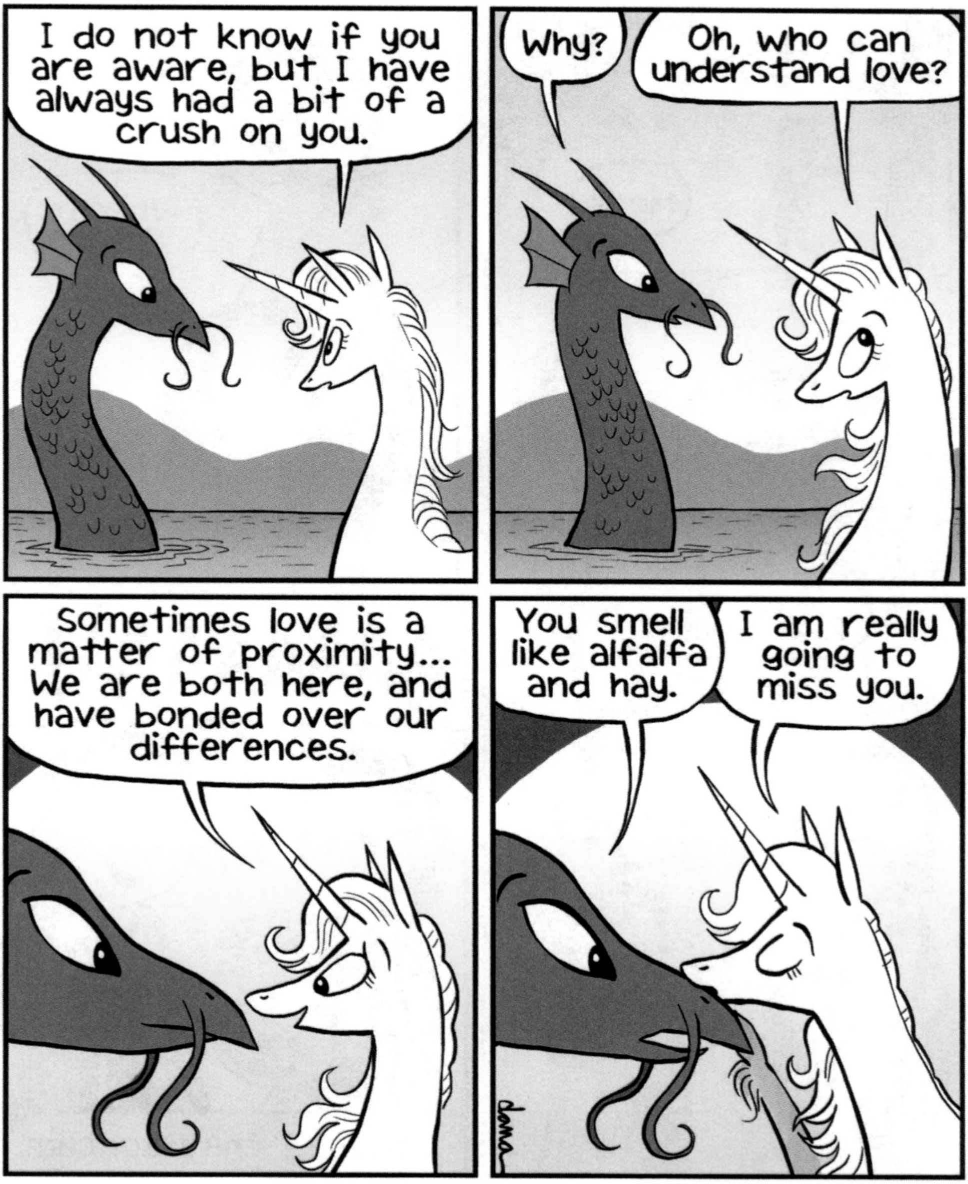
I do not know if you are aware, but I have always had a bit of a crush on you.
Why?
Oh, who can understand love?
Sometimes love is a matter of proximity... We are both here, and have bonded over our differences.
You smell like alfalfa and hay.
I am really going to miss you.
dana

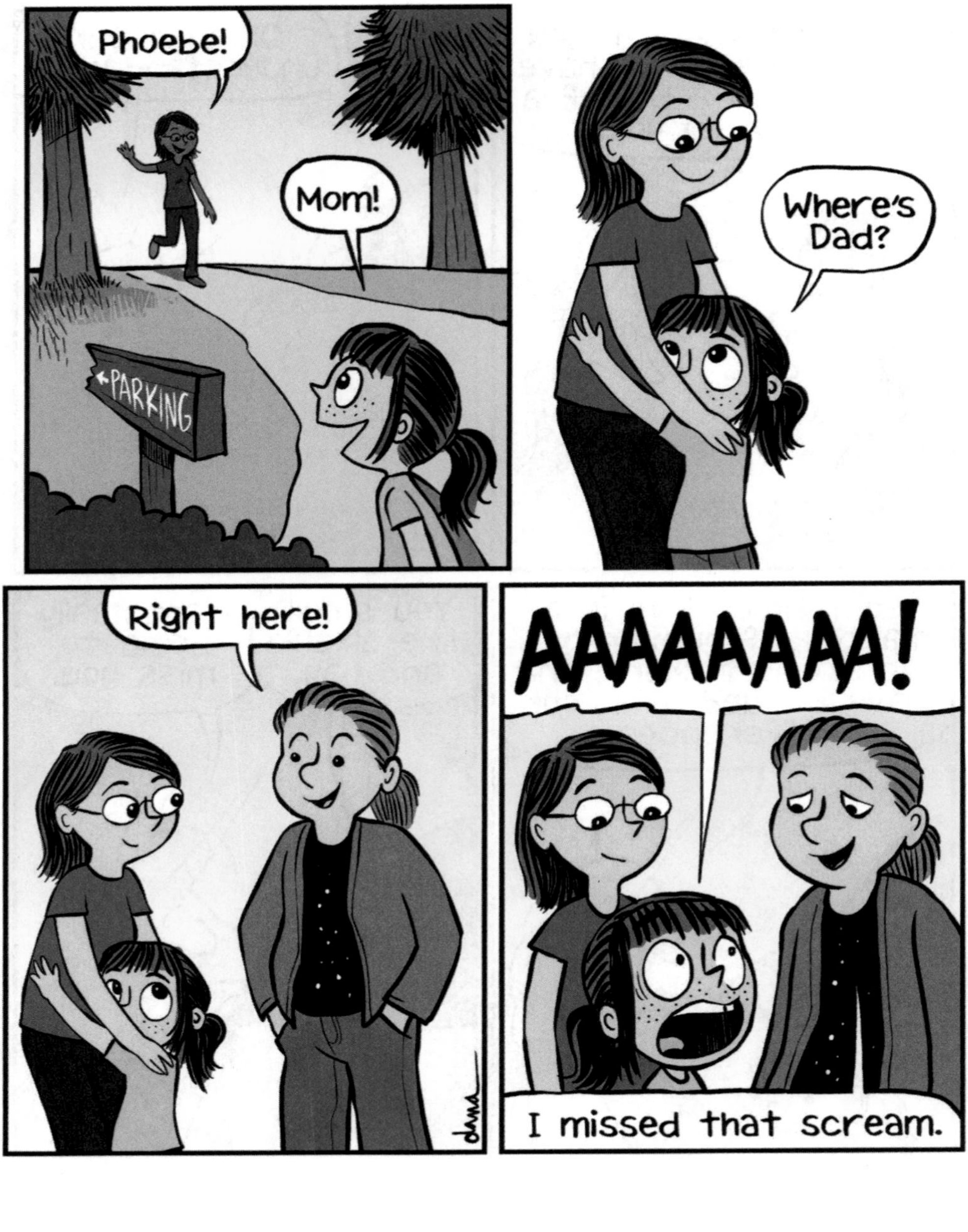
Phoebe!
Mom!
PARKING
Where's Dad?
Right here!
AAAAAAAA!
I missed that scream.

Learn the Creative Process

In the earlier books, I showed you some of how I draw Phoebe, Marigold, and friends.

Now, let's look at how I make comics.

For example, the one where Phoebe asked Marigold about her New Year's resolutions. (It's on page 34 of this book.)

First, I have to come up with ideas.

I like to leave my house to do that. My house is full of distractions.

Hm. What kind of New Year's resolution would Marigold make?

...well, what's HARD for her?

When I draw them in my notebook, they look like this:

Are you making any new year's resolutions?

I will inevitably fail.

That failure, in turn, will give me a much-needed dose of humility.

Your humility isn't very humble.

I am resolving to be INELEGANT.

Unicorn!

It doesn't have to be much, just enough to show who's talking and what they're doing. (Sometimes, Marigold is just an M, or Phoebe is just a P.)

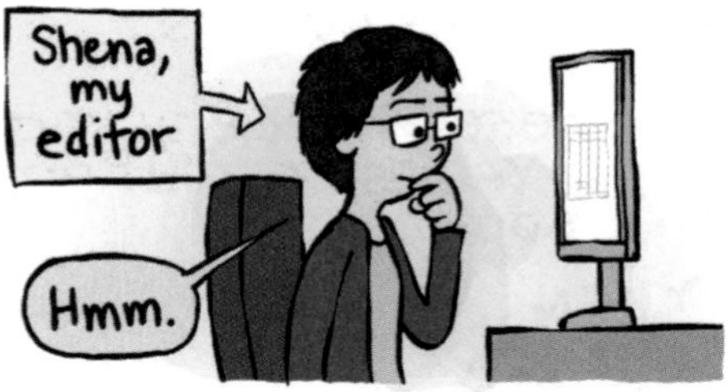
Shena, my editor
Hmm.

I take a picture of it on my phone and send it to my editor, so she can tell me what she thinks.

Sometimes she thinks something could be clearer, or funnier.

Other times, she just says:

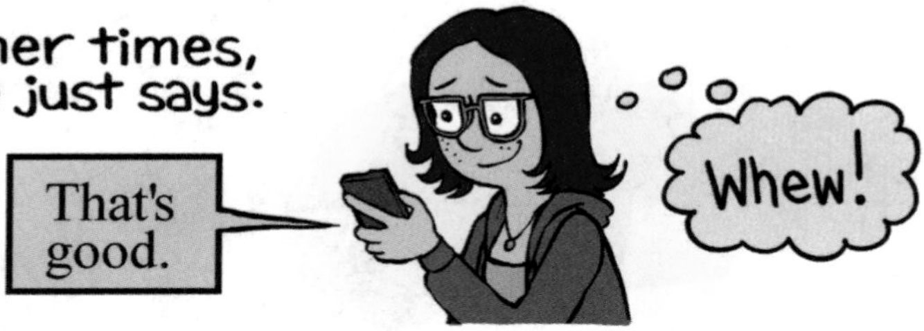
That's good.
Whew!

Once she approves, I get to work on the finished artwork. I do all that on my computer.

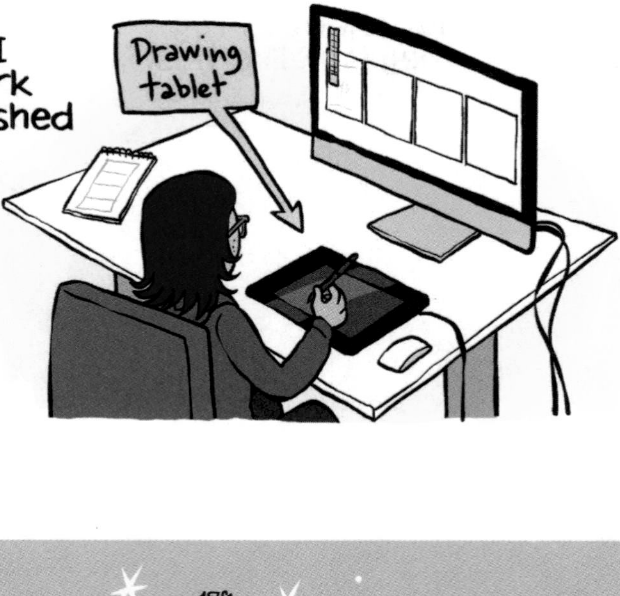
Drawing tablet

First, I add the lettering, so I know how much space I have for the artwork.

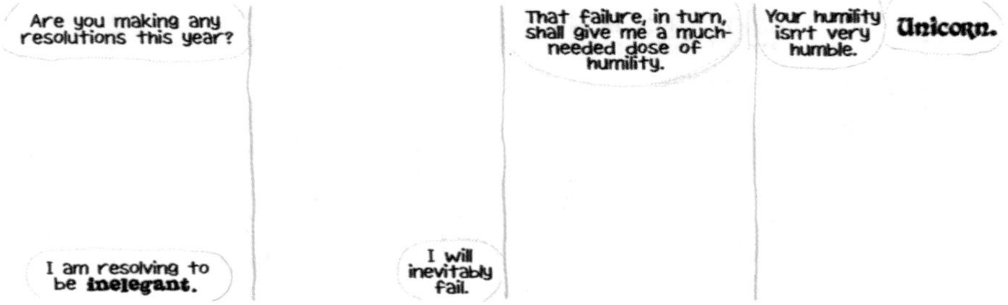
Are you making any resolutions this year?
I am resolving to be **inelegant.**
I will inevitably fail.
That failure, in turn, shall give me a much-needed dose of humility.
Your humility isn't very humble.
Unicorn.

Then, I add the rough "pencil" lines, usually in light blue.

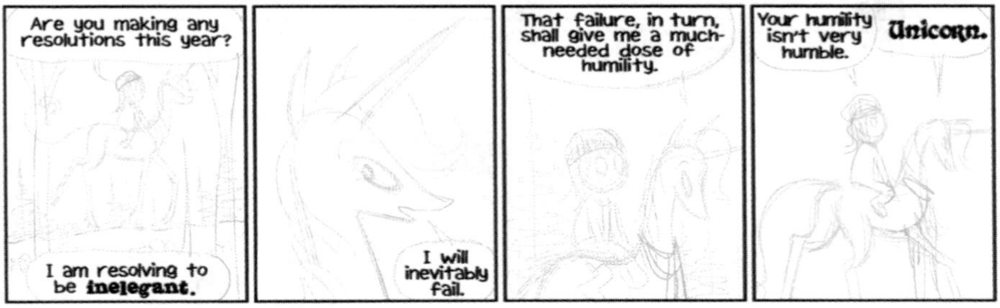
Are you making any resolutions this year?
I am resolving to be **inelegant.**
I will inevitably fail.
That failure, in turn, shall give me a much-needed dose of humility.
Your humility isn't very humble.
Unicorn.

Next, I add the black "ink" lines...

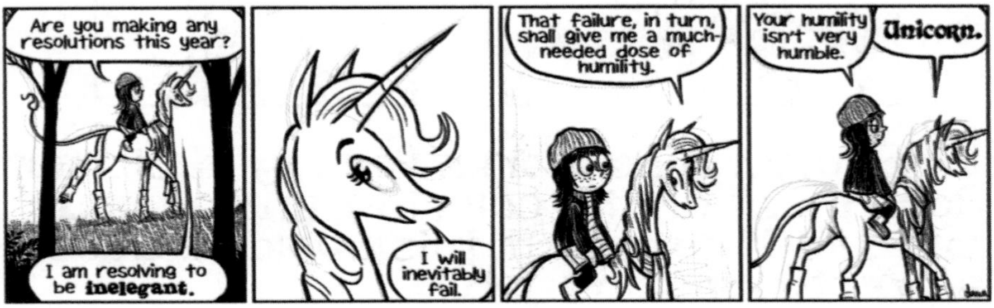
Are you making any resolutions this year?
I am resolving to be **inelegant.**
I will inevitably fail.
That failure, in turn, shall give me a much-needed dose of humility.
Your humility isn't very humble.
Unicorn.

Finally, I add in various shades of gray.

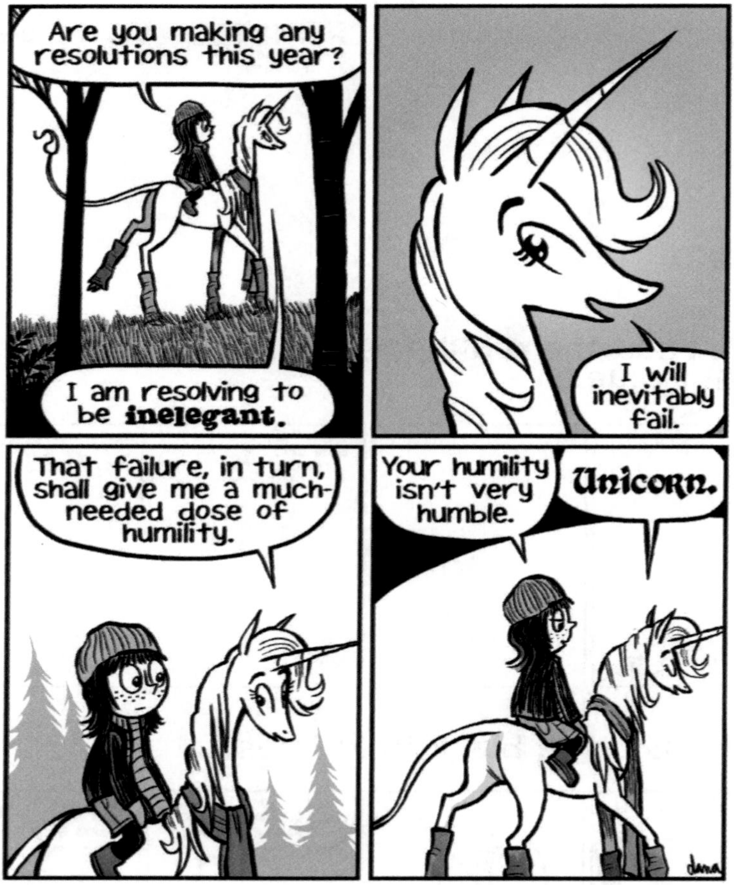
Are you making any resolutions this year?
I am resolving to be **inelegant.**
I will inevitably fail.
That failure, in turn, shall give me a much-needed dose of humility.
Your humility isn't very humble.
Unicorn.
dana

(A colorist who works for my publisher does most of the coloring, and as you can see throughout this book, he does a pretty amazing job!)

Glossary

calibrate: pg. 35 — verb / to plan carefully

context: pg. 163 — noun / the set of circumstances that surrounds an event

ensemble: pg. 163 — noun / a group of musicians

exoskeleton: pg. 82 — noun / a hard, external covering

feign: pg. 98 — verb / to imitate or pretend

hallucination: pg. 166 — noun / a vision of something that does not exist

incoherence: pg. 150 — noun / a state of not making sense

percussionist: pg. 164 — noun / a drummer or any musician who plays an instrument by striking or beating it

prescient: pg. 60 — adjective / having foresight

proximity: pg. 175 — noun / nearness

schism: pg. 98 — noun / a division into two opposing groups

scintillating: pg. 57 — adjective / brilliant or exciting

victuals: pg. 26 — noun / food or provisions

vortex: pg. 173 — noun / a whirling mass that draws things into its current

whippersnapper: pg. 37 — noun / an offensively bold young person

Andrews McMeel Publishing
a division of Andrews McMeel Universal
1130 Walnut Street, Kansas City, Missouri 64106

www.andrewsmcmeel.com

16 17 18 19 20 RR2 10 9 8 7 6 5 4 3 2 1

ISBN: 978-1-4494-8351-7

Library of Congress Control Number: 2016931068

Made by:
RR Donnelley & Sons
Address and location of manufacturer:
1009 Sloan Street
Crawfordsville, IN 47933-2743
1st Printing—8/5/16

ATTENTION: SCHOOLS AND BUSINESSES

Andrews McMeel books are available at quantity discounts with bulk purchase for educational, business, or sales promotional use. For information, please e-mail the Andrews McMeel Publishing Special Sales Department: specialsales@amuniversal.com.